NO ARMS, NO ARMOUR

BY ROBERT HENRIQUES

DEATH BY MOONLIGHT: *An Account of a Darpur Journey*

NO ARMS, NO ARMOUR

NO ARMS, NO ARMOUR

by

ROBERT HENRIQUES

"No more defenceless, maybe no less pleasant
Than the plump peacock or the prime cock pheasant—
A gilded company, a noble state
They keep . . .
No arms, no armour against fate."

FARRAR & RINEHART, INC.

ON MURRAY HILL   NEW YORK

With gratitude to
DOREEN MARSTON
in London
and
HARRY BLOOMFIELD
in Paris
Taskmasters

NO ARMS, NO ARMOUR

The mail and cuirass he was proud to wear,
The mace and cutlery he used to bear,
The broad-sword and the gaily pennant lance
Were fine against a gentlemanly foe.
The rifle, the machine gun and the tank,
The well-cut field boot on a well-cut shank,
Were better far for mucking about France;
But rather less becoming, don't you know?

But whether it's the one thing or the other,
A soldier has no arms against his brother.

Neither the clarion nor the fife
Can help a gentleman to keep his wife,
While Colonel, banker, lawyer, doctor,
The General Staff, the King's Proctor,
His bookies, politicians, tailors—all that lot
Put it across him, so he finds he's got
No arms, no armour against life.

No more defenceless, maybe no less pleasant
Than the plump peacock or the prim cock pheasant.

And We, especial Trust and Confidence reposing
In you, Trusty and Well Beloved, and supposing
(And this is hot)
That you are gents,
Do, by these presents,
Appoint you officers in our regiments.
So what?

Wine, women, horses,
Hear us sing.
And "Gentlemen, the King,"
We toast . . . A noble state
We know—wars, revelry, divorces;
And generals rule our courses,
On which we have no star, nothing,
No arms, no armour against fate.

A glittering company of officers and gents,
No arms, no armour, gilt accoutrements.

Author's Note A NUMBER OF PEOPLE HAD READ this book before it ever reached the publishers. One of them said: —"it makes me want to be a soldier." Another:—"if there's a war, it will be considered anti-army propaganda."

But it isn't in any way propaganda; and the army of 1928 is only the hazard setting of events that are happening elsewhere and at all times, in trade, industry, law, medicine and even politics. Wherever you go, the process of human emergence can usually be discovered.

Some of the men in this book were harshly treated by—and speak harsh words against—the army, the staff and the generals. I have just come from making personal acquaintance with the present-day staff at its fountain head; the change that it has undergone during the last decade is considerable. I am not competent to express an opinion on such very superior officers as generals. Nor do I want to. Like bishops, prime ministers, income tax inspectors or anything else, I suppose there are good and bad. The Secretary of State for War has certainly done some useful weeding. As regards the army, I can only say that I have now, once more, become a Regular (if only temporary) soldier. I hope that I may be allowed to work out my three years in undistinguished obscurity and in peace.

R. H.

August 15th, 1939.

To Our Trusty and Well Beloved

PERCIVAL ST. JOHN TRANNION WINDRUSH

Greetings

WE, reposing especial Trust and Confidence in your Loyalty, Courage and Good Conduct, do by these Presents Constitute and Appoint you to be an Officer in Our Land Forces from the *third* day of *September 1927*. You are therefore carefully and diligently to discharge your Duty as such in the Rank of *Second Lieutenant* or in such other Rank as we may from time to time hereafter be pleased to promote or appoint you to. . . .

Book One

1928

Chapter 1 AS YOU COME OVER THE CREST OF BEACON HILL from the direction of Andover, Salisbury Plain is laid out before you, until it touches the horizon on the western marches of your vision. Superficially it is entirely flat; and its color scheme is always a monochrome— green or blue, in grades of tint and brilliance that vary with the time of day, with the weather or with the season. The subtle shades of tone, the undulations, the distant fields and roadways, the trees and buildings, are none of them insistent; and it is only on a later impression that the flat downlands become contoured, scarred with woods, wrinkled carelessly into folds that hold a token of human dwellings, a spire rising from the trees, a suggestion of smoke drawn out by the wind from an unseen beginning. No part of it challenges the dominion of the Plain itself; for the Plain scarcely admits its own individual features, denies them indeed, allowing them membership of its body, but claiming their submission to—their dissolution into—its single uniformity.

You can see that the Plain is a fine, brutal piece of handiwork. Its parts may be grand or lowly, ugly or beautiful; Druids' stones, Saxon and Norman churches, the rippling Avon and its tributary streams and modest bridges; and there are army encampments blemishing the slopes with foul suppurations of corrugated iron. But, from the top of Beacon Hill, there is never anything more than the absolute Plain that shakes itself clear of the sky at sunrise and melts into it again at dusk.

3

From here, Bulford Camp is directly below you; straight ahead is Larkhill with its satellite gunnery establishments; beyond that again are the balloon school and the wide ranges. Because of the shoulders of the hill, you cannot see on the left the aerodromes or, far away to the right, the barracks and encampments that make up Tidworth. Airplanes circle and twist overhead or come past, flight by flight, in strict formation. Tanks nose their way up the slopes, and armoured cars slide through the lanes with the trees meeting above them. From the ranges there is the sound of shells bursting, the cough of the little guns and the deep reverberations of medium artillery. There is the simian chatter of machine guns and the crackle of rifle fire. A troop of cavalry trots over a crest, a squadron deploys into open order. A battalion in field service marching order tramps by on a route march. Everywhere, all over the Plain up to and beyond your horizon, men are marching and drilling and running and crawling and peacefully working their instruments of destruction. The Plain has been given over to the rape of soldiers by a public that has no further interest in its army. The army reciprocates this indifference.

Like the Plain, the army is itself a splendid and dominant body corporate. In its detachment it is proud; and proud, too, in demanding the submission and uniformity of its members. They may be handsome or ugly, tall or little, intelligent or stupid, brave or timid, kind or brutal, Godfearing or pagan, happy or miserable; but you may not know these finer districtions on a first, second or third inspection. They must be men in uniform with a uniform way of speech and a uniform way of thought and living. Whatever there is within them must be encased in a single military character. If the casing splits they are asking for trouble.

From Beacon Hill you might drop down into a score of army messes, into a score of ugly red brick buildings or dilapidated shacks of corrugated iron. In each of them you would—with few exceptions—meet the same people, see the same faces, hear the same speech, detect the same hackneyed stanzas of mechanical thinking. You might divine, with reason, that you had come amongst a race apart; a race that was kind and courteous and physically splendid, but otherwise subhuman. Your eyes and ears and intelligence would tell you that this was so; but they would instruct you falsely.

❦ The General's car was coming slowly up the hill from the camp. It was a big, grey, twelve-year-old car of the mid-war period, unwieldy, uneconomical, belonging to the Government and driven by a lance-corporal. At its age, it was all it could do to crawl sturdily to the top, a little steam coming from the radiator and laying a curtain of trembling vapor between the sunlight and the amber discoloration of the windshield.

The car suited the General, who was completely a pre-war soldier; who looked on the war as a pitiful era of confusion for the army, a lapse that must never recur and whose recurrence in the same monstrous form was so improbable that it need not be thought about. For a general, it had been a time of madness, with the tenets of decent soldiering slipped so far into the background that men, untrained and slovenly, were banished to the mud and left to the shells of heavy artillery; that officers were clerks, and accountants and the sons of nobody; that commanders lost reason, remembering horses and sabers only against a dim background of historic pageantry; that people dressed strangely and talked of duckboards and burrowed downwards instead of galloping towards the enemy; that the speed of the horse no longer dictated strategy; that even spurs were discarded.

At the time, it had been a nightmare for a true soldier. And now, ten years afterwards and the army sane again, the past could be comfortably forgotten. The next war would be of a more heroic, traditional pattern, with all the fine thunder of hoofs and clashing of sabers, with officers once more gentlemen, living as such, riding horses, going hunting as part of their training. That today they could not afford horses, that the Government housed them in ruins less habitable than a slum tenement, that the cost of messing and the upkeep of equipment exceeded their pay checks—these were their own misfortunes, sad indeed but too displeasing for a general's consideration.

The General thought of his officers, sighed and thought more happily of the lunch that awaited him.

The General's car had a ponderous dignity and was at least faster than a horse, so that it was easily ahead of the tempo of decent soldiering; but if the young lance-corporal (who was chauffeur) tried to gain too much by his motor, the General prized the upper half of his body forward from the whipcord upholstery and from the Brigadier beside him, panted himself forward to the dividing glass between himself and the driver and tapped with the end of his leather-covered cane until the young man in front half turned his head in respectful attention.

"A little slower, Blower."

Blower straightened his head and eased his foot off the accelerator. The General's breath rippled the ends of his grey moustache and he sank back against the whipcord. The car groaned on up Beacon Hill until, at the top, it gathered itself for the mild descent towards Andover. Lunch was half an hour ahead and eight miles distant.

The battery was climbing the hill in the opposite direction, returning to camp from the first route march of the training season. Seen from the crest, its approach had a curious appearance; it lacked the common rhythm of marching troops or driven horses, seeming at first a-rhythmic, but resolving later into an unusual meter of movement and countermovement. The dipping heads of animals, always irregular when seen in column, at first caught and puzzled the eye, until it became clear that the creatures were mules and that they traveled one behind the other and at no exact intervals, instead of in pairs or in ordinary gun teams of six well-matched horses.

Intermingling with the mules, the men walked stolidly, not in step and not marching smartly; short, sturdy drivers and tall gunners, strolling loosely, slouching even, each one to the gait that best suited his own disposition. There was insolence in their walking. Men of the Light Artillery, or of the Pack batteries—as they were known when they served in India and the East—men of the screw guns, the little short-nosed howitzers that took to pieces and traveled on mules, didn't march, they walked. But the knowledge that they held the marching record of the army, and that each gunner was specially selected by the doctors for his size and physique—and the romantic implications of that knowledge—gave them insolence.

The battery, a long serpent of brown, sweat-flecked mules and horses, of painted and burnished gun parts, of jingling chains and polished leather, writhed with the road towards the hilltop.

The General's car reached the summit at that moment.

🌸 Seeing the head of the approaching battery, the General leaned forward with interest.

"What's this, Arbuthnot?"

The Brigadier pulled himself nervously from the corner of the back seat and looked through the window. His promotion depended on the General's recommendation, and with relief he saw that there was no cause for anxiety.

"A battery, sir."

"I can see that."

"A light battery, sir."

"I can see that."

"I can't quite make out, sir. . . ."

"Who are they, Benjamin?" the General asked impatiently.

His A.D.C. twisted round in the small seat opposite.

"The Seventeenth Light Battery, I think; shall we stop and see them past us?"

"Have we time?"

"Plenty of time, sir."

"All right; tell Blower, will you?"

The three men stood by the side of the road; the General, heavy, stubborn, in his own command a bulwark against which dissension rebounded, impregnable in the rightness that was a general's heritage. Beside him, the Brigadier, Commander of the Divisional Artillery, in less than a year due for promotion or retirement, waited uneasily. It was difficult to find the middle role that his situation needed. He must be confident, knowledgeable, master of his subordinates; he must respect the General's rightness with proper humility. He must not know that Benjamin Ramsay, tall, dark and careless, one of his own very junior officers and the General's A.D.C., stood behind and laughed at the pair of them.

Along the road, the order to march to attention was passed down the column. The General heard it and composed his mind into a critical attitude, tapping the leg of his boot, waiting until the grey-haired major at the head of his battery should come— level.

It was not a military figure—slim, grey, fragile—and the General viewed it with displeasure, seeing an elderly gentleman who fitted his horse all right, but whose shoulders were bowed and who was somehow slumped into the saddle; seeing— as the major gave the order "Eyes Right" and swung his own head towards the group of officers—a worn face and soft, large eyes set in the tired whiteness of cheeks and forehead; seeing the face of an ascetic, a scholar, a hero even, but not that of a regulation soldier. The General caught the passive gaze but cast it aside, not admitting it, not daring to admit it.

When Sammy looked at you, you saw only the eyes, blue, childlike, full of power that was neither aggressive nor defensive. You saw a man without armour who was unafraid; a man without rancor whose knowledge challenged your misunderstanding. You saw a love that welled out and searched for a mate to draw back to it; an embracing love, not of life largely and widely, but of all its specific parts, of each human being, each animal, of the feel of leather, the stones of the road, the roundness of a pipe, the glitter of a breech block. It was not a deliberate emotion but an unconscious attitude to everything that was felt, touched, met with; an emanation no more controlled than the exhalation of an animal's scent glands.

When Sammy looked at you, the love came across and met antipathy without protest. You flinched; for you saw the unexpected, a man unbelievably human.

The General did not flinch; there was nothing in his making that either gave way or responded to outside influence. The laws of dynamics did not apply to him, and to an action there was neither reaction nor yielding. You could explain him only as a Yale lock affair, or perhaps as a solid block, through which ran a patterned channel; all that conformed to the pattern slipping through the channel, but bent and battered currency— currency that did not respond to his understanding—being stolidly rejected. That was the General; an expert, seeing through expert eyes a machine whose working parts he knew in detail but of whose uses he had little concern and little knowledge; a banker, busied over human arbitrage but considering human coins, in their infinite diversity, only in terms of his native coinage; a preacher, enthroned on his own pulpit, blazing the wrath of God without admitting the frailty of his congregation. Any, and each, of those comparisons gave you an idea of his strength and his weakness.

He must have been young once, that General, just as all generals started from pink and slobbering babies; just as every general owed an incongruous conception to some distant act of passion. But if the General looked through the wrong end of the telescope, thought back to the days of night-lights and a starched rustling by the cot-side, his memory stopped short at a dark November evening in the gunroom.

"His Lordship," the headkeeper diffidently suggested to the General's father, "thought we might blank Hog Wood into Jane Spinney . . . the birds'd fly better that way, coming home again."

"Blank Hog Wood!" the General's father answered. "My grandfather would turn in his grave at the thought of it." And, from that evening, the small, pink-cheeked, curly-headed, large-eyed boy became an embryo general.

But you had to suppose that the General once clasped small arms round a woman's neck; loved, hated, feared, wondered, trembled at the shadows; that once his mind threw out tendrils to grasp at the strange things that happened round him; to pull them back so that it could chew them, digest them and make something new out of them somehow. You had to try and understand the change, to find out when and why that mind—the mind of all generals, the mind of the army—shut itself against all but pre-conception and became a sausage machine, turning

out uniform sausages at one end, no matter what you put in at
the other. You had to try to understand, but you were left bewildered; bewildered that a man could be so inhuman that he
did not flinch at the pure humanity of the major.

The General returned Sammy's salute curtly and transferred
his glance past the trumpeter, the rosy-faced boy with an impu-
dent nose, to the battery staff that followed. The sun on the
horses' coats showed them hard and in good condition, so that
you had to admit there must be a horse-master somewhere in
the battery.

It did not look as if it were the major.

Riding behind the battery staff at exactly the regulation
distance, at exactly the regulation distance giving the order
"Eyes Right" in an ungentlemanly voice that rang like a sergeant-
major's, and—with exactly the right drill movement—flicking
his own head across, shoulders squared and back hollowed, a
sturdy, red-faced, short-legged little man rode in advance of the
leading section.

In the way that a banker who sees a strange coin might at
once appreciate its sterling value, the General assessed the
officer. That is a rough parallel, but it does not go far enough.
As an engineer, schooled in the supremacy of a Birmingham
product, might look without enthusiasm at a foreign automobile, the General glanced at the funny little man who was
passing. "May do the job . . . but no quality, no finish," was
the obvious opinion. And this grudging admission meant very
little, was strongly qualified. The job of an officer, as the General
could have told you, was not to be discharged by acquired pro-
ficiency; the care of horses not to be left to those who had
manual experience of its practice; the welfare of men not to
be tended by those who had served through the various grades
of non-commissioned soldiers. A battery could not be shot by
a man who had fought his gun at Le Cateau. The power to do
these things wasn't trained into a fellow but came from the
womb in his company; and the womb that had yielded this
officer did not bear consideration. That was the General's immediate verdict as he spoke over his shoulder to Benjamin:

"I say, Benjamin, a ranker, isn't it?"

"Yes, sir; Mr. Bertrand; rather a fine record. Trumpeter to sergeant-major and commissioned for gallantry."

The General did not answer. Very regrettable—those chaps who were so inconveniently valiant. He tapped his leg again as the battery came on past, the stocky drivers leading their mules, the gunners high above them. The sun displayed the well-cleaned steel and the leather of the pack saddles so that, in spite of the officers, it was undeniably an efficient unit.

❀ The General brightened as the rear section drew level. He jerked the butt of his cane at the large, fair second-lieutenant who led them.

"Who's that, Benjamin?"

"Windrush, sir, Tubby Windrush."

"Windrush . . . Windrush . . . I knew his father. Get him here, will you?"

The General, his head on one side, peered upwards. His glance was appraising. Good stuff this, in the rough; a likely youngster; pink and white face, eyes blue, all the features just beginning to mold themselves into the careless, precise and slightly disdainful fashion that meant good breeding. This rare blend of so many opposites, of modesty and arrogance, satisfaction and unpretentiousness, easy charm and utter lack of culture, was the perfect young officer. You had it here at last; tall, wide at the shoulders, thickset and heavy at the top; but, from the waist downwards, tapering quickly, legs slight, thighs flat—God knowing well that they were incomplete without a horse between them.

And, as for Tubby, he sat on his horse and looked benevolently down at the General. He had no trouble with senior officers and they, seeing him as an equal in embryo, spoke to him kindly. This General might have been an uncle by blood, as he was by upbringing. . . .

"Morning, Windrush; been here long, have you?"

"I joined six months ago."

"Only six months? Like it, do you?"

"Yes, thank you, sir."

"That's right; but you'd rather have horses, I gather? Hoping for Horse Artillery one of these days? More in your line, isn't it?"

"Of course we'd all like to have a jacket. . . ."

Of course: that was how it should be with a young subaltern. He ought to covet the blue-and-gold jacket that belonged to Horse Artillery and that went only to those who were specially selected for dash, efficiency, means or family, horsemanship and nice manners. It should, indeed, be inconceivable to him that an officer could have other ambitions; that he should desire further than to lead a section, on the right of the line, past the saluting base at a stretched gallop.

The General was pleased. He stroked his moustache and looked at Tubby, enjoying the satisfaction of finding a subaltern of perfect conformation, a good thoroughbred; one who was entirely a gentleman and the son of a gentleman, who would pick up the torch and carry it onwards, traveling the grades of promotion with easy familiarity until he himself came to generalship.

The General approved the look of Tubby. He was concerned with nothing deeper than face values, except to make sure that a man was no impostor—no second-rate stock posing as gentry. And there was nothing wrong with the face value of Windrush; a cricketer like his father, no doubt; a polo player like his uncle; a born sportsman like the rest of his family. As regards his career, the young man was as firmly planted as an industrialist's son entering politics. You could foretell it with certainty; Horse Artillery to major-general and even further. . . . But the boy was badly placed at the start in a Light battery.

"You ought to be with horses . . . mules not much catch, I imagine?"

"I don't know, sir; I like my mules. You get sort of fond of them."

❦ The General had not heard the answer; his eyes were fixed on the elderly subaltern who rode in the captain's place at the rear of the battery.

"Who the devil's that, Benjamin?"

"Watson, sir. Daddy Watson—you probably know of him. . . ."

"Get him here, will you?"

Watson turned his horse and saluted.

You could not have offered the General a sight less pleasing. There were all sorts of officers these days; some worse than others, more bad than good, but each with a use somewhere. For instance: the ones that turned religious—after a youth of admirable profligacy—could take church parades on Sundays; someone had to. The studious ones, who passed into the Staff College, filled the lesser staff jobs quite nicely; their further advance was checked all right by the selective panel of generals above them. The poor ones, who would not run up debts, were sent to guard those fortified islands that were scattered in forgotten parts of the Empire or to train recruits at the regimental depots. The ones who understood motors could be tucked away with the still rare mechanized units. And even those who disliked horses could be lost in the defended port of some distant colony or protectorate.

But this man, Watson, fell into no recognized category. He sat his horse and looked at you without positive disrespect but with a sort of sneering malice; a sour dislike, that was almost contempt, for your acknowledged authority. It was a heavy, clever face, belonging to one who claimed an unearned right to pass judgment on, and not to accept the award of, his superior officers; one who set himself up and challenged you to cast him down again, who sought war with you for the joy of battle, who balanced distress against the pleasures of complaining.

Don't make a mistake though! This one would not indulge in outright disobedience; he had the guts all right but he was too clever. He knew the law and he'd fight his battles within its limits. He was the sort they called a "barrack-room lawyer", bad enough in the barrack-room or the sergeants' Mess but a great deal worse among the officers. This was the type that raised the ire in you; about the only type that would put the General into active opposition, shake him from his stubborn passivity.

The General made no perceptible movement, unless you could sense the bull-like hunching-up as he looked Watson over slowly, coldly, from the ground upwards.

"Why haven't you got spurs on, Mr. Watson?"

The short, heavy, slovenly figure twisted in the saddle. The heavy pink face was lowered, and the small eyes looked back at the General with no expectation and so no fear, with only stolid resentment coming out of them.

"I don't wear spurs, sir. I have a bad ankle."

"You never wear spurs?"

"Not now, sir."

"All right, Mr. Watson, I suppose it can't be helped. It's unfortunate . . . looks bad on a drill order; spoils the turnout of quite a decent battery . . . That's all, thank you."

The horse was swung round, his hind feet skidding on the macadam of the roadway as the unspurred heels were driven hard into him.

"Looks bad, doesn't it?" the General said to Tubby.

"His ankle was smashed in the war, sir."

"Oh, was it?" the General said indifferently. "I used to know your father . . . Great pals we were at one time."

"Yes, sir?"

"We saw a lot of each other; knew each other at Eton, and afterwards of course; rode together in the Hunt Cup, I remember."

"Yes, sir?"

"You must come and dine with us some time. My wife would like to meet you."

"Thank you, sir."

"I hope we shall see something of you . . . Good morning, Mr. Windrush."

Tubby kicked his horse up the bank and cantered along the grass beside the road to rejoin his battery.

"Good chap that," the General said vaguely. "Good officer."

"The right sort," the Brigadier agreed with him.

"Tubby's all right," Benjamin said. "In fact, taken all round, it's a thundering good battery."

🌾 Tubby rejoined the battery as it was entering barracks. The subsections detached themselves one by one, forming up into line, while across the parade ground the major, still on his horse, faced them.

Alone, with only his trumpeter behind him, Sammy gained in glory. Humility faded as he ceased to be a man—a rather elderly gentleman—performing the duties of a soldier, and became a soldier—the quintessence of a soldier—invested still with the gentler human qualities. His presence grasped the waiting battery, as a martyr at the stake might hold the people. For a moment, he wore his full regalia and claimed their homage; drew them to his leadership. And they—the men, the noncommissioned officers, the officers—felt this drawing in, seeing him not only as their commander but as a human, whose quality they had tested. They stood, taut, unmoving, paying him the double tribute. It was a little theatrical; and, indeed, sensing the bonds that held them, you might have called Sammy an actor; except that no actor could have put the glamour of military discipline across the parade ground in this manner. It was the genuineness of the man that got you.

"Dismount . . . fall out the officers."

The officers doubled across the asphalt and formed up in front of the major in order of seniority; Watson on the right, his face still heavy but smoothed out now, almost tranquil; Bertrand, stuffed out, swollen-chested, solid; Tubby, a boy, self-conscious, towering above the others; the three of them saluting, stepping backwards a pace and ranging themselves behind the major.

He returned their salute gravely, dismissed the battery, and came to talk to them.

"The animals, Bert? They took it pretty well, didn't they?"

Bertrand was unsmiling. On the parade ground—and almost always—his body was by habit permanently at attention; it was only with a conscious effort that he divided his feet and relaxed his attitude. He answered in a voice that still had the sergeant-major tang to it: "Nicely, sir; not bad for the first route march . . ." He turned to Tubby: "Some o' them mules of yours in 'D' sub-section want hardening up, me lad. That pivot animal has a belly like a brood mare."

"Water and feed now, Daddy," the major said to Watson. "The men can go to dinners; we'll have stables afterwards." He walked off towards the battery office.

When he had gone, Watson put his hand on Bertrand's shoulder.

"I ask you, Bert," he said, "as one old soldier to another, doesn't that general make you vomit? Can you imagine a man so like a stuffed fish that he'll watch a battery march past him and his only comment is about an officer who hasn't got spurs on? And what was wrong with *you*, Tubby?"

"Nothing," Tubby answered. "Nothing I could help anyway. He said he'd known my father."

"He'd known your father, had he?"

"He said so. . . ."

He was uncomfortable about it. He had not sought, and did not wish, the General's favors. To him, the comradeship of Bert and Daddy, and the leadership of Sammy, were hot, living things that made soldiering beautiful. "I don't want his patronage; I'm on your side," he wanted to say. It was in his heart; but Daddy's face was strung tight; the eyes shrunken and full of malice. He was dangerous in this mood.

"He'd known your father, had he?" he repeated.

"He said so."

"He liked your boots, I suppose?"

"He didn't mention it."

"And he talked about the race tomorrow?"

"As a matter of fact, he didn't."

"He forgot that; he's going off a bit. I suppose he admired your breeches?"

"I hope so," Tubby said, at last exasperated.

Bert had stood silent with his face expressionless; a rock around which the current of Watson's resentment had to split to reach Tubby. By his silent neutrality, he broke the waters, keeping the flow impersonal, directing it against authority generally rather than against the junior subaltern.

"Come off it, Daddy," Bert said at last. "You can't change the army."

But Watson could not be diverted. His voice rising, he spoke across the neutrality of the solid, square little man to Tubby, who was standing beyond him.

"You're a blue-eyed boy with him now, aren't you? That's all a general cares about. Show him an officer and he looks first at his pedigree, then at his boots, then at the cut of his breeches, and sometimes gets his eyes up as far as the man's jacket. They're all the same; how can they help it? It's a sort of system of inbreeding, you see. One general gets his job on another's recommendation. The first one got there on boots and parentage, and you can't break the family circle; it goes on and on— boots and parentage making one general after another for ever and ever. What chance has a poor soldier like Sammy got? But the Brigadier now, his boots are a picture, and he's heading fast for promotion. . . ."

He turned away, as if drawing breath, and then swung back again. "God help the army," he went on; "it's only poverty that keeps a junior officer in it; and they wonder why we're forty per cent. under-strength in the Regiment. Fourteen years at thirteen bob a day as a subaltern! That's me; and I commanded a battery in France when I was twenty . . . I'm good for nothing else now and I daren't chuck it. I can't afford it. And if I *had* the money, or even a cousin in Parliament, or a peer somewhere in the family, or a job waiting in an uncle's business, I wouldn't want to go, would I? I wouldn't have to; I'd get on all right, you see. I'd be marked down for promotion. I'd be someone's blue-eyed boy, wouldn't I? Someone who wanted a directorship for his old age, a job for a nephew, a tip for the stock exchange, an invitation to Scotland . . . a general knows which side his bread's buttered."

Tubby shuffled his feet and looked down at them. Seeing his boots and the nice cut of them, he felt the true direction of Watson's criticism, felt discomfort, looked away and gazed awkwardly across the parade ground at the stables opposite.

"Well, I'm sorry, Daddy; I didn't want him to talk to me. . . ."

"Oh, don't be such a blushing maiden," Daddy said. "If you can get a lift from a general, for God's sake take it. You don't want to listen to me . . . I always get that way when I see anyone above the rank of lieutenant-colonel."

Looking up, he saw Tubby's face, anxious, worried, pained that anyone should be unhappy. He saw the big, fair, woolly man, rough in his youth, pink-cheeked, blue-eyed, taking life at its face simplicity. You couldn't look at Tubby without smiling.

"Forget it," Daddy said, his eyes widening again. "I've got to see the quartermaster-sergeant . . . Carry on, Bert, will you?"

❦ After lunch they went down from the Mess together, across the square where the cold wind swung in from between the buildings. The sun was shining and it was hot here in the lee of the stables; and the drivers in their shirt sleeves were formed up in subsections, with their numbers-one—that is, their sergeants—calling their names and looking them over. The officers stood some distance away, talking together, tapping their boots, flicking with their sticks at granite chips and wisps of straw, scrupulously not noticing what was going on. Until the sergeant-major reported to them that the battery was ready, the parade was his business and it was a tradition that they, the officers, did not interfere with him.

The sergeant-major stood truculently, his legs wide apart, in front of the battery. He was a big, fine, coarse man, with his virility gone obese, but still forceful. He was like an old bull, hanging heavy and solid. There was power in him and pride that came from the knowledge that he was feared and hated. Men obeyed him and he was hard and capable and a splendid sergeant-major. He was the focal point of the old-fashioned kind of military discipline. Below him, sergeants and bombardiers and lance-bombardiers ordered their men with lessening authority, each watched and controlled by his immediate superior. Above him, the officers comprised a governing body, benevolent, parental, knowing the family histories, the cares and peculiarities of the men in their commands. The sergeant-major was not troubled with these matters. As he saw it, the battery was a machine, the men its component parts, himself its driver. He was quite ruthless and entirely efficient.

A young subaltern could be frightened of the sergeant-major. The sergeant-major could be frightened of no one. His voice overrode the world as he called the battery to attention and reported to Watson.

❧ Tubby followed his men into one of the subsection stables. This hour, when animals were tended, was precious; an observance founded on a strictly prescribed ritual. Like the Lord's Prayer, you had it all by heart, so that it ran like a song at the least suggestion; feet, head, belly, legs; near-side, off-side, eyes, nose, dock; hoof-pick, body-brush, dandy-brush, sponge, stable-rubber, wisp. Behind it all, there was a long tradition that had built itself into the spiritual essence of a mounted unit. "Stables" hour was as sacred as the twenty minutes before the drawing room door opened and nurse came in to say that it was bed time; as hallowed as the last half-dozen casts in the growing dark of a June evening; as inevitably memorable as the walk back from church on a Sunday morning, the roast beef that followed and the Yorkshire pudding.

At this time, the unit was drawn together by its animals; its spirit blossomed. When jackets were off, you saw the man beneath the soldier. With the faint tang of ammonia and the sweet flavor of hay, the grate of shod hoofs on concrete, the hissing of men, the soft rasp of a brush on horsehide, the smack of a wisp on shiny buttocks, a soldier's life became grandly simple.

Looking down the long stables, through the long corridor of subdued light, you saw the doorway at the end framed against the hard brilliance of the day outside.

The sunshine and the brightness beyond were clear and free but without detail; out there, there was nothing more than a spring afternoon. Around you there was life; the men you knew, the mules you knew, the smells and sounds and sights that were familiar, that had adopted you into their family.

Making their way about the barracks, riding across the plain, sitting in the anterooms of the officers' messes, motoring into Salisbury, were all the other subalterns of Tubby's age, all living in the present and already forgetful of the complications of boyhood. It had suddenly become so easy. . . .

You had leaped into manhood, you see, with new and high-sounding duties, that were yet narrowed down to simple observance. You need not care about a way of living. You feared— and you laughed at—the Daddy Watsons, the sour and bitter old gentlemen who were left over from wartime. You vaguely admired Sammy with his queer affections. But you saw such people as cranks, who made living too much of a business, who were unable—it seemed—to clasp their hands about eyes and mouth and ears, to see and hear and speak only those things of the present that were thrust so clearly into their senses. Those men, the Watsons and others, had taken a wrong turning somewhere. They could not comprehend the straight and open path of a soldier, how he had left behind him the frequent crossroads of adolescence and, as a man, had come out on to the heath with the path running straight to the skyline.

Bert was right; that mule, Jane, had a belly like a brood mare. You must cut her corn; put her in the mess cart for a day or so.

Tubby strolled along, looking at the shoeing lists and feed scales that hung on the walls, keeping an eye on the men who were crouched at their mules, who were swearing under their breaths, trying to get at the belly of a ticklish one that was kicking, trying to sponge the dock of one that did not like these attentions. It was funny the way the mules and the men were both so individual. Each had his likes and dislikes, one got on with another and not with a third, so that a subsection became a family party of men and animals.

Later, the major came on his rounds, with Bert and the farrier-staff-sergeant and the sergeant-major in attendance. Tubby called up the men in each of his stables, the men standing to their animals, and Sammy waiting, tuning his eyes to the dimness of the building.

Somehow, when Sammy came in, the company was completed. It was not that there had been anything lacking before. The men, the animals, the ritual of the hour were glowing things; but a still brighter radiance had come with the slight, grey, stooping person who waited in the doorway. And yet, except for his eyes, there was nothing even to be remembered about Sammy's physical aspect; there was certainly nothing that struck you as vivid or forcible. He was neutral, almost negative; so that a stranger might well think him humble, unassuming and ineffectual. He didn't impress his personality on you, until you came to look for it. And then, with sudden vision, you found its clarity, beauty, austerity. You saw it, pure and true but colorless; cut-glass, crystal, diamond, full of reflections. For the character answered your own; and there wasn't a man in the battery who didn't feel this about him, finding in him something that was lacking in themselves, some need satisfied.

But, in the whole battery, it is probable that Daddy Watson alone could have put into words what it was that drew them all to Sammy. For there wasn't a general explanation of this power of leadership. You couldn't ascribe to him any of the standard qualities in more than average proportions. It was simply that each man—and there were eighty of them with eighty quite different characters—found in Sammy's quiet voice, gentle eyes and unobtrusive figure something complementary to his own nature. Perhaps you could say that, in a way, Sammy was universally feminine; but yet he was essentially male.

Perhaps, more truthfully, you could compare him with those exceptional people in whom birds and animals sense a love for themselves and respond immediately. For, in that way, Sammy loved all men, all living; and those who knew him well were in time aware of it.

He stood now just inside the stables, and every driver—and this is rare in the Army—was glad of his presence . . . "Go on, please," he said quietly to Tubby.

As his echo, Tubby repeated the order in his best parade-ground tones, and the men set to work again on their animals, Sammy walking down the stables, Tubby following after him, Bert and the others coming slowly along behind; a critical procession.

"That one, Kitty . . ." the major said.

"Mary," Tubby corrected him. "Kitty is the little chestnut in 'D' subsection."

"Of course, Mary it is. She's looking a lot better, you know, Tubby. She's coming along nicely."

"She's getting four pounds extra, sir."

"I remember. I should cut it to two. . . ."

They passed on to the big brown mule at the end of the stable. It took two men to groom him, one doing the work

while the other held a twitch of cord twisted round the upper
lip to keep him from kicking. The major stroked his grey
moustache as he watched.

"I saw Dynamite pulling the mess cart quite nicely yesterday. . . ."

Everyone smiled furtively, for this mule—Dynamite—was
the strongest and most unmanageable in the whole battery. It
had taken Bert, with the wiles of an old soldier and all the de-
vices of a cunning horsemaster, to get the better of him. Sammy
smiled too. "What have you been doing to him, Tubby?" he
asked softly.

Bert came quickly to the rescue. "Better not ask, sir," he said
briskly. Bert could not talk quietly; and in the effort to do so,
his words came out in spluttering jerks, like high-pressure water
through a narrow tap in the bathroom. It might have been a
sergeant-major speaking, but he looked hard at Sammy with
wide eyes that were blue and innocent.

"But I want to know," Sammy said, the smile still in his
voice, but pressing the question.

"It's like this, Major," Bert rasped; "he wants work, that
mule does. That's all he wants. We've been giving him four
hours a day up and down hill with the water cart."

"Filled?" Sammy asked quietly; for the water cart, when
full, was a load requiring two strong animals.

Bert tapped the leg of his boot with his stick and looked down
uncomfortably.

"You'll be in jug, Bert, one of these days," the major continued. "You wait till one of the Society inspectors comes
round and catches you." He turned to Tubby, taking his arm
between his thumb and fingers. "Well," he asked, "are you
winning this race for us tomorrow?"

"I hope so, sir," Tubby said. "The horse is fit enough; it'll
be my fault if we don't."

Sammy stood looking at Tubby. He had a quality of stillness,
of hesitation, as though a moment of repose had a positive
value. These halted seconds, when he seemed to balance the
scales, were like the catch in a song, a pause in the movement
of a dance. You drew breath and waited for what was coming

so that, when it came, it was heralded and of greater moment than its plain value suggested. It was simple enough this time.

"Well," Sammy said. "You'll be glad when it's all over. . . ."

"Glad!" Tubby answered, surprised, startled at the putting into words of something which—if it were true—was a product only of blushing thoughts, of secret tremors . . . "I hadn't looked at it that way. . . ."

"Hadn't you?" And again there was the pause before Sammy continued: "You don't look very carefully, very . . . curiously, these days, do you? You've rather forgotten how to peep round corners; how to be . . . inquisitive." He went quietly out of the stables, the others clattering after him.

Before following him out, Bert swung round quickly and stood facing Tubby, waiting for the others to go on past. He stood squarely, a stiff, solid, provocative figure; a short, square, square-headed, red-faced, little man, heavy as lead, hard as a pugilist. With the end of his cane he tapped the bottom button of Tubby's jacket. The button was unfastened.

"Smarten yourself up, me lad," he growled. "That's a cavalry trick. We don't want none o' that in this battery."

He went on out after Sammy.

You could not mind Bert's censure, scrupulously correct, always justified. There was no malice in it, no wish to humiliate. It was clean and medicinal as an astringent mouthwash. But Sammy's remarks, kind, gentle and apparently trivial, could not be brushed aside in the way that they seemed to merit. It was as if he plucked at a string, by extraordinary chance or insight on just the right note, to start your own inner tremors humming in sympathy. . . .

"You've forgotten how to be inquisitive . . . you don't look very carefully; don't peep round corners . . . you'll be glad when it's over." That's what he'd said in that quiet, smiling voice of his.

And that was Sammy's way. He carried everything a stage too far; twisted what should have been a series of casual questions and answers into a personal riddle; discovered corners and asked you, with a hint of reproach, why you had not poked into them.

And why should you trouble about corners, seeking the hidden when the obvious sufficed? The obvious seemed truthful enough; but these suggestions, that Sammy let fall so lightly, made you resentful of yourself, mistrustful of your own honesty. You wouldn't admit to turning your eyes from a sight that might be displeasing; you could not accept a charge of hypocrisy. You were a plain man dealing with plain facts, happy in the simplicity of everything—until Sammy came along, suggesting, insinuating, insisting even, that facts were not plain after all, that truth must be sought and was not, at least, to be had without the asking.

Tubby didn't reason this out. He didn't—you see—know how to reason. It was something he had learned in infancy and had spent the rest of his childhood and youth in forgetting. During his schooldays, certain things had been given to him as facts, certain codes of behavior laid down for him as incontestable. Accepting them, he had forgotten curiosity and lost doubt. He couldn't even have told you his own simple beliefs—that truth was a trollop common to anyone. He didn't bother about truth anyway. A thing was clearly what it seemed and didn't call for analysis. . . . Subconsciously (one supposes) a study of the few Daddy Watsons, whom necessity forced to stay in the Army, warned him of what happened to those soldiers who were not content to accept surface values. So why couldn't Sammy leave him alone in the safe and happy simplicity of the life he had chosen? Couldn't he even leave unsmirched the artless glories of race-riding?

You loved Sammy, but he made you angry with yourself and your anger rebounded against him. Why should he pretend—display—a knowledge of something that you, yourself, had not yet admitted, of the fears and tremors that fore-ran this first race of the season and the ones that would follow? How did Sammy manage to read those emotions, which you called excitement, as fear and apprehension? Just how much more than Tubby did Sammy know of the shadow happenings in Tubby's nerve centers? Did he understand how this race had become the focus of living, had diverted every thought and action to its own purpose? How a glass of beer, another helping of potatoes, was bad for the wind, would put on weight? How this exertion was good for the stomach muscles, but that other was dangerous, might make him slip, twist a cartilage, say, and be unable to ride tomorrow? How, if that wall behind the stables was part of the course, you'd have to take the hell of a pull coming into it . . . and could you take a pull with the grey mare tearing down the hill like a hurricane?

It was always that way before a race or a match or any of those athletic events which were the peak points of Tubby's cycles. Life went in waves, each great roller working up to some moment, some adventure, when every physical power—and the co-ordination of all physical powers—was directed to a plain and single purpose; when living was so joyfully obvious, so austere, so honest, that there was no trouble that could not be dispensed by the skill of muscles and nerves, by the proper functioning of the body. Man, then, was transported back to an animal age where all the queer emotions with which evolution had sensitized him were gone—and body was paramount.

Of course Tubby didn't begin to realize this. He only knew that during a race—or a hunt, say—when mind and body and all parts of him were, for a short time, confined to piloting a horse across a difficult bit of country, he was completely happy and came into powers that were his at no other moments. He was more than happy; he was joyful.

Of course it was a drug effect, for the senses appeared to be hyper-acute but were in reality limited. So little was required of them, and that on no plane but the physical. And of course it was a trance effect; for a man was taken out of himself, space and time existing only as factors of endurance, within the limits of which he watched his body perform miracles.

Consciously Tubby longed for these events; subconsciously he mistrusted and so feared them. Those who live on drugs, from one hypodermic to the next, crave but dread their influence . . . but how should Sammy know this, and why should he mar Tubby's conscious pleasure by exciting his subconscious apprehensions? Why should Tubby be forced now to remember that, when the race was over, he would know relief as the main pleasure to which anticipation had been directed? It wasn't fair. . . .

When you are about to take a woman, you think of the conquest, not of the fulfillment; certainly not of the still greater pleasure that may come with spent passion—even with disillusionment. . . . But Tubby could not view his temper in terms even of this simple comparison. For he had never had a woman. He had only talked about it. He knew no fulfillment beyond the races, the matches, the athletic events, for which he was constantly preparing his body. You might have said that, on his face value, he was more animal than human. But, to Sammy, face values were no more than transparent windows.

Tubby was a soldier, and a good soldier. But, somewhere beneath the uniform, a man was buried.

Chapter 2 A LITTLE AFTER DAWN, HICKS CAME IN TO call Tubby. He kicked open the door with his knee, kicked it shut with his heel, and stumped as noisily as possible across the creaking floor of the bedroom. He had greasy khaki slacks and was jacketless, shirt open at the neck and his grey, elderly hollowed face disgruntled from this early rousing. There was too much of this sort of thing with Mr. Windrush.

Tubby had been wakened by his entry; but the man came across and shook him by the shoulder until he got up quickly, gulping hot tea between shaving and dressing, pulling on jersey and breeches and going out into the April sunlight—much warmer than the draughty quarters.

Down in the lines, the men were cursing as they pulled out the horses, the Orderly Sergeant hurrying them on, all their voices harsh and throaty, the curb chains jingling, and the horses, hoofs scraping the concrete. Little sounds had enhanced value in the early morning; and until the day had found its stride, they were significant, striking the ear individually, passing through to the memory where they seemed fit to live for ever.

The Sergeant, the only man at that hour whose movements had the unselfconscious rhythm of long training, came up and saluted. "Exercise ready, sir. Thirty-three men and sixty-two animals on parade."

Not in uniform, Tubby touched his cap. "All right, Andrews . . . go on, please."

The men had two animals apiece and they had to ride on blankets strapped by surcingles to the horses and mules. They scrambled up, swearing at the animals that were fresh and restless, calling them bastards and bleeders, and then settling on to the blankets and sitting quietly. The groom pulled out the grey mare and Tubby felt the joy of a stretched muscle as he swung his leg over and came softly on to the saddle.

"Walk—march. . . ."

Leaning back, pushing his feet forward so that he saw his toes, Tubby watched the horses file past, the mules after them, filing off the parade ground and down the hill, between the stables and barrack rooms, across the Avon and up between The Sisters to the sweet turf of the plain beyond. Trotting on after them, he got the keen smell of ammonia that came from the stables out into the chaste morning. Consciousness was flooding up in him. He noticed now that the shadows were crisp and long across the road and that the sky was suddenly deep and cloudless. The ripples on the Avon glittered like the scales of a fish; and The Sisters—the clumps of blue firs on the hill beyond the river—were hard and scenic, as though cut out and pasted on to the flat downland. The shadows gave only a pretended third dimension.

He left the battery exercise and cantered across the slope. Taking a long slant up the hill, wind and sun together on his face and the grey mare strong beneath him, he felt the lyric of her movement come into him like music. Her hoofs drummed the beat; the muscles of his back and belly were relaxed and easy. The craft of living, then, was clear as the morning. There were no misgivings.

He was suddenly a man, and other men did what he told them. It was a brave plight; he, an officer, with a commission signed by the King himself; the King calling him *Trusty and well-Beloved*, reposing in him *Special Trust and Confidence*, sending him *Greetings*, giving him horses and servants, bands to play for him, plenty of honor, too little money and draughty and ramshackle quarters to live in. He grumbled and swore as men should; but in scarlet and gold, as gentlemen should, he drank to the King who was his only master. They made a joke of it, but it was a secret glory.

It was fine and easy; no room for doubts or worries. This was living. Up in his stirrups, he felt the mare lengthen beneath him. The grey ears flicked back as she slipped into a gallop. He let her go for two furlongs—a nice pipe-opener.

❦ "The little bitch," Tubby said to the groom; "she put in a beauty when we got to The Sisters. It was all I could do to stay there."

The groom, Murphy, greying and wrinkled, took the mare and patted her, stroking down her neck, squeezing the rubbery neck muscles of a fit horse, reassuring himself through his fingers that she was dry and well, had not suffered from her exercise. With the end of the girth strap in his back teeth, his hard little monkey face squinted up and grinned toothlessly at Tubby.

"She can put in one when she wants to . . . all but had *me* last morning."

"She's a grand little mare," Tubby said, his thoughts wandering. "Fit as the devil. . . . Let's hope she wins. She's got to. . . . No water now!"

He left her to Murphy, walked up in the sunlight across the asphalt square, between the corrugated-iron gun-parks, across the road that led to the Mess, up the weed-ridden path, up the two concrete steps, into the tin hut that he shared with three other officers. The quarters were cold, gloomy and falling to pieces. The roof leaked; the door flew open when the wind blew from the east; and the windows let the draught in. At the beginning of the month, before his ration of coal was finished, the stove smoked on five nights out of seven. The furniture, government issue, was as shoddy as the building. The drawers opened or shut with difficulty, the wardrobe was missing a hinge. The bed had a broken spring, and the Barrack Officer had noted it down to charge against you. You shouldn't be so heavy.

None of this really mattered while you were still young and illusioned. It was part of a soldier's life, the plain backcloth of his setting. It helped the glamour—which you didn't admit, but which you felt keenly. And the men, whose comfort had always to be considered before your own, lived in barrack rooms that were still colder and more draughty than the officers' quarters. They complained always, largely for the pleasures of complaining; but you did not add a reasoned anger to their unreasoned grumbling. You did not bother to argue that the whole barracks were put up hastily as temporary encampments in wartime, that they were built to last for a few years, and that —by patching and propping and for reasons of economy— their life had been prolonged threefold. You only knew that, because of something called the Labour party, or—as the Colonel said—those ranting pacifists, there was no money to be spent on soldiers. Acknowledging this, the matter was at once beyond consideration; for you neither thought nor talked politics. You were the King's man; and the politicians were graded contemptuously with shopkeepers, bankers, lawyers, plumbers, railway strikers, authors and other vagabonds, away below you. You imagined that the Conservatives, being gentlemen, were your champions; you knew that the Socialists— whatever they might be—were your foremost enemies. Because of their agitations, your men were underfed and under-heated, while you were underpaid and—unless you had private means, which they wanted to take away from you—reduced to penury. Even to a soldier, it didn't make sense somehow.

"Hicks," Tubby shouted from the window of his quarters, "Hot water, quickly."

Hicks appeared at the door of the servants' quarters, the next block of buildings.

"It's cold, sir. We ran out of coke last night, sir."

"Those bloody bolshies. . . ."

"Yes, sir."

"Well, bring my boots, and put on the gramophone."

It was just after eight o'clock, and Daddy Watson from next door shouted angrily. In reply, Tubby sang with the gramophone:

We'll travel along,
Singing a song,
Side by side. . . .

"That's you and me, Daddy," he called. "Traveling along and along with the dear old bongos."

Daddy was always surly in the early mornings, partly from the drink he had taken the night before, and partly because of his fourteen years of service as a subaltern. You can't be desperately poor, again and again disappointed, defenceless, subject to unfair treatment and unreasonable orders that toss you about the Empire like sea-borne wreckage, without getting sour and weary. And Daddy was intelligent enough to feel vicious about it, to nourish resentment. He came along now, flapping down the passage in his worn slippers and flannel dressing gown; his heavy face, just after waking, red and crumpled like a baby's; his pink head showing through the thin, mouse-colored hair that hung about his forehead. He limped slightly while his shattered ankle was still stiff from sleep. Already he had a sagging paunch, and the scar of a second wound ran down his throat into the open collar of his pajamas.

"Ruddy young swine," he said. "Wake me at six in the morning, and get me out of bed at eight with that blasted music box . . . turn the damn thing off, will you?"

Daddy was, of course, not really annoyed. But you never knew, with him, when his pretended anger might start on the course that ended in an uncontrolled outburst. Words were intoxicant to him. He loved them, flirted with them, let them seduce him until his play turned to passion. You could not explain what happened to Daddy when he started talking; and it was best to divert him at once from the path of rebuke—however lightly the rebuke was offered.

"It's duty," Tubby said. "I've been out with the bongos."

"I don't believe you've looked at a mule; you've been out galloping that race horse," Daddy answered. "I wonder it's got any legs left."

He crossed the room to the dressing table and took a cigarette from the packet that lay there.

"Who's this?" he asked, picking up the silver-framed photograph.

"Isn't she a peach?" Tubby said. "Tell me, Daddy, if that isn't a peach for you?"

It was a dark girl, with shiny hair and large wide eyes that were looking back over her shoulder, her head twisted in a studio pose, neck very graceful, breasts suggested by the fall of drapery from the shoulders. Daddy read the signature.

"Lydia? A fancy name—who is she?"

Tubby took the photograph from him. "Never you mind, Daddy. Keep your hands off her."

"*I* don't want her," Daddy said. "I've had one a year like that, since I was first commissioned."

"Not like that, you haven't."

"Just like that . . . they don't last; not ever."

"This one's lasted since Christmas. . . ."

Daddy was shuffling round the room, picking up objects— boothooks, the stump of a pencil, a compass—and putting them down again. He looked over Tubby's shoulder. "Fluff!" he said; "to pass the time of night with, after pay day."

Tubby looked fondly at the picture. "No," he said mildly. "She's got brains. She's clever. . . ."

"You don't want brains at your age," Daddy answered wisely. "You know what they say? Keep your interests below the navel. . . ."

"She's not that sort, I tell you. You wouldn't try to."

"Oh, isn't she?" Daddy said. "How can you tell if you've never tried it? And if not, you're a fool to be playing about with her. What do you want anyway? You can't take a wife for fifteen years or so . . . or is this Lydia a rich one?"

"She may be," Tubby answered shortly. "I don't know . . . at least, I hadn't thought of it."

"Oh, hadn't you?" Daddy said, knowing that this couldn't be true. "It's the first thing you have to think of. If she's rich, marry her quickly—before someone else gets her. If she isn't, it's bed or nothing. Otherwise, you're wasting your time and your pocket money . . . you'll know that I'm right in a year or two." He threw his cigarette on the bare boards of the floor and trod on it. "My God, you're young," he said crossly, and padded out of the room, down the corridor, to his own quarters.

When he had gone, you felt that he was like an old dog who

has picked his quarrel, met no enemy and gone his way satisfied. You felt no anger against him. He could not wound you. He was so old, unhappy, bad-tempered, generous . . . you felt rather pity, affection, sympathy, the tenderness you might have for an elderly relative.

Daddy was a good name for him.

All the same, after Daddy's remarks, shaving under Lydia's eyes was a coy sort of business. She watched complacently over her shoulder. But the disordered draperies, arranged by a society photographer, had an implication now. Even shaving had an implication. For, after all, you were a man; and she, from her portrait, very much a woman. Yet in no way was sex the medium of this friendship; and it seemed now that perhaps this very absence of sexual purpose was a shame to manhood; that perhaps she expected it differently.

And, from the beginning, she had seemed to be expecting something. When Benjamin first introduced them and she had come out from the crowded ballroom, away from guardsmen and young barristers, and had walked round and round the Square (the glow of London lighting the roof-tops), and had listened while Tubby told her how fine was the Army and how one day he would be a general and how a general was something, wasn't it . . . then, and afterwards, her interest had been more intense than his awkward, stumbling words could possibly have merited. She couldn't be really absorbed in guns, horses, mules, in the stories he had to tell of Bert, Daddy Watson, Sammy. But always those wide, remarkable eyes stayed gravely on his face, her lips sometimes trembling into a formal smile, her long hands moving in small, acknowledging gestures; and always, in her listening, there was a quality of waiting, of patience. It was as if she were making a diagnosis; as if what he was saying were of no direct or immediate importance, were important only as a herald of what was to come, as a symptom of what was hidden. . . .

You couldn't quite get the measure of it. But, whatever it was, it didn't make you uneasy or give you a sense that she found you wanting. Rather, that you had not fully esteemed yourself, that you were hiding something from her and that she was asking you to be more generous. . . .

And, remembering Daddy's words, he realized that it was hard to say just what he wanted out of her—or she out of him. They had nothing at all in common, but they were happy in each other's company. Their intimacy was based not on shared knowledge, interests, experience, but in the simple pleasures that each found in trivialities, the schoolroom funniness of things gone wrong, the knockabout humor in the spilling of the soup by a waiter . . . they laughed together.

That was as far as it went; and, after that, he couldn't follow her into the books, music, pictures, politics—all the interests whose representative literature, pamphlets, notices, invitation cards, were shown in studied disorder in the Belgrave Square "schoolroom." Nor could he find a part amongst the admirers who sent flowers and chocolates, nor his ease with the liveried footmen, the personal maid, the cars and chauffeurs that were always at her disposal.

It wasn't that the luxury of her life dismayed or impressed him. It recalled his own childhood, the bustling housekeeper and starched housemaids, the wide park from the nursery windows, the sugary smell of the back staircase that led first to the long, dark pantry, where two or three men were always polishing something, too busy—they said—to chatter. But, perhaps by reason of these associations, the splendor of Lydia's life made their relationship unreal, the stuff of dreams, of drama; a vignette hung glittering in the darkness of a theater; the spangled star at the top of the Christmas tree; something beyond his reach and to be enjoyed at a distance. That was what she must mean to him. But, as for her, she wanted something more than his fooling, the fun with streamers at a night club, his robust laughter at a paper cap pushed on the back of her head . . . her delight in these was the doctor's joy at a curious symptom.

"She won't last," Daddy said—and it was quite likely. With so much of her own, she would tire of him as soon as she found that there was no more to him than what he offered. And yet this friendship didn't seem to be slowing down; the curve was still upwards. Only yesterday she'd asked him for a weekend party; and today she was coming down to Bulford. Knowing nothing of horses, with the horses in her father's stable not looked at, unridden, she was motoring from London to watch him ride in the Command Meeting. And if he won, as he would win, it would surely please her?

And yet he had an unreasoned mistrust that his success or failure meant little to her. It was certainly not indifference on her part; but that, like Sammy, she wouldn't accept the standard values. She wasn't interested in triumph or failure, in a race won or lost. She was looking for something apart from that, something beyond his comprehension. She and Sammy ought to get on well together.

He rubbed his face dry, pulled on his jacket and, buttoning it up as he went, hurried to the Mess for breakfast.

❦ Half-a-dozen officers were ahead of him at breakfast: Bert, who was always early, nearly finished; Benjamin, helping himself at the sideboard. Standing beside him and looking at the row of dishes, Tubby found that already, so early in the day of the race, he had no appetite. He was not the kind of games player, sportsman, athlete, whose temperament is tuned low to meet the event in a frigid, businesslike manner. He was the other sort, whose senses are strung tight at moments of physical crisis but whose powers, long before this, start to marshal themselves, increasing in strength, carrying him up the curve of expectancy until, close to the peak, anticipation is so strong that he becomes organically disordered. He feels sick.

Tubby had been on the upward curve for some days, if not weeks. Anticipation had been the background of his life, the stained glass through which he looked at everything. He slept, woke, shaved, dressed, played and worked to it. His thoughts, consciously sometimes and subconsciously always, were busy on racing plates and racing saddles, bushels of corn, elastic bandages, weight-cloths, a last training gallop, and how you were going to steady the grey mare down the long hill to the open ditch at the bottom. Red and white flags fluttered before his closed eyes and appeared, all through the day, whenever he caught a glimpse of those colors. The memory of his first race strengthened, and he recalled the shame of his disqualification for cutting a corner. Bert, with the inability of many old soldiers to distinguish right from left instinctively, had advised him strongly about it. "Red on the right, white on the left," they muttered throughout the day on every inappropriate occasion.

"You ought to know it by now," Benjamin said, choosing a place at the end of the long table. "Of course it's very difficult. . . ."

"Don't worry the lad," Bert said. "He's going the right way about it. When I . . ."

"When you won your first race, Bert . . ."

"Red on the right. . . ."

The Adjutant, like all adjutants, came moodily into breakfast. "Good morning, Benjy; how's your General? Morning, Bert. Morning, Tubby. White on the right, isn't it? That's easy."

"Don't go up upsettin' the lad," Bert said seriously. "He's only acting like I told 'im. We're going to win this race, 'im and me between us."

🏵 "Is Lydia coming?" Benjamin asked as they left the Mess together.

"I can't think why," Tubby answered; "but she said she was."

"She's a queer girl, you know."

"I know. . . ."

"Don't think I'm butting in, old boy," Benjamin said awkwardly, "but I wouldn't take her too seriously. It's my belief she doesn't know what she's after. She's always trying something new; experimenting with people—if you know what I mean."

"Sort of vivisection?"

"Sort of. But it's a dangerous science for the unscientific. She'll burn her fingers one of these days. . . ."

"I doubt it," Tubby said with sudden wisdom. "I should have thought she held the safe end of the candle."

Benjamin laughed. "I don't know. She may lose her head with any one of you. And God help her and the lucky one!"

"Oh, I don't know," Tubby said, a little horrified; "wouldn't anyone be glad to have Lydia lose her head over him?"

"Well," Benjamin said, torn between two loyalties, "it'd depend how far she lost it. She'd be a grand girl for a weekend— but for a lifetime! I've known her too long, you see, ever since I can remember. And she's always frightened me somehow. She gets these fits of wild enthusiasm; mad about something one day and bored stiff with it the next."

"And you think I'm one of her enthusiasms?"

"I couldn't say, old boy; but I'm warning you. She'd never hurt anyone intentionally, but she's hurt a lot of people without knowing it. She'll never believe a man is what he seems. She gets her own idea of him, makes a sort of image of him—of what he might be—and that's the chap she's dealing with. Not the real fellow, you see, but the idea she's got of him. . . . It's funny; because now and again he turns out the way she's thought of him. But more often he doesn't and, as soon as she's disillusioned, she has to drop him. She can't help herself . . . and he gets hurt by the fall sometimes."

"I'm used to falls," Tubby said. "I bet I'll come a beauty this afternoon. At the open ditch for a certainty."

"That blasted race . . . is there nothing else to think about?"

"Not till this evening."

"White flags on the right then—or aren't they? See you in the paddock."

🌼 Every animal has some place of refuge, made safe topographically or by association; the dog, his special corner; the ordinary man, his house or room or even his particular chair by the fireside.

Coming across the parade ground, nerve strings taut, the race an imminent disaster that faced him singly, Tubby found comfort in the beat and murmur of the battery. All around him were soldiers, horses, mules that he knew individually. Each action was planned and had a meaning that he could recognize. Each man, as he could see, was a function of his neighbor and of his neighbors collectively. Whatever affected one, in some degree—however trifling—affected the others. A flash of unfair or ill-judged anger on his part could run through the unit, from one subsection to the next, in a series of explosions. A lame mule, a gun limber turned over, a dirty button on a general's parade, might send ripples into every barrack room, harness room and stable. You couldn't tell. You could only know that sometimes the stream flowed smooth and calm; at others, the surface was broken.

The obvious comparison was a machine, having—as many ardent engineers seem to claim for their charges—a soul and a temper. And, in a good unit, every part was as interdependent as each of the oily and shiny knobs, wheels and shafts of a big motor. But here the parts were living beings, men and animals, many of them contrarily minded, their natures working against each other and yet, by some mysterious welding of melody and counter-melody, coming together like a song. Whatever they— the all-powerful, all-hostile "they" of Whitehall offices—did to you, however much they took away your coal, discovered an extra calory in your rations and cut them accordingly, refused to paint and patch your buildings, slung you about the Empire —the song remained, fervent and beautiful as the song of negro slaves or Welsh miners. It gripped you, tore at you, comforted you, held you to its breast and, when all else had driven you desperate, kept you a soldier. When you were young, it was inspiration.

To enter at will this world, to pick up the domestic threads, to make the small housewifely decisions that kept a battery running smoothly, was—for a young officer—the army's solace. Simply to walk through the lines, identifying each man, animal, activity, settling a dispute, speaking in a fatherly way to a young culprit, and remembering all the time that this was no question of gain or wages or clock hours but a co-operative work to support living, was for Tubby a simple joy that he believed would never diminish. Without reasoning it, without even giving it recognition, he felt it keenly.

"Beg pardon, sir," said the Sergeant-Major; "there's Gunner Miles in 'A' subsection, absent at roll call."

"Again?"

"Yes, sir. He'll be up at office this morning . . . and, beg pardon, sir. . . ."

"Yes?"

"Will we be winning this afternoon, sir?"

"We'll have a try, Sergeant-Major—but don't go risking your money."

"My money's on you all right, sir. The best bet of the day to my way of thinking."

"I wouldn't say that. Are you coming yourself?"

"I hope to, sir. There's two bus loads from the battery. Two bob a head, it is—and most of the men put in for it. On your horse to a man, sir."

"I'm sorry about that. The horse is fit and well—but there's a lot of good ones running."

"Yes, sir . . . and, beg pardon, sir, I've changed round Sergeant Andrews. He was orderly sergeant, but I understand he's fixed up to give a hand with Murphy, saddling up for you."

"Yes. He knows a bit about it; he did five years in a racing stable when he was a youngster."

The Sergeant-Major saluted, and Tubby went on towards the battery office. The farrier looked out of his shop; a long, gaunt, hollow-faced man, almost toothless, completely bald. His words came out half born, only intelligible with practice. "Them racing plates fits a treat, sir," he said. "Will you be up to see them?"

"I'll meet you in the stables, Staff-Sergeant."

Further on, outside the signal store, the signal-sergeant was squatting in the sunshine fitting batteries to a Lucas lamp. He was a round, red-faced little man, a hairy chest showing through his open jacket. He started to rise.

"Don't get up, Hines," Tubby said quickly.

Hines grinned up at him. "Fixin' up a couple o' lamps for this afternoon, sir. . . ."

"A couple of lamps!"

"We're sending Hiscock down to the turn, sir; to let us know how it's going . . . so as we can keep an eye on the bookies."

Today the battery was focussed on the race, on the grey mare, on Tubby. He believed that it was not only for the money they had on him, but that they'd be glad to see the battery win the Command heavyweight. He wasn't sure about it.

Inside the battery office, a third section of a corrugated-iron hut, Bert and Sammy were talking together. Tubby saluted and stood waiting.

"'E'd best be gettin' along, sir," Bert said, looking up.

"What—our jockey?" Sammy asked.

"That's 'im, sir. 'E's got a lot to see to and 'is girl's coming."

"Oh—it's women . . . women now?"

"Wine, women and 'orses, sir. The soldier's motto."

"Is it?" Sammy said dryly. "How elevating."

"If 'is 'orse can keep to its legs, that's all the elevatin' *he* wants."

"Very likely, Bert . . . he'd better slip away then."

"There's that man of mine, Miles," Tubby said; "absent from roll call."

Sammy hunted through the pile of paper on his blanket-covered table and pulled from the bottom the blue-and-white conduct sheets of the day's defaulters. He laid them in front of him, tapped them square with one finger and lit his pipe slowly. Every movement was gentle and tranquil, as if he found joy in it and beauty in what he was touching. His words came slowly, lingering sometimes on his tongue, as if he tested them before he let them loose, and as if they had a double meaning, one for himself and the other for whoever else cared to listen.

"Your Gunner Miles is a persistent gentleman," he said, looking through the conduct sheet.

"Yes, sir. It's the third time. . . ."

"It's that man Patricks," Bert said savagely. "No matter how we change 'is subsection round, there's always crime in it."

Sammy lifted the burnt match from the tobacco tin, the battery ash tray, looked at it lovingly and put it down again. "I do like that word 'crime'," he said. "The atrocious crime . . . you remember, Bert? It was Pitt, I think. . . ."

"No, sir. Not in my time."

"Of being a young man, Tubby." Sammy smiled to himself and picked up the conduct sheet. "But Gunner Miles really *is* becoming something of an habitual criminal. A girl—I suppose?"

"'E wants detention, sir," Bert said. "That's what 'e wants. Why not take 'im up to the Colonel?"

"Whatever I do," Sammy answered, "I think I'll transfer him to Sergeant Andrews. He has a way with criminals . . . how many have we given him? And most of the recruits as well. Yet he always has the best subsection—and how do you account for *that*, Bert?"

"'E's the best sergeant."

"Exactly," Sammy said, leaving no one quite sure of his meaning. "You'd better get along now, Tubby. I may see you on the course—and, one moment. . . ."

"Yes, sir?"

"Just to please me, stop looking so unhappy. Whether you win or lose, whether you break your neck or not, it doesn't really matter a scrap to anyone—least of all to you, Tubby."

"Oh, I don't know, sir. . . ."

"Well, get along with you now, anyway."

To reach his stables, he went between the barrack rooms, set back from the concrete path behind an edging of whitewashed bricks, green plots of grass and then white concrete foundations with red-painted corrugated-iron buildings on top. Red and white again were mixed and, unless he kept himself to realities —away from the sort of remarks that Sammy dropped in front of him—it became very confusing.

There was a crowd by the grey mare's box: Murphy, Bert's groom, Andrews, the farrier—and Daddy Watson. Daddy was speaking: "You'll put the plates on as soon as she gets there. Walk her about to see they're easy."

You didn't connect Daddy with racing, for he was an open denial of all that went with it. He looked all right on a horse; but, when he spoke of horses or racing or hunting, it was sarcastically and with contempt for those who thought such things important. There was even courage, you thought, in the attacks that he made in the Mess, preferably before the senior officers, against all that they—with a queer but true integrity —thought sacred in a mounted unit. But, unless they were strangers or generals, they only smiled at him, enjoying the wealth of his assault. No one who knew him well failed to smile when he became aggressive. When he started to go too far, they left him alone quickly.

Seeing the crowd in the stables, Tubby felt a moment's apprehension. "There's nothing wrong, is there?"

"She's fine," Daddy answered. "The farrier's made a lovely set of plates." He groped for his watch, a cheap, heavy, gunmetal one, which came from his pocket with difficulty, together with a very dirty handkerchief and a very worn pocketbook. Somehow, so many of Daddy's trifling actions were pathetic, his clothes and possessions shabby and inexpensive. You felt that there had never been anyone to give him the nice trinkets, the good leather and gold and silver things that men usually collect. Fumbling awkwardly for the watch, he dropped the notecase, spilling faded letters and yellow photographs on the stable floor, stooping rather foolishly to pick them up, everyone trying to help him. Without reason the scene held pathos. . . .

"You'd better get along now," he said, looking at the watch at last. "Bert and I will see the horse off."

Tubby gave a last look to the mare and left the stables, Andrews following. "Mr. Watson says, sir, as he's never seen a horse looking fitter."

"Oh, did he?" Tubby said vaguely.

"And he ought to know, sir. . . ."

"Ought he?" Tubby said, not very interested in Daddy's opinions about a race horse.

"Why, yes, sir," Andrews insisted; "the best jockey as we've ever had in the Regiment, since I've been serving."

"Who?"

"Why, Mr. Watson, sir."

"Mr. Watson!"

"Yes, sir. He rode in the National, you know; saw him meself, me and the missus. We was on furlough at the time in Oldham. That's where she come from."

"Mr. Watson never rode in the National!" Tubby said. It didn't seem possible.

"Excuse me, sir . . . just after the war he was riding all over the country. Sandown, Cheltenham . . . he had a horse called Nier Vale that he won no end with."

The world was all wrong today, broken up, shuffled up, like the pieces of jigsaw puzzle that (you are told) can be sorted out into some sort of unimagined picture. Daddy—cynical, rather fat, shabby, bad-tempered, benevolent, paternal old gentleman—riding in races. And winning them! Sammy's odd remarks that broke up complacency: "The atrocious crime of being a young man . . . it doesn't matter to anyone . . . least of all to yourself, Tubby. . . ." Lydia, unaccountably coming to see him ride. Daddy's sneers about her, and Benjamin's warning. Nothing was in its place. White and red were jumbled. "Red on the right anyhow. . . ."

He looked at his watch. In exactly three hours they'd be starting.

❀ "Hicks . . . Hicks . . ."

"Yessir—all ready, sir."

Everything was laid out on the bed and on the rug beside it: white cotton breeches, black-and-red jersey (he had never afforded a racing silk), ladies' silk stockings, thin—almost cardboard—boots, an old tweed coat, an old tweed cap, a mackintosh.

"Put on the gramophone, Hicks."

"Yessir. What shall we play, sir?"

"Anything you like, Hicks."

"*My Sweetie's Gone Away*, sir? That's one of your favorites; a good tune, sir. It's got a tune to it, if you take me." The gramophone played the foxtrot and Tubby started to change quickly.

He could never put on a pair of girl's stockings without a sense of guilt left over from schooldays. The cool silk, stretched over the hard muscle of his calf, made what he couldn't help feeling were unhealthy, almost immoral, suggestions. He wished he had thought of borrowing a pair of Lydia's, instead of sending Hicks into Salisbury to buy them.

"How much were these stockings?" he asked.

"Well, sir," Hicks said, embarrassed. "As a matter of fact they wasn't anything. They belongs to a young lady. . . ."

"You mean you borrowed them?"

"Yessir, in a manner o' speaking. But she was proud to lend

them . . . most ladies is, sir; it's a souvenir like, for afterwards."

Even the knowledge that the stockings belonged to Hicks' young lady didn't prevent his thoughts slipping from races, horses, red and white flags, to a still more disturbing quarter. What sort of a girl would an elderly man like Hicks, grey and getting on for forty, go about with? The clinging silk led him up to a round thigh, the silk and lace undergarments (that he had never seen except in a picture, never handled except in rare, dark fancies), to the curves and the pale flesh, the folds in the flesh and the tempting shadows, small breasts of course (he had never seen a woman's breasts), a neck twisted round, an oval face, dark hair and wide eyes looking backwards at him over her shoulder. . . .

"Are we going to win, sir?"

"What's that, Hicks?"

"Do you fancy we'll win, sir? They're saying down in the lines as you're the best bet of the day. Some o' them likes that big brown 'orse of Mr. Cutting's. And there's others that fancy the little chestnut mare that Captain Jago's riding. But the bulk of 'em is on you, sir."

"Don't go and put your pay on me."

"No, sir. I've had my flutter . . . steady with them stockings, sir. Your boot's caught 'em."

"They've split or something."

"Laddered, sir, that's what the ladies call it. They gets in no end of a stew if you ladders their stockings for 'em. You can do most anything else; but that sets 'em at you proper."

"You're a bit of a one with the girls, are you, Hicks?"

"I wouldn't go so far as that, sir. But I don't like to see a laddered stocking. When I was a nipper, there was a jockey down our way—Stockbridge that is—he *was* a lad now. Used to borrer 'is stockings all round the village. 'E wasn't arf a one, but he'd get proper worried if he laddered a stocking. Something always went wrong, 'e told us. 'That'll be a death,' he'd say. Or—'My 'orse will cop it at the water.' That's bad luck, that is. . . ."

"Get on with you, Hicks. That's an old woman's tale."

"Maybe, sir, maybe not. . . ."

"Have we got everything?"

"I took leave to borrow a pair of gloves from Mr. Benjamin. Yours was all washing."

"Borrow's the word, Hicks. Have you got my socks back?"

"There wasn't a lot left to 'em."

"There never is. . . . Come on, Hicks, I can't keep Miss Mervinne waiting."

❧ He went up eagerly towards the Mess, in front of which Lydia's car might already be waiting. He would see when he turned the corner. He walked quickly, with Hicks half running behind but losing distance—burdened with a suitcase, a five-pound racing saddle, whip, gloves, spurs and a crash helmet.

"Hurry up, Hicks."

"Coming, sir, coming. . . ."

His sudden ardor to be with her was not reasonable, unjustified by anything that had passed between them. They had said prosaic farewells and, since their last parting, there had been nothing to draw him on beyond her photograph, the sentimental tunes he played on the gramophone, Daddy's cynical suggestions, Benjamin's warning—and a pair of ladies' silk stockings. But he felt now the quite elementary symptom of love, that the world was not entirely complete without her presence. It was no more than that, but even so it was new to him. No woman had before been a serious factor in his life; and now, in her absence, this particular woman had all at once become a necessity. Or so he felt at that moment.

You can't explain this sudden last stride up the path of adolescence. He was strung tight, of course, with the fear of the race bearing on him, the constant thought of it piling up the pressure. And there is always a last straw, one supposes; a last ripening, a gust of wind, that allows the fruit to drop from the heavy branches. There is some instant of sudden change in many gradual metamorphoses: the butterfly and the chrysalis, the tail of the tadpole. And again, all sorts of unexpected reactions can take place when the conditions are right and the right catalytic is added. It is a matter of chemistry; but this was a matter of a large, fair, healthy, exuberant boy and a sophisticated young woman. The fruit was ripe perhaps; or the silk stockings a catalytic agent?

❧ She was sitting in the driving seat of the long, black car, a book open on the steering wheel, so that, absorbed in her reading, she would not have to make contact with the officers who were passing into and leaving the Mess, some of whom would have known her and some not. Waiting is a very difficult social art, but no social art was beyond Lydia's accomplishments. She sat, elegant, expensive, detached, entirely occupied with her novel. She was very beautiful, with a rich, formal loveliness, with a fur overlapping her hat, framing her face, holding her small, delicate chin in its setting. The silver-tipped hair of the fur, mounted against the soft glaze of her cheeks and neck, mingled with the glossy, darker hair that looked so well in the photograph. Her absorption in the book, her general composure, were almost smug; the whole effect so deliberately hazard, such a carefully pretended repose, so purely feminine, so provocative.

She heard his step, his pause, his bending down to speak to her. She looked up, marked her place deliberately and shut the book, made a show of adjusting hat and collar.

"Good morning, Hicks," she said, speaking first past Tubby. "Good morning, Tubby. You're looking pale; feeling nervous?"

"A bit, but I don't admit it."

Interested at this, she watched him calmly while he put his things in the car, taking them from Hicks and arranging them carefully on the back seat, finally going round behind the car and getting in beside her.

"Remembered the lunch?" he asked.

"I've got a lovely lunch for you."

"All wasted; I shan't eat any."

Clouds came across the sky, and the morning darkened as they drove out of barracks and up the hill behind. At the top there was a long, straight road stretching down and up again to the horizon beyond the dip. The windows were spattered with rain and, up here, they could feel the heavy car edging sideways away from the east wind that was blowing.

"Oh God!" Tubby said suddenly.

"It's only a storm," she said. "It won't be more than a few minutes. We shall have the sun again."

"I wasn't thinking about the weather. . . ."

"Well, what . . . Tubby, it's not the race that's racking these awful groans out of you?"

"As a matter of fact it was."

"Tubby, you *can't* be so silly," she said almost crossly. "You can't take this race in such mad earnest. Can't you see it's a sport, a pastime, something you needn't do if you don't want, that you *do* do for pleasure? You're a human being, Tubby. A lot of people aren't, I know, but there *is* something human in you. You can't tie up your whole life, every hope and fear, to a race, to ten minutes' galloping across the country. . . ." She spoke urgently, but Tubby could not answer. "Of course," she said reflectively, "there is some danger. You might get hurt, I suppose. People have even been killed, haven't they? That's the one saving thing about it . . . 'Exposing yourself to danger elevates the soul. . . .' Stendhal said that, didn't he?"

"Stendle?" Tubby said. "Stendle . . ."

"Welsh Guards, I think," she said viciously.

❦ The last hour before the race had the quality of a dream but was less realistic. You had it all: the proportions wrong, a need for haste and no power to hurry, feelings and actions indistinguishable, thought and words melted together so you didn't know whether or not you had spoken. But there wasn't the clarity of visions; and all that passed was in shadow happenings behind a ground-glass obscurity.

The horse had as many seconds as a boxer. Murphy, Andrews and the farrier-staff-sergeant were busy around her, with the sergeant-major keeping the crowd from the battery at a distance. Bert came to the weighing-in tent and saw to the saddling. Benjamin came up and said that he never saw anyone so pampered, that Tubby had nothing left to do but take the cup from the General's wife . . . "But turn your head, old boy, her breath smells."

Daddy had walked round the course and was looking important. "I don't want to bother you," he said, "but it isn't the jump down the hill you have to worry about. That's nothing. But the fourth fence from the end wants watching. You ought to be coming up by then and you land uphill. You need to take it steady. . . ."

"There's that brown 'orse of Cutting's," Bert said. "He's a good 'orse. You'll have to stick to 'im. . . ."

"And watch that chestnut of Jago's," said Benjamin; "he jumps crooked."

"How do I do it?" Lydia asked, as Tubby bent down to her, the strings of his cap hanging.

"Just a bow, a tight bow . . . tighter."

"How's that?"

"Fine . . . you do smell good."

"Better than hay and leather?" she asked wickedly.

"You'll never let me forget that. . . ."

"I don't expect so."

She stood back to view him. "You don't look really well in racing things," she said. "These sort of theatrical clothes are for dark people, like me and Benjy. That's what's so sad about the poor Germans. They do so love being pink and white and they do so love dressing up, and the two just don't go together. Even a very fine specimen of a white mouse ought to be got up as soberly as possible. . . . There's something rather German about *you*, Tubby."

"The bookies are getting the wind up," Benjamin said. "You're two-to-one on now; it was threes against you half an hour ago. There's about twenty of your Pack Battery stiffs have made a circle round Mr. Alf Higgins and one or two others. They seem to be detailed off to stay there. I saw your Hicks with an ugly look in his eye and a brickbat. . . ."

"Where's Bert?"

"Just gone on down to the paddock; so has the horse. We'd best follow."

The rain stopping, a burst of sunlight sharpened the colors of the riders and added a gloss to the flanks of the horses. The grey was going round quietly now, but the dark stain between

her buttocks showed where she was sweating. The crowd was
pressed tight against the ropes and Bert pushed his way through,
signaling to the groom to bring the horse into the center of the
paddock.

"I want that saddle more forward," he said. "Hold on to
her now, will you?"

The mare pivoted away from Bert, Bert following round loos-
ening the surcingle and girths, and Tubby standing on the far
side with his weight on his outstretched arms and his hands on
the grey flanks, trying to keep the horse steady.

"Just stuffed with corn," he said over his shoulder to Lydia.

"Lead him round," Bert said to the groom; "I'll get the
girths up that last hole in a minute."

Sammy came into the paddock and shook Lydia's hand
shyly with nothing much to say to her.

"How are you feeling?" he asked Tubby.

"Our last joined recruit's feeling nervous," Bert said. "Got
the wind up proper . . . But 'e'll win all right."

The bell rang and the groom led the horse into the center,
Bert going up to tighten the girths again.

"Well, good luck, Tubby," Lydia said.

"I must hurry round and get back to you."

"Good luck and I know you'll win."

He crooked his leg and Bert, putting his hand under it,
tipped him into the saddle.

"I'll be back soon. . . ."

"Take it easy to start with," Daddy said. "You can't rush
the first fences with that devil."

"Take care of Lydia," he called back; "see you all in hospital.
And ginger up that ambulance."

They rode out of the paddock, through the lane that the
police cleared for them. The blue arm of a constable was pressed
across Sammy's chest but he looked up and caught Tubby's
eye.

"Good luck, Tubby; enjoy yourself."

"Thanks, Major."

He saw the sergeant-major and Sergeant Andrews, Sergeant
Hines and the farrier and some of the others in the crowd.

"Good luck, sir."

"Thanks, Sergeant-Major, thanks, Andrews."

"You'll win, sir, you've got 'em stone cold, you have."

"Thanks, Staff-Sergeant, we'll have a crack at it."

Tubby stood up in his stirrups and let the grey kick and bucket her way up the hill to the start. At the top, there was a large field and several of the horses were restless.

The starter pushed his bowler hat forward over his eyes and spoke to them: "Red flags on the right, gentlemen, white on the left . . . I shall say *are you ready—go* and drop my handkerchief."

"That's easy," Tubby said to his neighbor. "White rhymes with right, you see, but you have to forget it because it's the other way round to make it difficult."

"Tubby, you're hopeless. God, I haven't half got the wind up."

The other man was sweating under his cap and his face was pale and tight like Tubby's.

"You don't need to worry," Tubby said; "I shall put you all down at the first fence. This brute always jumps crooked."

The grey was fidgeting about and going backwards into the big brown horse, the brown horse letting fly with a sudden, vicious spasm of its hindquarters.

"Curse your soul," Cutting said. "Can't you control that bloody animal?"

"Not in the least," Tubby said, "you don't mind, do you?" He saw the starter raise his handkerchief and he pulled the grey round so that they faced the wrong way and the starter had to wait for them. "One moment, sir. . . ."

"Hurry up, Mr. Windrush."

The dream was over now—except that there was no past, the future was dim, unlit and pressing, the living moment vivid. But impotence had gone. He was no longer nervous. This was a game that he knew, and all the power of him, mind and body, was collected in his legs and arms, with him jockeying for a start, playing to get the grey mare facing the right way, all bunched up between his legs, half cantering forward.

"All right, sir."

The starter let them go and flicked down his handkerchief.

Up and out of the saddle, a vast press of horses and the grey mare amongst the leaders. The first fence not far ahead, but everything beautifully clear, unbelievably simple. No fears, no doubts, plenty of time and a knowledge of what must be done quickly. The beat of the world had quickened.

You might have been driving in the dark through country lanes, all twists, humpbacked bridges, right-angle turns, the headlamps lighting first one side and then the other, throwing their futile beam into the sky, glowing back from the grey wall of a barn that seemed to block your passage. And then, at last, you had come into the long, straight highroad. Ahead, a clear path of light down which you could roar unthinking. By comparison, the immediate past, cantering to the post, jockeying for a start, was lost in dreamland happenings; and all before that was of no account whatever, deeply buried in time, forgotten in time, decaying now with the spent hours and minutes. And, in this brave new world, time is nonexistent. Time is drawn out, swollen, stretched like a lady's stocking, laddered, broken into fragments. In life, in true living, there is only the time that you make; it is your servant and, when you are ready, it may move on behind you. Its movement is no limitation, for you limit its passing. You are not tied to time, only to a sequence of actions. You are master, all powerful, power coming up and responding to your order. You are all-knowing, all-seeing, looking down from above, making moves on a chess board.

You live. Up and out of the saddle, weight on knees and on the fragile irons, weight of the horse on your arms, the movement of the horse working into you, through thin cotton breeches, through thighs and loins deep into you. The helmet binds your brows, the peak of the helmet blanking the upper sector of your vision; below the peak, grey ears, grey neck, grey moving muscles of her powerful shoulders. Her hoofs flash forward, entering your vision as they chop the earth, turning green turf to brown fragments, swinging backwards and forwards, into and out of your vision, adding their beat to the general percussion.

It is clearer now in the growing daylight; with the end of dawn, night is forgotten; and the dream, sharp in the moment

of awakening, has gone too from memory. The awakening itself,
bright and vivid when the handkerchief fluttered, is now in
shadows and is suspect. Always the past is false, and only the
present is true living. All around you are friends of the past,
present enemies. Beneath you, the grey mare is your only ally.
The rest is easy: field after field, fence after fence, with you
poised steady on your knees, down in the saddle as hoofs rattle
the brushwood, up again with the fence behind you, quiet and
still as the grey muscles beneath your knees carry you rhythmically.

Red on the right. Round the flag with your knee on the pole,
the pole shaking and the fence all too soon after. A chestnut
draws level, is past, the grey mare lengthening her stride to
catch up, but you checking her. A bay is past and another, and
Cutting's brown horse, that had kicked at the start, comes up
and stays level so that you go into the next fence stride for stride,
taking it together.

Halfway round, and the long hill down to the water, and
Cutting still with you, the chestnut and one other in front. A
glimpse of metal, the water below; the hill beyond, a strip of
plough, the chestnut tiring and the others out of it. The chestnut
goes wide round the flag, comes slowly back to you, jumps
slantwise across you, crashes the fence, pecks, stumbles and has
fallen beneath you. The grey swerves to miss them, bumps the
brown horse, you curse. Cutting curses, the two of you cursing
hoarsely and taking the next fence with knees touching. Knee
touching knee for a long, dangerous moment.

Glance sideways. The grey is strong beneath you, but the
brown horse is full of running. Eight fences to go, seven, six, and
the wind is cool in your face, a numbness in you, a vast exaltation . . . glorious, joyous moment of time, come from timelessness with eternal value. You know nothing but you know all.
You feel nothing but you live. You cannot feel the rubber of the
reins, but the ridge of short hairs, where the grey mane is
clipped, is rough on your knuckles. Four fences to go, three
fields, and the brown horse still with you . . . what did Bert say
about the brown horse? What did Daddy say about the brown
horse? What did Daddy say about a fence somewhere? "Stick to

the horse . . . the fourth fence from the end—take it steady . . ."
How could you? How the devil could you?

Let the mare go! Down in the saddle now, forcing your will
into her through the power of your thighs, through the feel of
the reins and the touch of your hand on her withers. Round the
last flag; you and the brown horse together, with the fence
ahead and the grey's stride lengthened out, low and smooth,
in the dregs of strength that gush from her. Life is music. Vision
has narrowed to the grey neck and ears and the black fence
beyond them.

He heard Sammy's voice first, speaking gently and calmly.
"That's right," he was saying, "that's right, we'll have that out
of it."

Then, from some way off, there was Bert, gruff and abrupt,
shouting to someone. "This way," he was calling. "Come on,
can't you?"

Then he smelt the warm, sweet scent that was strangely
familiar—better than hay or leather. His muscles, his senses,
his thoughts were lost to him, jumbled together like the curb-
chains, the bits and the irons that you threw in a sack and shook
together for cleaning. He could not disentangle them. Seeking a
muscle, pain flooded him. He lay quiet, with pain and the sweet
scent filling his knowledge. He wanted sight, fought for it and
opened his eyes, seeing that all about him there was a dim
whiteness. He asked the conventional questions.

"Where am I? What happened?"

"You're all right," Sammy said. "Just lie quiet a bit. The
doctor's coming."

"Lydia!" Tubby said as he saw her beside him. "What
happened, someone?"

"You must lie quiet and not worry."

He got cross with them and started to lift his head, but the
pain in his shoulder went shooting through him, all down his
chest and the side of his body. Then he was angry and he tried
to shout, but his voice came out a croak, unreal, as if from a long
distance.

"What the hell happened? Won't someone tell me?"

"You had a fall, dear," Lydia said soothingly.

"I guessed that," he answered, trying to grin. "I had that damn race in my pocket."

Bert edged into the circle of his vision. "How is he?"

"Grand," Sammy answered. "He'll be all right in a minute."

The doctor came in, the R.A.M.C. major from barracks. He knelt down beside Tubby and started to feel him. "Does this hurt . . . this . . . this . . . ?"

"All of it . . . hell." Tubby answered with the sweat cold on his forehead. Then it was hard to breathe, and the whiteness was closing down on him.

"God, it's hot."

"This tent *is* hot," he heard Sammy saying. Then Bert was speaking again, then Daddy Watson. "Can we get these flies open?"

"I'll do it."

The breeze came in, and Lydia's hand was cool on his forehead.

"I'll give him a spot," the doctor was saying.

"They've got the hurdle," Daddy called loudly.

"I'll give him a spot first," the doctor answered. "It'll be easier to move him."

"Don't bother about the jersey," Sammy suggested.

"A knife, someone?"

"Have you got one, Daddy?"

"Bert?"

"I've one in my bag," Lydia said surprisingly.

"Cutting my throat?" Tubby tried to grin at them.

The knife touched the flesh of his arm and the doctor was back beside him, very important. "Can't see in here," he was muttering.

"Make it a double, Doctor," Tubby said, still trying to be funny.

There was a prick in his arm and the doctor was dabbing iodine. Then everything was quite clear all round him. "Could I have a cigarette? Just while the dope's working."

"Rather, old boy."

"Turk or gasper?" Daddy asked briefly.

"Turk for preference."

Lydia was fumbling in her bag.

"I've got one." She lit it for him and leaned over him, and the scent came strong, and he saw the red marks on the butt of the cigarette as she put it between his lips.

"Don't move," she said. "Tell me when you want to puff and I'll take it out for you."

He drew in the smoke and smiled at her. The others were getting far back and there was only he and Lydia. He still tried to joke: "I never want to puff. It just sticks to my bottom lip like a . . . like a . . . like a . . ."

He struggled for thoughts and words, but his voice was very distant and foreign.

"Yes, dear," Lydia was saying.

"That's fine," the doctor said loudly and suddenly.

❀ Sammy went with him in the ambulance, and several of the others followed in a private car to the hospital. As they were unloading his stretcher, he could hear them talking together, their voices lowered and restfully indistinct, the general hum of their speech coming as a soft accompaniment to what was so strangely happening to him. Now and again, a few words flashed out at him, like blazing lights, he seizing them and turning them about so that, against the dark background of his mind, they were impressed unforgettably.

"We'll get a cup of tea," Bert was saying.

Bert and a cup of tea were at first incompatibles, till suddenly they whirled round and clicked into place, Bert and a cup of tea being then an obviously suitable connection.

"If we come back in an hour . . . it's no use your hanging about here, Miss Mervinne. . . ." That was Daddy. It was not like Daddy, this practical argument. Then Bert and Daddy came together in one big red face with a cup of tea sternly before them and Lydia, cool and smiling, softly behind.

Sammy and Lydia were talking together gently, and Lydia was giving a telephone number of four figures that mixed themselves up in a hopeless jumble. They went round and round, like a wheel that told fortunes, and resolved themselves at last into the house where Lydia was staying. It was suddenly clear what was happening.

"Major, you naughty old man," Tubby said, making a joke of it, "at your age . . . asking her telephone number." It was necessary, at all costs, to keep up being funny. In this last extremity, it was the only token he could give of self-mastery, of manliness. He turned his head slightly to smile, and the pain came through him like a sword, turning and twisting. The breath came out of him suddenly and all his body seemed to be relapsed into the unendurable pain and the sweat cold on his forehead. He felt Sammy's hand lightly on his hair, and the pain that was everything was dulled down and melted into the warmth of his stillness.

"You're all right, Tubby, old chap, you'll be better in a minute."

Absurdly, a small tear was trickling from one eye down his cheek, but he dared not turn his head to hide it.

"Gently, gently," someone was saying.

"You'll have to tip it, matron. Go easy, orderly."

"Up here, a little more . . . more . . . that's about got it."

There were men in white smocks about him, someone in uniform, a young nurse and an elderly woman.

"Just one more," said the radiologist.

The black lamp affair that was hanging above him filled the world and started to revolve about him. It was all dark, because of the whirring of the lamp, except for the shiny nickel handle that was turning fiercely, coming towards him and filling his vision.

"Sal volatile . . . brandy . . ." a woman was saying.

"Another shot, to get him into the ward," a man answered.

Later, there was another prick of a needle. Then, as they moved him, the pain came wickedly through the furred darkness, fighting the waves of warmth that were sweeping up in him. A strange voice from a long distance was calling hoarsely. People were moving about, quietly, persistently, and hands touched him lightly.

❦ His father came into the ward, tiptoeing naughtily, like a child bent on mischief. Tubby had not seen him for a year, and did not want to. His father was smoking a cigar and wore that ridiculous monocle. He was not very clear, but big and red-faced and heavy.

"Hullo, Father," Tubby said. "Where have you sprung from?"

"Hullo, John; I flew from Le Touquet."

"I'm sorry, Father."

"That's all right, my boy, I like flying."

"I'm sorry to be such a nuisance. . . ."

"Not at all, my boy, I wanted to get back to England. Lost all my money at Le Touquet and had to recoup somehow."

"I'm sorry, Father."

"No, no," the man said with irritation, "I like flying. I'll get you to London."

"No," Tubby said. "Don't move me again, for God's sake. I'm fine here, Father."

"Better in London."

"I'm fine here. Couldn't be better."

"Of course you're fine. Anyone can see it."

"No," Tubby said weakly and heard them arguing. The doctor was there, and the radiologist and the matron. They were all against his father, but his father kept on talking of London. He hated his father, and hated the cigar smoke and the big red face and the argument that annoyed him. They were going out of the room, and their voices dwindled like a car driving away in the darkness.

❦ The nurse rustled into the room, carrying her white enamel tray and moving briskly.

"What is it this time, sister?" Tubby asked her.

"Just a little something to get you ready."

It was the day that they were going to operate to try and manipulate his arm into position. At ten o'clock, they were coming to give him the anesthetic that would take away the pain, the almost unbearable pain that had been his companion for the last week. The morphia that they shot into him every four or five hours dulled the pain and threw it into the background but left it there, in his shoulder and arm and side, filling his body in waves till it was omnipresent throughout his consciousness. For all of that time, he had scarcely slept. He craved unconsciousness, begging them to operate for the relief the chloroform would bring. He could not think beyond the oblivion of the anesthetic. It was only oblivion that he wanted.

"What is it?" he asked. "Not the usual morphia stuff?"

"It's got that in it."

"What else?"

"We are inquisitive, aren't we?" she said brightly, speaking to a child.

"I don't see why I shouldn't know what you're putting into me."

"Just something the doctor's ordered."

"It's my arm you're putting it into," he said petulantly.

"Of course it is," she teased him, drawing apart the pajama jacket that was pulled over his good arm.

It was now extremely important that he should know all about it.

"Sister, you're not to put it in till you tell me what it is."

"It's something very special for good, obedient patients. It's got morphia and atropin and one or two other things that they mix up all together in the dispensary. Now you know as much as I do." She nicked the top off the capsule and was holding it and the needle up to the light.

"What's atropin?" he asked.

"We always give that before an operation like this."

"Why?"

"Because the doctor orders it," she said, absorbed in filling the needle.

She gave him the injection and then moved quietly about the room, putting it straight. Almost at once the drugs began to work. He was lifted up, looking down on his pain, knowing it was there, but feeling aloof and rather proud of it. It was in this way that, during the race and at other moments of exaltation, he had become a spectator to his own actions. It was a pleasant, godlike feeling.

Later, the anesthetist came in with a stethoscope to make his

examination. He was a clean-shaven, sober-looking man, with a
face like a dentist and a grave, suburban manner.

"Vetting me, Doctor?" Tubby asked, grinning at him
foolishly.

"That's it," the doctor said without smiling, busy with his
stethoscope.

"Lame on the near fore, I make it."

"That's it."

"Otherwise sound in wind and eye."

"Near enough."

"Perhaps it's more like an execution," Tubby said, arguing
with himself. "Getting the drop right and that sort of thing.
Giving me a hearty breakfast, only they wouldn't let me have
any."

"I don't expect they would."

"Or perhaps, again, it's more like a human sacrifice. It's a
neat point, Doctor."

"Yes?"

"You mustn't mind me, Doctor, I'm just the least little bit
drunk."

"Ah."

"Pretty near sozzled on that stuff the nurse shot into me."

"It takes some people that way."

"I call it a shame, getting a chap into hospital, fixing him up
in bed and then making him rolling tight like this."

"You won't do much rolling."

"That's just it. Tight without rolling. That makes it all the
worse."

"Nice feeling, isn't it?"

"Fine, but it's all wrong. Morally wrong. I object on principle. I asked the nurse what she was putting in, but would she
tell me?"

"I don't expect she knew."

"That's what she said, but it was a long time before she'd own
to it."

The doctor finished his examination.

"Send me the certificate," Tubby said. "I suppose it's the
usual two guineas."

The operating-room sister came in and talked with his nurse. "He's all right," the nurse was saying softly.

"I can hear every word," Tubby said. "All your innermost secrets, sisters."

They moved out of the room and then came back again with an orderly. Then the surgeon and the anesthetist and another young doctor came in and the room was full of people.

"This *is* an execution," Tubby said. "I'm as drunk as a lord."

They pushed a wheeled stretcher alongside his bed and were arguing how to get him on to it without hurting him. They tried moving him gently, drawing him gradually across. He closed his eyes.

"Does that hurt?" someone asked.

"Like hell," he said. When he unpressed his lips to answer, all his breath was drawn out of him with the words. They stopped moving him and were talking together again.

"I've got an idea," Tubby said.

They took no notice.

"I've got an idea, a bloody good idea," he said again, crossly.

"Yes, yes," someone said impatiently.

"*Will* you listen to my idea?"

"All right, old boy," the surgeon answered, putting his hand on Tubby's forehead. "Let's hear it."

"Why don't you give me the anesthetic here? Then you can push me along without worrying about hurting me."

"We might do that."

"Do what you like when I've had the anesthetic. Finish me off quickly. But for God's sake give me the stuff."

They discussed the suggestion together, standing by the doorway, and talking as though he were a child and could not understand their words.

"All right, that's what we'll do," they said at last.

"Broadminded of you, Doctor," Tubby said feebly. "Very decent I call it. Letting the patient teach you your business."

"That's about it."

"Don't mind me, will you," Tubby said anxiously. "I'm just a bit tight so you mustn't mind what I say. I didn't want to get tight, you know. Tight on parade, that's very serious."

"That's all right."

The anesthetist held the pad to his nose and mouth.

"Breathe deeply."

"What filthy stuff."

"Never mind, breathe deeply."

"What a smell. Lovely, lovely stuff."

"Breathe deeply."

"Lovely, beautiful stuff."

He was looking up into a cone-shaped whirlpool, the outer edges of which enveloped him completely. The water was composed of dung-colored, distorted swastikas. In the center of the whirlpool was the hard brightness of the pain that came back to him; and, as he looked at it and tried to understand it, it came down through the whirlpool and smothered him completely so that, from a long distance, he heard someone screaming. For a moment there were people very close to him, doing something to him, and then the hard center of pain went back and, still fiercely bright, was incomprehensibly distant. The dung-colored swastikas enveloped him again. Years passed, and the hard bright center moved across until it was no longer over the whole of him but concentrated on the left side of his body. As if through a glass, that converged the rays of the sun, the black, dazzling pain was at last fixed in his left shoulder.

"They've made a mess of it," he said at last.

"Everything's splendid," the nurse answered. She was leaning over him, and holding a small piece of ice between his lips.

A long time afterwards, he started to think it out. After the anesthetic there should have been no more pain. The anesthetic brought unconsciousness and, while he was unconscious, they put him right. The pain should not have been there; but it *was* there, a thousand times greater than before.

"God, they've made a mess of it," he said again.

"No, no, everything's quite all right."

"It's still hurting. They must have made a mess of it."

"It will hurt a little at first. You have to expect that, but it all went splendidly."

The nurse was fluttering her hands about his pillow, speaking automatically, words of routine assurance.

"God, how it's hurting."

"You'll be better soon. Would you like some more ice?" She brought the bowl of ice towards him.

"I'd like a drink."

"No, only ice."

Later again, he put his good arm across and felt his left shoulder. It had all gone hard.

"Sister," he called. "Sister . . . sister . . . sister."

She was out of the room but came hurrying back again.

"Hush now, you'll wake everyone else in the hospital."

"What's happened, it's all gone hard!"

"It's quite all right; quite all right; just how it's meant to be. I'm sure the doctor will be very satisfied." Again that automatic reassurance.

"But it's all hard," he shouted.

"Hush. You'll wake up all the other patients. It's the middle of the night, you know."

He twisted his head, and saw stretched out beside him on a table a long, white-covered tube where his arm should have been.

"What is it?" he whispered.

She moved the light for him to see.

"It's the splint they've put on. It's quite all right. It's what they call a Thomas."

The Thomas splint was a sort of skeleton tube, the framework wound with bandages. The near end of the tube was hard against his shoulder and armpit, the swollen flesh of the shoulder almost enveloping the ring of the splint. His arm was stretched through the tube, his wrist fastened to the far end of it.

"God, sister, is it meant to hurt like this?"

"It always hurts after an operation. You're very lucky not to be sick. That's because of the ice we've given you."

"It can't be meant to hurt like this. It goes all through me."

She looked at her watch. "It's nearly time for another injection. Another ten minutes."

"Give it to me now."

"In another ten minutes," she repeated firmly, her lips pinched up together.

"Why not now? Ten minutes can't matter."

Rather than argue, she pretended to give way to him. "I'll go and get it—immediately."

She was a long time away, and waiting for her was almost unendurable. When she came back, she looked at her watch again.

"It's time now," she said, and gave him the injection. It was a strong one, and began to work quickly.

"Now we'll have a nice sleep," the sister said through the mist, the quiet mists that were wreathing the trees and creeping quietly up the valley.

"They never rise when there's mist on the water."

"What's that?" the nurse asked, bending down to him.

"It's a waste of time, staying down by the river."

"Of course it is," she agreed. "Ever so much better to have a really nice sleep, isn't it?" She gave the pillow one more little pat, turned out the lamp and left the room quietly.

"Sister . . . sister . . ."

She didn't answer, so he lost consciousness.

In the morning the surgeon came, a tall, bleak man, with a wide forehead, a hard, dry, incisive voice that crackled. He looked at you with pale, almost colorless eyes that gave no comfort, that suggested rather doubt, uncertainty, that nothing existed unless proved scientifically and that hope was not a scientific emotion. He regarded you, you felt, as the subject of experiment, a case not without interest. You might, indeed you should, recover. He made his examination, renewed the dressings himself, while the nurse held your head turned so that you could not see what he was doing, and left quickly. You asked him questions, and he, evading an answer, increased your unhappiness with all the fears that imagination could conjure. "I can't say that . . . it's early yet . . . after the next photograph perhaps . . . really I can give you no idea, no idea at all; not at present. . . ."

The pain, the mist of pain, was all about you with the memory of the anesthetic that recurred like sardines or onions. The day was endless with pain, and with pain-borne fancies. Of all the possibilities, the surgeon had eliminated none; had done nothing to lighten the burden. There was so much he might have said, so many assurances he could surely have given: "You won't die, anyway . . . you won't lose your arm . . . or the use of it . . . it's a matter of weeks, months, years . . ." anything. But in no way would he commit himself—he who could so easily have parted the mists to let in one gleam from the future.

Still those mists; sometimes thickening to the yellow fog over London with the sun lamps suspended overhead; but, much more often, the gentle mists hanging low on the river, lapping the trees, the frost-bound twigs crackling beneath your shooting boots . . . "They won't come now, Benjy," . . . And then the whisper of mallard in the darkness . . . and the mist lay on the plough, but it was clearing. "We'll hunt by twelve," the Master said . . . "There'll be a scent, I shouldn't wonder," Tubby answered.

"What?" the nurse asked, bending down to him.

The nurse came and went through the mist, shattering each pleasant fancy as it began to grow substantial. Each time, she was carrying something, a basin, a cloth, a kidney dish, the apparatus for a caffein injection. Every hour they did something to you, something unpleasant, humiliating. The visits of this cold, aloof, competent, loveless woman were the day's landmarks. They were nothing more. She was nothing more to you than a hired guardian. And you were lonely.

"Oh fat white woman whom nobody loves. . . ."

Suddenly, the memory came back to you of a master, rather a sissy master, reading poetry to you in English hour. Wednesday afternoons, he remembered. That line hadn't been in his head for years; but now it had come back again. It was queer what you held without knowing it. Like the conjurer's glass that went on and on, pouring out bucketfuls of water. Didn't he remember, though, how they'd all laughed in the servants' hall on Boxing Day, when the conjurer (who'd been caught illicitly fishing before now) kept on pulling rabbits out of the head-keeper's pockets? And the final insult when he found there a dummy bottle of beer, to follow the rabbits . . . dear old Will Ramsay, who'd taught you to shoot and who loved his five or six pints in the evening. You could hear him now: "Ye're behind him again, Musterr Johnnie. . . ." And couldn't you hear Menzies laughing at that conjurer and at the way he'd discomforted Will Ramsay; funny, whiskered old Menzies who wouldn't let you try out his billhook.

The nurse came rustling back again.

"Why do you walk through the fields in gloves?" he said, remembering triumphantly.

"What's that, dear?"

Goodness! She was a new one; a dark, kind Irish woman, the maternal sort. But still you wished she'd go away, for she only increased your loneliness. You, who had so many friends, were alone with your pain, uncomforted, unsupported. Grief and pain flooded your body. You wanted a soft hand on your forehead, a quiet, cool hand against your cheek, a soft breast in which to bury your face and weep out your misery. You dare not loosen your pain with tears for fear of the plump, hard, soulless woman—or even of the little dark one. They would not leave you alone, but you were lonely.

During the morning they brought in a portable X-Ray apparatus and took photographs; and in the evening the surgeon came again with Sammy. With Sammy sitting on the end of the bed, his quiet smile and gentle eyes absorbing your misery, the mists cleared and pain receded.

"I suppose you can't tell me," Tubby said abjectly, "but do they think it's serious?"

"Serious?" Sammy answered, as if he were surprised at the question. "I've talked with Dr. Barret and he tells me it's an unpleasant accident. But not serious. He doesn't expect that your arm will ever be as good as new. You may never have any movement in the shoulder joint. But that doesn't matter, does it?"

He put the question as a declaration, converting you at once, so that you had to know with him how little it mattered. Without reason, you were convinced by his simple, quiet statement.

Even to Tubby, it was as if Sammy had said: "Birth, you know, is only the first stage of death, which is the first stage of . . ." So that these wayside incidents could be of no great importance.

"Will I . . . will I be long in the hospital?" he asked later.

"A goodish time," Sammy said cheerfully. "Several months, I'm glad to say. It's a wonderful chance for you, Tubby, to do— so many things that we never have time to do in the army."

Once again, it was not that he was sugaring the pill. He was, instead, stripping its reputation for nastiness, showing you that in truth it was good and desirable. While he was there, sitting on the bed, dropping the slow words that had a strange weight in their fall, it was hard to doubt the honesty of what he was saying.

"We'll move you to London, of course. . . ."

"Oh no, sir."

"I think you'll be better in London. There's a fair amount to be done to you . . . besides your father wanted it."

"Oh, him. . . ."

"Well, he's your father, after all—though he does seem to have gone abroad again."

"Has he? I'm glad of that."

"He went to Cannes to recoup from Cheltenham races. He seems to do a lot of recouping."

"I don't see that his wishes have got anything to do with it."

"Perhaps not," Sammy said mildly. "But if any human being has anything to do with it, it's Dr. Barret. And he doesn't want to travel a hundred and fifty miles, two or three times a week, to come and look at you."

"No," said the surgeon. "No, I can't do that."

"But . . . but what have I broken? Dr. Barret has done his operation, hasn't he? He mended me when they gave me chloroform. . . ."

"I think Dr. Barret had better tell you about it."

The surgeon cleared his throat, and spoke dryly, as though delivering a lecture. His uninterested eyes were fixed on the window, across the room and away from Tubby. He kept it quite impersonal. There was no distress or sympathy. He was a workman, refusing to take any fraction of the weight of other people's troubles, no more kindly—less kindly—than a plumber, who at least commiserates on a flooded bathroom.

"It is a compound fracture of the humerus," he said, "that is, the upper bone of the arm. It is not unlike an umbrella, with a knob at the end of it fitting into the cup of the scapula—that is the shoulder blade."

"Like an umbrella," he repeated happily, as if making a somewhat whimsical comparison and, by this descent from the strictly scientific, a concession to the two laymen. He nodded to himself, clearly resolving to continue in this frivolous strain.

"Like an umbrella . . . and if you snap off the knob . . ." He shrugged his shoulders, spreading out his hands palms upwards. "Well, the umbrella is out of action for many of its . . . less obvious purposes. It might keep off the rain, it's true; but for carrying or holding . . . very awkward."

He allowed a short, effective silence, balancing himself with a gentle, rocking movement on the balls of his nicely pointed feet.

"That is what you have done," he said, swinging round on Tubby, scoring a quick point, finished with this benevolent nonsense. "You have fractured the humerus at the surgical neck. The shaft has entered the brachial plexus and pierced the brachial artery. The brachial plexus is an important nerve center. That is why the pain you feel may be extensive and general. The piercing of the artery is an interesting complication. It has caused considerable internal hemorrhage and, as you can see for yourself, external swelling. We shall not be able to operate until the swelling has subsided. . . ."

"But you have operated . . . you operated yesterday."

The surgeon cleared his throat again in disapproval of this interruption. Question time was at the end of a discourse. "We made an attempt," he said severely, "to manipulate the shaft into position. We also made an incision, largely for the purpose of ascertaining the possibilities of plating. I am glad to say that these are considerable. We succeeded in clearing the fracture from the artery, and in a few weeks—say two months—we should be able to make a fresh incision and put a plate on the joint. We must give the artery a chance to heal, of course. . . ."

"So you see," Sammy said, "you've messed yourself up a bit."

"Throwing himself about," said the surgeon, at last getting really jolly. "And now, I'm afraid I must leave you to your senior officer . . . an operation in London tonight . . . another case of interest. . . ." He turned round quickly, and gave them a curt nod, said "Good-by" and was gone.

"I call that good value at ten guineas a time," said Tubby. "That unmitigated ass."

"You mustn't start getting intolerant at your age," Sammy answered. "You will find that many clever specialists are like that—a little foolish, a little lacking in humanity. Some call it a mark of genius."

"The nearest that man ever got to humanity," Tubby said, "is an umbrella with a knob on it."

"Perhaps—but a clever surgeon by repute. Your father insisted on employing him . . . I only hope he'll have recouped somewhere by the time the bill comes in."

"Oh yes," Tubby said bitterly. "My father lives on my capital. It was quite a lot once, when my mother died. I'm always signing things—I suppose I'm a fool about it. . . ."

"I don't think so," Sammy said. "I'd rather be too poor than too rich. I have to be, anyway . . . and I once wasn't."

"Look here, sir," Tubby said, bursting out with it, "can't I stay here? It doesn't cost anything, and I expect these chaps are all right. Let's finish with that idiot."

"I'm afraid it would hardly do," Sammy explained. "Your father rather antagonized the medical staff here. I must confess he only gave them my own views. . . ."

"What did he say?" Tubby asked with interest.

"He said that, if they hadn't changed since his day—and he understood they hadn't—the R.A.M.C. doctors were better at funerals than surgery. The Colonel here told me all about it . . . regrettable; especially as an officer is not officially entitled to medical attention. He gets it as a privilege. . . . No, Tubby, I'm afraid you'll have to go to London."

"You—you'll come up and see me, sir?"

"I'll be up often. You know my wife is in a nursing home—has been for years, poor dear. I'm up in town twice a week in any

case. And—you know—I'll always come if you want me . . . and
there'll be your Miss Mervinne. She rang me up about you. And
Daddy goes up fairly often. He has—an attachment of sorts
there."

"And Benjamin," Tubby said. "He's always beating up
London."

"There, it won't be so bad, you see . . ." He rose to go. "I
must be getting back now. I'll come again tomorrow." He
stood at the door, a slim, bowed figure, his face pale and
translucent, so unlike a soldier. "And remember, Tubby, a lot
of interesting things can happen in a few months in hospital
. . . I shouldn't be surprised if this weren't one of your more
fortunate encounters."

While Sammy had been there, talking gently, the pain had
died down, so that it was a background to all that happened,
always in consciousness but controllable. But when Sammy
had gone, the pain swept up so that Tubby could think of nothing but the pain, the core of which was concentrated in his left
shoulder, but the outer edges of which extended to, and were
conquering, the whole of him, mind and body. He rang for
the nurse. The pale, fat one answered.

"Couldn't I have some more of that morphia, or something,
sister?" he begged her. "It's rather hell at the moment."

She looked at her watch. "Not for another half hour, I'm
afraid."

"Couldn't I just have it now?"

"In half an hour," she said firmly.

When the door had closed, he found he was weeping into his
pillow.

Chapter 3　FROM HIS BED, TUBBY COULD SEE THROUGH the window a patch of sky joining the top of a grey building. It was a sad landscape. In the bottom sector there were two mute windows, opaque, sealed, truncated by the frame of his own lattice. Above them, the façade rose stupidly, heavy with Victorian embellishment. There was nothing to be said for that building, overdressed, pretentious, its stone weathered drab yellow by the London climate, except that it served as a foil to the sky above it. Its sole distinction was its skyline; and from the imprisonment of this small bedroom—a servant's attic before the mansion had been converted to a nursing home—it was only through the changing sky, the small parcel of sky in the upper part of the window, that any one day varied from any other.

Considered objectively, there was nothing in the least extraordinary about the few acres of skyscape to which his eyes were constantly returning. Their grey elements changed formation, of course, from hour to hour and, when you watched closely enough, from minute to minute. They rolled orgiastically one upon the other; they danced and tripped together, catching and rejecting the sunlight; they performed all the human antics that a mind, not otherwise busied, can attribute to cumulus movement. Yet their importance was not in this ability to occupy the mind, but in their further penetration, their making of a deeper, more mortal impression; their breach of the outer defences to attack the spirit.

Tubby's spirit was suffering. The emotions that racked him had outpoured reason, and now he was hurt by misgivings that mind could do nothing to dissipate—even if mind had been practiced. For, when for four months you had lain and examined the furthest marches of your vision, discovering that—limited as it was—it extended to infinity, you had to start feeling something. On your left was a screen with the door beyond it; facing you, a table, a windowless wall and a rather stupid picture of a stag surrounded by staghounds; behind you, where you could not see it, a very suitable reproduction of "The Angelus"; and on your right, an armchair for visitors, the window and—through it—the grey top of the building and the sky above it. Only the sky changed and, except for it, people came and went before a static background.

At first you were a man, immensely important, fixed to a bed between screen and window. Then, as the weeks passed, your attachment in space to screen, bed, window, lost significance; your relationship to the small patch of sky displaced it. Quite simply, your own existence became insecure, when considered against that sky and when you had understood that you were no measurable distance from a sky whose depths themselves were immeasurable. You fled from the thought, but it pursued you, overtaking and passing reason. What were you? A vital, incomprehensible Tubby. But, with the sky going on and on forever, you were less than a pinpoint, as immeasurably small as the sky was infinite; yet still—curiously enough—Tubby, a man with endless and unexplored regions within him, the vista within being—maybe—as vast and unlimited as the vista without. The thought, the fear of the thought rather, drew you out of yourself, allowing you once more to see yourself complete and at a distance, showing you yourself as a poor creature in a cage that you had come along to watch and to feed buns to.

In considering how banal and elementary was this experience of Tubby's, you have to recall that emotionally and mentally he was a child, all tendency to abstract thought and honest feeling having been schooled out of him since infancy. And, when at first he felt this way, it was as frightening as a child's first sexual manifestations. It was the way chaps went nuts, he remembered, recalling early warnings and the similarity of the two discoveries. But the thoughts and the feelings (in each case) had kept on coming back to him; and he had shrunk from them, as if he had been on a cliff edge and, looking down, had found the height made him dizzy and had scrambled away but was drawn back again and again to its dangerous fascination.

He clung to himself then; to his fine powerful body, laughter, wind in his face, and the joy of exhaustion, to smells of horses and hay and leather, and the warm security of good friends around him. Then that, too, came away in his hands. His body was wasted and there was no power in him; smells were antiseptic and disinfectant; every movement was controlled by others. The hay and the leather and the steam from sweating flanks and the feel of rhythmical movement were a long way distant. These were things that were part of Tubby, and Tubby was little else beside them. They were gone, yet Tubby was still remaining, desperately vital but quite insignificant. So what was Tubby?

The door opened quietly and the nurse entered. "Time for your medicine," she said brightly.

❀ The nurse came into the room quickly and smoothly, moving like an expensive car that was carrying an invalid inside it. She was no longer irritating to Tubby, and he did not mind the starched rustle of her movements. When she spoke it was in a cheerful, professional voice.

"Your medicine, Mr. Windrush. You don't mind this one."

"What is it, sister? The 1912 vintage?"

"That's right, Mr. Windrush. It's one of your favorites."

"Here's luck," Tubby said, taking the glass with his good arm and emptying it quickly. He was getting rather tired of jokes about medicine but he quite saw that appearances had to be maintained, self-respect considered, like the stories of Empire-builders dressing for dinner in the heart of the jungle. The relationship between himself and the nurse could not be confined to her humiliating attentions. All the same, it was difficult, after twelve weeks of lying flat, encased in a steel

jacket and with an arm at full stretch in a Thomas splint beside
you, to think up new jokes for the nurse and not to reserve your
sprightliness to ease the visits of the friends who came to see
you. The nurse had known you in the depths, when restraint
was vanquished, and it was not really much use keeping up
pretences before her. She moved about, tidying the room and
smoothing his pillows and bedclothes with competent, automatic hands.

"We must make you nice for your visitors."

She brought him a hairbrush and held the looking glass while
he tidied himself.

"Visitors . . ." he said wearily.

"You know you like your visitors, now."

"I shouldn't like *not* to have them, I suppose."

"That nice man, Mr. Watson," she said; "and Miss Mervinne. . . ." She looked at him slyly. She was a queer woman,
the nurse; or perhaps a woman in a queer position would be
fairer. She knew all of his body, all of his moods, his tension, his
breaking point. In a lot of ways she was more than a wife, yet
she called him Mr. Windrush and knew his friends only formally
as Mr. Watson and Miss Mervinne. "And perhaps your father
will come again soon, and that nice uncle, the Admiral. . . ."

"God forbid," Tubby said gloomily.

"Now, now. . . ." She wagged her finger at him. "We mustn't
be naughty. Where should we be if your friends and relatives
didn't come to see us?"

Tubby's only acknowledged male relatives were his two
paternal uncles, who—as general and admiral—had retired
from the Army and Navy respectively, and his father, no more
than a colonel, who had retired almost permanently from his
creditors. In England, the Colonel's debts were heavy, in the
best tradition; but his credit was still elastic, and when he chose,
he returned for the major race meetings and those lesser ones
for which he had a long-established affection. He was a curious
man. In retirement now, and without speaking more than a few
words of any continental language, he flitted from one European resort to another, received everywhere in the best semi-

diplomatic and society circles, living on Tubby's capital, his own very limited knowledge of the English tongue, excellent clothes, nice manners, a permanent cigar and a really genuine eyeglass. His Sackville Street tailor, never daring to decline his orders, sent suits by the half-dozen to most of the capitals, sometimes to Biarritz and Le Touquet, very often to one or other of the better resorts on the French Riviera, Cannes, Juan or Monte Carlo. From time to time, on his periodical home-comings, this tailor was permitted to record Colonel Windrush's increasing measurements and to be reminded of the numerous foreign clients he had gained from his recommendations. But the Colonel never asked for a commission.

That was Tubby's father. Tubby scarcely knew him, disliked him, but resembled him closely, for the Windrush sires were proverbially prepotent. He met his father perhaps once a year, at the funeral of a great aunt, or at the office of the family solicitors, when an expensive lunch followed. From time to time, Tubby was asked to sign some fresh document which, he understood perfectly, deprived him still further of his maternal inheritance. On these occasions, his father was uncomfortable; the lawyer quieted his conscience with a formal warning, and Tubby, not interested in money, signed quietly. If the surrender of a birthright could prolong and cement the separation from his father, it was worth the sacrifice.

Except for one photograph, Tubby knew nothing of his mother. She had been Italian—not very high-class Italian, but well-dowried—had died fortunately at Tubby's birth and was never mentioned. Neither were her family, who had been legally minded, but ill-advised by a Milanese lawyer. The capital was put in trust for Tubby; but the trustees, who were not very honest anyway, were given wide discretion. They held that, with Tubby's consent, the support of his father in a decent social position was primarily in the son's interests. In this—being mostly soldiers—they were not without reason.

Tubby in no way resembled his mother, who had been slight, with a narrow pelvis unequal to the birth of a nine-pound baby. And when the Colonel (in the Edwardian way) had been asked by the country doctor as to which should be saved, he had replied: "The child of course," and thought no more about it. The mother may perhaps have sharpened her son's emotions— or his capacity for emotion; but her main contribution to his welfare was financial, in that the House, Park and grounds (though annually diminishing and the remainder increasingly mortgaged) had been retained for the first eight years of his life. He was thus brought up in traditional and happy surroundings, to which he must partly have owed his manners, his charm and his self-confidence.

This, then, was Tubby's origin; and these three old men were the only relatives who came to see him in his garret-like room at the top of an expensive nursing home. The general and the admiral, feeling that an accident arising out of a horse was creditable, paid several calls, usually together. Both were bachelors and were embarrassed by the sick-room, still more embarrassed by the flowers they carried, and glad to be off again as quickly as possible. This suited Tubby, and they gave little trouble. It was his friends, of whom a dozen paid regular visits, whose coming he feared increasingly. It was easy to understand this apprehension on the basis that Tubby must have had, somewhere in his darkest corner, an Italian sense of inferiority and a hyper-sensitive nerve of Latin origin.

At first, when you are hurt, you rally your defences and try to make light of it and to disguise your fears from yourself and from others. Then you are like a child, bewildered at your incapacity, at your dependence and at the personal indignities that go with illness. Later, you become either egotistical or acutely self-conscious. Tubby had become self-conscious and he suffered from knowing that he was now an object of pity and, as a result, one with whom so many of his visitors found it difficult to be at ease. He was like a man who has fallen off his horse in public, or like a Jew who hears his neighbors talking anti-semitism, or like a prisoner being led along the streets with a policeman at each elbow. Feeling like that, singled out by circumstance as something not quite human, expelled from the herd of his friends, he suffered keenly from the constant restraint that he had to impose on himself. He could no longer say or do what first occurred to him; his actions were not now controlled by habit; he could not laugh when he felt happy, swear when he felt cross; he must always disguise his feelings, hide the pain, the indignity, and the helplessness that were his new states.

Of all his friends, there were only three whose visits he really welcomed. It was not bad of course, with either Bert or Benjamin. You could laugh at Bert, his hushed voice that refused to restrain itself, his tiptoe entry, his terror of sickness, his shrinking from bandages, bedpans, injections, medicines—all of which were so clearly a woman's business. You could laugh *with* Benjamin. You had known him for so many years, were both attuned to the same humor, shared the same jokes, knew the same people, were of accord on what was right and what was not permissible. A year or two older, and distinctly more clever, he was one of those people you will always admire and never catch up with. And—even so—Benjamin, with whom you had shot, fished, hunted, climbed mountains, risen at dawn to wait for duck, retired at dawn after a night's dancing, who was always so gay, so confident, so charming a leader, was no longer at ease in your presence. He came to Tubby, as he would to a friend in prison, to affirm his loyalty. Between these two, who knew each other so well, there was restraint and discomfort. Iodoform, lysol, picric acid, sear very easily the tissues of friendship.

The three people whose visits Tubby always anticipated with pleasure were Lydia, Sammy and—perhaps unexpectedly—Daddy Watson. Daddy was not the sort of person whom you could imagine would be welcome in a sick-room. But it was for the very reasons which would lead you to this conclusion—his egotism, tempers, pride, constant dissatisfaction—that he was good company. His speech, when he was not dealing in the drab currency of an officer's vocabulary or not confined to the Officers' Mess syllabus of accepted topics, was often violent and bitter, always amusing, sometimes clever. He acknowledged no authority, saw nothing dispassionately and rarely saw anything without displeasure. He disapproved of the world and fought the world. And yet, for all his egotism and pugnacity, you knew that he was on your side and that, however often he might bruise you with his tongue, unleash on you his wicked uncontrollable passions, he would never seriously hurt you. He would feint, threaten, raise his hand against you; but the blow would not be delivered. If he did not like you, you could go to the devil. As his friend, he might well go there with you.

In most ways, Sammy was the exact reverse of Daddy Watson; and yet there was something elemental that they had in common. It was their independence that made them alike, and in the ingredients of their independence that they differed. Sammy was self-sufficient, invulnerable, because he had a belief—so profound that it was knowledge—in the omnipotence of human beings, in the fragment of divinity within them. For him, man's only problem was development, emergence, the sloughing of those sheaths that clothed and trammeled the immortal core. Man was divine and eternal. You could not harm him.

Daddy arrived at the final conclusion quite differently. His only belief was in the limitations of man, his finiteness, his mortality, his essential badness. Man was an animal that lived, died and was finished, like any other of the earth's creatures. If he feared misfortune, he would suffer. If he refused to capitulate, he became invulnerable. Refusing to acknowledge injury, he could not be injured. Or again: since happiness and peace were unattainable, unhappiness was a normal condition. Admit that, and you could not be unhappy. Daddy would tell you that he had suffered so much, he could be hurt no longer. He could be angered by incompetency, idiocy, obtuseness; but the pain he felt was vicarious. That was his story, anyway.

These were now Tubby's two greatest friends; that is to say, the friends whose influence he felt most deeply. Sammy's creed was positive, metaphysical, logical: know this, and no one can hurt you. Daddy's was negative, changed from time to time, often illogical and did not bear a too close scrutiny: you have no cause for hope; it is useless to be frightened; above all, don't submit.

Tubby had no idea of all this; it was far beyond his understanding. He only knew that Sammy and Daddy Watson were two remarkable people of an independence that he was learning to envy. Sammy, he loved and admired. He was frightened of Daddy, but found him entertaining—and had for him a quite unreasonable affection. Daddy, like certain poisons in small quantities, was a stimulant. Sammy was at once a sedative and a tonic. You couldn't say why, but when he slipped quietly, unobtrusively into the room, the whole world changed—softened, widened. Standards were new and broad. It was as if he had brought his own world with him.

※ "Daddy!" Benjamin said. "He's a queer fish if there ever was one. That man's got a first-class brain, but he won't help himself with it. He *will* use it for provoking generals. He's the little boy at the zoo who sees 'Don't molest this animal' and goes and prods it."

"But I'm fond of him, Benjy. . . ."

"No one could help being fond of him. He's the most generous man I know and with so little to give."

"He's a good soldier. . . ."

"I don't know what he's like in peace time; but, I tell you, Tubby, there wasn't a better wartime soldier in the Regiment. Recommended for the V.C. they say, and got his D.S.O. as a subaltern . . . commanded a battery in Palestine—when he was our age, I suppose."

"And a bit of a jockey, according to our Sergeant Andrews. . . ."

"A bit of a jockey! Good heavens; he walked off with every race in the country. Bought an unbroken four-year-old from somewhere in Ireland, breeding unknown—probably stolen in those days . . . I tell you, Tubby, that man could do *anything* . . . *could* have done anything, that is."

"What put him wrong?" Tubby asked.

"Everything. He had a wicked deal; not a picture in his hand. I don't know the whole story but, from what I've heard, if ever a man had real, honest bad luck and real shabby treatment, it's Daddy."

They lapsed into silence, and while they sought words, the ardor with which they had been speaking seemed false, as if they had not dared let the play falter. Then the nurse came in with her tray and dishes, and Benjamin stood up quickly.

"Don't go," Tubby said halfheartedly.

"I must, old boy. I've got to be getting along."

"This injection only takes a minute. . . ."

"Honestly, Tubby, I've got a date. I'm late already. I've brought you some papers by the way; you can study society and see what you're missing. There's a lovely one of the Brigadier at a race meeting; quarter of a page to himself, giving ancestry, titled connections, exploits and manly pastimes. The General noticed it yesterday and was no end pleased about it . . . try showing it to Daddy."

He threw two or three illustrated papers on the bed, seized hat and umbrella, smiled sheepishly at the nurse, gave an awkward flutter of his hand and (usually so self-possessed, so suave, so polished) turned, half tripped and almost stumbled from the sick-room.

Thinking of it afterwards, Tubby knew that, with the positions reversed, he would have been the same about it.

"Snob papers," Daddy said, turning over the pages. "I'm ashamed to find them here."

"Benjy brought them."

"Benjy . . . Benjy!" The repetition of the name was a simple detonation, undirected, a puff of colorless smoke. You couldn't have said whether it meant scorn, dislike, resentment—or even admiration.

"You like him . . ." Tubby said.

"I like him all right; you can't help liking him. What annoys me is the easiness of his success, and the way he makes sure of success by trying nothing difficult. He's no fool, you see; but if ever anyone hid his talents, it's that young man. He's got brains and ability and he wastes his time, dancing attendance on that half-witted general. Really half-witted, Tubby. When one's talking about generals, none of these ready-made epithets are overstatements."

"Here's something for you," Tubby said, searching quickly. Conversation with Daddy was always like playing with an

unknown assortment of fireworks, you lighting one end but
never being sure what sort of star, spray, rocket or flare is going
to come out of the other. But on the subject of generals, you
applied the match with reasonable safety. Tubby pushed over
the Brigadier's picture.

"Ah," Daddy said slowly, a hungry man approaching the
sideboard. "I see. Our Brigadier, our 'Commander Royal
Artillery,' gone all social. But look at his clothes, Tubby, lovely
clothes! Old floppy hat; woodcock pinfeathers, no doubt, in a
slightly grubby hatband; those hats are the despair of foreigners
—they just can't do it. Then that little bow tie; it wouldn't look
right, you know, if you bought it in Paris or Hamburg. Yellow
waistcoat, I think, though it's hard to tell in the photograph . . ."
(He held the page to the light, examining it joyfully.) "Old
tweed coat; check breeches, my word! Newmarket boots . . .
what a perfect ensemble! It fills me with envy. *You* could do it,
Tubby; Benjy could do it. But not me or Bert or Sammy."

But now Daddy was pulling the conversation—the monologue
—in a dangerous direction. The wind seemed to be changing,
he tacking to fill his sails again.

"The General . . ." Tubby began, puffing hard from the old
quarter. But Daddy had already put about.

"Tell me, Tubby, how does one manage never to wear anything but old clothes? It's the mark of aristocracy, of course, but
how do you get them old? Does the butler wear them for the
first year or two?"

Tubby refused to follow. "The General," he said firmly, "was
very pleased with that picture. Benjy said so."

"Oh," Daddy said happily. "Very pleased, was he? That
means the Brigadier is all set for promotion. It was a toss up
before, but this ought to make it a certainty. I think that photographer earned his little something."

He took one of Tubby's cigarettes and lit it slowly, enjoying
his own deliberate movements. "You have to understand," he
said primly, "the way a general looks at things. He sees only
part of them; he sees them on one plane and just can't understand a third dimension. But he's sure he's getting the whole
picture of course. . . . Perhaps he's like a fish with a limited cone

of vision. Or like a servant girl in a basement, only able to see the legs of the people who pass above her. But the servant girl and the fish have an idea that there's a part of the scene outside their vision. You'll be able to correct me, Tubby, but doesn't the fish move from time to time, to see a little further?" (He didn't wait, of course, for an answer.) "But not so the General," he went on at once. "*He* takes up his stand in one place and believes what his eyes tell him: 'Nice pair of boots, good breeches —all we can see—but undoubtedly a good officer.' Not the slightest element of doubt, you see. Not a chance that a general could be fallible—else he couldn't be a general. A general who might be mistaken! Bless my soul, no good to anyone. . . ."

Tubby laughed. Not only because Daddy meant him to laugh, but in a sudden burst of happiness and satisfaction; the way that a baby crows when you shake before his eyes a diverting toy that need not be very original or very ingenious.

"Why do you laugh?" Daddy asked fiercely; a pretended ferocity, near enough to the real thing to stop you short and stifle the laughter. "Why are you laughing? You don't know. Because you're entertained, of course; but you've no idea why you find me entertaining . . . or have you?"

"I don't know," Tubby said uncomfortably.

"You don't know, because you don't think. You don't think, do you?"

"I must say I hadn't thought about that. . . ."

"But you ought to think about everything," Daddy said severely. "If you thought, you'd know; and you ought to know why you do things. *I'll* tell you why you laugh. First of all, I'm acknowledged rather a queer chap—a sort of court jester. I have all the advantages of a professional humorist and when I come under the spotlight, you sit back ready to laugh at the first thing I say that can possibly be considered funny." He leaned forward and pointed his finger at Tubby. "And remember," he said solemnly, "the sorriest hag can seem entrancing to a prisoner." He leaned back again, satisfied, triumphant, like counsel who has scored an unanswerable point against a witness.

"Meaning," Tubby said, "that I'm the prisoner, stuck here in bed by this splint affair?"

"Nothing of the kind." Daddy leaned forward, urgent to dispel this suggestion of a wounding reference. "I mean that intellectually every soldier is a prisoner. His mind is confined to the narrow limits of what is considered proper for it. So he convinces himself—not without pride—that he hasn't a brain, that he's a stupid sort of chap and that, after all, it's rather a decent thing to be stupid. Try and recall the conversation you hear in any Mess; not just now and again, but always, always; in the hall, anteroom, dining room, billiard room, lavatories. Its limitations are appalling. If you think, you'll realize it never goes beyond immediate life and habits; what we've done today, what we'll do tomorrow, sport, women, drink and horses, horses, horses . . . all nice, gentlemanly subjects, none of them requiring one grain of pre-consideration. A soldier opens his mouth and speaks, just as a dog wags or droops his tail or pricks his ears at his master's footsteps."

He stood up, crushed out a cigarette, hunted in Tubby's box and took another. His face was more than usually red and just glistening, and he was speaking now with conviction, almost passion. Whether or not you agreed, you had to admit that his words were the fruit of thought, that the thought might have been misdirected but was, in intention at least, wholly truthful.

"Matches—where the devil are they?"

"On the mantelpiece."

"As for thought—abstract thought," he went on, slowly, lazily now, speaking from before the fireplace, "the soldier regards the idea of it much in the way that a savage regards an airplane: a queer possession, belonging to someone not necessarily better than himself, perhaps worse, quite possibly a little ridiculous, and certainly altogether different, and this isn't an exaggeration . . . you watch a soldier listening to an economist! I've done it—I gave a party once . . . I don't say he was a very good economist and he *would* talk philosophy, but he'd got a first in Modern Greats and had a University lecture-ship. . . . And I saw three soldiers listening to him—and *seeing* was the word for it; for of course none of them opened his mouth. You could see the smile of tolerant amusement just suppressed by good manners. All their nice upbringing would allow was a grave display of admiration. 'Clever fellow,' they were thinking; but with the reservation that to be clever is a form of dishonesty and bad taste, incompatible with sportsmanship and manliness. . . ."

Daddy paused and looked inquiringly at Tubby, inviting an answer, an argument. Once again, he reminded you of an old dog, quivering, hackles up, tail stiff, a low growl coming from his tummy. But Tubby wouldn't fight; couldn't. Daddy's words had a terrible ring of truth. Had they come from a stranger, a civilian, Tubby would have attempted a denial, made a show of opposition; but from a soldier . . . D.S.O. as a subaltern, commanded a battery of twenty-two, rode in the National. . . .

"Well, why are we such nitwits?" he asked plaintively, admitting defeat, groveling. "Why shouldn't we have brains the same as any of the others?"

"*What* a shame," Daddy said sadly. "Why shouldn't you have brains? Why are you intellectual outcasts?" He came forward briskly and spoke urgently once more, bitterly, every word born of conviction. "*You're* not outcasts," he said. "*You've* rejected the rest of the world. You—we—are as clever as any other set of people. It's utterly untrue that only people who haven't the brains for anything else come into the army. That's a nice lie, propounded by all the men who are jealous of a soldier's social position, his look of physical fitness, his success with the ladies . . . The soldier doesn't start stupid; it's only that he vaunts stupidity so much, he forgets how to be clever. Look at your own friends . . . we've all got more brains, more ability, than half the men you'll find hanging about a stockbroker's office on half-commission, or nicely placed in a family business, or even deviling half the night for successful barristers. . . . But Benjamin tells himself, and everyone else, that he's stupid: 'I'm a stupid sort of chap . . . horses are more in my line than ledgers, old boy . . .' and in five years he'll become so—and be well on the road to generalship."

"Yes, yes," Tubby said; "that's true enough about Benjy."

"Don't interrupt," said Daddy, now well committed. "On the other hand, look at me and Sammy. I always said I was clever; I proved it at school, at Oxford; and now I'm finished as

a soldier because I've made myself conspicuous without either
money or family to back me. And Sammy—has a brain and a
spirit . . . you can't describe them, they're tremendous. He's a
born leader and he'd rule anywhere, except in the army. Even
there, he's as good a regimental soldier as you'd find—but he
won't even make a colonel. He makes a general feel small, so
the general stamps on him, to show he isn't. It's the army that's
wrong, you see; rotten at the top, and fine and sturdy the lower
down you get. It's like an inverted pyramid, balanced on the
point, everything depending on the point; and the point a
parcel of nit-witted, well-bred, nicely-dressed, formally-educated,
really sporting old generals . . . a survival of the least fit . . .
that's what makes me so savage."

"But . . ." Tubby began, and subsided. He had been told so
much in half an hour's conversation: that he was a fool, that he
wasn't; that he was a better man than those clever fellows who
"made money in the city." He had something to think about
and to puzzle out slowly at his ample leisure; something not
unrelated to that patch of sky above the grey building. What
was he? A soldier, a man, infinitesimally small, infinitely important. His own ideas, conceived of long suffering, fought each
other—even as Daddy's. Truth seemed to be buried in contradictions, not lying on the surface. He couldn't have put that
into words; but somehow, somewhere, in some distant part of
him, he was beginning to feel it.

The nurse came in with a jigsaw puzzle, two books, a box of
flowers, a bundle of papers, and a glass of medicine. "What a lot
of nice things for you, Mr. Windrush." She turned severely to
Daddy. "I'm sure you've been here quite long enough, Mr.
Watson. I mustn't let you tire my patient." She went out again.

Daddy stood up slowly and prepared himself to go, finding
hat and umbrella, smoothing the creases in his trousers. Watching him, Tubby saw the change pass over him quickly. The
preacher who thundered in his pulpit, becomes in the vestry
a poor priest—shabby, hungry. The schoolmaster, mortarboard
and gown discarded, is a sour, weary, underpaid, pathetic
individual. Daddy, in his silly bowler hat—holding his genteel,
pretentious umbrella—short, a little fat, was a commonplace

person; the sort of little man you bumped into in a crowd and scarcely bothered to beg his pardon.

"I must be off, Tubby. That nurse is quite right; I've been here too long altogether."

"Don't take any notice of her."

"I have to go. My girl's waiting for me."

"Your girl!" Tubby said in surprise. "I didn't know you had one."

The heavy face swung away from the bed, a slow, tired movement, the dull eyes looking wearily out of the window.

"Didn't you?" he said; and then, in a voice that was almost querulous, "What do you think I am—a blasted eunuch? Of course I've got a girl . . . sensibly chosen with enough money to support herself . . . I gave her some pictures . . . otherwise she's not much of a thing, with a stupid Shakespearean name to her. You shall meet her one day. I like her. She suits me; dresses nicely, undresses nicely . . . I do hate woolen underclothes on a woman, and acres of elastic. . . . She's quite amusing, quite well-educated, a little common—like I am. Her father was a grocer in a big way. She's waiting, anyhow. . . ."

By the time the door had shut behind him, he had lost all glory.

❧ "I doubt if it really hurts," Sammy said.

"Oh, doesn't it?" Tubby groaned.

"No. Not really." There was a smile in his face from behind the features; a flutter of wind just stirring the lips. But he wasn't joking. "It causes pain, but it doesn't hurt; it doesn't matter, you see. It doesn't injure any part of you that matters . . ." The smile emerged, not making light of your pain, but saying—"Take my words or leave them; rather farfetched, you may think, but my belief . . ." No! Not that. Sammy's face, bearing his whole character, never allowed an expression of belief. His lips used it, but the rest of him transposed it to "knowledge. . . ."

"One thinks these things hurt . . . one confuses hurt and pain . . . pain is nothing. Hurt you must consider as injury, vital injury, the loss of hope or courage. . . ." Sammy's words continued to fall lightly, vaguely; gentle rain, a sort of Scotch mist on a parched garden. Mrs. Evans, pressing on with her work, turned her head slightly and said in a hearty voice, "That's right, Major, you tell him. Such a fuss he makes. . . ."

Mrs. Evans, the masseuse, a widow of course, Welsh of course, but—in spite of being Welsh—large, fair, blue-eyed and Nordic, squarely built, firm in her movements but (so she said) gentle, aged between forty and fifty, once (you might think) handsome, thin-lipped, cruel-to-be-kind, a purposeful woman, came every afternoon about tea time. Usually visitors were not allowed till she had finished; or nowadays till half an hour after she had finished, when Tubby, screwed to a high tension by the pain she inflicted, had subsided again. But Sammy was an exception. He had come early because he had a train to catch later. He had wanted to go when Mrs. Evans arrived but had stayed when Tubby begged him to. "It'll help me through the rough and tumble, sir. Do stay if you can spare the time. . . ."

"It doesn't really hurt," Sammy said, from the edge of the bed where he was sitting.

They were all of them, then, close together; and with the June sunlight catching the façade of the building opposite and darkening the room by contrast, there was a certain mystery in their intimate grouping. It was rather grim, almost allegorical; Tubby, the central figure, supine on the bed, fastened there by the splint, the strappings of which had now been loosened; Mrs. Evans, crouched beside him, in white overall and red tie, sleeves rolled up, muscular forearms and plump wrists traversing the splint in rhythmical movement. On the other side, Sammy was reclining towards the foot of the bed, pale, quiet, gentle, you might say priest-like, almost sexless or feminine in his fragility—but with a hidden power that was the essence of manliness superimposed on his more pallid qualities. You could never describe or explain or even understand just how you felt with Sammy. It was nothing that he said or did; it was more probably what he gave, what emanated from him.

Tubby lay back, remembering how once he had doubted that sweat could gather on your brow through pain; through the effort to suffer pain and to maintain control; the purely negative achievement of doing nothing, of not succumbing to the pain, of not groaning, weeping, shouting the place down. The agony was intense. Mrs. Evans took the hand—the one that had been fastened to the splint for so long that there was now no movement in the fingers—and worked on it. She moved the thin, rigid, almost brittle fingers, little by little, one by one, and then —sprinkling French chalk on her palms—took the whole of his hand within hers and slowly closed it. This was the core of all pain, and following on the months of dull, purposeless pain that had gone before there was a certain purity in it. It was a clean fight that you had when you came to conquer it.

"You remember," Sammy said slowly, "what you described as 'all that nonsense' you'd been thinking about that patch of sky over there and yourself . . . you remember that? That's worth remembering. It's something you can't think out, you can't read in books and nobody can tell you. It's something you feel. It's not a product of the brain at all. . . ."

"That's just as well," Tubby said, forcing his words through the pain, "considering Daddy says I haven't got a brain . . . that soldiers just don't have them."

"Daddy never said that." It was a quiet statement, not an exclamation.

"Something like it." The words struggled in the current of his breath; his chest was rigid.

"He might have said that they don't admit to a brain," Sammy said looking away; "that they find it serves them better to be stupid, to glory in a lack of cleverness. There's truth in that; there's truth in a lot Daddy says . . . I've known him a great many years, and whatever else he is, he's always truthful. He's narrow, hard, egotistical, conceited, but he's a generous friend, and he has a great comprehension. He'd understand about your sky. He'd know that you were so minute, and yet so vital and—don't you know, Tubby—that that's why nothing can hurt you, that's why pain can't hurt you? You don't have to understand that—it's beyond comprehension perhaps. You have to *know* it, and you're beginning to know it, and one day you *may* know it. Your power to know that is the most precious of your elements. And just because it's strong, because you're able to get at it, you have the chance of making something out of life; you have the chance of living."

"If one could only believe. . . ." Tubby whispered.

"Believe, nowadays, is a very difficult word. It implies reason, logic, argument, mathematical precision, scientific deduction. Trust, feeling, knowledge are more old-fashioned and easier than belief."

"Then you think . . ."

"Mrs. Evans seems to have finished and you can do the thinking."

They had ignored Mrs. Evans, and she, with rather a resentful expression, had risen, taken off her overall, packed up her things, put on her hat and coat, and was going. "Well, that's over for this afternoon, Mr. Windrush. You've been so busy talking, you've hardly noticed me . . . hardly felt anything, *have* you now? You see it's mostly imagination. You see it doesn't *really* hurt, does it?" (You might think that there was almost disappointment in her voice.) "Until tomorrow then . . . Good afternoon, Mr. Windrush. Good afternoon, Major."

"She's a grim woman," Tubby said when she had gone. "A frightening sort of woman. Think what it must have been for her husband."

"Yes," Sammy agreed; "but out of the mouths of grim women . . . you noticed what she said, Tubby?"

"I noticed."

"Keep on noticing things then; it's good exercise. If she says it and I say it and you feel it—perhaps it's true, isn't it? It can't be proved any other way . . . there has to be something you take on trust; just one fundamental stone at the bottom. . . ."

But, when he had gone, there only seemed one certainty: that Sammy knew, that you could trust and love him.

But afterwards, Tubby was angry that he felt no shame. He was a man. The long months in bed, that had little by little eroded the flesh and muscle from his limbs, had not made him any the less a man. Acid pain, slowly dissolving the mucus that choked perception, had freed understanding and widened the scope of what he allowed to be possible; but it had not reduced him to the frailty of woman, to the meek anemia of an acolyte.

He had suffered, wept and cringed; but, surviving, there was still manhood. And what had happened was shameful.

Sammy had preached. He had talked to Tubby, at Tubby, of matters that concerned the soul, humanity, God. He had hedged them at least, letting his tongue enclose them but without the courage to admit its real target. His words were a sermon; and sermons were affairs of childhood, of hysteria, of women. To make matters worse, the text had been drawn from Tubby's own indiscretion when, in a flooded moment, in the warm intimacy of Sammy's presence, he had chattered unblushingly his thoughts and fancies. That fragment of sky above the grey building, and himself—vital, insignificant—these had been seized by Sammy almost as if here, at last, was the treasure he had long been seeking. The halting words had been clutched, fondled like porcelain, until out of them had come the sermon . . . it was indecent.

But it had been Sammy talking; and somehow you knew that what he said, whatever he said, was true and honest. When he had gone, his conviction lingered behind him, a nimbus that faded slowly. Unlike Daddy, he did not lose his glory on departure. And yet you were angry, ashamed that his words had meant so much to you, that you had wanted so much to hear them. Or ashamed that, true as you knew them, you had understood them so little? Or not ashamed at all—only angry?

A curious man—a wonderful man—Sammy.

He could shave himself now, the glass propped against his humped knees and all the paraphernalia on the table beside him. Unaided, his good hand could manipulate soap and brush, put together a safety razor, and, in the course of ten minutes, complete the whole business.

It's funny how things strike you while you are shaving; how, scraping away at those obstinate hairs along the line of the jawbone, you achieve a sudden clarity of thought, a clearing away of litter, a quick understanding. It is a painful but important time. Perhaps its sordidity unclothes for you the passions, the violence, you have recently permitted. Naked, they become ludicrous. You see at once the ill-covered ribs, spindle legs,

potbelly, the protuberant Adam's apple. You are disillusioned
about your overnight passions. Values are upset and reassorted.
Shame predominates in the new arrangement.

In the morning, the feeling of discomfort, of shame, was so
strong that it went straight to the belly. It might have been the
day of a race, the last hour before a big match. You were tense
with feeling. But, this time, it was not anticipation but reproach.

All emotions were much the same then: fear, hate, love, pity,
shame, remorse? What was it you felt last night when Sammy
left you? Anger at your own shamelessness; or shame at your
own worthlessness? Self-pity, self-hate, resentment; reproach
that the soil of yourself was not ready for the seed sprinkled in
its furrows? You could not know—only that its violence was
pathetic and, in itself, shameful. But you knew, with morning
certainty, that Sammy was pure and true, and you unworthy.

And yet . . . and yet you couldn't prove that. Why shouldn't
you scoff at unproved knowledge? Doubt it, anyway? All your
development led you to demand proof; that was why God had
been discarded. And Sammy, what was he? Just a quiet, gentle
man who slid through life scattering these clergyman's plati-
tudes? A man who had never lived hotly, known the ecstasy of
fierce living? Untouched by pain, he had drifted gently like a
pampered woman, like Lydia. It might be that way; and, if so,
his beauty faded. But you couldn't tell; you knew nothing about
him. Himself was the one topic that had never been talked
between them.

❦ Next time he came, he entered so easily, with such a quiet
assurance of his welcome, that all your discomfort vanished.
He sat, as usual, on the side of the bed, calm, grey, tired and
entirely Sammy. After a little he picked up the latest photograph that had come that morning, held it to the light and
looked at it closely.

"Ah, Lydia," he said. It was just a quiet comment, without
the suggestive note, the suggestion of a wink, a smirk, that
might be natural when one man discusses the woman friend of
another.

"It's good of her," Tubby said. "I like it."

"It's interesting," Sammy agreed. "He must be a good photographer. It's touched up a lot of course, very polished, very beautiful, but somehow he hasn't painted out the expression; the feeling that there is behind the expression."

Behind the expression . . . it wasn't that these things Sammy said were clever or in any way remarkable, but always he seemed to put into words the half-formed thoughts that were moving you at the moment. As though he read you. More than that, as though he were part of you, sharing your own perplexities and feelings, wondering himself what there was behind those quick, momentary expressions that came and went on Lydia's face without the transmutation of a crease or dimple, with scarcely a movement of the large, dark eyes, and often without reason.

"I can't understand that girl. . . ."

"Why should you?" Sammy asked quickly. "How could you? Why, how do you expect to understand people? Do you think a human being is a simple, straightforward arrangement of bits and pieces—like the mechanism of a breech block, that you can teach a recruit gunner in three lessons? Can you understand pictures, poetry, music—just by seeing and hearing them? You may like them, they may strike you as admirable; but you don't get much further. Can you understand a chemical reaction by watching the crystals dissolve, the liquid change color and start fizzing? A human being is more than a work of art, and very much more complex than a scientific experiment . . . who *can* you understand? Bert, Benjamin, Daddy, the Brigadier, the General, Hicks, Murphy, the Sergeant-Major? I'm blessed if I can!"

"No," Tubby said, "you're right, as usual. And as usual I look such an idiot. I can't make the simplest remark without finding out how little I've thought about it."

"Don't worry," Sammy said cheerfully. "This is real progress, the first step to knowledge. Not one of us opens his mouth without saying something that somebody can prove idiotic. . . . Only, Tubby, if you don't want to be very unhappy, very violently disillusioned, don't start hoping to understand people. What do you know—I'll ask you again—about Daddy; about what goes on in his brain, even about the history, the physical history of his life? I daresay he'll tell you himself one day. It's a sad and terrible story, but it's so extreme that it's almost beautiful; so sordid that it's fine—and he comes well out of it . . . you see, you just don't know about people. Not about any of us . . ." He was looking steadily at Tubby as if weighing out the measure of his physic. And he seemed, too, to be filling himself with resolution.

"And myself. . . ."

He said the words, and then was silent; a long, positive silence in which things were made, things happened. It was as if he had closed one book and were opening another, one whose contents were painful. He rose from the bed, still without speaking, and walked to the window; and the simple movement, lending weight to the silence, was surprising. For you were used to the stillness and tranquillity that were more to his speech than music is to a song; the premeditation of every thought and word. But in this action, he, too, knew pain and uncertainty. He stood by the window, looking out of it, and somewhere the clouds parted so that the evening was lit briefly.

"That sky of yours . . ." was all he said in a low, sad voice, and then again was silent. When he turned, he was older, the lines deeper in his face, the eyes wounded. "You've never met my wife," he said. "No . . . she doesn't meet people now . . . and she was once the most lovely woman you ever saw . . . once. And the terrible part is that you can't see the change—only know it. And it isn't age, for time hasn't touched her at all. She won't acknowledge it, you see. Nor is it sickness—because she isn't ill. . . . But for nine years she's lived in nursing homes— from one to another." He turned away again.

"And if it were *my* fault . . . if it could be . . ." The words were his own unrestrained whisper, but as if he purposely unlocked himself, stripping, wounding himself, not doing it for his own relief, but for Tubby's succor. "And she altered the whole direction of my life," he said gravely; "not in any way that you could imagine, that I could explain to you. She turned me round and set me off on a new path altogether—not intentionally . . ." He seemed shrunk into himself, but grand rather than pathetic. He didn't ask for sympathy or pity; you couldn't pity. Whatever he said, whatever he might be, you had always to admire him.

"And of my life," he went on, "just the plain historical facts of it, you know nothing. Nothing . . ." The word lingered, and then the tempo quickened: "Nobody does, because my old friends aren't my friends now. The people who knew me when I raced, played polo, shot, fished, went hunting, did all the things you do, drank a good deal more—all of those friends, they're mostly what is called successful. And success and friendship don't go together . . . so it's as it should be. And my friends nowadays see only what's come out of the past; not the past that created it. And now . . ." (A sigh trembled but never came.) "*You* don't know anything about that either, not even the material things. How half my pay and all of my private income go on nursing home bills, and on moving my wife from one part of the country to another—as the fancy takes her . . . No! No!" he said quickly, "I didn't mean that, I shouldn't have said it. Because, you see, I love my wife very, very dearly . . ." He paused and then made a last struggle. "But there's a lot more you don't know. I once wrote a book, nearly went to prison, won a prize for poetry, a cup at Olympia, made 'a possible' at Bisley, was cited as corespondent . . . and debts! I nearly shot myself for debts. . . ."

He was up off the bed again, standing by the window, shoulders bowed, so tired looking. "And you know nothing of my thoughts," he said very quietly, "only what I tell you, what you can read in my face, my words, my actions . . . if only they were all of me. . . ." His voice trailed off, the last words gentle as the breeze that scarcely moves the foliage. He was sad, beautiful, lovable and purely human. "That sky . . ." he whispered again.

Then he came back to Tubby. "And I doubt if you know any more about Lydia," he said briskly. "I don't, of course. But I can tell you, she's a clever, interesting, truthful, sympathetic and very beautiful woman."

Before he left, he stood rather gravely by the bed, his back to the window, silhouetted against the bright evening. "You'll

feel better now, Tubby," he said. "We're quits you see. You've
told me about your troubles, and I've told you something about
mine. The confidence isn't all—one-sided . . ." Again the voice
brightened; a doctor prescribing now. "But if ever anything
I say to you is of any importance, it's this: use people all you
can; use their brains, their feelings, their spirit. And let them
use you—if they are able to and want to . . . but don't hope that
either of you will understand the other. If you can begin to
understand *one* person—yourself—you'll have gone a long way
for one lifetime."

He went round the bed to the door and, when it was open,
looked back sadly. "Once again, when I've gone," he said,
"you'll feel hot all over. You'll tell yourself that I'm an old
woman, a clergyman, schoolmaster . . . but I think you're
in a draught."

He went out quickly.

Chapter 4 SHE DROVE THE CAR CAREFULLY ACROSS THE traffic, slipping her clutch so as to avoid jarring him, and drew it up under the trees close by the Achilles Monument.

They were in sunlight, a beam having found a breach in the foliage above them, and the afternoon was light and scented. It was midsummer, which in England is late spring, and London was buoyant. Those ponderous qualities of the city, that weigh upon and squeeze dry the individual, had been drawn out of it by the trembling of the earth and by the sweet, slightly luminous haze of dust that surmounted everything, joining the clear-cut tops of the buildings to a cloudless sky. That pretentious jumble of houses and important people and underpaid, self-satisfied clerks and overpaid, dissatisfied workmen had gone frivolous, grown young again. The soft afternoon absorbed the clamor of their business, the squeaking of their pens, their agitated chatter, the yapping of their horrid little lap dogs, the blare of their horns, the steady rumble of their traffic; so that the town was almost quiet, even in the flow of its own tumult.

In the park, the more genuine quiet was made a particular delicacy by the curtain of absorbed sound that surrounded it. It might have been the humming of bees, the drone of summer insects. Only occasionally, the yelp of a dog that had been trodden on or kicked, or the remarkable horn of an especially gaudy car escaped the solution, reaching the ear as an individual outcry. Otherwise, you might have been in the country.

95

Lydia drew in her breath slowly: "Glorious, isn't it?"

He shifted his position with care, holding with his good hand the pile of cushions and folded blankets that supported his splint. For a brief instant his face was twisted from the pain of moving. "No!" he said; and then more violently, "No! It's beastly, it's sham, it's a fake. If you've got to be in a town, I'd rather hunt out the worst block of slums in Whitechapel, the narrowest, dirtiest little street—wherever it is—then you *are* in London. This is neither one thing nor the other; it's nothing . . . the sunlight is good, though."

She looked at him swiftly. The passion in his voice was something new that she had not heard before, that had been remarkably absent. She was glad of it and, not bothering to answer, sat contentedly in silence. It was all right to be silent with him these days, with their friendship running smoothly without the lubricant of talk. Unless you had something to say, it was no longer necessary to keep up a conversation. Silence was now a token of repose and not of comfort or estrangement.

A party on horseback approached, riding towards Hyde Park Corner; and Tubby, careful not to move his body or his shoulder, twisted his head to watch them pass him. Striped and patterned by the sunlight that came through the overhanging branches, they walked quietly; a groom or a riding master leading a child on a small pony; two girls, a young man and an elderly lady. You heard their subdued, well-mannered voices and you heard the muffled hoofs on the tan surface. You saw the white, cream-washed sweat fringing the horses' girths, the flecks of saliva about their bits and curb chains. Then, for an instant, you smelled the keen, sweet tang that belonged to horses, to warm horses, to horses packed together in stables, to horses that were—or had been—sweating. Round the other side of the Park they had been cantering. In and out of the shadows, the shadows striping them. The soft wind of their movement full in their faces. The joyous movement.

"Tubby . . . Tubby," she said desperately, "you're not to look like that; I just can't bear it. They're not even very good horses, are they?"

"Not very . . ."

"Then why, *why* . . . ?"

"They're horses," he said shortly, his eyes still following, his shoulders rigid to the front, his neck twisted, almost grotesquely.

"Tubby, stop it! Stop it, will you?"

"Why?" He asked the question harshly, brutally, putting into it sufficient insolence to challenge her right of interference.

Again she looked at him with surprise. Within a few minutes it was the second time that his voice had held this new, bitter violence.

"Why . . . ?" she repeated, responding to his temper; "because it's mad, ridiculous, stupid. What *are* horses? Animals with legs and a tail and ears that go backwards and forwards. . . ."

"And a soft muzzle and large, generous eyes, and with characters that you can learn and know; not like human beings; you can't hope to understand human beings; they're complicated things, much more difficult than pictures or poetry or—or— chemical experiments."

"Tubby!" Her sudden cry was surprise, not dismay, not annoyance.

"Horses are decent, straightforward creatures—" (he was looking straight in front of him) "they're not like people who have brains or haven't brains, who are clever or stupid; who tell themselves they're stupid, who glory in being stupid; like I do, like we all do in the army."

"Stop it, Tubby!" she began indignantly; indignant not of his views but that he had reached them without her, that she was outside, excluded from his temper. "What have you been reading—or thinking—or who have you been talking to?"

It was some moments before he answered; and then the words came slowly, reluctantly: "Sammy, and Daddy Watson, and Sammy. And I've been thinking; lying and looking out of the window and thinking. . . ."

He didn't want to have to tell her this; he didn't want to hurt her, not to talk of it at all. But he was angry and resentful with her, with himself, with all of them; with their views and their way of thinking; with the way they made simple things difficult, looking for difficulties and complications, searching behind doors, poking and prying into hidden corners—like a Barrack

Officer hunting out deficiencies and breakages and surplus chairs (and the odd coal scuttle Hicks had "made" somewhere), on his annual inspection. They looked at him, Tubby—he knew it now—and said "that man can't be such a damn fool as he seems." They watched his movements, peered into his thoughts, seized on his words, to prove that he was not just the simple, happy person, the good soldier, athlete, gentleman, he had been before this accident delivered him up to them. He didn't want them to find him different; he didn't want to be more clever than anyone else. He denied this alleged duality of his nature. There weren't two Tubbys, one lurking behind the other. There was the Tubby that everyone knew and had liked well enough, who rode hard, laughed and was happy and honest. You could rely on him; you could previse his actions, his words even (why be ashamed of it?); you could trust him to do the decent thing, to say something bright that would hurt no one. He was a quite simple article in a shop window, well made and with the price marked in plain figures. You could take him or leave him; but you couldn't go prying into him, fiddling about his works, searching—as if he were one of those Chinese cabinets —for hidden drawers and cupboards.

People were always singling him out: Sammy, Daddy, Lydia, because they wouldn't believe their eyes; even the General, because he had known his father! They were all at it. And he wanted no more than to hide himself in the warm herd of his friends, to be as them, better at some things, worse at others; to be entirely comparable in a vertical scale, so that you could write a report on him. "Good with recruits, no good at survey; not so clever as Benjy but a better horse-master; and yet without the experience to be a real horse-master like Bert. A good shot, good at hitting a polo ball." It was all so simple. Why make things difficult?

That was how he felt. But, even now, the process by which feelings were transmuted to thought, and thought to speech, was slow and cumbersome. He was still primarily driven by instincts. Give him time—perhaps a day or two—and his brain would work out something; but, for immediate results, that which he felt or experienced, both with his senses and the still deeper parts of him, struggled to escape in speech and to by-pass the filter of the brain. Or perhaps that is a bad simile. Perhaps it was more like trying to work a steam engine without lighting a fire beneath the boiler. Nothing much happens.

"Don't you see, Lydia . . . it's all this interference; all this looking for things . . . so unnecessarily difficult. . . ."

She was a clever girl, had followed him part of the way. "But things just *aren't* easy and simple," she said.

"Horses are. . . ."

"Oh, horses!" She spoke with weary disgust.

"Yes, horses," he said. "Horses! You can understand them, feel them. You know what they're going to do—that is, most of them, usually. . . ." Even here he was insecure and of course she seized on the weakness.

"*That* isn't true either," she said; "*I* don't know what a horse is going to do. *You* do, because you play with them, live with them. Horses, not humans, are your real affinity. You become an animal. You give up all the rights you've inherited as a human being; throw them away and become a creature of instincts, an animal."

"And what's wrong with being an animal?" he asked quickly, looking for some sort of foothold, feeling for the crevice into which he could prize a finger.

"Nothing," she said; "because we're all animals. But we're something more as well. There's an animal side to us and a human side to us and . . ."

"It isn't that," he cried, seeing that she was swinging back to the old argument, the maze that led always to the same final perplexity, the conclusion that you wouldn't admit because it made life too difficult. "It's much more than that—or less than that—you'd call it. Horses mean all the clean, decent things that make life fresh and simple. The air going through you, cleaning you. . . ."

"Like a person," she broke in, "who washes his face every day and takes a bath once a fortnight. He looks clean . . . *what* do horses mean that is clean and decent? That's what I can't discover. Racing! The sport of kings and gentlemen, is it? A clean, decent, honest game; none of the dirty tricks you'll find in the Queen's Hall or the National Gallery. And healthy too—more healthy than football, say, because you don't stand in one place exercising only the lungs; you're on the move, running between the grandstand, the bookies and the paddock. It's a wonderful thing to be a sportsman. . . ."

"That's not fair," he said. "I mean riding in races."

"Oh, no you don't. You ride in one race to every ten you go and watch . . . but it's off the lines a bit, this. Let's go right back to them . . . horse-coping; that's at the root of all this horse business. The be-all and end-all of it. Such clean, decent people . . . Hunting! Thirty dogs, two hundred people—most of them scared stiff and chattering like monkeys—and one miserable little fox chased into a hole and dug out with spades and a terrier. . . ."

"All the old arguments," he said scornfully. "Nothing new after all. You can argue against hunting till you're blue in the face—and I admit there's no real answer. But you can't get away from the thrill that it gives you—that *is* clean and decent in a lot of ways. It makes you forget. It's simple and straightforward. It helps you to . . . to . . ." He couldn't express himself. That was where all these people scored. They knew words as he knew horses; and they could talk, talk, talk, hiding their lack of understanding under all this talking.

"Helps you to—what?" she asked him, taunted him, pinning him down like a butterfly. "To what does hunting help you?"

"Oh, hell!" he said, cornered, tired of it. "It helps you to get away from everything, out into the open air with the wind and the sun and the rain and the frost coming on in the evening. You don't have to think; you don't have to be clever. It helps you to . . . to . . ."

"Escape, Tubby?"

"That's it," he said, eagerly, gratefully. "That's what it does. It helps you to escape. . . ."

"From what?"

"From everything that's uncertain and complicated and difficult; from everything you can't trust; from people talking; from having to think and worry about what's true and what's false, what's right and what isn't; from . . . from . . ."

"From being human," she said suddenly. "You escape from being human and become entirely an animal. That's why you go hunting."

"And who wants to be human?" he asked angrily. "What's the use of it when you can be a decent, honest animal? What is there so wonderful about being different? What *is* a human, anyway?"

"A human?" she repeated and looked out from the car at the deep shadows and heavy foliage, seeing the children's play, hearing laughter. "A . . . a pulse in the eternal mind, no less . . ." she said softly.

"Ah. . . ." Then they were both silent until he said defiantly—"Even *I* learned that once, you know. I . . . I used to think it—the whole poem—rather beautiful."

She turned at that, resting her arm on the driving wheel and looking at him. "When?" she asked.

"Oh, at school, I suppose. During the war. When I was quite young. . . ."

"And when, Tubby dear, did you start forgetting it?"

"How can I say?" He was getting exasperated. "When I grew up, grew past it, I suppose."

"When you grew up," she said. "That's it! When you grew up and started hunting and found this wonderful new, clean, decent way of forgetting that thoughts and ideas can be fine, can be—your own word, Tubby—beautiful."

He sat quietly; defeated. Once more he had met truth; and recognition came swiftly. It was no good. You couldn't get away from them, all of them—Sammy, Daddy, Lydia—and again and again they led you back to the water. You can lead a horse to the water, though . . . but he tried to be honest with himself. That proverb wasn't true, was made up by someone who didn't understand horses. . . .

"Tell me," she said gently, "all the beautiful things that you saw and read and heard as a child. . . . There was a man called Shakespeare . . . no!" she said quickly, laughing. "*Not* the one in the Regiment, *nor* the one who rode Sweet Corn at Leicester . . . but isn't the name familiar? Don't you ever remember?"

"I remember sometimes," he said sulkily. "When I've had a glass or two, when I'm very tired perhaps, when I can't sleep . . . odd bits come back to me. There are times in fact," he said proudly, "when I can quote quite a lot of Shakespeare and . . . and" (and this was a real scoring point) "Benjy can go on spouting it for ages."

"And you still find it beautiful?" she asked.

He paused for some moments before answering: "I suppose I should—if I thought about it."

🌼 He had his back to the long invalid chair in which Tubby was sitting, but you knew very well the smile to which he was speaking.

"So Lydia said that too . . . I'm not surprised really. But how you must have hated to hear it! How you begin to hate us!"

He looked round, as if to reassure you with that smile; to show you the pale, tired face that was always the same, that concealed nothing, having nothing that needed concealment.

"You aren't sure of yourself, Tubby. You may be right, or may be wrong. Or *we* may be right . . . that's how it is, isn't it?

"How angry you are with us for disturbing you; for taking away your complacency and that gay, easy way of life that you enjoyed when you were—(how does the song go?)—a handsome young soldier. And yet you've no cause to be angry with *us*. You've been ill for four or five months—isn't it?—and in that time we, you and I, have had three, perhaps four, of . . . of these very earnest conversations. You've done the rest for yourself. And—remember—you started it!

"No," he said, "be angry with yourself, Tubby. Hate yourself because you haven't the guts to believe in one thing or the other. You've lost self-satisfaction and found doubt. That's the first stage of a very, very long journey. . . . You'll rest for a time now. You'll hunt in a few weeks, as soon as you're out of this. Next spring you'll race again. But, once you've started to doubt, you've started something that makes life hard but makes it worth living. Most soldiers start it at fifty—when they've retired on an inadequate pension. Then it's hell for them!

"Some time, somewhere, somehow," Sammy said, "when something goes wrong again, you'll come back to this moment. Then you'll move on again, further on the journey . . . it may be years; it may be in the quite near future. One never knows —does one?—just what will happen in the army. And when things go wrong—that's when you need the part of you that can otherwise lie dormant. That's when the preacher gets you, isn't it?"

"Don't hate us, Tubby," he said later; "because I must be off now. I just came in to say good-by on my way to Yorkshire. Six weeks with the Territorials and we'll all be back on the Plain again together . . . if you get there first, don't quarrel with Daddy while he's commanding the Battery . . . give my love to Lydia . . . get well quickly."

The commonplace ending, the last few words of farewell, were reassuring. One man, an ordinary, sane, healthy man, had spoken to another. That was cool, solid reality.

Apart from that, it was true—so wickedly true—what Sammy had said to him. He'd put up a fight all right; but, now that he'd started to doubt, he could believe in nothing; living could never again be quite the same easy, simple business. The hate, the fear, the resentment were dying now. He was almost— grateful.

These last few weeks, he had looked to the past and considered the future. The two had drawn together and the present had lost value. The firelight flickered, lighting up the less dark corners of memory, recalling adolescent childhood, babyhood fears and happiness. They were days of contrasts, those; not of the flat, toneless pleasure that had come later.

So he'd started a journey, had he? Doubt, Sammy said, was the first stage; what was the second? And where was he going to?

He was vaguely excited.

❦ "Where are you going to?" the house physician asked, standing by the window in his white jacket, hands in the pockets, joggling up and down on the balls of his feet, looking through rimless glasses at Tubby. "That's the question, Windrush. Barret says the bone's healing nicely—at last. We can stop our osteolin injections, violet ray, Mrs. Evans, and leave the rest to nature . . . a nice, long convalescence in the country where there's someone to look after you . . . you don't want a trained nurse; just someone who'll wash their hands before they change the dressings. . . . Quiet, and afternoon rests, sunshine, medicine, and some help with your toilet. One of your rich friends, perhaps. . . . Where are you going?"

"I'll think of someone . . ."

"Anything in mind?"

You could tell that the servant of this expensive nursing home disliked riches. Behind their rimless glasses, his eyes saw Tubby in terms of comparison: the sterile impersonality of a hospital, against the floral pamper of so many overfed, overheated, overinjected hypochondriacs, who would be better knocked on the head and have done with it. This Windrush, a decent fellow, ought never to have come here; would have been better off in the discipline of a general ward; and it was wrong that wealth should lap him about with so many luxuries and fancy treatments which, if anything, impeded recovery. It wouldn't be bad to take him down a bit . . .

"Well—what's it to be, Windrush?"

The question had for some time been searching for an answer. There were so many houses to which one went to shoot, for a few days' fishing, a hunt ball, a race meeting . . . but where could you invite yourself as a privileged guest for a long period? Benjamin's father had a sort of Gothic castle and acres and acres of grouse moor, fine when you were a child, but ratridden, full of beetles, roof leaking, no light, and the water rarely warmer than tepid. And the old man was half imbecile, subject to violent passions and guarded by an attendant. That seemed to be about the general form of his possible hosts. There was Uncle Arthur, admiral, with a flat in Half Moon Street and a small sailing boat at Hamble; Uncle George, general, with a minute cottage close to the Royal Berkshire and clubs in Pall Mall, St. James's and Piccadilly. Beyond that, there was no one.

"I . . . I don't really know," Tubby said, bewildered when he came to analyze the popularity that was an essential part of his character—as he saw it.

The hands, withdrawn from the pockets of the white coat, were rubbed together pleasantly. "Well, Windrush, there's always Osborne . . . I've got a friend at Millbank, at the Military Hospital; I daresay we could fix it up for you."

"Osborne . . . the Isle of Wight!" An island where there was no hunting or shooting, where people went—of all effeminate amusement—for sailing. "Not that place!"

"What's wrong with it? Ever been there?"

"No, but I've heard about it. It's for people who are dying; moribund old generals flirting with middle-aged nurses; and old frauds who go there again and again for a free holiday. Retired commanders who get a room for Cowes week; admirals and their wives who like croquet . . . why I've heard the Queen visits it once a year, and everyone has to play croquet and ping-pong and arrange themselves in the garden to show how much they're enjoying it. . . . And it's full of statues, with fig leaves put on to please Queen Victoria. And it's all rules and regulations; and everyone talks about what's wrong with them, and how important they used to be, and what they used to do at Poona. . . ." It seemed impossible to Tubby.

"Well," said the doctor; "if that's how you feel about it . . . of course, if you can find anywhere better . . . a rich friend or someone. . . ."

Lydia, of course, knew about it that afternoon. There was nothing hidden from her. On each visit, and she came almost daily, she talked with the nurse, the doctors, the radiologist, Mrs. Evans, even with Dr. Barret; with anyone, in fact, who could not resist her charm and would answer questions. She had this habit, common to women who are born in luxury and with dependents—tenants, and the children and wives of outdoor servants—that she made everyone's affairs her business, questioning them, searching for ways to help them, and applying the traditional remedies for all ills—jellies, milk, eggs, coal, cakes, from the house, discarded clothes and cross-examination. It had been all right a generation before, when the owners of property had these genuine responsibilities; but, now that the State had assumed their liabilities, leaving them only diminished assets, it became little more than patronage, sometimes gratefully received, more often suspect. And, even now, it was all right for Lydia in her youth and loveliness, with her rather imperious charm—itself a solace. Even the house physician, rimless glasses, left-wing views and all, could not resist her.

"Tubby!" she said, as she came into the room, "you're coming to Calcott. We could go down Friday." She always entered like this, filled with some urgent resolution—even if it were only that the sweet peas were dead and should have been thrown away yesterday.

"On the contrary," he said. "I'm going to Osborne to-morrow. I'd like the car at ten to take me to the station."

It was the technique that he and Benjamin employed when Lydia, her fragile, porcelain beauty so ludicrously fired with competence, came bustling upon them. It stirred her naïve sense of humor and she laughed at once; the low, slightly hoarse, happy laugh that was altogether a guileless expression. She was her most attractive in laughter, with all pretense abandoned.

"Tubby, *please* come to Calcott. You can't go to Osborne . . . moribund generals and people from Poona. . . ."

"Damn you," he said, "you've been talking to the doctor. I only said that to annoy him."

"You know you didn't."

"Yes I did. Osborne's a swell place really."

"That's just not true, Tubby," she said. "Please. . . ."

"Of course I can't come. It's out of the question."

She sat on the bed looking at him. She was really very beautiful; the closer she was to him, the more beautiful. And her scent was by now strong with memories; and her eyes were just as they always had been when they looked back over her shoulder in the photograph. Feminine charms were still strange and alarming to him; and he could only particularize the emotions they provoked—that she now provoked—from what he had heard or read, and not from experience. He knew so little. He'd never seen a girl do her hair, make up her face, clean her teeth, struggling with a dress, lying curled on a bed or stretched in a bath, or in any of the intimate abandon that explains woman. Nothing that had happened since his accident had lessened his timidity at even the thought of these things. In fact, with his physical confidence gone, his limbs wasted, face pallid, and all of his body subject to the degradations of nursing, sexual demands were driven still further into his darker corners, divorced more completely from the women he actually encountered.

"There just isn't any reason why you shouldn't come," she said. "Really Tubby, there isn't . . ." Her voice had always the quality of cream; a rich, consistent tone—larger than herself—to which it sank from excursions up the scale, made to express surprise, pleasure, amusement, indignation, very rarely anger. She was free with exclamations, not exclamatory words, but ordinary words or names, used with emphasis to express emotion . . .

"Tubby!"

"No," he said; "how can I? Your mother . . . your father . . . I hardly know them."

"Daddy's in Scotland, Mummy's in Marienbad, and Calcott is lovely in October," she said, as if finally dealing with that argument.

"But you and I . . . we can't be alone in the house." The suggestion really frightened him. He shrank from a situation in which something else, new and unknown, might be thrust upon him; feared it but yet wanted it.

"There'll be a dozen servants or so," she said dryly.

"They're never supposed to count. . . ."

"Tubby!" she cried in amazement; "you haven't gone all prudish! There's nothing wrong about it . . . I promise I won't seduce you."

This was more than he could stand. He blushed, got angry and she was laughing at him; but there was nothing he could do or say about it. "But . . . but . . . it isn't fair to you," he stammered, changing ground. "You'll be saddled with me . . . someone will . . . dressings and things." And then he felt suddenly that he must get at the truth of it, find some basis on which he could understand their friendship. "I mean," he said, looking away, "if it were different . . . if we were more than just friends . . . if you really cared for me. . . ."

She leaned across the bed and turned his face towards her, still laughing at his blushes. "Tubby—you silly old man—of course I care for you a lot . . . I think you're a dear. Why else do you imagine I come here to see you every day?"

"Sort of slumming," he said with quick perception, and there was too much truth in that for her to counter it quickly, haphazardly, without a thought of where the answer might lead them.

"We once had forty slum children down there for a fortnight," she said cleverly.

"And you want me on that basis?"

"Yes, Tubby dear—if I can't have you any other way. . . ."

Chapter 5 THEY STOOD ON THE STONE STEPS, BETWEEN the grey fluted pillars, on about the third step from the top and the fourth from the bottom. Coming from the dim hall and the smell of cigar smoke, lavender and floor polish, they paused in the autumn sunlight, the breeze blowing sweetly into them.

"A nice October day," Tubby said; "we ought by rights to be killing something."

She refused to be provoked. "We probably shall," she answered; "if I'm not careful. . . . It's a nice car, isn't it?"

"Not a bad sort. Leaves you nicely. . . ."

The new car, grey this time, stood in the drive with the chauffeur beside it. Like the last one, it was long, low, heavy, expensive; money thrown recklessly into a product so that it should feel money, radiate its cost, force on you the irresistible pleasures of wealth and privilege.

"How I hate the rich," Tubby said.

"So do I, Tubby. . . . She's lovely, isn't she?"

"Not a bad birthday present," he said. "I remember my father once sent me a fiver."

The chauffeur, clearly once a coachman, touched his cap and opened the door for her.

"What about her, Walter? She takes a bit of grooming, doesn't she?" Tubby said to him; and the man stood back, bending back from the hips, looking the car over as if for the first time he was considering the question. "She *will* do, sir; she *will* do.

When the first polish wears off . . . I'd as soon have a pair of horses."

"You hear that, Lydia?" Tubby said. "Trot her up for us, will you?"

"Come on," she answered. "I'm dying to try her. . . . It's all right, Walter, we shan't want you."

"And you have the nerve," Tubby said, settling himself comfortably, "to taunt me about horses."

She took the car out of the drive, down the short hill with chestnut trees meeting above their heads, through the stone gateway and along the wide curve of the outer drive towards the highroad. The grass was still long in the park, the park trees heavy still, their leaves just turning, the dew glistening, the deer taking sudden fright as the car went past them. The morning was so close to perfection that to breathe it, to live it, was nearer to memory than to a present experience. Each moment was rare, could never be exactly repeated. It was sad that you would never get again just that view of the stone tiled lodge, light against the elm foliage, the grey and white garments on the clothes line, children playing beside the chrysanthemums, smoke from the chimney taken slantwise by the breeze till it died in the pearl blue, blue-washed haze of the autumn morning.

He felt it, felt keenly, the flawless beauty of the morning. It was a conscious appreciation, linking the present to everything in the past that was beginning now to make memory precious. Perfection destroyed time, leaving nothing that you could say was yesterday, today, tomorrow. Always emotion gave him this knowledge of timelessness, and still he had not admitted the knowledge; for, though thought and reason were growing, they had not yet caught up with experience. There was a lag of days. He thought tomorrow that which he had felt yesterday . . . and this negative aspect of Tubby's character has constantly to be stressed. Feelings had always nourished his life and now they were growing deeper and more poignant. But how can you describe them except in terms of the thought that would follow?

For the feelings themselves were little more than purely physical; a constriction of the larynx, a swelling of whatever lies within the upper ribs, a melting of the loins, tightness inside the stomach; so that if you knew only the symptoms, it might have been indigestion.

In their intimacy, she was aware of his joy, knowing—as he could not—how much keener and deeper it was than any emotion he could consciously have felt six months earlier—that is before his accident. And in the last few weeks he had changed so much—or the ratio of their friendship had changed, as he increased and she remained constant. He was finer, gentler, keener and even fiercer; a blade that has been sharpened . . . she wondered what he had lost in the process.

Outside the park, she drove more quickly and soon they turned off from the main road, going by lanes along and across the Cotswold valleys, through grey villages that grew out of the valley sides, buildings huddled together, piled up one upon the other, all painted with deep shadows, the tithe barns surmounting them. They crossed and re-crossed the fast-running Coln that watered the soft meadows. They slid over narrow bridges, between stone parapets; always the same grey limestone of the Cotswolds, hewn from the hillsides, holding in itself the colors of all the seasons. Sometimes the heavy woods came down to and bordered the road. More often the hill rose steeply beside them, field after field of shallow soil, chrome stubble, sepia plough, or light, gamboge-washed pasture, all patched together by the grey walling.

At last they left the valley and came up on to the main road that joined Cheltenham and Oxford. "We'll try her out," she said and pressed down the accelerator.

It was a straight, dark-surfaced road, seeming wider than it was, with trees on each side to start with but later running along a naked ridge, a spine of the uplands, with pale fields and broader valleys stretching away each side for a long distance. At once the car was tearing down it, noiselessly, without a tremor.

"Steady," he said, "we're a lot over ninety."

"Frightened?"

"No, not frightened; apprehensive. If I remember rightly, the road curves in a moment."

"She'll hold any curve at ninety . . . she's wonderful."

"I hope so. . . ."

He saw the wheel quiver, her knuckles white as she held it over. He heard the high whine of new tires on macadam. He felt the car swing, its hind wheels slipping away from them. They were round, they were all right. Then, for a long moment, he saw the motorcycle, coming from the opposite direction, skidding, swung out on to the wrong side of the road, heading straight for them. He saw the cloth cap, worn the wrong way round, peak backwards, the leather coat flapping loose, the red muffler, the man's face, as he passed.

She pulled the wheel over hard, taking the grass bank, the broad verge that rose in a short but steep slope to apparent safety. He saw the telegraph pole well ahead, felt the crash of the springs, the car rock sideways . . . then a tire burst. The wheel spun out of her hands. He heard the thunder of something broken, tearing at the turf of the roadside. He got his hand to the wheel and, as the stone wall faced them, wrenched at it. There was no hurry; nothing was happening quickly. Broadside on, the car hit the telegraph pole and, as the world burst about them, turned over.

For some curious reason, he knew and remembered afterwards exactly what happened. Each stage was clear in his perception and memory. Only the senses failed him. The four separate blows were individually recognized by some part of him, but his sight, hearing, feeling, had only the shuddering knowledge of disaster. He was aware of the scream of the tires, the sharp crack of the blowout, the thunder of their rocking progress; but his ears knew only the general tumult. He could count the motions of the car, the lateral swings to left, to right, to left again, full sideways for some distance and then a complete turning; but he saw only a quick sequence of quite vivid but meaningless pictures: stone wall, roadway and telegraph pole, succeeding each other again and again, mixed together, flashing across his vision in hieroglyphics that to the eye itself were unrecognizable. At the last instant, when the telegraph pole broke, when movement ceased and momentum was in the end conquered, he lost consciousness. In a tiny fraction of a second, it slipped from him slowly, so that he could smell the chloroform, hear the anesthetist's order ("breathe deeply"), hear Bert's, Sammy's, Daddy's, Benjamin's, Lydia's voices in the tent, and watch with interest (that which had been hidden from him before) the grey mare going too fast into the fourth fence from the end, coming all wrong, he pulling at her to put her right, kicking her into it, the hoofs skidding, the brown horse bumping her in mid-air, the uphill landing, she pecking, reaching out, giving it up, and the slow somersault afterwards.

Then there were only the dung-colored swastikas of anesthesia.

He was unconscious for an eternity of two seconds. And his first knowledge was that his bad shoulder and his bad arm, strapped to his side, were not hurting, were uninjured. Almost at once, he knew then the smell of petrol, that he was lying on his side, that Lydia was speaking, was fixed somewhere beneath him, the steering wheel bent between them. He struggled— gingerly at first—found surprisingly that there was no pain, that the door opened with a kick of the knee upwards, that he could climb out of it on to the roadside.

At once it struck him that the spectacle of the car was indecent, upturned as she was with her vitals showing. The side of her that was uppermost appeared uninjured, except for the wheel, the wing and the headlight, which gave the impression of being generally battered, like the face of a pugilist. The engine was still foolishly running, and glass from the headlights was strewn everywhere; he felt it beneath his feet as he stepped out quickly. Then his face was wet—from sweat or water? He put up his hand and it returned bright with blood, wide, shallow rivulets of blood, thin, ample, delicious. There had been no visible blood in his last accident. Blood made it more genuine; much more exciting. It did not occur to him that it suggested an injury.

The experience was clean and pleasant. There was the long extension of time that provided the same physical ecstasy of polo, racing . . . you acted quickly but at leisure.

It was the top of the car and the windshield that had suffered most obvious mutilation. The roof had been torn apart, shattered completely, and the windshield—a broad star of cracked glass—was flattened back against the steering wheel, which was itself bent grotesquely towards the driving seat. He saw, then, the particularly indecent feature of the whole accident: the telegraph pole. This had fallen and had broken in its fall, the top sector being swung on to the road by the tension of the wires, and the butt dropping across the car, splitting the roof, almost bisecting it. In the driving seat, imprisoned in a cage made by the butt of the telegraph pole, the bent steering wheel and the flattened windshield, lay Lydia. She was quite conscious; her face was completely white, eyes wide open, and she was speaking. It was now perhaps as much as three seconds since Tubby had scrambled from the car and his feet had found the roadside; perhaps ten seconds since he had recovered consciousness; thirteen from the last phase of the accident. Lydia was ending the appeal, the beginning of which had been among his first impressions on awakening. "Tubby . . . I'm stuck here . . . Tubby, it's going to catch fire . . . do you smell the petrol?"

Yes! he smelled the petrol; had smelled it all along from the first instant. So he climbed in beside her, climbing up the side of the car and plunging head-first in by the window. He thought he must stop the engine; but the dashboard was bent under; the switch was rigid, refusing to move in any direction. He felt behind, searching for some wire or something electrical to get his hand on and to tear at. His fingers, prying where there should have been space, found only the sleek, blank surface of enameled metal.

"The petrol tap . . . where is it?"

"I don't know . . . I'm stuck, Tubby. . . ."

He took hold of the steering wheel, then, lying bent over the side of the car, head downwards (ridiculous, he must look, he thought at that instant), bending his thighs so that his knees found purchase against the sharp edge of the running board. . . . "God! for my other arm. . . ." Even as the words were pulled out of him, he felt they were melodramatic, regretted them, blushed for them. He strained again, but the steering wheel would not move towards him. He could only free Lydia by breaking the back of the seat and letting her slide out that way.

So he climbed in completely, lying sideways, hunching himself up sideways, knees to chin, his back to the dashboard, his thighs compressed like a spring, his feet against the back of the driving seat. In here the smell of petrol was very strong; and it was also hot, the heat coming upwards from somewhere beneath them. And he was close to Lydia, parted from her only by the steering wheel, her face very white and large, the stump of the fallen telegraph pole a black arm raised above them. "Now for a feat of strength," he said; another calm, melodramatic remark, immediately regretted.

He felt drumming behind his forehead, pressure in his eyes and temples, the glorious rigidity of all muscles, a slight pain in his injured shoulder. The tumult inside him increased with the swelling heat and with his greater, greater, impossibly greater rigidity. At last there came the crack; a knowledge of splintering, that something had broken. The back of the driving seat collapsed suddenly as the spring of his body uncoiled and his thighs straightened.

He got an arm round Lydia's shoulders, slipping it down, his fingers for the first time touching her quivering breast, and he, suddenly—with the world swelling in his loins—conscious of it. Then the impression blacked out; everything blacked out except a sudden knowledge of heat, of urgency. . . .

His hand clutched and held beneath her armpit, and he wriggled backwards, his legs protruding further and further out of the car, until once more he could bend his thighs, find purchase with his knees, and regain the roadside. She came out easily.

"Like sardines," he said, "that's what it is, you know. . . ."

❧ They sat on the grass and she dabbed at his face with a handkerchief. Sickness came up in him but got no further than his chest; and he let himself sink backwards, lying flat, his head on the grass and the grass tickling him. It was very peaceful.

"Oh, Tubby . . . I wish we had some iodine. . . ."

"In my pocket," he said. "No, the little pocket; what my

tailor calls the ticket pocket . . . can't think why . . . never keep tickets anyway. I just don't hold with them . . ."

She found the metal tube that covered the glass iodine ampoule. "*Whatever* do you carry this for?"

"Always carry it. Always wanting it with horses. . . ."

"What horses? Tubby, you haven't been near a horse since April. There aren't any horses. . . ."

"Never know when you'll meet one. . . ."

She was examining his face, wiping away the blood, as it came, with his handkerchief. "I don't think it's serious. Except for one cut, it's mostly sort of grazes. It must have been the driving mirror or the headlights. I can put iodine on the grazes . . . not on the cut, I don't think . . . it's too deep, and right across your cheek. It wants a stitch or two . . . Oh, Tubby! What have I done to you?"

"Nothing that matters . . ." (Had he said that or had Sammy?) Everything was very odd, very indistinct and rather amusing. The car was blazing nicely some distance away from them.

"You were so disgustingly competent," he heard her say. "You said such dreadfully calm and proper things. You did it all so beautifully. Oh, Tubby. . . ."

It was curious how, in these crises, you always got facetious. Resistance, tried beyond its normal powers, summoned as reserves your sense of humor. ("Take the first shock of assault," it pleaded.) And, by being funny, you parried the blows, diverted them. "What did the surgeon order me?" he murmured. "General convalescence, complete rest, quiet, sunshine, semiskilled attention . . . I seem to have everything."

"That isn't kind," she said.

He smiled up at her: "No—honest, Lydia—I mean it."

She was running her hand through his hair . . . "And there's an awful bump here," she cried. "And that's bleeding too, quite badly . . . it's quite a deep cut . . . Tubby!"

"Don't worry," he said. "It's all right . . . I like it. . . ."

Knowing exactly what he was doing, feeling warm and contented, he abandoned the effort, let consciousness slip from him and quite happily fainted.

❧ The automobile accident welded them together in the memory of a shared experience. He had seen her for the first time as frail; and she knew at last the strength of that part of him which dealt with emergency, which directed his body to meet the needs of a crisis. She could respect him now, and his fear of her was dwindling. Her hard, glittering surface had been shown as so much varnish, with a soft and tender woman curled up beneath it.

The days at Calcott became uneventful until they followed each other in identical pattern; the fixed pattern preventing boredom which is dependent on the speed you travel between landmarks, on the passage of time which itself—in an active life—is always too fast or too slow for your personal tempo. Either way (too much rush or too much leisure) can bring boredom; and only a strictly ordered life can subvert this regime of discrepancy. And at Calcott they fell into a tenor of living as level—if less exacting—as that of a religious order. They met and parted and met again; they read, talked, took walks, ate and she played the piano to him or, more often, the gramophone. He began to like Mozart and to appreciate silence. The silence between them grew rich and golden like the days of autumn. So that they might have been two long-married people, tranquil, scarcely noticing each other but complementary; each impassionately needing the other—but without a physical bond left between them. So that sex was not an open factor of their intimacy. It doesn't sound likely, but it happened.

In the first place, both were virgins and ignorant. If either had been insistent, the other would probably have agreed to an experiment. For it would have been experiment for them, the outcome uncertain, each fearing the experience that was bandied so lightly in words. Again and again, in the dark privacy of his bedroom, Tubby thought of a woman's body, soft and naked. But somehow the face didn't attach itself; he couldn't personalize his fancies or his urgency. His thoughts, you see, couldn't make anything practical out of it. They could picture a pale body, without clothes, beautiful; but they couldn't undress a smart, lovely woman, with plain, severe, expensive

satins, or still plainer tweeds. To start with, he didn't know how
your hand first approached her; how on earth you found the
courage to undo the first hook or button; whether it was a hook
or button and on what part of her person it was to be found
and fumbled for. The difficulties were so great, the embarrassment might be so acute, that the risks weren't worth taking.
That was the conclusion you came to.

Besides, there were no opportunities to make the moment
propitious. They sat together in the library on each side of the
fireplace, a masculine room with no sofa. They walked together, with dogs hunting in the gorse or lost in the rhodo-
dendrons, and there was always a terrier or spaniel to be looked
for and whistled. They met tenants, woodmen, keepers, gar-
deners, and stopped to talk with them; one, so to speak, handing them on to the next; George working at the top end of the
copse and Tim Painter mending a wall at the bottom. And
they came back to find footmen laying another meal, and
Thompson padding about the house, making up the fire,
bringing letters, drawing the blinds, asking for orders. The day
went on like this until, quite early, they went to bed, Thompson
and a footman still up, locking up after them. At the top of the
wide, oak staircase, their corridors were different. They stood
beneath the antlers and armour and scarcely looked at each
other. That way it was always safer; there was no fear of embarrassment or starting anything you couldn't finish.

"Well, good night," she said.

"Good night. It's been a grand day, hasn't it?"

"Lovely . . . don't forget the lights, will you?"

And then, in the dark bedroom, fancies and urgency might
come tearing up in him. What had she said in the nursing
home? "Tubby—I promise I won't seduce you . . ." That surely
meant that the contrary was possible . . . but it was too late
this evening. She'd be undressing now, cleaning her teeth,
climbing into bed, already in bed, curled up, sleeping. He
couldn't just barge in and say "Lydia, I want to come to bed
with you . . ." She'd answer: "You must be mad, Tubby. . . ."
or more probably: "Poor dear Tubby! Go and find the house-
maid. The pretty little one sleeps in the big bedroom at the **end**

—with two others. And I'm afraid the boards creak on the top landing. . . ."

❧ And then—he discovered with almost horror—she believed in God. "Not a religious god, Tubby; not one that you have to thank and sing to, and go to church for an introduction. Not a personal god; but something divine somewhere, to which the little bit of divinity inside ourselves is making its way slowly . . . so slowly."

"But you can't prove all that."

"I don't want to. I know it."

"But *I* don't know it, Lydia. I don't believe it either. You can't make *me* believe it."

"I'm not trying to, Tubby. You'll know it for yourself one day; it's not for me to have the presumption to try and teach you. . . ."

"It's about the only presumption you haven't got."

"That's unkind—but it may be true . . . but it wouldn't be any good if I *did* try. You can only help people by being yourself, letting them use you—if they want to. If I'm no good to you that way, there's no other. . . ."

"But you are, you are," he cried. "I don't know what it is, but I'm happy with you. I know where I am, what's right and what isn't, what's true. . . . You make things difficult because you're so hard to satisfy, never satisfied. But you make things easy too. You do something to me that makes life simple. . . ."

"Like horses do?" she suggested, smiling.

He thought for a moment. "Much more than horses," he said solemnly. "It's a different part of me that you touch. . . ."

"Horses touch your instincts and your body," she said. "And me?"

"I don't know, Lydia, I don't know. . . ."

And all this made her still more untouchable.

❧ She was sad when he went in the middle of November. The last week of his leave had to be spent in London; and, in any event, her father was coming down for the covert shooting. Tubby could have stayed on, though there was yet scarcely sufficient movement in his shoulder for him to manage a shot-gun; but it seemed to them both that their time together at Calcott was already precious, would be spoiled by the intrusion of others. It must end as it had started, something entirely personal between the two of them, a period of growing intimacy, a steady growth from seedling to blossom. It was something that—if they never met again—had a fragrance and color quite unforgettable.

In the last months, the change that had taken place in Tubby had become very evident. Before that, the effects of his opera-tions and of the long, drugged recovery had so devastated him that what was left bore no resemblance to the man he had been in April. At Calcott, the improvement had at first been rapid. Then it had slowed down as his general condition began to stabilize. The car accident had taken little physical effect and left no visible marks except for the scar down his cheek, from which the stitches had long been removed. And you could see now just what he was; tall, well-made, amply-framed, but much less thickset and awkwardly solid than before; less rough, less loutish, finer. His face was thinner, more interesting, not only because of the scar, but from the wearing off of the freshness, the newly-bought glow of (for instance) stained leather, that makes a just-purchased article of that substance less attractive than an old one. The uses of pain, unhappiness, dissatisfaction, had improved him.

When he left Calcott in the middle of November, it would have been absurd, of course, to have compared him with the pale invalid who had gone there six or seven weeks earlier. It was, however, interesting to consider him against the man who had suffered the racing accident. If you could have seen the two together, they might have been brothers, one considerably older than the other, or even more distant relatives with a family resemblance. Undoubtedly they were not the same person. The difference was much more radical than the mere passage of time could account for. Time smooths down some parts of a man and makes rugged others. It alters him, of course, changes the pitch of his thoughts, feelings, words and actions. But this was not a change of pitch; rather, a change of instruments.

"Good-by, Tubby," she said. "We shall see a lot of each other, of course; but this is the end of something that has . . . made us rather happy."

"Yes," he said, standing on the grey steps. "I feel I've grown . . . grown right back to a child again. I feel as if the sun had come out . . . as if there were shadows. Bright sides to things and shadows."

Chapter 6 "YOU'VE ALTERED A LOT, OLD BOY," DADDY said, when they met at the club where the taxi had dropped Tubby and his luggage. "My word you're different! One can see it now; couldn't in hospital." He spoke almost with admiration, uttering a compliment: "Less of a cavalry officer, Tubby . . . you'll have to live up to your looks, you know."

(Calcott was already dim in the past.) "Or down to them. . . ." Tubby said doubtfully.

That one affectionate outburst seemed to finish the matter. It drained off their pleasures of reunion so that during lunch, over their glass of port and their coffee afterwards in the smoking room, words came sparsely and with an awkward hesitation that was new between them. At last, with large brandy glasses in their cupped hands, they looked at each other solemnly, like two strange children, quite speechless. Something was clogged. The pressure within each of them was increasing but the flow could not overcome the obstruction.

"Look here," Daddy said, "I'm going to take you to see Ariel. You'll come, won't you?"

"Ariel?"

"I told you it was a stupid name . . . my girl, you know. She'd like to meet you."

"I doubt it," Tubby said, "but I'll come with pleasure."

It was, all the same, surprising that the invitation had been offered. Friendship with Daddy had always been one-sided, its aspect an objective view of only one of them, of Tubby; its conversational aspect confined to criticism, implied or direct, of wealth, authority, systems or individuals. Very often Tubby himself was the subject of attack; and it was new for Daddy to let the battle surge his way, to disclose the weakness in his own defenses. It was a pity, too, for Tubby did not enjoy the discovery of weakness in others. It was more secure to feel your friends impregnable. And for some reason, he thought of Daddy's girl as an entanglement, a break in his armour, lessening his independence. Again, as once before at the nursing home, Daddy had lost valor. Abandoning the assault, he became pathetic. And, as they left the club and started to walk down Piccadilly, he was almost common; a stout, rather vulgar little man with a bowler hat too small for him and too much on the side of his head, brisk, pert, commercial. Tubby was almost ashamed of his company. It was a terrible feeling.

"By jove, Daddy," he cried, to convince himself, "it's good to be with you again. It's good, isn't it?"

Once it was said, it began to gather truth to it. As they turned left up Down Street, he *was* glad to be with Daddy. He wished that Bert were there too—all of them—to make a party of it.

"It's not much of a flat," Daddy said apologetically, "but she finds it cheap and convenient. It's hers, of course—*I* couldn't afford the rent—but there's a lot of my things in it. . . ."

"Grand!" Tubby said with violence but quite meaninglessly. He couldn't bear to see Daddy apologetic. You had to fear him. Once he became pitiable, you were forced back on to patronage.

"A lovely Georgian doorway," Daddy said, fumbling for the latchkey. "A shame they had to make all these places into flats. The outside is the best part of it . . . I'm afraid you won't think much of it . . . I mean it's not . . . not what you're used to . . . after Lydia . . ."

They went in then, into the dark and narrow hall, past the table with its three or four piles of envelopes—mostly halfpenny stamps, clearly bills and circulars—up the staircase immediately in front of them (reproductions of Alken prints covered with dust and scarcely visible in the grubby twilight), past the first three floors, with yellowed visiting cards tacked to the doorway (nearly all "Miss" somebody—Tubby noticed) and stopping at last on the fourth landing.

"Another key. . . ." Daddy rapped on the door, a peculiar conspiratorial knock, and threw it open.

The room was empty. It was large but low and, though it was early in the winter afternoon, scarcely lighter than the staircase. Daddy moved about, switching on standard lamps that stood on the desk and tables. "Rather nice lighting . . . the whole place isn't much, but not bad really." He took off his coat and hat and knocked—the same knock as before—on the door at the far end, presumably the bedroom. "Only two rooms," he muttered, "and a sort of bathroom-kitchen—but quite convenient . . ." He opened the door, found the room empty and came back to light the gas log. "It wants a sixpence," he said, when nothing happened.

"Here you are," Tubby answered, fumbling quickly, anxious to do something.

"No, no, old boy . . . I've got one, I think." Then he saw the note left for him on the mantelpiece. "She'll be back at tea time," he said. "We'll wait, shall we? It's nice here, isn't it? Warm and cozy."

It was terrible. Everything that Daddy said and did made him more vulgar, more pathetic. Awkwardly Tubby removed his coat and, wandering about the room, became suddenly, gratefully aware that it was nicely furnished. He stopped in front of a picture, and Daddy came quickly and stood beside him. "A Renoir landscape," he said; "reproduction, of course, but rather a nice one." He seized Tubby's arm; "But here's one of his drawings, the best thing in the room . . . I got it in Paris. I'd just won a race on an outsider . . . a Renoir drawing, Tubby!"

"Renoir?" The name seemed in some way familiar.

"Good God, boy. Good God! Haven't you ever heard of him?"

Ah! This was better. This was Daddy way up above you again on the unattainable level of Lydia. It was good to hear his violence. He had hold of your arm and was pulling you about the room. "There's a Manet reproduction here; and this Picasso drawing, and this sketch by Sickert . . ."

"They're pretty, Daddy. But the names don't mean a thing to me." With overwhelming relief, with gratitude, Tubby admitted his ignorance, wallowed in the shame that at last put him back below Daddy. "I despair of myself," he said. "I can't ever catch up, I can't start to. It's the same when I'm with Lydia . . . I just don't know anything. Everything that she knows about—and you know about—it's gibberish to me, a foreign language."

Daddy half turned with the old, quick, battling movement, with the old smile, not the bashful, ingratiating twist of flabby features, but the kind smile with a light of war in it, the generous smile of a combatant, humane, ruthless, compassionate—everything mixed up in that large, heavy face, and that small, heavy body, head on one side, and the loose flesh, the sagging chin and paunch no longer evident.

"That's foolish, that's humble," he started. "Never be humble; don't be weak. If you have a weakness, glory in it till it becomes a virtue." (It was the old, entirely illogical, inconsistent opening.) "It's gibberish to you . . . it's a foreign language . . . you don't know . . . how *can* you know? Who taught you? How do you think knowledge is acquired? Through the nose, with the air you breathe? Through the food you eat, the drink you take in the weary evenings? Whatever there is in those things, there isn't knowledge. No! You can't expect to have knowledge; but you *may* have, *should* have a sense of beauty. . . .

"Didn't anyone," he asked, as they sat down on the sofa, "didn't *anyone* ever tinkle to you on a piano, show you a picture, a view even, a bit of a sunset over the hill, or the moon on the sea from your nursery window? Didn't they say: 'Look! Isn't that pretty?' Didn't they read to you; bits of poetry, bits of the Bible? Didn't they slobber about the beauty in them?"

They were sitting on the sofa, and Tubby stretched himself, wrinkling his forehead in the old bewildered, puppyish expression. "There was a master at school once who taught us English. . . ."

"Well?" (A sharp, challenging question.)

"He used to read us bits of Shakespeare, over and over again, and ask us if we didn't find them beautiful."

"And did you?"

"Some of us did. I did. I remember the bits still at odd moments. They *are* odd moments, too. You never really know when they'll crop up suddenly."

"You wouldn't—and what happened to the master?"

"He didn't last. He had to go after a term or two."

"You mean that you—all of you—discovered his inaptness for discipline and threw paper darts and ink pellets?"

"That's about it."

"I thought as much," Daddy said triumphantly. "You see the whole of your schooling was not educational in any accepted sense of the word. It wasn't development but suppression. Instead of trying to make you into something, it was trying to stop you being anything else." He was leaning back, hands clasped about his knees, rocking himself backwards and forwards. "It stopped you being anything more than a pleasant young man with nothing to be pleased about but an enormous amount of self-satisfaction; with—shall we say—a fair appetite for pleasure and no equipment for ever attaining happiness; with a nice eye for a gentleman, later to be developed to include a horse—for they're much the same thing, you know—but none whatever for a picture . . . stop me if I'm wrong, won't you?"

"Oh, certainly," Tubby said. "Go on telling me, I'll contradict afterwards."

"You won't contradict this; it's so much a truism that it scarcely bears repeating." (Daddy was working up to it nicely.) "The whole of your education—from your first incompetent governess—was devoted to making you exactly as your father had been before you, which was exactly what his father had been before that. It allowed you certain minor modifications of course, to keep you abreast of the times; a new taste for speed, a little less drunkenness; it acknowledged the airplane and not the Moonlight Steeplechase. . . . But, as regards your brain, your character and your tastes, it had to turn you out in the same set pattern. And, Tubby—and this is immensely important —you fashioned remarkably easily. You were nice, plastic material.

"You were remarkably good at games," he went on, thoroughly committed now; "your muscles responded quickly to those impulsive demands which your eye made upon them; and your eye, without the slightest difficulty, could follow a ball right up to the moment when you hit or kicked it. For that excellent reason, you were a successful schoolboy with all the attributes and failings of a successful anything else—business man, soldier, lawyer, doctor. You were rather pompous, generous, autocratic. And you adopted a pose of diffidence with such assiduity that in the end you began to believe in your modesty. *You* know, Tubby . . . healthy, hearty, muscular-Christian modesty. . . . You were immensely popular, of course, with nearly everyone; with all those who couldn't afford not to be friends with the successful. You were a jolly good fellow—and I expect they sang it to you pretty often; after a house match, a school match, some sort of match, anyway. I don't know about that . . . I wasn't at a good enough school myself to get all the details. . . ."

He slewed himself round, hands still clasped about his knees, head on one side, his large face happy, a lock of thin hair fallen over his forehead. You didn't mind what he said in this temper. He was so obviously doing it for his own enjoyment; without malice, making a virtue of his own lack of a public-school education; working off, in the words he loved, thoughts that had been born in goodness knew what moods of darkness.

"But, anyway," he went on, "as a jolly good fellow, you didn't have much truck with the horrid little bookworms—except of course those who had also a certain talent for hitting a ball in the right direction." He chuckled to himself, as if that somehow applied to his own schooldays; a grammar school, as far as Tubby could remember. Or it might have been one of those places in the West Country—"Jolly good schools," you said heartily, trying to suppress the patronage that guided your tongue at such moments. . . .

"Then," Daddy went on happily, "you were naturally made a prefect—or whatever they called it. You were pushed into a position of considerable and quite unwarranted authority. You were given every cause for self-satisfaction at an age when self-dissatisfaction, doubt, searching, discovery, are the natural, vital elements . . . Am I right so far?"

"Near enough," Tubby admitted happily; "near enough to the facts to make your conclusions quite ridiculous."

"Ah!" Daddy wriggled with excitement. "You see the progress you're making? You've started noticing things. You've observed that right conclusions come either from right facts or wrong facts—but not from facts that are neither one nor the other. Not from half truths . . . but I don't believe you, anyway. Where do you quarrel with my conclusions?"

"I wasn't self-satisfied—for one thing."

"Oh yes, you were! No man can say he isn't. Only others can judge that particular quality of a human being. You've always been self-satisfied; right up to the last six months; until you had your accident. Up to then, everything that had ever happened to you had driven you into self-satisfaction. It was only because you were born to a certain feudal authority, bred for this destination, prepared for it, that you managed to retain the natural niceness of a young animal.

"And mind you," he said, pointing a finger at Tubby's belly, "your sort of schooling isn't necessarily too bad for those who go on to a University—especially if they are shown soon enough that athletic prowess and popularity can sustain them for perhaps a third of their adult life, but certainly no further . . . but you didn't! You went to Woolwich, you were called a Gentleman Cadet—with emphasis on the 'Gentleman'—and were treated all over again, and for at least the third time, as a first-term schoolboy. Once more, of course, your physical strength and your pre-eminence at sport helped you." He threw up his arms and said, with real pain in his voice: "You see, Tubby, up to the present we might have been training a navvy, a pugilist, a professional footballer . . ." He sighed deeply—though whether or not it was part of the play, you couldn't be certain.

"Again you were immensely popular," he said in his argumentative voice, "and in no time you joined with the others—led them, no doubt—in hounding from the place all those poor, original, intellectual misfits who might otherwise have saved the army and who seemed to have strayed there by accident.

. . ." (He was working himself up now to real indignation. No animosity—you understood—but impersonal fury against a system.) "And even there it didn't end," he went on hotly, "for after Woolwich you went to Larkhill, to that ridiculous 'Young Officers' Course', where they line you up, march you about at the double, and—instead of turning you into men— push you back again into infancy. But your reputation had preceded you and—I don't doubt—you were the darling of that hearty, idiot-boy Captain, who's good at cricket or something, who bottle-washes for the Chief Instructor and who does schoolmaster to all the dear, rosy-cheeked, healthy little officers. *He* didn't mind that you couldn't do survey, couldn't learn the gun parts, couldn't look up a simple logarithm, couldn't utter two consecutive sentences of correct English or scarcely write a literate letter. It wasn't counted against you that you could never learn to work out a code telegram, handle a director, give out a fire order quickly, or even understand the simplest principles of ballistics. That didn't matter, because you learned the cries parrot-wise and could conceal your ignorance; and because you were good on a horse, had nice table manners, played football, got honestly drunk on guest nights and smashed up the furniture like a gentleman . . . you were reported on as a 'thoroughly suitable young officer'—and how Sammy and Bert and I laughed at that report—and you were sent to our Battery.

"And it was then, Tubby—only then—that God intervened. He sent you to us, where Sammy and Bert and myself could knock you into something resembling a man and a soldier. You liked us—I expect; nobody below the rank of colonel can help liking us. But you thought us cranks, and it wasn't till you fell off your horse and got pinned down in the hospital that you started to wonder, began to have doubts about who *were* the cranks of the party and who were the normal people . . ." He paused—almost for breath.

"I never thought Bert was a crank," Tubby said, swept off his feet in the torrent, clinging to something.

"Bert? He's a crank in the sense that he's unusual. You don't get many ranker officers, and most of them are pretty awful, anyway. But Bert isn't. He's fine. He's solid and reliable and efficient. A wonderful friend and a bad enemy. A true and straightforward man and a beautifully dishonest soldier. It's through his thefts that we get more forage and blankets and coal than the rest of the Brigade put together. But he wouldn't borrow a sixpence and he'd lend you his last tenner without a moment's hesitation. . . ."

"Good old Bert," Tubby cried, uttering without thought one of the affectionate expletives that, in the old days, had been the greater part of his conversation. They answered any argument, set an obstacle to the run of any conversation.

But, before the silence grew noticeable, there were feet on the stairs, the brief suspense of someone pausing on the landing. Daddy rose quickly. "That's Ariel . . ."

The door was opened noisily and she bustled nimbly into the room. This, then, was Daddy's woman. As he had once said, she was the least he could have borne with and the best that his social qualifications and insignificant income could procure for him. There was nothing to her beyond a dull but very pretty, weak, insipid face; nice, cheerful eyes and a beautiful body. Her dress was tight and her untied breasts quivered very slightly at every movement. Her hair was blond with a touch of red in it; her clothes vivid, cheap but amusing. She was vivacious, sympathetic, but clearly not, as Daddy had claimed for her, either interesting or clever.

"*Two* men in my flat," she cried. "*What* a pleasant surprise." Her voice was educated but common, with emphasis overstressed on all the obvious words.

She shook hands with Tubby. "I've heard *ever* such a lot about *you*, Mr. Windrush. You're *Tubby*, aren't you?" She took off her hat and shook her hair about her head with a movement (Tubby realized with dismay) exactly Lydia's. "I must *just* go and make myself lovely," she said and went into the bedroom.

"A widow," Daddy said, leaning against the mantelpiece; "married very young to an airman who got killed—like most of them—in a motor smash. He left her a few hundreds a year —not much. I like her all right . . . but she's nothing, you understand?" He was looking away from Tubby, speaking defiantly. "A man *has* to have a woman, you know; though I don't think that a woman need necessarily have a man. A woman can be intimate with a friend of the same sex, but a man can't. He has to have something to . . . to humiliate. In his own mind, that is. And he has to be intimate sometimes, physically, mentally, spiritually. Intimacy seems to be an out-pouring of all that's superfluous, like the waste pipe at the top of the tub that only comes into use when there's too much water. . . ."

He moved his feet uncomfortably, as if he felt that he must offer this explanation; as if he wanted sympathy and did not realize that Tubby would look for and find a sympathetic aspect to any situation. Or, as if the story were repeated more for his own conviction than for Tubby's enlightenment. "I take the Moslem view," he added. "I regard woman purely as the complement of man. Apart from him, she has no independent existence. She is his crock, his possession, and he need be under no restraint in her presence. You see what I mean? The Moslem will unclothe himself before his womenfolk but not before his male friends or relatives, neither his brother, his son, nor his father. And, in the same way, we can also unclothe our souls before them . . ."

"And Ariel?" Tubby said, without meaning to.

"Ariel . . . she knows more about me, the present me, than everyone else put together—except Sammy perhaps; and he is more concerned with the past and the future, with the time-less, undetailed aspects of people. But Ariel doesn't take it in. She's a waste pipe, I tell you. Things run through her. She listens without hearing, looks without seeing. Only her body is fully receptive. Without me she's nothing. *With* me, with some other man before me and still another man after me, she *is* something. She's a man's complement, you see. She's part of him. While she's with him, she's living. . . ."

"A rather conceited view," Tubby said. "I'm afraid it shocks me rather. I wouldn't dare take it."

"You wouldn't dare!" Daddy said scornfully; "of course you wouldn't. How could you? You're a male animal that hasn't yet developed. What knowledge have you of women? None!

You've met girls of your own age, I suppose; danced with them, joked with them, managed some sort of conversation. But you've never got any further. Apart from Lydia, whom you don't begin to understand, you've just shown no interest. And they reciprocate your indifference. It's only women of some age and experience, and not many of them, who find attraction, stimulus perhaps, a challenge—if you like—in an apathy to their own allurements.

"Of course," he said wisely, "you're quite unusually virginal . . . you were abnormally plastic, you see, and all your schooling —designed for more stubborn material—kneaded you too thoroughly. After all, it's only in the last eighteen months that your access to women hasn't been thwarted all along the line, both directly by the rules and regulations of your various places of education, and indirectly by the way of living they prescribed, the physical aspirations they inspired in you. And, above all, you've got to remember the general attitude that they, the authorities, adopted; the way they assumed—and made you assume—that sexual intercourse is no more than an unfortunate and shameful necessity for procreation, something that the cleanest and decentest people practice only with their wives and husbands—and then with their eyes turned in the opposite direction and their nightgowns disarranged as little as possible. . . .

"You believed all that, didn't you?" he asked, taking hold of Tubby's arm. "Of course you did—subconsciously; even if consciously you knew it as nonsense. And you went further. You told me once that you hated—saw no point in—all this flirting, necking, petting—whatever you like to call it—that has to be undertaken in a taxi by every manly sort of fellow. That's a good mark for you! That's because the male urge is strong in you, though you haven't acknowledged it. But you've sensed prematurely that this fumbling and fondling isn't the play but only the overture . . . but you daren't ring up the curtain. . . . My poor boy," he said with pretended sorrow, "you've had a rotten deal. You've been pruned ruthlessly by the schoolmasters and you've blossomed not as nature intended but as they purposed."

Tubby was silent, struggling for speech, the words at last

coming ponderously, jostled out by his swelling indignation. "Because I believe in what you would probably call an old-fashioned sort of morality, is that any reason that I'm more likely to be wrong than you? Why is it better or finer to believe, as you do, that you've just got to hunt up a woman—any woman as far as I can make out—and throw off your clothes in front of her? That's your view, isn't it?"

"Almost," Daddy admitted cheerfully. "It's a good view; and I adopt it for my own convenience and to suit my income. We're not rich enough, you see, to pick and choose; and we're not poor enough to get it for nothing from our neighbor's daughter. Or not very often . . . of course one strikes a bit of luck now and again. One rarely draws blank on a steamer. . . ."

"You're disgusting," Tubby said, with much more violence than usual. "You disgust me."

"Because I mean to," Daddy answered quickly, "and because," (he poked his finger into Tubby's chest) "because a lot of what I say rings true to you. I have to exaggerate and elaborate to get it home, you see. But something tells you I've talked a lot of truth, doesn't it?"

"No, it doesn't!"

"Doesn't it? You might be a general speaking."

"I'd rather be a general than a tomcat."

"I'm not sure about that . . . But I'm not a tomcat anyway, I'm a Moslem. And don't you ever feel the spark of truth in it? Don't you feel that *we* are men with something divine in the core of us, something godlike that demands victories and conquests? And that woman is a lesser animal, subhuman, without the godlike quality?"

"No! Quite definitely not," Tubby answered truthfully.

The bedroom door opened and Daddy swung round to see Ariel. At once he was kindly and paternal; open and radiant, as though invested with a sudden tranquillity. She had a tea-tray in her hands, silver teapot and jugs and pretty china. He was a warrior with the battle over, returned home, his arms discarded, his armour thrown into a corner. It was only with his woman that he didn't need arms or armour.

"I'm not sure I don't agree with you," he said to Tubby.

❦ As soon as tea was over, Tubby left the flat and made his way slowly to Pall Mall where Benjamin's club was. Once more he had been roused by Daddy's violence, by that torrent of nonsense, in the center of which a thin current of truth seemed to flow always.

Those ridiculous theories about women! And yet, when you really considered them, away from the hot blush of shame that they brought when you first saw them personalized—the man and the woman together—they were only traditional. In this case, it was Daddy who was conservative, while yours was the progressive outlook! For the things he had said linked themselves closely with a soldier's precepts, with the songs that they sang on guest nights and with the wisdom of the Mess— "keep your interests below the navel", so often repeated, so much a catchword that it began to swell with truth. And, all along, there was this belief that woman was in some way inferior, put on to the earth for man's uses, herself nothing, by her very design a complementary article.

That was how they regarded woman. And when you came to think it over, it wasn't such nonsense. After all, though you shared your life with her, it *was* your life. She bore the children; but it was you who got them; and you did it as and when it pleased you. . . . He knew no more than that about it.

These theories, when applied to Lydia, unraveled a lot of tangles. She was, then, above all a woman, a complementary being. All the rest of her was only the clothing, could be stripped from her with the clothing, to leave the woman, pure woman, naked and waiting . . . if only he knew about that first button! Or, if only he could bring his tongue to utter any one of the stereotyped phrases that led to marriage. But, in spite of the new inferiority with which she was invested, he knew that this would not be enough for her.

And, further, he didn't want to get married. . . .

❦ "Is Mr. Ramsay in? Mr. Benjamin Ramsay?"

"I think so, sir," the porter said. "I'll send a page. Will you wait here, sir, please?"

Benjamin *would* belong to a civilian club, and one where they put you into a chair in the hall, instead of showing you into the smoking room. And they didn't even give you a newspaper; so that you had to sit uncomfortably on view while arriving members allowed themselves a quick glance at you, a smooth appraisal—too often through tortoiseshell glasses, for this was a weak-eyed set of fellows. He hated waiting but remembered Daddy's words: "If you've got a weakness—glory in it. . . ."

He thought about this. At first it conflicted with all that had been said, so long ago now, about the stupidity of soldiers. But then it became clear that, if soldiers really had been stupid, their attitude was the right one. But they weren't; and, since they had minds and feelings like anyone else, they attributed to themselves an imaginary weakness. He was as good, then, as anybody else; as all these distinguished-looking men with greying hairs, high foreheads, stooping shoulders (like Sammy's), weak eyes, and their polished assurance—quite different from the brusque satisfaction of the army, more convincing perhaps, but no better. He returned their glances and doubted it . . . and, according to Daddy, he was in the same way certainly good enough for Lydia. But he doubted that also. . . .

"Hello, Tubby!" a voice said behind him.

"Why, hello, Alastair! It's good to see you." (It *was* good, too; for, if Alastair were a member of this club, there couldn't be so much to it. You could recall giving him six good ones on the bottom. Dirty little beast he'd been in those days.)

"What are *you* doing here?" Alastair asked.

"Waiting for Benjy," Tubby said. "They've gone to find him."

"Well, come on in and let him find us later. It's a beastly system here, putting guests in the pillory." He pushed Tubby gently before him. "You've changed a lot," he said, as they sat down in a corner of the room. "I'd never have thought you'd turn into such a sober, sensible-looking person. I always considered you as rather a pleasant madman. And I'm not sure that I'm glad to see my almost-contemporaries growing old so quickly and gracefully. . . ." He ordered drinks, and went on talking. "And I shall never forget, Tubby, your beating me for not cleaning my teeth . . . ever since then I've been the despair of dentists. They can't find anything."

Benjamin came in almost immediately. "Well, well, Tubby, they've let you out again," he said, putting his hand on the back of the chair, the utmost affection that club manners permitted. "And you've healed beautifully. Distinguished, I call you . . . what do you say, Alastair? . . . I can't believe it's the tubby little boy I beat for letting my fire out."

"We all seem to have beaten each other," Alastair said, "except me. There's only one of my victims a member of this club; but perhaps another guest will come in later." He looked round the room hopefully.

"It's not a bad foundation for a lifelong friendship," Benjamin said; "that is, in those rare cases when it's absolutely fair and impartial." He lit a cigarette and said: "But it's a bad system all the same. I'm getting tired of all this tough stuff . . . but then I'm getting tired of a lot of things. In fact . . . I'm sailing tomorrow . . ."

"Sailing tomorrow!"

"Where? Why?"

"For the Sudan. They've taken me in the Sudan Defence Force. I hope to get to one of the Arab corps."

"But your general . . ." Tubby said.

"I got fed up with him," Benjamin answered airily. "Gave in my notice. He didn't like losing such a good valet, but he had to put up with it."

Later, when Alastair had gone and they had dined together and were sitting quietly with brandy and cigars and their old friendship strong between them, he said slowly: "One day, Tubby, I'll tell you all about it. All about why I'm really going. But I don't want to discuss it till it's clear to me just what I *am* doing. . . . It was partly the General and partly that I felt I couldn't go on soldiering in England—wasting these rather precious years—any longer. And it was partly a girl. I fell into the old, old trap of thinking she meant it, losing my head over her and then finding she was just playing about with me. . . ."

"And Daddy says they're inferior beings!"

"So they are, Tubby . . . but not if they can help it. It's that way you've got to treat them. Either get what you want out of them or leave them alone. Either they can give you every-thing and make life wonderfully right for you—or they are just takers. And the funny part is . . . that receptive women, the women you *want*, take only what's superfluous, what you have to get rid of . . . *That's* the kind to look out for. And I think, Tubby, that these are words of wisdom. . . . Tell me in twenty years' time, will you?"

"I may tell you the day after tomorrow. . . ."

"You won't, old boy. I'll be heading for the Bay of Biscay. I'm getting out of it. I want to study my own company. . . ."

Chapter 7 YOU MOUNTED FIVE WIDE AND SHALLOW steps to the front door of the house in Belgrave Square. Tubby knew well the five rather furtive strides, always excessive for the mild ascent, the furtive glance at the lace-curtained windows of the morning room (on ground-floor level) and the cowardly fear that Mrs. Mervinne, thin, graceful, but forbidding, might peer through the curtains at the sound of the doorbell. But the bell had to be pressed; and with the certain knowledge, too, that its tones— low and dignified though they were—would be heard by Lydia's mother if it happened both that she was in the morning room and that the morning-room door was open. And somehow, these were the prevalent conditions, whenever he paid a visit.

It was not that Mrs. Mervinne disapproved of him in particular. Indeed, judged on the standards of many of the queer, long-haired, red-tied gentlemen whom Lydia asked to the house, or of the lissom and more beautiful people who brought her flowers and chocolates, Tubby was among her more desirable specimens. It was simply that Mrs. Mervinne regarded any man as a possible suitor, and all suitors as suspect of having an eye primarily on the Mervinne riches. She was well aware that she would have no say whatsoever in the choosing of Lydia's husband, but she was determined to be forewarned of the worst at the earliest possible moment. She was a pessimistic woman, and each time that the doorbell rang, she envisaged the arrival of a future son-in-law.

It was a corner house, facing south, stretching back to the mews and presenting to the square a rather defensive aspect. It suggested exquisite taste, exquisite manners, quiet and expensive gentility (rather than the photographed people of fashion), inflexible rules of behavior and morals, political and religious orthodoxy, a general assurance of rightness within certain narrow limits and a steadfast disregard for all that exceeded them. It was almost impossible not to feel a poor relation, a hanger-on, a parasite, when you approached this smug and well-bred house in which Lydia had spent those times when she was not in Paris, Rome, New York, St. Moritz, Cannes, Madeira, or Calcott.

After ringing the bell on the right, you waited impatiently sometimes for quite a long time, annoyed that the wealth of your host could not provide more expeditious attention for his daughter's visitors. At last the door was swung open by a footman in dark livery, with Thompson waiting discreetly back, a few paces behind him. It was carefully rehearsed and perfect. You never knew which of the two took your hat, coat, gloves and umbrella; but they were clearly removed according to a long-established ritual, swiftly, neatly, before you had realized that they were superfluous. The knowledge of all this inner etiquette, many strata of tradition extending downwards through pantry, hall, kitchen, to the lowest innermost sculleries, clothed your host in a still more radiant security. You basked in it too; but at the same time, made aware of your own insignificance, found it a little too dazzling. You understood that you were not wanted, but that, since you had come, everyone was making the best of it.

"And how is the arm, sir?" the man asked. It was a question uttered as part of his duties.

"Much better, thank you, Thompson."

"Miss Mervinne is out, sir; will you wait in the schoolroom?"

"Yes please, Thompson."

A long way back from the front door, through the glass doors, past the doors of the morning room, dining room and study, the Adam staircase swung up gracefully to the first floor, to its series of rooms each with its Adam ceiling, chandeliers, and

Adam fireplace, each furnished sparsely with Chippendale chairs and tables, Chinese rugs, an occasional Chinese lacquer cabinet, and case after case of Chinese porcelain, Ming and Khang Hsi, famille verte, jaune, or noire, a little powder blue, a very little eggshell and self-color, nothing that was not made between 1620 and 1780 when, with the accession of Kien Lung, the porcelain industry had gone to pieces. The knowledge of so much that was superb, priceless and irreplaceable resting over your head on the floor above you made you tread as softly as dignity would allow, along the thick-carpeted passage that led to the schoolroom.

But it was useless. As you passed the morning-room door, a civil, not unpleasant, but slightly querulous voice called invariably: "Who's that, Thompson?"

With a sad smile and a glance that might have been sympathy, Thompson went to the door and answered: "Mr. Windrush, madam."

Mrs. Mervinne came out then, tall, straight, handsome, taking your hand with the utmost cordiality and open disapproval.

"My daughter's out, I believe, Mr. Windrush." Her voice was unfortunately nasal, and either rose rapidly or fell rapidly on the last syllable of each phrase or sentence.

"Oh . . . good afternoon, Mrs. Mervinne," he said. "Lydia asked me to come at tea time."

"Well—I suppose you'd better wait for her." The emphasis on the second syllable of "sup*pose*," and the rapid lifting of the voice on the last word (pushed up almost as an afterthought, suggesting that there was something very nearly funny in the situation) just saved this remark from being unpleasant.

"Will you wait in the schoolroom?"

"If I may, Mrs. Mervinne. . . ."

"You know your way, don't you?" She turned to go and then, feeling the call of politeness, asked over her shoulder, "And how is your arm doing?"

"A lot better, thank you."

"I'm glad . . . well—I hope that my daughter won't keep you waiting *too* long." The door shut behind her, leaving the suspicion that the wish was hypocritical and that Mrs. Mervinne hoped—and thought it quite probable—that Lydia would have forgotten all about you, and you would wait till dinner time.

The schoolroom, right at the back and with only a back window opening on to the roof over the kitchen and the kitchen skylight, was really rather disgraceful. You could, perhaps, think of it as the last native reserve in an otherwise civilized country; a little parcel of territory where all was confusion and all around which unimpeachable order dwelt with disapproval. It was a small, low room, over-filled, gloomy, with the door opening the right way so that you could see immediately the desk, the window, the piano, a few chairs and occasional tables, but not the large sofa that occupied the whole of the wall space between the doorway and the fireplace. That sofa annoyed Tubby, for he knew that, virginal as she was, Lydia had gone a good deal further than himself with sofas; had allowed many fumbling embraces which he (as Daddy had remarked) regarded as nothing in themselves, but as undisputable preliminaries. That sofa shamed him too, for why should he hold these rare views, be moved by such unorthodox feelings; and why should he be so backward at what other men took for granted?

But apart from the sofa (and if you wanted to be polite), you could only describe that room by the French word *intime*, except that all of the furniture that you could see—all, that is, which was not covered by papers, books, chocolates, gramophone records, weird musical instruments and general litter— was so solid, so Victorian, so English, that such a very Gallic word is too daring. The room was obviously occupied by a woman, and by one woman exclusively; was obviously loved with the same possessive affection that is bestowed on a favorite dog or on some particularly long-harbored and very personal belonging. Otherwise it was frankly garish. Strange toys, dolls, fluffy dogs, night club mascots, hung from nails, from chair-backs, and on the gilt candlesticks of the piano. The furniture and bric-a-brac were clearly unwanted relics, pushed here in the first instance when Lydia was in early childhood, but by now so cherished and familiar that they would never be ejected. There were all the useless combination-articles that rich people give as presents: A calendar and clock together, a cigarette box with a barometer, a pen-pencil, a scissors-paper knife. There were things that looked like other things; a frog that was a tape measure, a silver peacock that was a corkscrew, a pack of cards disguised as a leather-backed volume. There were cases of stuffed pike, of unbelievable size, caught by Lydia's father; a stuffed squirrel over the doorway. There was a widely-strewn collection of boxes, carved jade, ivory, bead, tortoiseshell, Battersea enamel, and even a shell box. And there were numbers of musical instruments which Lydia would buy, knowing at the time that she would never learn to play them; a ukulele, a Swanee whistle, a guitar and a concertina. She had once ordered a harp, but Mrs. Mervinne, seeing its arrival from the morning room, had met it on the doorstep and soon sent it back where it came from.

Tubby had been here many times before; but now, while he was waiting, he realized suddenly that this room *was* Lydia in all her moods and all her shallowness, in her sincerity and pretensions, in her childishness and wisdom, in all the contrary things that made her first, and above all else, a woman whom— he now knew—he loved deeply. The books in several different languages, the stacks of music, from Bach to Hindermith, the cards and papers that lined her mantelpiece, warning her of committee meetings, inviting her to concerts, private views, first nights, lectures, congresses, political gatherings, did not dismay him now. He thought them no less trimmings than his own occupation with horses. For, beside Lydia, horses had now dwindled to small importance. Suddenly she had become a part of him. Without her, he lacked something vital. He needed her.

She came into her room like an animal, a vixen returning to her earth, a dog to his basket. For an instant there was the suspicious wavering, the uneasy hunting about, the quick exploration, and then the careful settling down into tenure. A few letters, newly arrived, were found, glanced at and put aside. An ornament, a photograph, an inkstand, were straightened with quick, nervous movements. Coat, hat, bag, gloves, parcels, were spread about the furniture. She talked as she moved: "Hello, Tubby . . . I'd forgotten you were coming . . .

have you been here long . . . have they given you tea? I'll ring
for it . . . I'd have been earlier if I'd remembered. I'm so sorry."
Then she gradually became herself, tuned down to their old
intimacy. It was as if she had asserted herself, her accomplishments and versatility, in the litter and knickknacks of the room
and that—this done with—she could be, more than at any
other time, simply a woman. Over tea, they were both entirely
happy and, when they had finished, they sat together quietly
on the sofa.

"It's my last day of leave," he reminded her.

"No," she said. "No, Tubby; it can't be. . . ."

"But it is. . . ."

Sitting beside her, the afternoon growing dark but the lights
still unlit, the firelight behind her face, creeping round her face,
not putting it into silhouette but molding it with soft shadows,
tinting softly the delicate, pale hue of her cheeks and neck, his
sadness and his need for her flourished rapidly. There were
present all the parts of sentimentality; everything was ready,
topographically, chronologically and by association. Memory
became unrestrained and active, thrusting before him quick
pictures of his quarters, of himself shaving, dressing, going to
bed before her photograph. His past feelings for her, unacknowledged desires, yearnings, returned to him singly, each
connected with an incident of their separation, piling themselves
upon each other into a force which, urging him onwards, gave
no hint of direction, left him feeble and hesitant. It was as if
they had parted already, and already he was mourning his loss.

"Lydia," he cried.

At the tone of his voice, she made a quick movement, but
did not answer.

He didn't know what he wanted. His two yearnings, that
should have been correlative, were struggling against each
other. There was his need for her, for their intimacy, for her
leadership, her simple presence. Forgotten were Daddy's
theories, confirmed by himself, confirmed by Benjamin. There
was his need for a woman; no longer the vague desires and rest-
lessness of adolescence, the products of all the fake stimuli of
pictures, novels, chorus girls, alcohol, nude thighs and senti-

mental music; but the urgency for woman, her spirit, mind and body, handed over to his tender possession. And still this woman would not identify herself with Lydia, so that still the two yearnings did not run together.

"Lydia!"

"No, Tubby," she said, as though her thoughts and feelings had been linked with his. "You want, first of all, a widow; a kind, sympathetic, adequate widow. Until you've had that, you can't know the truth of anything that there is between us. I can't help you, you see. I'm the same as you; we're both ignorant. You can't come to me for experience and I can't come to you. We've nothing to give each other *that* way; and *that* way is troubling you most at the moment . . . we know each other too well to spoil it by fumbling about together . . . it isn't, you see, like married people, who recover from it slowly, because they know they've got to. . . ."

She turned and took hold of his wrists, one in each of her small, long-fingered hands. "I like you such a lot, Tubby . . . I think I love you. . . . If it would help, I'd sleep with you. But I know it wouldn't. If it were kind, I'd marry you; but I don't think it would be. And I've thought a lot about it because I've known—I've thought I've known—how it was coming up in you, how it was coming up between us, joining us together, forcing us into it. . . .

"I oughtn't ever to have started it," she said a little breathlessly, "but at that dance, when Benjy introduced us, you looked so strong and fit and clean beside all the other men that I see everywhere, with their white faces, their beautiful manners, and the way they find everything so easy, know everything— know just what to do always . . . I can't explain it. I wanted you as a friend, because you were fresh and rough and different. . . ."

"Because I was a soldier," he said, not bitterly, but anxious to help her, to help them both. It was the same thing, suddenly.

"Oh, I'd known plenty of soldiers," she said.

"Guardsmen," he said scornfully, "professional men-about-town; some of the more exclusive cavalry regiments. Not honest-to-God soldiers like the poor, simple gunners, who haven't got any money or any social graces; who aren't anything but—just soldiers." And still he wasn't bitter. Defiant, defensive perhaps; but, for her, he had only a great tenderness.

She considered this gravely. "I think that's true," she said slowly. "They're all just men in the army—in the smart part of the army. You *are* different. You've got a sort of vocation for it. . . ."

He smiled then. "*I* thought so," he said, "but you all laughed at me for it."

"*I* didn't, Tubby, you know I didn't," she pleaded. "I wanted you for it, wanted you as a friend, as an acquaintance."

"Well—you've got me. . . ."

"I know, Tubby—and so much more than I reckoned on. . . ." She pulled at his wrists to stop him speaking. "But just hear me out for a moment. . . ." She sat thinking, collecting her feelings, trying desperately to get at the truth of them. "You see," she went on at last, "when I'd met you once or twice I got curious. I was amazed. I couldn't believe anyone could be so clear, so single-minded, so entirely *one* character . . . one not very interesting character too . . . but there was somehing in the way you did things, and spoke sometimes—perhaps it was in your eyes all the time, perhaps it was a little drop of Italian blood, of Italian sensitivity, of arrogant humbleness— that showed you up, that showed there were things inside you that would have to come up one day. I wanted to find out what they were, to see if I couldn't stir them. Have you ever prodded a chrysalis and seen the life inside it wriggle? A girl I knew, who was going to have a baby, used to slap herself and make it kick her tummy. I wanted to prod and slap your feelings, your mind, your imagination."

"You're all the same," he said wearily, "you all want to make something out of me. You want me as a subject for your experiments. You want me for something that I'm not—that I don't think I ever will be—ever can be."

"No, *no*, Tubby! Listen to me! Because later, I saw how it was . . . only just lately I've really understood it—since the car smash perhaps. . . . There's everything in you, just as there's everything in every human being. But it's strong in you, alive . . . and it *is* coming up in you sometime." There was a catch in her voice, a trembling, as if tears were near, as if she were frightened. "But when it comes . . . when it *does* come," she said in almost a whisper, "the thought of it is quite—frightening. For what *will* you do, Tubby? You won't be able to go on being a soldier, you know . . . so what *will* you be, Tubby?"

"God knows," he said grimly. "But I'd lay odds I'll still be a soldier—a general probably. Just to annoy Daddy." (Once again, you see, in the stress, in the moment of encounter, he had to be funny.)

"That's just it," she cried. "You *aren't* made for anything else. I said it just now—you've got a vocation to be a soldier." She spoke breathlessly, hurriedly, to stop him interrupting. "And I couldn't be a soldier's wife, you see. I must have possessions and a home and a fixed sort of life and lots of interests. A gunner is the worst of all, isn't it? He gets moved all over the world, from one brigade to another. I couldn't follow you round making new friends all the time; all of them such nice, drab people. And we'd have more money than the others; we'd have to entertain; we'd do it comfortably. But that would make it worse. We'd never have a life of our own, like we had at Calcott; and I couldn't share you with all the other dreary, dreary men and women in the army . . . there'd be a trio of us all the time; you, me and the others."

They were silent for a time, and then she said slowly, dreamily, in that low rich voice—"But *when* it comes, Tubby, *if* it comes and if you can't go on being a soldier, and if I'm not in love with anyone else, and *you're* not in love with anyone else— then we might do it.

"But you see, Tubby," she said, desperately trying to convince herself, "you don't really need me now—not as anything more than a friend in one way, or as anything more than *a* woman in the other. If you're really honest with yourself, you only think of me as *the* woman, because I've got no competition." She laughed—she was able to laugh at last—and said briskly, "And anyway you couldn't be a soldier and married at your age. You're too young . . . perhaps we're both too young . . . there's too much against it—for the present."

He didn't know how to answer. Daddy could have told him;

Benjamin could have told him; but it was he, Tubby, who had to manage this situation. He sat silently, his wrists in her hands, looking back at her. If he'd known what he wanted, if he'd known the dullest, simplest, most hackneyed procedure of lovers, he could then have had anything. He had only to say that he needed her, only to refute the single argument she had used, that they weren't ready. . . . She loved him and she was generous. She would have married him or slept with him . . . but that wasn't it. He wanted nothing that had a name to it. Only the satisfaction of his desperate yearning.

She let go his wrist, looked at her watch, and stood up quickly. "Good heavens," she said, "I'd no idea it was so late. I must rush and change. We're dining early and going to the Ballet."

He clambered to his feet and stood, his arms hanging, looking at her. She stood on her toes, pulled his head down and kissed him on the forehead. "You poor, dear dumb animal," she said. "When do we meet again? This weekend? Saturday?"

"Not Saturday," he said; "I'm hunting Saturday."

Chapter 8

"LOOK!" DADDY SAID, "JUST LOOK AT THAT General! Half baked, isn't he? Wouldn't there be a row if you served him to the troops for dinners?"

"Shut up, Daddy," someone said; "have another?"

"My turn this time . . . waiter!"

Tubby, leaning against the wall, looked through the curtains at the Brigade trumpeters. It must be cold outside with the wind blowing a drizzle off the Plain; and the small boys, and the sergeant in charge of them, were packed into bulky greatcoats that made them bottle-shaped. They stood in the half-light from the Mess windows, and their trumpets flashed as they raised them, the Mess call then coming to the anteroom faint but, like all trumpet calls, beautiful.

"Getting quite musical these days," Tubby said critically.

"Musical!" Bert said. "Good God! These young officers don't know nothing—musical! Those *aren't* trumpeters."

"Good old Bert!" Daddy said happily, emptying his glass. "Now when *you* were a boy . . ."

"I'd have had my backside tanned if I'd made a noise like that. 'Orrid!"

Daddy was signing another chit for drinks. "Good old days for a trumpeter, Bert; or weren't they?"

"Look at 'em," Bert said, pulling aside the curtain. "Just look at them, will you? They don't even learn 'ow to 'old them-

148

selves. They don't learn nothing in the Regiment . . . it's them new theories at the depot."

"Bert, you must have been a rosy-cheeked little cherub as a trumpeter," Sammy said, coming up to them. "Have a drink, Tubby. It's nice to see you back with us."

"Pale but handsome," Daddy said.

"'Andsome, my foot," Bert said. "What is it, Tubby? Gin, sherry?"

"This is on me. . . ."

"The night's young yet . . . what's it to be, Major?"

One of the guests, a cavalryman with silver chains on his shoulder, came away from the group of senior officers by the fireplace. "Hello, Tubby," he said. "How goes it, old boy? You're looking a bit thin . . . Still got your arm fixed up, I see."

Tubby's left arm was strapped to his side with a black tape that cut across the scarlet facings of his mess jacket and his white shirt front.

"That's only for guest nights," he said, "in case of rough stuff . . . I'm leaving it off altogether in a week."

"Otherwise fit and well, are you?"

"Fine," Tubby said. "Lost a lot of weight; easier to mount and everything."

"Here's luck," Daddy said, raising his glass.

"God bless," Bert said.

"Fast women and fast horses," said Tubby.

Through his alcoholic happiness, Daddy looked at Tubby slyly, laughing at him, at the aptness of his toast, but saying nothing. But Tubby did not notice. Swollen with the joy and comfort of having his friends close around him, he stood silent, withdrawing himself from the talk and laughter that flowed and rippled warmly. Good, biting talk of all the things that were sweet and simple, that didn't hit back at you, that demanded nothing. "Corking little horse," someone was saying, "nine miles without a check, I tell you . . . and didn't he take it at the bullfinch . . . at it again, Daddy . . . arse over tip on the plough . . ." They were friends, herded not by choice or suitability but by their calling and the peculiar chance that had thrown them together.

As they moved towards the door, the band started the gay, brave tune to which they went in to dinner on guest nights. After the trumpeters, it was the ceremonial start of the evening, and all that followed had a traditional pattern, proud, childish and invariable. For this one night of the month, they filled themselves up with drink and emptied themselves of those dark yearnings that were supposed to get rolled up inside a soldier, that made him want to sing, to abandon all restraint and, above all, to break things. That was the official view; and, though the greater part of those present disliked, and were bored by, the ritual, they must pretend to enjoy it. It was easy, too, if you started getting drunk well before dinner. And, if you did it thoroughly enough, pretense vanished.

"Shall we split a bottle?" Tubby suggested.

"I'm drinking whisky," said Daddy.

They sat at the long table which had two narrow strips of tablecloth each side and, in the middle, an uncovered part that reflected the silver cups and trophies and candlesticks. The General and the Colonel and one or two of the elder guests were at the top end, on each side of the Mess President—a heavy, florid Major with moustaches brushed upwards. Daddy, as Vice-President for the evening, faced him at the lower end, Tubby on one side, Bert on the other, and Sammy next to Bert. Already their voices were occasionally loud and happy. The band was playing in the lobby, between the anteroom and the dining room. The mess waiters, in striped jackets, walked swiftly about, always at an angle as if leaning against a storm.

Bert ate stolidly, his face expressionless and set to a placid fashion adopted years earlier to serve most occasions. It rarely showed amusement, pleasure or anger. Daddy, slightly tipsy, smiled blandly, his head on one side, his fingers drumming a fork on the table in time with the music. "Dear old Bert," he said, "what would he do with his ears if he were a mule? Would he put them back when he got angry and prick them when he heard the feed call? Or would they just stay straight upwards so as not to show that he was thinking?"

"You're tight, Daddy," Bert said.

"Wise in my cups, Bert."

"Come on, Daddy," Tubby said. "Tell us some more about Bert. How does his tail go? Wouldn't he be a lovely bongo?"

"My lips are sealed," Daddy said primly.

"Give him another drink," someone suggested.

"No—I've had enough for the time being."

"These young officers," Bert said. "Had enough after the fish course."

"Come on, Daddy."

"Waiter!" Bert rapped out. "Another whisky and soda, double, and the same for Mr. Watson."

The ritual of the evening was beginning in the second degree. The table was cleared of the two long cloths, two waiters going to each end, twisting them quickly into ropes and whipping them away with a long-practiced flick that disturbed none of the glasses or ornaments. The port and madeira were brought and each glass filled and left untouched, the ruby light glowing back from the table. Conversation dwindled; the Mess President was on his feet, rapping with a mallet; chairs scraped the floor as everyone rose briskly; there was a quick, important silence. The President's voice rang through the room as he made his declaration: "Mr. Vice—The King!"

Daddy was suddenly steady, facing the President. His voice was clear and young and happy. He had regained the age that his years made him. "Gentlemen—The King," he replied solemnly.

In the short minute that they stood, glass in hand, rigid and silent while the band played the National Anthem, there was emotion. Like the trophies on the table, brave, cherished, more subtle than appearance suggested, these seconds were charged and recharged with power, long hallowed. Passed from hand to hand, they were swollen with valor. They were weighty with time, with courage, with vows repeated.

Tubby looked down the table at the blue and scarlet and the gold and silver trappings, at scarlet jackets with white facings, one yellow facing, the deep purple of a Padre, the blue of an Air Force Officer, the dark green of a Rifleman, but mostly the dark blue and scarlet of the Royal Regiment. The band and the drink and his memory—the memories of his father and grandfather and generations stretching darkly backwards— showed this to him as precious. This was the lure that made son follow father in their queer, gilded calling. . . . He looked at the faces, brown against the white of collar and shirt front, stamped (he thought) with this moment of dedication. He wondered what they would be like with the shells bursting and their vows challenged. Or white in death amongst the craters. . . .

The Anthem was finished. "The King," they murmured, sipping at their glasses. "God bless him," a major or two added —a field officer's privilege. They sat down again, and the talk started and grew in volume, half dissolved in the tune that the band was playing. Odd remarks, chance words, stood out like rocks in a torrent. Absently Tubby filled his glass from the decanters that had reached him on their circuit. He left the glass untouched on the table.

"Why so silent, Tubby?"

"Poor old Jenkins," someone said.

"You've heard about poor Jenkins, Tubby?"

"No . . . no . . . what?" Tubby said, waking suddenly.

"Such a nice fellow," Sammy murmured gently, "such a sad end; he wouldn't pass the port, Tubby."

"They don't know nothing," Bert said. "These young officers."

❧ The sober-minded senior officers had retired into the card room and were playing bridge inexpertly but with solemn disregard for the racket that accompanied their game. In the anteroom, most of the furniture had been cleared for safety. The officers, who intended business, had removed their spurs and taken them to the lobby to hide in their greatcoat pockets. Somebody called Jerry was playing the piano.

Sammy stood by quietly, a glass in his hand, not drinking, smiling. Tubby was beside him, aloof and rather superior on account of the arm that, strapped to his side, prevented his joining in the revelry. Bert and Daddy were cock-fighting on the floor. Daddy, jacketless, made a joke of it but he was flushed and sweating. Bert was stern and serious, for whatever he did was business. They lay on their backs, arms interlocked, and swung their legs, sparring for position. Once more Daddy was upturned, his backside round and shiny in his tight, worn overalls. His legs waved impotently like those of a squashed spider and someone smacked his buttocks loudly.

"Go on, Ginger," Bert urged, "give him another . . ."

"Don't you know the rules?" Daddy gasped. "Bert, you devil! Let me up, blast you." He struggled free and, with the crash of a table and the glasses that were on it, he and Ginger were locked together. "Learn your commandments," Daddy shouted, jumping up and down on Ginger's belly. "Honor thy father, you redheaded monster."

At the piano they had started singing. The songs were obscene, their themes sex and lavatory, absurd, not very funny, but accepted as formal amusement. They meant very little, but a guest night was incomplete without them. To deny their humor was prudish, indecent. It was fun to join in the chorus, and the piano could reasonably be smashed up afterwards. At last they were finished, and Jerry was sounding chords, waiting for inspiration. It needed courage to start on something that lacked obscenity.

"The screw guns," someone bravely suggested.

"Come on, Jerry, the screw guns."

"Come on the bongos. . . ."

> *Smoking my pipe in the mountains,*
> *Sniffing the morning cool. . . .*

They were all singing, Tubby, Bert, Daddy and Sammy; Sammy leaning back against the piano, his face happy, lit by some new comfort, fired with an old inspiration, an old memory.

> *I walks in me old brown gaiters*
> *Along o' me old brown mule,*
> *There's seventy gunners behind me . . .*

The Pack Gunners were gathered together, joined in the fellowship of the mule, scorning the Field Gunners who pulled their guns with horses instead of carrying them on bongos. To the tune of the Eton boating song they swept into the chorus:

> *For we all love the screw guns*
> *And the screw guns they all love you,*
> *And when we come up with a few guns*
> *My God, you will know what to do;*
> *Just send in your chiefs and surrender,*
> *It's worse if you fights or you runs,*
> *You can go where you please, you can shin up the trees,*
> *But you can't get away from the guns.*

As—completely happy, with unashamed abandon—they sang inaccurately the Kipling words, Tubby could see, could pray for, the hot sun on the desolate frontier hillside, the kick of dust as bullets hit the ground beside him, and the tall gunners slinging the screw guns into action at his order.

> *With a wheel on the horn of the morning,*
> *With a wheel on the edge of the pit,*
> *With a drop into nothing behind you,*
> *As straight as a gunner can spit. . . .*

It was unbearably exciting, if you were made that way, this crude, simple song. This was what they lived for, for the day when they could slew their guns against a real enemy. This was what lay behind the wine, the women and the horses.

The air was thick with tobacco smoke; it stank of beer and whisky; and, outside, the rain spluttered onto the windows. A smashed chair and bits of a table lay derelict on the carpet that was scattered with ash and broken glass, soaking up spilled alcohol. Tubby could see the childish futility of this deliberate destruction and the equally deliberate intoxication. In words, it was inexplicable in grown men. But it was justified by the moment. It was symbolical. It was as purely ritualistic as Masonic ceremony, as cabalistic observance. Everyone, red-faced and happy, was shouting the final chorus.

"You can't get away from the Guns. . . ."

"Good old Jerry."

"Good old Bert."

"Sammy, you're not drinking."

"What's yours, Tubby?"

"Waiter . . . waiter. Where the hell has he got to?"

"My God, Daddy's a captain," someone said suddenly.

"Daddy a captain?"

"Not till tomorrow. I'm not a captain," Daddy said plaintively. "I ought to be a captain. I ought to have been one years ago. Promotion in the Regiment is a scandal. But, boys, I'll tell you a secret. I'm not a captain. Not till tomorrow."

"Tomorrow's in ten minutes," someone shouted. "Bags off, Daddy."

Daddy was on the floor with a welter of people above him. His spidery, overall-covered legs, dark blue with a broad red band down them—the overalls close-fitting and strapped tight in the instep of his Wellingtons, waved frantically. Two people were pulling at the boots. They came off, the overalls with them to a sound of rending. Then Daddy was up, his straggling locks of scant hair hanging over his face, his face red and crumpled like a baby's, his bare legs pink and wobbling slightly with the superfluous flesh on his thigh and calf muscles. With his shirt tails flying, he threw himself at someone and hurled him on to the sofa. The others fell on top, and the sofa, giving under the weight, subsided gently in two or three stages. First the legs went, then the arms and then the back, until it was flattened into complete destruction.

They all stood panting and exhausted, Daddy naked except for his socks, Jerry still playing gently on the piano. Daddy seized the end of the hearthrug and jerked it violently, it coming at his tug and Sammy going down with it. Clothed in the hearthrug, Daddy squatted down happily before the fireplace. "*Y'Allah, Allah, Allah,*" he chanted in the voice of an Egyptian beggar. "*Allah karim, anna maskeen, anna agooz, m'andi haga.*" He went on, and they fetched an enamel jug of water and let it pour gently onto him, onto his head and splashing off onto the carpet. They emptied ash trays on his hair and dressed it with beer and whisky and they squirted soda water. Bert brought in rolls of toilet paper from the lavatories and wound them rapidly round Daddy, turning him into a paper-covered chrysalis. Tubby took another drink and smiled foolishly. The room was rotating slightly. "*Y'Allah, Allah, Allah . . . m'andi haga*," Daddy was still chanting.

Sammy had gone. The adjutant had come in and whispered to him, and they had left together hurriedly. It was time for bed. Leaving the anteroom, Tubby found it best to keep his eyes steadfastly on the door for which he was making. With an effort he found his greatcoat and forage cap. He looked back through the open door, and the smoke hung like shreds of fog over the broken furniture, the smashed glass, the upturned chairs and the whole pathetic shambles. "*Y'Allah, Allah, Allah. . . .* What's yours, Daddy? Go on, Ginger. . . . Waiter . . . where's that man got to?" Three people were on the piano. With a particularly lovely crash it fell into pieces.

It was desperately cold outside and, spurs tinkling as he walked, his feet scrunched the frost-bound gravel. The roadway was not entirely steady, and he walked solemnly and carefully, making his way between the sullen buildings back to his quarters.

"Wine, women and horses," he said grimly to Lydia's photograph before he turned the light off.

❧ The blackness of nothing that was all around him swayed cruelly. His bed rocked and then seemed to be turning, going in a half circle one way and then reversing. Between the curtains there was a shaft of light, but even that was not constant. The darkness itself was wickedly solid and bewildering.

He was desperate at the futile impotence into which he had allowed himself to slip. He fought, wrestling to gather himself together and to control his senses. He turned on the light, climbed out of bed, retched painfully and was very sick in his slop-pail.

For a long time he lay with the light on, still feeling sick, at last being sick again, being remorseful, deeply penitent, vowing fiercely that it was the last occasion.

"Oh God, let me sober down. Let me be sick properly. I'll

never be drunk again, oh God." He hadn't drunk much either; just steadily, and only when he was pressed, throughout the evening.

As if to his prayer, the room slowed down in its motion till the bed was scarcely swaying. He switched off the light and slept deeply.

❦ He woke to find the light on. His head was pierced with arrows of pain, his throat was glued around some sort of solid obstruction, and in his mouth there was the taste of vomit.

"Poor old Tubby," Sammy was saying.

Sammy was still in mess kit, his face drawn and white with fatigue, but smiling at Tubby.

"Good God, sir," Tubby croaked, "whatever time is it?"

"After six," Sammy answered. "I've some news for you."

"News! What news? No news will take away this blasted headache."

"A couple of aspirins," Sammy was saying and rummaging on the washstand. He found them and brought across the bottle and a glass of water.

"What news?" Tubby asked again.

"I'll tell you in a minute. I want to get hold of Bert and Daddy."

"Daddy's next door. Bert is the end quarter of the next block."

"I'll go for Bert," Sammy said. "Fetch Daddy, will you?"

Daddy was sleeping peacefully, a hand under his pillow, the other flung across the bed outside the eiderdown. It was strange to see the complete, pure repose that could follow the drink he had taken that evening. Tubby watched him a moment and then shook him regretfully.

Daddy awakened quickly and cleanly. He sat up in bed and, for an instant, was wide-eyed and childish, gazing surprisedly about him. Watching him, Tubby saw the change come swiftly, travel across and through him, a wicked transformation. The sleeper, awakened to the fresh purity of his youth, was returned harshly to the present. The stale drink came up in him and his face was furrowed. His youth, regained for a subconscious instant, had left him. He was Daddy again, thirty-four years old, a man of fifty or even older.

"What the hell do *you* want?" he asked. He groaned and stretched himself. "God, what a head. That filthy whisky."

"Sammy wants you," Tubby told him. "God knows why, but he wants us all quickly."

Daddy looked at his watch, closing first one eye and then the other, blinking miserably at the dial, turning his arm so that the watch face was towards the light. The light shone on the faint ginger hairs of his wrist and forearm, making them glow to the auburn tint of the hair that was Ariel's. That arm (and Tubby ever afterwards remembered the thought that came in this moment) had encircled Ariel at many awakenings.

"What the hell . . ." Daddy said again. "Nearly six in the morning."

He sat on the edge of his bed, his feet groping for his slippers. Tubby threw him his dressing gown from behind the door. It was striped flannel and pathetically shabby.

"Come on, Daddy," he said, "snap into it, can't you?"

They went back to his room where Bert and Sammy were waiting, the strange gathering at this hour weird and exciting, Bert ruddy as usual, his face unchanged, stubborn, unrevealing, as though this were a normal occurrence.

"God, my head," Daddy said by way of salutation.

"Good morning, Captain Watson," Bert said sarcastically. "How is the Captain? These young officers; a drop of drink and they go to pieces."

Suddenly the night had gone and day was threatening. There was no visible indication that this was so, and the darkness was thick outside, pressed against the window. But the depth had left it. There was the cold, sickly pallor of pre-dawn creeping upon them.

"There's a certain amount of hurry," Sammy was explaining. "I've been all night with the Colonel and we've got it settled . . . we're sailing the day after tomorrow, catching the troop-ship. We'll just about do it. . . . They're making us up to strength from the other batteries, six guns and the bongos . . . Daddy, of course, comes as Captain; but they can't spare us another subaltern. . . ."

"Sailing for where?" Daddy asked wearily, without the least surprise.

"The day after tomorrow?" Tubby stupidly repeated.

Bert said nothing; his pipe was already going.

"Yes," Sammy said. "There's some trouble somewhere . . . in the Red Sea, I gather." He had a bundle of papers in his hand and he put them down on the table. "The Adjutant and I—we've worked it out between us. . . . You, Daddy, the guns . . . indent for ammunition and spares . . . check up on muzzle velocities . . . Bert—you'll see to the bongos; we're not taking draught equipment. And Tubby . . ."

While he talked, the day crept upon them, edging away the night, washing into it drearily.

"Oh, boys, what a lark," Tubby said, rejoicing.

"You think so?" Bert asked in a voice that was quite expressionless.

"Lark!" Daddy said. "I think it's completely bloody. There'll be a row and we'll get shot up or something. And the Red Sea—Christ help us."

"It's a change, after all," Sammy said mildly.

❀ They started to entrain sometime after midnight and got into Southampton just before dawn after a slow, irresolute night journey. The carriage windows were misted over, and Tubby let one down and looked out to find the hard, bright station sliding up to them, the cold wind blowing down the platform, rocking the arc lamps.

The men, crowded in the third-class compartments, were asleep or just waking. They fell out onto the platform, buttoning their greatcoats and pulling on their caps, foulmouthed, bleary and needing a cup of hot tea to put them right again. There was no hot tea, and they formed up, the sergeants and bombardiers giving sharp, quiet orders, the Sergeant-Major shouting and Bert's voice loud above all the other noises in the station. Daddy, fastening his belt as he went, sour and bad-tempered, stumbled up the gangway after his squad of drivers and went down to the hold to see the animals into their stabling. The rest of the Battery formed up on the cold platform.

They came on to the quay, and the cranes were black against the paling sky, the arc lamps dimming as the day lightened. The side of the troopship towered darkly; and knowledge of the sea came with the cold that bit into them. The wind tore at a cap, at the skirts of a greatcoat. Dim shapes drifted against the sky and melted again into the grey twilight. Voices broke out and were silenced; muttered words, low oaths, quick orders. "Stop talking there . . . take that man's name, Sergeant." That was the Sergeant-Major, driving the Battery.

Figures came to you out of the daybreak, burly, mysterious shapes, resolving at last into familiar people. Sergeant Andrews, quiet and efficient: "Left Section guns aboard, sir. . . ." Hicks, miserable, weary, solicitous: "I thought as you might like a scarf, sir. I kept this out for you." The farrier, long, lean vulture of a man: "Beg pardon, sir, Mr. Bertrand's compliments and he'd like a word with you." The Sergeant-Major again, closer this time, then beside you, heavy, threatening, his voice subduing all others, defying the wind to tear it from him: "Stop talking there . . . What the 'ell is it, Sergeant Patricks?" And Sergeant Patricks' flabby whine, "Pivot's stuck, Sergeant-Major . . . can't get 'im in nohow. . . ."

"'Oly Christ," said the Sergeant-Major, "a lot o' puking infants. . . ." The Quartermaster-Sergeant, an elderly man, stout; the wind ripping off his hat and rolling it like a hoop along the quayside, he stumbling after it, clutching at it, like an old woman following a chicken. And Sammy, standing quite still, apart from it all, saying nothing, doing nothing, for all had been said and done beforehand, somehow drawing the Battery together by his presence, watching it as—quietly, smoothly, efficiently—it transferred itself according to his orders from the bitter quayside into the foreign bulk of the troopship.

Baggage, harness, guns, ammunition, mules, horses . . . Bert and the farrier peering up at the crane, drawing a chalk cross on the quay, marshaling their picked drivers.

"Come on with 'im, lead 'im up . . . right up, boy. . . ."

Hoofs skidding on the concrete; the smack of a hand on a

horse's buttocks. "Who is it? Kitty? A bandage, farrier . . .
drag ropes, let's have 'em . . . above 'er 'ocks, me lad. That's
got it . . . 'eave now, will you? 'Eave on her. . . ."

The chain hung down, swinging gently in the wind, the canvas sling brushing the ground as they groped for it. As it touched
her belly, the mare lashed out quickly. "Hup there. . . ." The
crane engine clanked a half turn and the sling tightened.
"Gimme that breast collar . . . get a hold of that breeching. . . ."

"'Eave, will you—'eave there. Tighter . . . tighter. Do you
want to have 'im kick 'imself out of it?"

"Right away. . . ."

The crane clanked steadily, the engine gathering speed till
it found its normal rhythm. As they left the ground, the horses
—and more so the mules—lashed out at its last touch with re-
doubled apprehension. In mid-air they hung, black, grotesque,
carcass-like in hopeless terror.

Then it was day, with the sky heavy and grey and a drizzle
blown in on them. The Battery was embarked, and the men
came ashore again for breakfast in the big, open warehouse on
the quayside. Daddy came down the gangway, speechless with
bad temper, grimy with the white grease and scurf off the
animals, hands stained with saddle soap off the ship's head-
collars.

The four of them stood together, silent, chewing bacon, sipping at hot coffee, watching the men and hearing their voices,
loud with oaths now that their task was finished. The coffee
warmed your innards. The scene was precious with the quality
of a cub-hunting morning, the dawn mists bright in the cover,
the fox slipping away at the lower end of it.

✦ The precious, unwanted minutes passed slowly.

The quay was shining with the bleak misery of a wet afternoon of departure. The day had never blossomed; its bud had
been nipped by the early winter evening. Low clouds hung
above them, joining the mud-grey sea at the near limits of their
vision, so that they felt confined, dreary, denied even the glamor
of new adventure. The ship at its moorings needed painting;

it was dirty white, smeared with streaks of an obscene rust-yellow. The rain pattered on to the tin roof of the vast shed under which they were standing.

They stood in groups—artillerymen, infantry, signallers, engineers—among the bales and packing cases, one uniformed person to a number of civilians. There were old women and elderly men and young girls and even babies. Most of the officers had only their wives or a single woman friend with them; but the men were surrounded by parents and brothers and sisters, who had come for the excursion in the special train provided by the War Office. They stood uncomfortably, waiting for time to pass and for the order to embark that would bring release and separation.

🌼 "My dear," Daddy said, "you'll soon find someone better. It's been a grand time while it's lasted."

She looked at him dumbly. Her clothes, a little too smart, were made tawdry by these wrong surroundings. She saw Daddy in profile, looking away from her, standing unhappily in his worn uniform with its frayed medal-ribbons. Already she was locked outside him. Already, smiling deliberately, he was in the current of this drab, unhurried departure.

"I thought . . . I thought . . ." she said, her voice trailing off uselessly.

He did not answer.

"It will be nice . . ." she tried again later. "It will be fun . . . sometime . . . we'll write, won't we?"

"No," he said quickly, with unmeant violence.

Now there was nothing between them. The leash that had held them was parted and only the waste minutes kept them together. Somewhere a bugle was sounded. The siren trumpeted mournfully, touching them and echoing past to the grey town behind and the grey sea before them. At last they could take their leave and break the tangle of this trivial friendship. It had run its full course from seed to blossom. To each, knowledge of the other had come quickly and fully and was soon disillusionment. Now they could go their ways and seek fresh illusions, their hearts clear of regrets on the score of their parting. It had not come by choice but suddenly and without the sadness of contemplation. They had been spared the torture of final occasions, the last night, the last breakfast, the last dance, the last everything that had grown into intimate custom. A bell was ringing.

People hurried past in such preoccupation that they, the two of them, were left in solitude. Standing square in front of her in a dark corner, he took her by the elbows. They were much the same height and he looked into her face, trying to make his regard sardonic, to renounce its drama. The appeal in her eyes strengthened the sadness that he had imprisoned within him. For a moment, it aroused regrets that he would not own to. She was not pained by his hardness; she had learned to know it.

"You can have the pictures," he said harshly. "But don't sell the Renoir drawing unless you have to . . . not for less than fifty pounds anyway . . . it's worth double." But it didn't help; it was all so cruel, so useless.

She couldn't answer; he heard the breath catch in her throat as she tried to.

"Ariel. . . ."

"Bill . . . Willie . . ."

"Good-by," they said and kissed briefly.

He did not look back as he walked up the gangway and, as she saw him go, it seemed to her that his shoulders were square, his body sturdy and manful.

❦ There was a strange syncopation about the clanking of the crane that had a hidden, unreasonable rhythm. Bert looked upwards, his eyes glad to fasten themselves to some detailed movement. Watching the crane was a purpose to speed the passing of these long minutes.

"Well, Jane," he said briskly, "same old story, same old trooper, same rain, same everything."

He stood with his legs apart, his hands in the pockets of his breeches, his boots and belt polished superbly. She was several inches taller, nearly his age, pale and awkward.

"It's a long time, Tommy," she said obscurely.

"Never you mind," Bert answered. "I've stood you for ten years; I'm not likely to change that sudden."

"We ought to get married," she said dispassionately. "There's no point in it this way."

"When I make captain . . . or don't, as the case is. One way or the other."

They stood in silence, looking out from the dark shed across the shining quay to the white troopship.

"It's no bloody joke bein' an officer," he said angrily. "It's a bloody liability. I was a sight better off as sergeant-major . . . we could ha' married as sergeant-major, easy. . . ."

A gust of wind blew in to them. He was solid as granite, not swaying to the wind, not giving an inch to anything. She clutched at his arm, a nervous uncompleted movement.

"You're a good girl," he said suddenly with unusual affection.

She smiled at that, and her plain, pale face embraced him. He felt tenderly for her; for her faithful simplicity that he could understand; for her thin, fragile, complaisant body; for the long years of intermittent companionship that they had enjoyed together. She was his wife, except for the act of marriage. Their thoughts ran together.

"If anything happens, you're as well not married," he started explaining. "We've a tidy bit put by and it's yours to do what you like with."

"I'd like to be married," she said wistfully. "When you're here, I don't mind—though it isn't a lot we see of each other. It's when you go that I mind it."

"So we shall," he said again without impatience. "In two years' time—one way or the other."

A bell was ringing.

"That's about it," Bert said quickly. "It's good-by, my girl. Good-by, Janie."

He held her forearm, fingering it gently. They did not kiss and he looked at her without smiling, with the same unchanging face that he wore in the Mess or on the parade ground. They moved out into the rain. He had no coat and she no mackintosh, but neither seemed to notice. For a moment, they stood looking seaward, their eyes beyond the horizon, their only contact his hand on her forearm and their quiet understanding.

"You don't want to get wet," he told her.

"No," she said. "Nor you either."

❀ "Look, Tubby . . . look, there's Sammy. How pale and tired he is. . . ."

"His wife's worse," Tubby said; "really ill this time, he thinks. It's hard for him leaving her . . . I said you'd go and see her sometimes, it's the Wigmore Clinic. . . ."

"How sweet of you, Tubby. . . ."

"Don't let's try to be funny," he said wearily, inconsistently, "it doesn't help—this time."

After that, they stood silently in a corner of the vast shed. They leaned against a pile of packing cases, waiting for the time to pass, waiting uncomfortably, hoping for some chance thought or a sudden, shared emotion to round off this parting. There was a lot that they wanted to talk about together, but the knowledge that their time was limited to a few brief minutes made conversation impossible. But it was desperately important that these moments, during which the circumstances of departure ought to have brought them into a last spasm of intimacy, should not be wasted in time-passing trivialities. The concord that lay in their silence was better than that.

"Tubby . . ." Lydia began to speak and then felt lost and unassured, bewildered by the inflation of these dragging minutes.

"Yes?"

In her smart furs and dark, neat clothes—standing among the hurrying, uniformed figures, but apart from the bustle of embarkation—she was alone with a foreign people who spoke an incomprehensible language.

"Why do they give you such grubby, worn-out boats to go in?" she asked desperately.

"Search me," he said. "It's good enough for the brutal and licentious soldiery."

That helped her to laugh. "Dear Tubby—so brutal and licentious."

"Do you want me brutal and licentious?" he asked quickly.

"Not a bit. I like you as you are, sweet and innocent."

He was suddenly fierce and insistent. "Do you want me at all, Lydia? I must know. How much do I mean to you? Shall we write to each other? When I come back, in two or three years, shall we meet again . . . or will we have forgotten each other?"

"I don't expect we shall have forgotten each other."

"Lydia," he said without restraint, "it can't matter to you the way it does to me. I know that. You don't realize . . . there just *aren't* any other women for me. I can't be bothered with them, they aren't important."

"I don't think I'm really and honestly important," she said gently, "not necessary to you; not as *me*, myself, Lydia . . . you just feel you ought to have a girl for sentimental times like this. I'm like a sort of roadhouse. You pull in for a meal when you're tired of driving."

"You don't know," he said; "you *can't* know. . . ." And once more, words were too much for him. "I can't explain . . . but you see what I mean? Lydia . . ."

"Perhaps," she said brutally, "perhaps there'll be a Piccadilly where you're going. Cheaper, too, I expect. . . ." But she wasn't really unkind; she didn't mean to be. Time was now too short for anything but the flippancy of their easiest relationship. She tried to step right back to the days before the accident.

The ship's siren had called and now a bell was ringing.

"When I think of you . . ." he began, in a last hopeless effort.

She was seized in the stream of his half-uttered pleading, left without foothold in the spate of his urgency. Time, clock time, that had dragged so slowly and was now slipping from them, had become his ally.

"*Do* you want me?" he pressed her.

"I think I do," she said helplessly. "I daren't . . . I don't know . . . I couldn't . . ." She struggled to find what she meant and to tell it to him. Why was it so hard to know the truth of a sudden emotion? "It's so, so hard," she said. "That last time, in the schoolroom—we had a lifetime then, ahead of us. Now we've a few minutes—hardly that . . . it's time for you to go, Tubby. . . ."

"I want you, Lydia," he cried. "I love you."

His feelings were true, but the words sounded false to him. The language of love was crude and hackneyed; you could not believe in it. What could you say to a woman? You could only tell her you loved her, you wanted her—like out of a story. You couldn't explain the hurt, the deep-biting need, except with words that use had made common.

The bell rang again and someone was shouting; Bert's voice, coming crisp and hard from the gangway, telling Tubby to hurry. Lydia clutched at it, to escape from the tide of the moment. She took Tubby's hand between hers and stretched up towards him.

"You have to go now, Tubby. You're sweet and I'd hate to lose you. We'll write often and often. . . ."

For the first time, she opened her lips while he kissed her.

"Run off quickly," she said. "Go on, Tubby dear—or I might cry in a minute."

She watched him run out of the shed, across the quay and up the gangway.

❀ The rhythm of departure was quickening; the pulse of the ship beating within her. The men, signalers, sappers, infantry, gunners, crowded to the rails, hats on the backs of their heads, jackets unbuttoned, singing, shouting, whistling, keeping it up, keeping it up so as to give an outlet to the pressure that, rising within them, pounded in their chests and throats and stomachs, shook their bodies, threatened their manhood, threatened a tear, a sob, that had to be turned into an oath, into an obscene joke, a personality, a catcall.

The crowd on the quay surged forwards, the wave of them broken by the line of red-capped military policemen. Women were crying; open, luxurious tears. Men put their arms round them; old, grey-haired fathers, comforting their wives and daughters with staunch protective gestures. Small children identified fathers or brothers, pointed excitedly upwards, became insistent, were slapped and started to bellow. The rain had stopped and the band, emerging from the shed, began to play on the quayside. The widening gap, between the ship and the sea, was bridged by the tumult, by this enchanting misery.

"It's the first time for you, Tubby," Bert said, "but it won't be the last. Not by a long chalk—eh, Major?"

No one answered him.

"My ninth trip East," he said proudly, trying again to break into them.

The crowd swayed, individuals fading, faces white in the gathering dark, under the relit arc lamps. Lydia wasn't there; not part of that heaving substance, not one of those squirming insects that shared their tears, their cries, their fluttering of hands and handkerchiefs.

A press photographer, a flash, a particular flicker of light, seized his glance and drew it to her, there at the back, she and Jane, standing together on a packing case, beneath a lamp, beside a tall policeman. She waved delicately—she must have seen him—spoke to Jane, pointing, Jane leaning over her shoulder and following the line of her outstretched arm and finger.

"See Jane? There—with Lydia."

"Ah—I seen her," Bert answered, and raised his hand slowly.

They had seen each other. There was a thread between them; Jane, white and awkward, waving frantically; Lydia, her hand lifted, still delicate. The two men, Bert and Tubby, holding themselves tight and gruff on the deck of the troopship.

"You can't go on waving," Bert said viciously, crossly. "I wish to hell they'd take us out of it."

For an instant, the siren drowned the band as the ship's movement became obvious. And when the sad trumpeting ended, the band was lost to the ear. Then the beat of the big drum, the strains of music and, at last, the actual tune that the band was playing, pushed their way back to you.

"*The Girl I Left behind Me,*" Bert said. "That shakes you, Tubby, me lad."

"Oh, go away, Bert," Sammy said wearily.

The photographers were busy on the quay and they saw a reporter go up to Lydia and saw her wave him impatiently away. It was a tiny, defenceless gesture, breaking through the self-control of her smart easy carriage. Seeing it from the deck,

Tubby recaptured the strong, artificial sadness of their ship-side parting.

The troopship drew away slowly. The band was playing *Auld Lang Syne*, and the men on the decks below were singing in tune to it. The crowd took it up and their voices joined across the water. Handkerchiefs were fluttering and the figures were becoming indistinct, the band, too, growing fainter.

"I need a drink," Bert said. "Come along Tubby. Coming, Major?"

"You go on," Sammy answered. "I'll follow you down in a minute."

"So will I," Tubby said, his voice coming unexpectedly hard, from a long way inside him.

The band died and trailed off as they thought they could follow it, and then knew that it had stopped playing. "It's all false and sentimental and God knows why we do it," Sammy said, with the first violence that Tubby had ever known him use in conversation.

"The troops love it. . . ."

"And so do we . . . why, I couldn't tell you. But there it is. We work up this tremendous, unbelievable emotion. We feel the insides of us bursting with our own tragedy—and then we love it."

The drizzle had started again and they stood in silence, eyes puckered against the wind and the rain, gazing out into the blurred twilight. England was there, somewhere, invisibly receding in a half-sensed jumble of dockside buildings and moored shipping and lights that were just appearing.

With the dark tight around them, and the lights, mysterious, exciting, smudged by the rain, they dropped their pilot and slipped into the Channel.

Book Two

1929

Chapter 9 THE PEAK OF THE NIGHT WAS TOPPED, AND the darkness had that thin and hostile quality of early morning. It was anticlimax. After the solid resistance or solid comfort of the night—whichever way it took you—this atmosphere sucked at you and left you feeble. The unfulfillment of waking from a brief sleep, the taste of sleep sour in your mouth, plucked at nerves, upset reason. The lessening of your powers and the loss of balance put you on the defensive, so that, as a good soldier should, you became immediately aggressive and looked for trouble.

In two hours it would be sweating hot; but now, well before dawn, the cold wind made them huddle into greatcoats and stay close to the blazing fire. Hicks was waiting to kick apart the logs and stamp on the embers, but in the meanwhile they sipped at their coffee, forcing the hot liquid past sensitive lips, finding comfort and strength in the hurt that it did to throat and stomach. At once, your system was put into motion, eyes cleared, sounds had a meaning, words came to you.

"As a socialist, Daddy," Sammy said, "you ought to be drinking tea the same as the troops. I'm sure there must be something bourgeois about an Englishman drinking coffee." It wasn't often that Sammy made this sort of remark, rather pointless, almost provocative. He felt, perhaps, that the silence wanted shaking; that he must break the apathy that had hold of them.

"I don't agree," Daddy answered. "They prefer tea, we like coffee." He spoke crossly, clearly in the worst of his tempers.

"All parties are happy then," Sammy said and walked off into the darkness.

"I'd sooner have a cup of tea meself," Bert said for no apparent reason.

"It's this condensed milk that makes tea so filthy," Tubby suggested. "You don't have to have it with coffee."

"There's no need to have it with tea either," Daddy argued. "You can drink tea neat, can't you? Why shouldn't Bert have his tea if he likes it?"

"Why shouldn't he?" Tubby agreed. "He can go and get it from the cookers if he wants to. He can send Hicks for it. He can tell me in advance and I'll see that he has it. . . ." He knew that Daddy was started again on one more attack against himself as Messing Officer. At any other time of day except before dawn, he would have thought out a plan of pacification. Now he felt quarrelsome.

"Why should he have to get it from the troops?" Daddy asked nastily. "You're running the messing, aren't you? Go and get it for him."

"I'm fed up with the messing," Tubby said.

"Oh, you're fed up with it, are you?"

"For God's sake leave the messing alone," Tubby said. He knew how it was going; the way it had gone almost daily for this last week or two.

"Are you running the messing or aren't you?" Daddy asked.

"Yes, I'm running it."

"Well, why the hell can't you do it properly? It's easy enough, isn't it? Even a bloody idle second-lieutenant ought to be able to run an Officer's Mess for four people. Why don't you make a job of it?"

The hurricane lamp shone on the table by which they were standing, and Daddy was back beyond the fringe of light so that his voice was coming out of the darkness.

"I make a darned good job of it," Tubby said.

"You think you make a good job of it?"

"Yes, considering."

"Considering what?"

"Considering all there is to contend with. You're always

grumbling. The others are satisfied. Why do you always have to be grumbling? There's no reason to."

"Somebody's got to grumble if you can't do it properly."

"I *do* do it properly."

"Like hell you do. You can't even get Bert a cup of tea when he says he wants one."

"I don't want a cup of tea," Bert said. He made the statement in an aloof, disinterested sort of way and then—as it were—turned his back on the argument. He didn't mind trouble but he kept out of it. The glow of his pipe lit his face rhythmically, showing it calm and stolid, set against interference. The quarrel didn't touch him. Let it run its course, expend itself.

"You said you did," Daddy persisted. "You *did* want one too. Go and get him a cup of tea, Tubby. Go on, hurry up and get it."

"Damned if I will."

"You're damned if you will, are you? Well, go and get it, see? Go and get it, that's an order."

"Don't be such a fool," Tubby said.

"That's an order."

"It's not a lawful order, anyway."

"Don't do the barrack-room lawyer on me. Do what you're told, blast you."

"Are you bickering again?" Sammy asked, coming back to the table. "I'll have to forbid you two to talk to each other. What is it this time? Messing again? We've been arguing about the messing for two months and I'm fed up with it. Shut up, both of you."

For the last few weeks Daddy had been very difficult. It had been hard for everyone, living in tents with a midday temperature of a hundred and twenty in the shade; but when they had run out of whisky, which Tubby rarely drank but which Daddy needed continually, the trouble had really started.

Hicks came up and started to collect the coffee things.

"Is that pot empty?" Bert asked.

"No sir."

"Gimme half a cup, will you?"

Hicks filled the cup.

"The Sergeant-Major would like a word with the Major," he said. "He's waiting, sir."

"Ask him to come along, then," Sammy answered.

The Sergeant-Major came up and saluted. He had got a lot thinner in the last few months. His obesity had gone entirely, and his front was no longer convex. His virility was as forceful; but now he was like a young bull, full of fight, suppressed power, and not like an old bull that was hanging heavy with his strength ponderous. You had to admire him in these bad times with the men getting difficult. He was always the same, fierce and ruthlessly efficient, caring for the men as a matter of business, showing no sympathy or kindness, doing nothing from kindness, never actuated by so weak a sentiment but only by pride in a duty that allowed him to override others, to bend and break them.

"Cup of coffee, Sergeant-Major?" Bert suggested, pushing his cup forward. "It's freshly poured out."

"Thank you, sir."

The Sergeant-Major took the cup and started to drink from it. He held the saucer in one hand, and the little finger of the hand holding the cup stuck out straight, like somebody very refined at a tea party. Tubby noticed it as extremely ridiculous. It helped to send away the anger that had mounted during his conversation with Daddy. The anger had come up in him, slowly at first and then quickly, leaving a feeling of sickness when it had gone again.

"What is it, Sergeant-Major?" Sammy asked.

"There's two men under arrest, sir. Been fighting again."

"There's been a lot of that lately."

"Yes, sir."

"I wish you could put a stop to it."

The Sergeant-Major looked uncomfortable. "It wants an example making," he said. "There's been a lot of trouble, I'm afraid, sir. The men are fed up with leaving home at two days' notice and hanging about here for two months afterwards."

"I know, Sergeant-Major, it's been hard for everyone."

The Sergeant-Major looked at the ground and spoke doggedly. "It wants an example, sir . . . if I might make a suggestion?"

"Yes?"

"Field punishment. . . ."

"No," Sammy said, "I don't like it."

"It's the only thing, sir."

"It never did any good in my experience. Savage punishment only makes them savage. I know all the arguments. . . ."

"Beg pardon, sir, but if the men was to see a lad or two lashed to a gun wheel for a couple of mornings, it soon puts the fear o' God into them."

"The fear of you, Sergeant-Major."

"It comes to the same thing, sir. . . ."

"Well, we're moving now," Sammy said. "I'll see the men when we get into camp. They'll have to march with their sub-sections in the meanwhile."

"Very good, sir. What time shall we be moving?"

"Almost at once."

"Very good, sir."

The Sergeant-Major saluted smartly and went off, and they heard him curse to himself as he stumbled in the darkness. Then they heard his voice, strong, tremendous, ringing through the bivouac. He called the sergeants by name and you heard them answer, "Yes, sir . . . Yes, sir . . . Yes, sir . . ." the wind carrying their voices. You heard Andrews' voice, older and more controlled than the others, "Yes, sir . . . 'A' subsection ready now, sir."

"A good man, Andrews," Sammy said.

"An' a good man the Sergeant-Major." Bert's voice was challenging. He didn't care about his tea and he didn't like trouble, but he minded about the Sergeant-Major.

"Yes, Bert," Sammy agreed. "A good sergeant-major, at any rate."

"One an' the same thing, to my way o' thinking." That was Bert entirely. For him, life was soldiering; and soldiering did not admit humanity. Humanity suggested that a soldier was an individual, an all-time individual with passions, tempers, frailties and personal characteristics. He wasn't. He was nine-tenths a soldier, a gunner, driver, signaler, officer. The other tenth of him concerned nobody, concerned only a fraction of his own kingdom, utterly immured from his uniformed self. Humanity only came into soldiering so far as it increased efficiency; make the men happy and you had a better unit. Beyond that, all such things as kindness, pity, love, were inadmissible. That was the ranker outlook, applied by Bert to himself and to all subordinates.

"We'd best be getting formed up, sir."

"All right, Bert," Sammy answered. "See to it, will you?"

When Bert put on his topi, he rolled himself up and pushed himself down into his uniform, becoming entirely uniformed with all ten-tenths of him. He was the senior subaltern, the chief executive of the Battery. He knocked out his pipe, pulled out his torch and moved solidly into the darkness.

"Loads-on . . . fall in . . . column of route facing West. . . ." The voice quelled all other activities, admitted no hesitation. You knew what to do, and you did it quickly and without error.

The sergeants had torches, each torch making a small circle of light which flickered sometimes on the flank of a mule or on a gun load or on the men who were loading up the animals. The clang of the gun loads, as they were put on to the pack-saddles, and the clink of breeching chains came out of the darkness.

"We'd best walk," Bert said to Tubby. "We'll have the horses led behind with the staff, shall we?"

Sammy had joined them. "I'll walk too," he said.

❧ The first battalion of infantry started to come past, marching well, falling at once into the rhythm of a long journey. You could hear the steady, muffled beat on the sand; a resolute tune that left no issue in doubt, that fired you to join their purpose.

"As good as a band. . . ." Tubby spoke half consciously; as though, in this dark morning, his lips were the servant of any trifling impression.

"Not bad. . . ." (This was Bert's gruff approval.) "They come from India. They learn to march *there*."

From the back of the battalion, the adjutant swung his torch along the head of the battery until its beam touched Sammy. "Nice morning, sir," he called; "are you following us?"

"We have that pleasure," Sammy answered.

The battery slid into the column behind the leading regiment. Once it was moving, it drew breath, became a living being. You could feel its single life stirring, moving through the sub-sections. The irregular beat of hoofs and marching boots, the snort of a mule, the tinkle of chains on breast-collar and breeching, the gentle clank of gun parts, the smell of warming animals —all this made joyful knowledge. You had lost identity and were part of the unit.

It was rather fine marching through the dying night with the Southern Cross on your left and the wind behind you. Soon that weakness of early morning, that water-in-the-blood feeling, wore out of you. But things weren't quite real. The ground, even the air, was muffled. It was cold; but once your muscles had stretched and were working in that drugged, pendulum sort of way, the chill couldn't get into you. You marched with an easy calm, finding pleasure in the movement and in the sounds of the march, the hushed voices loud in the night, the crackle of burnt grass as you stepped on it. Your feelings were keen; they quivered like the nostrils of a horse; your senses missed nothing. But it was all rather sad. You felt that it was something fine—a single, fine thing—so much a first stage of death, a sharp, biting, ecstatic hour which you could not again encounter in its exact purity. There had been just this feeling one September morning at Calcott.

For a long time, Tubby walked beside Sammy without speaking. Then marching became difficult as field-boots, unnailed, slipped in the thickening sand. Sammy missed a half pace, almost stumbled as he reached forward to catch up again. "We'll ride after the first halt," he said; "we've made our gesture."

Every now and again Tubby dropped out to watch the first section, his own section, file past. Andrews would be somewhere towards the end of the leading subsection, always seeing to something; and a torch, flitting across the men and mules, picked out his sergeant's chevrons.

"All right, Andrews?" Tubby called.

"All right, sir . . . going nicely."

When the section was past, he waited beside the track for his horse that was coming along behind the guns but in front of the battery staff, the ammunition limbers, the cookers, water carts and transport. Bert was walking by one of the mules of the center section, stooped down, walking sideways, struggling to adjust a breast-collar without stopping. Sergeant Patricks, a long streak of a man, walked beside, shining his torch on the place where the collar was rubbing.

"That's about it," Bert said, straightening himself and slipping out of the column. "An' why the 'ell you can't do it yourself, Patricks . . ."

The last gun was past and, a short distance behind, the darker, more homogeneous bulk had in it the files of battery staff horses.

"Murphy . . ."

The little man pulled out, riding one charger and leading the other. "Yessir. Here we are, sir."

"I'll ride June," Tubby said. "Follow me up, will you?"

Riding was a new motion for this morning, one for which the walk had deranged his muscles. Trotting beside the track, back to the head of the battery, muscles stretched pleasantly. The mare shied at a thickening of the darkness, a thorn bush, bunching herself up and bucking as he kicked her straight again.

"Skittish little bitch," Murphy said from behind. He was talking to himself but in hopes that you'd hear him. He felt the need for more intimate company in the darkness. At the head of the battery, Tubby dismounted, Murphy taking the horses and bringing them along behind the leading section. In this way, Tubby could pull out when he liked, watch the section past and ride to the front again.

Up there, Sammy was walking alone, you might almost have said strolling, his pipe in his mouth, his head bent, his arms clasped behind him. The day was just coming and, in the first light, his was a forlorn and not very military figure. But Sammy couldn't ever have been a martial sort of soldier.

"How were they?" he asked.

"All right, sir."

"No trouble?"

"Bert had a breast-collar. . . ." Tubby said.

"Patricks, I expect. I never ought to have made that man a sergeant. It's far and away the worst subsection. . . ."

It was disappointing. There was no glorious act of dawn. The day just came and found them still walking. At first the darkness grew weaker, diluted, but without light coming. The sand showed lighter than the darkness above it; men and horses came out of the shadows, thicker and bolder, until they could be distinguished as men and horses. Small objects beside the track, stones, rocks, scrub, a burnt stick, became visible; then you could see the men in front and, after that, the day grew quickly. The wind dropped and the sun burst suddenly on your back, so that by the first halt you were sweating.

Daddy came trotting up, his bad temper gone, smiling. "Hello, Tubby . . . stretching your muscles nicely?"

You could never resist his way of making up a quarrel by just assuming that it had never happened. His brain had turned over a page, and the quarrel was buried in the part of a book that is read and forgotten; the way you can skim through a novel, forgetful of what you've read, concerned only with a new mood, the next excitement.

"Well, Tubby?"

"You're an idle devil. I don't believe you've been off that wretched animal."

"Captains' union . . . captains don't walk. It's the only rank in the army that's permanently mounted—one way or the other."

"Bawdy old brute . . . get back to your cookers."

Going on again, riding now, the sun was up properly but the morning still cool and the march pleasant. An hour ahead, you could see the hills that had to be crossed before evening. Hills always have a fatal appearance. . . . The dawn mists were just disappearing and the folds and complexities of the slopes were suggested by hints of the long, slanting shadows. The higher peaks shone brightly.

Those hills, beautiful as they were in the morning light,

seemed to hold a warning. They were like sirens, beckoning you on to disaster.

Years later, Tubby was quite sure that this was not an afterthought. He remembered the impression, keen and vivid, coming to him as he rode beside Sammy.

❧ "A man called Hemingway," Sammy was saying, "wrote a book about bullfights. I remember chiefly how he explained the artistic side of the thing; the way the fight progresses, one stage after another, while the bull is prepared for killing. His mind and spirit and body are all prepared together. The whole of him, you see? When the bull is finally killed, it is the climax of the fight; the *Moment of Truth*, I believe they call it . . . does that answer you? Does it go any way towards answering you?"

"It makes sense," Tubby said. "The moment of Truth, the stages . . . the pattern, as you were saying. The way life has a reason, a design in it. It's fantastic, of course. . . ."

"Fantastic?"

"I mean, sir, we say all these sorts of things—at least we don't very often . . . but when we do, we believe them for the moment. Afterwards we feel as if it was all nonsense. We're rather inclined to blush about having said them."

Sammy lit his pipe again. He sat his horse easily and looked well on it. He needed both hands for his pipe and the reins were looped loosely over his left wrist while he leaned slightly forward, struck a match and puffed intently.

"You're rather apt to blush about speech, Tubby. It isn't necessary, you know. It's a shyness you ought by now to be overcoming. . . . You see, you said just now that something made sense. If it does that, it will equally be sense this evening or the day after tomorrow. That is, if it isn't something dependent on changing circumstances . . . and our knowledge of life and death isn't likely to change in the immediate future, is it? Tell me," he added a moment later, "why *do* you shut up your brain and your perception for most of your life and only let it out on rare occasions? Why, Tubby, why? There must be some reason."

Tubby shifted in the saddle, leaned down and ran a finger under the girth, leaned forward and gave the curb chain a flick. Anything to gain time before he had to commit to words the feelings, the half-thoughts, that came up in answer.

"It *does* make sense," he said at last, ignoring the question. "It's hard to believe it all happens by accident. Looking back . . . my accident, you, Daddy, Lydia . . . it seems as if there really had been a sort of pattern. . . ."

"As if," Sammy said relentlessly, "we were fattened like turkeys. As if we were prepared all our lives by a series of events which come to a climax—a moment of truth—when we are ready for death, when the pattern is completed. Some patterns are uninteresting, drab, dull colors, very simple, the highlights a holiday to Margate, a family wedding. Others are more complicated, more exciting; racing accidents, hospitals, love, war . . . and the pattern of this life, you see, is only a tiny corner of the whole pattern of ourselves. And that, in its turn, is an infinitesimally small part of the whole great pattern of the universe . . . but it *is* a part. That's the important thing to remember. . . ."

They were in the hills now and Sammy's eyes were far over the new horizon. He spoke on gently in his soft, halting speech; a teacher, diffident but certain, propounding a doctrine that his pupils could take or leave according to whether or not it seemed good to them. A teacher, though, speaking from knowledge, not from untested belief, not from theories. Here, on a plate, was the fruit of knowledge—if the pupil were ready to take and eat it.

"Don't be misled, Tubby," he went on quietly; "that's only one way of putting it and quite a crude way. It goes such a little distance that it's really confusing. It's obvious, you see, that all of us—each individual one of us, each of our thoughts and actions and feelings—are a part of the universe. The other side of it isn't so obvious; that the same thoughts, words and actions contain the universe within them. . . .

"The universe is in *you*, Tubby. You have the seed of all-power, all-knowledge. One day—a long, long time ahead, perhaps so far that we cannot conceive it—that seed will grow to a plant, blossom and die. That is the hard part; for when it has died, when you are no longer self, when you are no longer grasping or needful, when there is no Tubby—he will be all-powerful. He will be all love . . . that is the way you are traveling, the thread you are weaving in the pattern . . . and this lifetime—however far it takes us—can be no more than an insignificant stage of the journey. . . ."

For one moment that was truth, strong like flood waters, strong with the flood of your own spirit. Feelings, unborn thoughts, hopes, fears, memories, stormed within you. Where was the key to the gates; that gift of tongues that made you human? What God could hide this power within you, could leave you swollen with this spirit but without the means to unpent it?

"That's it," Tubby cried, "that's how it is. It's all there, you see. You can learn things and know things and do things—you *must* be able to; you *are* able to. But you can't get at them. You know what I mean? I can't say it, I can't put it into words; I wouldn't even be sure what it is that I want to find words for . . . it's not reason, it's something you recognize; a familiar face; you get a glimpse of it in a crowded room, in a street and you can't put a name to it . . . that isn't it either. . . ."

His words drifted helplessly, uncontrolled, undirected. He looked at Sammy, appealing to him, knowing that *he'd* find a key that would loose the waters. He'd understand; he knew the words, the way of words, the way of knowledge.

But Sammy did not answer. He had gone. He was there beside you, but his eyes had come down from the hills, his face was twisted and anxious.

With a quick movement he pulled open his map case.

"They're wrong, Tubby," he said, "I'm certain of it. . . ."

The wave that had been at the crest tumbled over, taking you down from the ridge of bright, glittering bubbles into the trough of the grey sea, into the level of a rough hillside and the hard sun high above you, the narrow track that had somehow found a shelf to follow, the hill—all rocks and scrub—towering upon your left and, on your right, dropping less steeply to the narrow valley, the dried-up bed of a river.

Ahead, some way ahead—for they had left an interval to make marching easier, without the halts and pauses that happen in a column—the leading battalion was twisting up the mountain.

"They're wrong, Tubby; see where the track divides?" (This was Sammy speaking; the same gentle voice, that had talked of death and the universe, come down from over the hills to the level of the hillside.) "Do you see, Tubby, how one branch of the track goes up and the other down? The upper, the one they've taken, it looks wider, but it's wrong. It's the lower one that we ought to be following. . . ."

The map lay across his horse's withers; there wasn't a wisp of breeze to stir it. It was very still, with the small noises of their progress so loud that they scarcely touched the silence. The silence was heavy, overpowering; the more noise you made, the more it bore down on you, the more it became untouchable. It was a silence that was a better undertone to death and the universe and the pattern of life than to a question of map-reading.

"Nip along, Tubby," Sammy said; "give the Adjutant my compliments; tell him he's wrong; tell him I'll halt the battery to give him room to get back again."

The clatter of your horse starting, his legs pulled under him by the drive of your knees, by the kick of your heels in his ribs, smacked into the silence and rebounded back again. A stone went rolling down the hillside. The dust spurted up as you broke into a gallop. The movement of the horse pulled you back to the thing that was happening.

"Hello, Tubby," the Adjutant said, "run out of whisky? Why else this pleasure?"

(That was the way to talk; that was better than death and the universe. This was a chap you could trade with in your own currency.) "My old man says you're on the wrong road. Can't you read the ruddy signposts?" (That came out pat enough, but when you wanted to answer Sammy, the words fled you.)

"I was thinking the same myself," the Adjutant answered. "I'll see the Colonel . . . he never could read a map, anyway."

The men in front pulled into the side, huddling into each other as he shouted to them to make way and cantered past them. "We've stopped to give you room," Tubby called after him.

Trotting back down the hill, he could see the battery laid out just below him. Daddy at the back there, walking slowly up the column; the sergeant-major, a pace up the hill, calling to someone, an arm stretched out in a Roman gesture; Bert and the farrier, bent together over a brown mule that must have a gall somewhere; Sergeant Andrews, shifting a load from one mule to another; the trumpeter, up at the head, dismounted. And then Sammy . . . and this was strange, this brought you hard to reality, banged you into the idea that something was happening—Sammy sitting on his horse with the battery halted; Sammy, still mounted, when his law, his one implacable law, his one foible, ran that every horse and mule must be relieved of its load the moment that the battery stopped moving. That was curious. It was disturbing. . . .

He was looking worried and he had out his compass, propped on the front of his saddle. "I don't know that this map's right . . ." he said. "See here, Tubby . . . I don't quite like it . . . if there should be any trouble—a nasty spot to be caught in . . . no scouts out, no flank guards, nothing. . . ."

"Trouble! What a hope, sir—"

"Yes," Sammy said, his eyes on the hill tops, scanning them carefully, "it would be funny, wouldn't it?"

The bowl of his pipe was in his cupped hand, as if he were going to relight it. Then the pipe was on the path, its stem broken to pieces.

That was the opening bar of the music. In Tubby's senses there was the sharp, electric click—perhaps the click of a gearchange—as time went once again into slow-motion. He started to speak. He started to say "bad luck, sir," and all his life he never knew how far he got with it. At the same time he heard the crack, not a sharp incision in the silence, but soft and muffled; and, as Sammy slipped forward, the shot was echoing back from across the valley. Very slowly Sammy slid to his horse's neck, his arms hanging each side of it. Then he twisted sideways and fell to the ground.

Almost as he fell, Tubby was on his feet beside him. The

reins of his horse were slung over his arm and he knew at once
that he must get rid of the animal. He called to the trumpeter,
who was the Major's orderly. "Take these horses, both of
them . . . get Murphy."

He noticed that his voice was calm and easy, as though it
had taken charge of him. He noticed everything that happened,
not just vaguely, but remarking its smallest particular, linking
it up with the past, with odd bits of knowledge, with memories.
Each instant contained pictures, charts, that were laid in front
of him. There was a burst of firing and a mule in the leading
subsection went down kicking. Sammy was doubled up on the
ground and Tubby kneeling beside him.

"Get them off the path, Tubby . . . off the path quickly."
The voice was very faint, nearly all air, but very urgent: "Go
on, Tubby; *right-take-ground* will do it."

You had to stand for that; in this racket you must give a
signal, clear and unmistakable; the order first, the signal afterwards. . . .

"Right-take-ground . . . get off the track . . . get down the
hillside. . . ." He turned, facing up the path with his back to the
battery, punching the air at right-angles, giving the signal for
the battery to turn right and drop into the valley.

Andrews got the order and acted quickly, passing it on, calling, signaling to the next sergeant, swinging the head of his
leading mule to the right and smacking it hard on the buttocks:
"Git on, Jenny . . . keep a hold on her, Harrison. . . ."

Tubby heard and saw and knew exactly what was passing.
All along the line, the mules went skidding down the slope,
over the convex brow of the hill, down into cover, their drivers
clinging to the reins and sliding after them.

"Well done, Andrews . . ." (Tubby scarcely knew that he
had called to him.) "Get the load off that mule . . . give him a
bullet. . . ."

Andrews and two gunners were cutting at the saddle of the
kicking animal. Tubby saw that, and bent again over Sammy.

"What is it, sir—what is it, Major? . . . Sammy!"

Sammy could not speak. He lay on the ground, scarcely
breathing. Kneeling beside him, you were helpless, foolish. . . .

But there was someone shouting and the clatter of hoofs as he galloped up to you, stones flying, the red dust spurting; Bert, strong and square and efficient; Bert, knowing just what to do, galloping up to get you out of it.

Just behind you the horse skidded, stumbled, fell and rolled over.

"God blast it," Bert said, staggered for two paces and fell across Sammy . . . "Get them bloody guns into action. . . ."

"Bert! Are you hit . . . you're not hit, are you?"

"Oh no," he said. "What in hell am I lying here for . . . get into action. . . ."

You got an arm round his waist, feeling the solid weight of him, the firm, rubbery body of a ferret; "I'll give you a hand. . . ."

"Get them guns into action. . . ."

"The Major . . ."

"Do as you're told . . . get them guns . . ." He rolled over, twitched, half rose, and lay still again.

Running down the hill, sliding, tripping, jumping from one boulder to the next, keeping your weight back and running aslant so as not to stumble forwards . . . (The physics laboratory at school—will it slide or topple? . . . work it out, draw a diagram, verify it with experiment: "you draw the picture, Benjy . . .")

There was the battery, littering the hillside, some of the mules stopped, some of them even grazing, some of them sliding on down into the valley. It was a mess; it was a rabble; it was pretty hopeless. Andrews had collected his subsection. Could he hear you, a voice thrown through cupped hands, in all this racket?

"Action rear . . . the best place you can find for it. . . ."

He was a fine man, Andrews; he might have been on the gun park; his hand touched his topi and shot up above his head in the drill acknowledgment of an order.

The Sergeant-Major was still on his horse, somehow galloping along the hillside. It wasn't possible what that horse was doing, feet slipping in all directions but he somehow remaining upright.

"Into action, Sergeant-Major. Alongside Sergeant Andrews. . . ." Your voice was lost in this tumult, the words gone, scarcely spoken, torn from your lips as if a high wind were blowing.

But the sergeant-major had heard and kicked his horse into a turn, facing straight down the hill, his horse sitting on its rump and skidding into the valley. Down there, the battery was taking shape in the hard sunlight, collecting itself into little groups, each making contact with its neighbor, the groups fusing then into larger globules; globules of mercury glistening in the sunlight; a globule of eight mules there—another gun completed. You could not hear the sergeant-major's voice, but you could see, as he reached the bottom, the process of assembly quicken.

Andrews' gun had taken shape. The loads had flicked together into a shining, snub-nosed howitzer. The mules, freed of their loads, were dragging their drivers down into the river bed. The sergeant-major, standing in his stirrups, cap raised high above his head, was collecting them together. Everywhere else, men and mules were struggling up the slope, drivers tugging at the reins, gunners beating from behind and pushing; some of the mules going up freely and the gunners clinging to their tails to get help up the steep places. Look at Dynamite, the unmanageable mule, burdened with the heaviest load, charging the slope like a mad elephant. . . .

Out on the left a Lewis gun started, then another. They were quite close, so it must be Daddy with the wagon line guns already in action, beating the infantry with their own weapon. There were horses, galloping along at the bottom of the valley, the battery staff, signalers, telephones . . . a director. That jolted him up, brought him to his senses. He wasn't the audience, to sit here watching; he was principal boy with his cue approaching and his lines not ready . . . lines of fire, an angle for the director . . . compass, glasses. . . .

Up the hill again, just below the path, a thorn bush, a boulder. A bullet smacked into it just as he got there, but from behind its shelter he scanned the hillside. Far above him a flutter of white, a shelf perhaps, a patch of scrub anyway, a thin veil of dust, of smoke, of suggested movement. He had it; the white was the clothes of natives. An angle with his compass, another back to Andrews, a sum, a simple subtraction. He was ready.

Plump, red-faced Hines (who had taken the lamps to the races, who had put his money on the grey mare and lost it) came toiling up the hill, giving out wire behind him, like a spider.

"My God, you're soft, Hines! You want a few runs before breakfast!"

Hines lay on the ground, oiled with sweat, his face streaked with sweat and the marks of burnt grass, his chest and stomach heaving. He unclipped his reel, unslung his telephone, wrenched out the cork of his water bottle and emptied it over the earth pin.

"Oh, good man . . . I'd never have thought of it."

Hines grinned silently, fighting for breath, conserving it for speech down the telephone. "Battery . . . battery . . . battery . . . four guns in action, sir."

The question of orders! Steady now, don't rush it—what did they say—"clear orders make good drill; good drill makes good shooting. . . ." And Daddy laughed at these clichés! "Time spent in reconnaissance is seldom wasted. . . ." No! That was the wrong one. TALD CAP MIPEF, the initial letters, the sequence of orders. He could hear Old Bandy talking. (Old Bandy, the gunnery instructor, grizzled and twinkling, who looked like a sheep dog and got a prize at a gymkhana for being the person most like his dog, which *was* a sheep dog.) "Gentlemen," he said, "you don't want magic. Learn it! But take it down if you want to. It might be useful one day . . ." TALD CAP MIPEF . . . magic letters. Target, Ammunition Line, Deflection, Concentration, and so on. . . .

"Shot one, sir. Shot two," Hines said to him, before he was aware that he had given out the orders. It seemed that, in the general measure of the dance, the guns had gone off without his direction; the two dull thuds and the whine of shells as they passed over; the burst, too high up the hillside, just a brown-black flurry of dust and rubble; the long, low *boom* . . . that followed long afterwards, showing that a shell had gone over the crest and burst in the valley beyond—all had happened, it seemed, apart from his agency. He lowered the range, adjusted the line and got his bracket. "Not much ammunition," he thought, "unless Daddy has done anything about the limbers. . . ."

"The Captain, sir . . ." Hines was saying.

Daddy was crawling along the hillside just above them. Streaming with sweat, he lay beside Tubby and watched the shooting.

"Nice work, old boy," he gasped. "Hitting 'em nicely."

"Hitting 'em in the beak," Tubby said with joy; "seeing 'em properly."

"God, it's hot. . . ."

"Yes," Tubby said. "I hadn't noticed it."

Daddy gave him a quick, curious glance. "It's like a race, isn't it?"

"Just like a race," Tubby said gratefully. For it was clear now, all that had happened in the last ten minutes. Then he remembered . . . "Bert . . . Sammy. . . ."

"I know," Daddy said.

"You've seen them?"

"I found them on the track . . . patched up Bert and got him under cover. *He'll* be all right. . . ."

"And Sammy?"

"Dead," Daddy said briefly.

✿ They had been told that they were to bivouac at the railhead; and, for the last two hours before they came to the town, the wide roadway of ever-thickening sand, scored with tracks and tire-marks, lined with dung and the relics of campfires, cut straight as the Legionaries through the spare scrub and the rare, drab and utterly shadeless trees that made up a harsh landscape. It was bad marching. Till early evening it had been hot, breathless, with the men plowing on, grim, silent, goading the mules, goading themselves with the knowledge that there was no alternative but to finish the journey. The heat of the day was piled up behind them, a last, fierce gesture. The night was long in coming.

At last, with no evident change, it became cool. The sun

was in their eyes and the shadows of men in front were long and sprightly. A breeze came through the thorns, touched sweat runs on cheek and forehead. Feet regained a rhythm; and quietly the day slipped away, leaving the trees and scrub as darker shadows in the twilight, the sand underfoot pale, with the memory of light in its texture.

Some time ago, Daddy had ridden on with a staff officer to be shown the site of their bivouac, and Tubby was left alone, the only officer with the Battery. He rode up and down the road doing what he could, getting a smile when he could, sometimes—following Bert's example—dismounting and shaming a sergeant by discovering a mule whose saddle was galling. At the halt, which came a little after nightfall, it was easy to tell the good men from the bad. And it was fine to see the sergeant-major, up and down the column, threatening the surly, mocking the frail, laying a confidential hand on the arm of a flagging sergeant, knowing that a touch of the familiar paid on these rare occasions; or the farrier, without his topi, his bare skull, beak nose and horsey teeth flashing in the torchlight, following quietly, helping with a shoe here or with a pad there, where nails had worked loose or where girth or crupper was rubbing. Patricks, the long, wet sergeant, lay on the ground with his men, numb with fatigue, idle until the sergeant-major roused him.

Inactivity allowed fatigue to ravage you; but if you kept doing things, the disease was powerless. And Andrews, knowing this, was as brisk as early morning, his men chaffing each other, finding something joyfully obscene in all that happened. Then Hicks came forward from the transport: "You'll be wanting a jersey, sir; best put it on . . . come on, sir." He wanted orders for the night: "I thought a nice tin o' sardines, sir, a tin o' tongue and we might end with a tin o' peaches . . . or would you as soon 'ave stew from the cookers?" And Murphy was fussing with the mare: "Ye little bitch . . . ye'd fussick yer soul out . . . 'Aven't ye 'ad enough, 'aven't ye?" All down the column, matches flared, torches flickered and here and there a pipe glowed in the darkness—for wasn't a pack battery the last stronghold of the pipe in the army? You could smell tobacco, sweat and leather. A laugh was as loud as a rattle. It was all swollen, as if you had turned the volume control of a wireless.

They were approaching the town and had come to the long suburbs. They moved on past groups of camels, barracked in twos and threes, the bitter scent of their cud coming sharply sometimes before their heads and thin, monstrous necks could be seen beyond the campfires. Long, scraggy, yellow dogs, all ribs and mange, ran out and barked and snapped; crowds of them slinking from behind the towering refuse dump, the lower slopes of which were scattered with the bones of cows, goats, camels. And more dogs came bounding across the cemetery— unpretentious mounds of sand, a rare mud tomb, a grass mat shelter harboring the old, old woman, the custodian of a holy sepulcher. Dogs and more dogs; and women running out, giggling, uttering their high-pitched trill of welcome, stinking of their rancid hair dressing, emetic but—some said—aphrodisiac.

Soon the town started with its undesigned clutter of native *tukuls;* lights shining through the conical roofs and through the grass mats that covered the doorways; more and more dogs, more and more women, naked or almost naked children, men standing silent, sometimes an arm lifted in greeting; an old hag in fits of laughter pointing a withered finger. A crowd of young girls, quite coy, their blue *tobs* drawn up about the lower parts of their faces. . . .

The huts changed slowly to mud dwellings, to a brick-built bank, a post office, away to the right the station. The shops, kept mostly by the semi-European races, Greeks, Syrians, Italians, occasionally a Turk, Arab or Egyptian trader, had the peasant squalor that is not particularly African, that can be found in the back streets of any small town around the Mediterranean; white, pale pink, pale chrome dwellings with iron-work balconies and slits of doors through which the lights shone indirectly. Black, grey, buff, sepia men were grouped in the doorways beside, and in front, of the piles of merchandise, bales of cloth, china, galvanized iron buckets and cooking utensils. . . . They looked out at the passing troops with little interest. Their muddy indifference to all that did not concern their living, the vignette of their heavily-shadowed selves, framed by the doorways which were black wounds in the pale façades of the buildings but which had in their depths the breath of the house, the light that came from far inside them— all this quickened Tubby with a curious tremor of fear, wonder, excitement. This, again, wasn't real. Where was reality? It was a play, and he was, at the same time, audience and player. And so were they. It was perfectly reciprocal. Neither concerned the other, in that there was no thread whatsoever between them. Neither was human to the other, neither was better than the other. They were apart, in different existences. There could be no blending, no common knowledge. Tubby and his men were lords of the earth; and the others, these dark ones, knew that this was so but felt no envy. They had a kingdom that the lords could not enter. They had lives which could only be touched superficially. As you stroke a dog, throw a stone at a cat, shoot a rabbit . . . life didn't matter; was nothing.

All this had happened before and would happen again. The tramp of tired soldiery; Athens . . . Rome . . . now England . . . all of no moment. Except that this hour was fragile, precious, easily shattered. And it filled the inner parts of you with all that had gone before and all that would come long after. This present was tiny, insignificant, vital; like yourself in hospital, lying between door and window, with a patch of sky over the grey building . . . "You know what I mean, sir?"

Sammy, walking beside you, knew all right. "Ourselves," he said, "our own moment, are nothing. You know that, don't you? It's all humanity, truth, spirit, love . . . love, Tubby, the spirit essence of the universe. . . ."

But no! He hadn't said that; that had been coming. He said it now for the first time. His feet were beside you. His pale face was lit now and again by the lights that filtered out from the doorways. His voice was patient. His words didn't break in upon your reason—you were too low and ignorant. They touched you like a kiss and went straight to the spirit with a promise of sadness, and of great beauty. You could weep for your lowliness, for your unreadiness to greet the spirit that swelled within you. "Yes, yes . . . but if only . . . it's hard to explain . . . you see what I mean, sir?"

"Beg pardon, sir," Sergeant Andrews was speaking behind him, "the Captain . . ."

Daddy was riding back, looking for the head of the Battery. "We go left here," he said, "through a particularly noisome locality."

🌸 The glow of the town was behind them; and they marched on in darkness, aiming at a single star that hung some way above the ground, still well in front of them. Slowly, very slowly, the star drew nearer, until they halted at last beneath it, and found it a hurricane lamp tied to a thorn tree.

"This is your promised land," Daddy said, "I hope you'll like it."

"I'll like anywhere where I can get horizontal."

"You're an optimist," Daddy said. "That's hours away. . . ." He became at once brisk and efficient, giving out orders, disposing the Battery for the night. "Sergeant-Major, Farrier . . . mule lines between those trees . . . two limbers and the wire for the horses . . . Subsection bivouacs . . . Tubby, take the animals to water, there's two pools in the *wadi*. Take Andrews."

This was a different man speaking. As captain and second in command of the battery, he hadn't had much need for this sort of blatant efficiency. His tasks were done darkly, with the quartermaster-sergeant and ledgers, bundles of blankets, bales of hay, cookers, water carts, ammunition limbers. And Daddy, even while still a subaltern, had filled the role of battery captain since long before Tubby joined them. So that the arrival of this new, precise and competent person came as a shock and started, for the first time, a crystallization of that unadmitted knowledge —that Sammy was no longer with them in body. Or rather—a hardening of the suspicion, the fear, that he had left them.

"Where the hell is that Sergeant-cook? Go on, Tubby, get *on* with it."

Plunging away from the lights, numb with fatigue, going off once more into the thick darkness, Tubby felt panic come up in him. Authority had drained away, it seemed. Muscles obeyed all right, but the mind longed to be given orders, simple orders, "Do this, go there, stop talking. . . ." Instead, there was this wicked darkness, full of confusion and impotence, shouts, oaths, and a hundred animals straining at their head-collars; one man to two thirst-ridden brutes of mules, who knew what they wanted; animals plunging down the banks of the *wadi*, steep banks; the thunder of hoofs, the trampling of scrub and branches; exhausted men pulled off their feet, not knowing what to try for, no one telling them, no one giving them orders. He felt helpless, frightened. "Come on, Tubby, give an order" (Sammy was speaking). "If there's any sort of muddle, always give an order. Right or wrong, it doesn't matter; so long as it's clear and possible . . . *how* many times have I told you?" Yes! That had always been Sammy's particular teaching.

His torch swept over the shambles, picked on the men he wanted: "Bombardier Price . . . Jones . . . Harrison . . . form up in subsections. Horses on the right, mules on the left . . . Murphy, get those grooms right out of it. And *stop* talking there. Andrews—stop them talking."

"You see, Tubby, a man has everything in him. There's nothing he can't do, nothing impossible. . . ."

All that evening, the feeling, the knowledge of Sammy's presence was unmistakable. There was nothing eerie about it, you understand; it wasn't a Spirit snooping around in your outer consciousness. It was Sammy himself, more vitally with you than ever he had been in his lifetime. You realized, then, how little his bodily presence had meant to you, how frail had been his bodily existence. He might have slipped away like that any time.

Their table was under the tree, two deck chairs by the table, a hurricane lamp on the table and another hanging from the tree's branches. Beyond this light that was intimately their own, was the night. Beyond the night were the dying fires and the lights of the sleeping battery. The servants brought dinner, two servants waiting on two, on three, on two officers . . . only Bert was absent. There was soup out of a tin, sardines, tinned tongue, tinned peaches . . . "Or would you sooner have stew, Daddy? . . . I'm not sure I wouldn't."

"I'm not particular."

"There'll be some left in the cookers . . . we could send Hicks. . . ."

It took them back across the span of the day. "Why shouldn't Bert have his tea . . . well, why shouldn't he . . . you're running the messing, or aren't you . . . but I *do* make a job of it. . . ." He had never known tiredness like this, that had hold of the mind, body and spirit. That lapped him and lifted him up, that cradled him in the night.

"He'll be all right, won't he?" Tubby asked.

"Bert?" Daddy answered, his voice firm and real. "Yes; I don't think it's much; he took one in the ribs and his leg's broken. Lost a lot of blood and so on. He's for home all right. . . . Before we're through we may envy him. . . ."

"What'll they do with us?" He didn't really care; but the question occurred and was put half-consciously.

"God knows," Daddy said. "But I'd wager it's something stupid. It's odds on they'll hide us away in some God-forsaken place and forget us. But I don't mind. I'm past caring . . . for tonight anyway."

"We shall miss Bert."

"We shall miss him with the animals," Daddy said. "They'll want watching. You don't realize how much he did, till you haven't got him."

"No . . . he was good with the animals. . . ."

"Hicks," Daddy called into the night. "Tell the sergeant-major I'd like a word with him. And bring another chair, will you?"

The sergeant-major came almost at once. He didn't seem tired. His power and glory were in no way diminished, were no less than when he had last come out of the darkness to talk with Sammy. "A good man, the sergeant-major . . . no; a good sergeant-major . . . One an' the same thing to my way o' thinking. . . . No, Bert, not to your way of *thinking*, to your way of *living;* to the army that is so fine a way of living and so dangerous an animal; to the army that gobbles you up, Tubby, and takes yourself away from you. Just as you have to lose self to find truth . . . to find love. . . ."

The sergeant-major sat down gingerly and Daddy gave him

a cigarette, pushing across the matches. For a moment they sat in silence, looking away into the darkness at the orderly ring of dying fires that marked the bivouacs. Only an occasional whispered word came to them, and the soft thumping noises that belong to tethered animals. The Southern Cross was just above the tree-tops, permanent, indestructible. A light wind stirred the tablecloth and blew to them the scent of wood smoke. The sentry passed, his footsteps muffled in the sand, his tread solemn.

"Sergeant-Major," Daddy said, still looking into the darkness, "we must fix up about this funeral. It ought to be early . . . as we're not moving, I think we'll do it properly. . . ."

"Yes, sir," the sergeant-major said, "and when will you see the defaulters?"

Daddy did not answer. It seemed that he hadn't heard the question.

"Beg pardon, sir . . ."

"Yes. What was it you said, Sergeant-Major?"

"When will you see the defaulters?"

"What defaulters?"

"There's the two men I spoke to the Major about this morning. Fighting, sir. And there's two men been at it again at the first halt, sir. . . ."

"Oh . . ."

"It's getting bad, sir. If I might make a suggestion . . ."

"No, Sergeant-Major," Daddy said. "There'll be no field punishment. I'll see them after the funeral."

Sammy took several days going. It was as if he were packing up, and you met him hanging around odd corners. "That mule, Kitty . . ." he said. "Annabella, sir," you corrected him; he always made this mistake. "Kitty is the little chestnut in D subsection. . . ." "I remember. She's looking a lot better. . . ." Or he might be on that patch of clear ground you had made into gun parks. "You *must* see these sergeants keep their sights tested, Tubby. It's a subaltern officer's job, you know. Patricks' gun was shooting all over the place the other morning. . . ." He was tidying it all up, saying good-by to his friends, and even the sergeant-major met him. "The Major won't have *that*, sir," he said once to Tubby; and then stammered and coughed, for the first time embarrassed.

The funeral made no difference. Sammy watched it and, as often at funerals, wouldn't take it seriously. He was always ribald on these occasions, so long (he said) as the sorrowing relatives couldn't see or hear you. And now the only sorrowing relatives were the hundred and fifty members of a war-strength battery. And, when his charger came along with the boots back to front in the stirrups . . . "I'm quite sure Hicks had a hand in that polish," he said. "My man could never get them like that, not even when the General was coming. . . ."

That awful ragged volley, with a few shots going off long after the rest had finished. "That'll make Bert angry. It always does. He can never forget the depot . . . but it's no good; our chaps are gunners, not riflemen. You can't set a mason to mending lavatories." But he was quite annoyed about the trumpeters. "I don't see why they can't sound the Last Post decently. They'll make a worse mess of Reveille. Have a word with the sergeant-major. . . ."

As the days went on, you saw him less and less about the place. His voice grew fainter, and he spoke less often.

"Don't go yet, Sammy." (You had called him that to his face for the last day or two.)

"I've got to go sometime, old boy . . . it's a fine battery."

"But, don't you see, sir, when you go, you're taking the ground from under my feet; you're taking the inside out of me."

"I'm taking nothing . . . I'll leave you your inside, Tubby." Of course he was smiling, pale and happy as usual.

"But, sir—one moment, sir—don't you see what it's going to mean? Before—that is, when I joined the battery—it was all so easy. I was happy; I didn't have to worry. Then you started talking, and all the old ideas went to pieces."

"The old lack of ideas, wasn't it, Tubby?"

"Yes. That was it all right. You made me dissatisfied with myself. You told me that it was the first stage of a long journey. You took me a few paces. You told me what I *could* be . . . but you didn't tell me how to be it; or how to know the main road from the side tracks. . . ."

"But you're a *man*, Tubby. Not a mule to be led. You have to find the road for yourself. I couldn't have shown it you."

"I'll take the wrong way without you—just like the infantry did. I'll slip back again. I'll have to retreat; and you've left me nothing to fall back on."

"No! You never slip back; I can promise you that. You may mark time for a few years; and I told you that from the start, didn't I? But—when the time comes—somebody, something, turns up to give you a push in the right direction. . . . But it may be hardship and sorrow; it may be adversity. You must be ready for that. Or it may be Daddy, Benjamin, Lydia . . . you've got some good friends, you know, Tubby. And there's yourself. Don't forget him, will you?"

"You're leaving me nothing . . ."

"Oh, yes I am. Keep on feeling things, keep on noticing things. Don't you remember in hospital, what that Welsh woman said? It doesn't really hurt. It doesn't really matter. Nothing matters, except *you*. Not what you *are*, but what you can be, will be. . . ." The voice was very faint now. "It's truth and love, Tubby, that matter. . . ."

"Don't go yet, sir. . . ."

"I have to be off sometime. . . ."

It was nothing but a whisper.

Chapter 10 AT THE FORT, TO WHICH THEY HAD BEEN sent shortly after the death of Sammy, there was no recreation but dispute, no assuagement but whisky. You couldn't think; there was no time for thinking. You ate, and with a swollen belly you tried to sleep. When sleep had at last come, it was time to rise, to attempt some sort of languid work, to eat, to drink and to go to bed again. And through all the hours you sweated. The sweat didn't only take out the whisky; it drew your powers, your mind and your spirit out of your damp, flabby body, letting them waft in the current of the fan away from the gloom of your room to the wicked sunlight outside. So that nothing remained but a large, beefy lump of sweating flesh that suffered discomfort, misery, pain, but no other experience. That was the way of living in this place to which, for no apparent reason and for no crime that they could identify, they had, three months earlier, been committed.

"God blast the generals. . . ."

Sometimes Daddy, with outstretched arms, shouted this into the night. More often—to start with, at any rate—he attempted a bright, irreverent mood that would keep up their spirits. "This fort," he would say, looking up at the battlements, "of vast antiquity, possibly sixth or seventh century . . . additions made from time to time, the most notable about 1860. . . . Observe the happy confusion of pseudo-mameluke and neo-Gothic ornament. And our neo-Farady Searchlight! Ample scope for archaeological research here, Tubby. How would you place, for instance, the stained-glass panel in the doorway of the officers' earth closet? A bright thought of the Royal Engineers, about 1910, I fancy. Altogether a little gem of military architecture."

You couldn't really surmise when, why, how or by whom the fort had first been built or last been occupied. The older inhabitants of the village, a mile away, said that the soldiers had left in the year of the big lion, and the big lion had come the year that the soldiers left. It had clearly been disused for a decade at least, and was so verminous that the battery had lived for a month under canvas while the place was scrubbed and lime-washed and while two listless Royal Army Medical Corps corporals and one mutinous private made a pretence at fumigation.

"The R.A.M.C. all over," Daddy said, "just the wrong way round to the rest of the Army; two corporals to an orderly, four sergeants to a corporal, and about twenty ruddy doctors to four sergeants. . . ." He emptied his glass and carefully filled it again with whisky and tepid water. "I asked one of the corporals what he knew about fumigation. He told me that he belonged to an Anglo-Catholic church and used to light the incense. . . ."

The R.A.M.C. detachment disappeared on the train one morning; the senior corporal came to Daddy and said that he was going. Ordnance demanded return of the tents and there was no alternative but to occupy this fort whose existence seemed allegorical, heraldic, but not otherwise credible. It neither marked nor defended anything; no town, no strategical point of the least importance. The village, from which the barking of dogs could be heard at nighttime, entirely peaceable, controlled by a Sheik, a native doctor and a native schoolmaster, was on the Red Sea Railway along which a train ran once weekly. But the fort had obviously been built before steam had come to East Africa. There was no military or civil station near it. The next white man was sixty miles to the east and had paid one courtesy visit; the first town was a hundred miles in the opposite direction.

"It's sensible," Daddy said, "and I can understand it. A staff officer, or perhaps a native clerk, or perhaps a general—yes, it was certainly a general—received two disturbing informations on one unfortunate morning. They told him of an unwanted fort and an unwanted battery. It fitted perfectly. . . ." He filled his glass again.

In between whiles, Daddy's tempers were quite unpredictable; and, as each entirely uneventful week followed one that—in retrospect—seemed a burden too great for man, his unprovoked outbursts of rage against Tubby became more frequent. Even so, Tubby admired, and in a way loved him. For he had to love someone. The instinctive side of him predominant, he was like a dog, having to find a master on whom to depend, from whom to get an illusion of safety, around whom his life could center.

Sammy was gone; Daddy remained to him.

The days had no beginning and no end. They ended at four in the morning and started a couple of hours later, just after sunrise. Or they ended at two in the afternoon to recommence at half-past four, two hours before sunset. They were double days, each little twin as heavy and monstrous in pain as a week of normal living. And the officers and men became babies, waking and sleeping and feeding, impotent in their discomfort and with no one to comfort them.

Sometime after midnight—if there had been no quarrel to curtail the evening—Daddy and Tubby parted on the common veranda that served as living room and dining room and joined their two bedrooms. There had been a happy, half-drunken imbecility that started one evening and became a ritual: "Well . . . lovely ladies," one wished the other.

"Like hell!" you answered. "Good-night, sleep tight."

"Mind the mosquitoes don't bite."

"Like hell!"

But they always did, of course, even though for three or four hours you hunted sleep around the inside of a closely-fastened mosquito net. You flirted with sleep all that time, pleaded with her. Or rather she did the flirting, demanding all and giving nothing; always dancing just out of reach and revealing the most seductive vistas; until, just before the first light, she'd give herself at last, and with utter abandon, lapping you, fondling you, letting you sink down, down into her sweet embraces. . . . Then Hicks was beside your bed with a cup of tea, with his old-family-servant pretences and with his barrack-room joke all ready. "Rise and shine, sir. Six o'clock of a nice sunny morning." And the little black boy, Ibrahim, pattered in with shaving water.

Going out on to the veranda, barefooted, carrying a cup of tea, smoking a cigarette, the memories of sleep dying, its taste growing less bitter, you looked across the compound. The sun came over the main gateway, the squat arch surmounted by a concrete way on which the sentry worked out his time. On one side of the gate were the guardroom, stores, magazines, gun parks; on the other, the barrack rooms and cookhouse. The sun, coming between the steel girders of the searchlight tower and through the branches of the single tree which grew from the sand of the compound, was full in your eyes. In an hour it would be immediately above you; but, now, you turned to right or left to see the long, sloping ramps that led up to the battlements—real battlements, in the best toy-soldier tradition. Then you might step out from the veranda to feel the still cool sand in your toes, to send the tame gazelle scampering away, unafraid but frolicsome, and to throw a friendly stone at the monkey who swung himself into the tree, or at the macaw who scolded from its lowest branches. If you walked out to argue with the bird, you could look back at your own bedrooms, the battery offices next door, and the sergeants' and bombardiers' Mess adjoining. Above that block of buildings, the ramparts were continued with machine-gun emplacements and, in each angle, the long-nosed, old-fashioned, 4.7 guns on their fixed mountings.

The armament of the fort was all obsolete and must have been in fashion at the time of Gordon's death, if not earlier. "That's never a machine gun," Daddy said, when he first inspected his command. "It's the gatling that jammed for Mr. Newbold . . . Sergeant-Major, what is a gatling anyway . . . send for the fitter, he'll tell us."

Locked behind four doors, steel, each with a separate key, there were three hundred rifles, mostly of Belgian manufacture, a thousand cases of very old small-arms ammunition and two crates of cavalry sabers marked "not to be opened." And outside, in the few acres of orderly sand within the barbed-wire entanglements, there was a small cemetery, a fallen-down revolver range and a disused midden.

When you had blinked long enough at the morning and thought how the cloudless sky, the soft haze, the sloping sunlight—if they were only rolled up into an entity of time, isolated from what had gone before and what would follow immediately—might have been summer at Calcott, you went back to the wash house behind the bedrooms and rubbed yourself down with tepid water. You shaved and dressed quickly; shorts, shirt, shoes and stockings, and topi; always, from six in the morning till sunset, that hated topi. You went, then, across the compound and out through the gateway, to take the animals on exercise around the prescribed route within range—according to regulations—of a bored Lewis gun detachment who mounted watch on the parapet.

You were out for an hour while, back in the fort, Daddy found ways to divert the rest of the Battery. The gunners pretended "alarms" and scampered up and down the ramps, while the sergeant-major timed them; or they pretended fire and unreeled long-decayed hose and made chains of buckets; always pretending some impossible eventuality; pretending so hard that they grew like children, naughty and quarrelsome.

"Eh, Sergeant," a tall gunner argued, "but it's *my* turn to have a hold on the nozzle."

"Give it him up then, Wilkins," said Sergeant Patricks.

Breakfast was long drawn out so as to shorten the morning; for it was hard to keep the children occupied. Gunners and drivers were taught to signal, and signalers were practised in gun drill. But none of them liked it. "It's the guild spirit," said Daddy. "They're born trade-unionists. . . ." And they hated the thought that others could acquire their skill so lightly; and still more they hated that, for the same pay, they should be asked to become doubly proficient. Everyone was happier when, in the full, devastating heat of noon, the trumpet called the drivers to stables and the gunners mustered on the gun parks to repolish their already overburnished equipment.

After lunch—dinner it is in the army—the whole garrison, except for the guard and the pickets, went to bed to sleep off the afternoon. Every room was heavily shuttered; and the fans, which worked off the same plant as the searchlight and the lighting system, revolved slowly. Often they failed; but sometimes they made a state of semi-consciousness just possible.

Though it was afternoon, the heat grew and grew to reach a peak some three hours or less before sunset. Even the tame monkey and the tame gazelle and the queer, unclassified parrot, discovered what shade they could and huddled there. You could walk right up to them and stroke them.

❦ He lay flat and still, eyes closed, a towel round his belly to save him from colic. Directly above him, the fan turned slowly, as big as an airplane propeller. The room was dark but not cool. Outside, the day had halted; the afternoon wasn't hurrying.

Neither awake nor asleep, he was aware that a fly, penetrating the mosquito net, had alighted, was walking between his eyebrows, down the ridge of his nose and across to his cheek where it met a trickle of sweat from his forehead. He brushed it aside at last and rolled over.

Propping himself on an elbow, he groped for a cigarette. It was just light enough to read in the shuttered bedroom and he picked up the book that was beside him, a limp, sham-leather-covered edition of the Ingoldsby Legends, brought from England because (somewhere in a story) someone had said that, if he had to make do with three books on a desert island, they would be Shakespeare, the Bible and the Ingoldsby Legends. He had read Shakespeare, the Padre would have a Bible, and the book he had brought had been a confirmation present. Even at the fort he had not been able to bring himself to read it. As he turned over the pages now, he remembered that, when he had been packing, active service had seemed quite as ro-

mantic as a desert island—and had certainly turned out no
better. The Ingoldsby Legends had, at least, a number of sepia
illustrations with captions underneath them:

> "*The Maiden is stately and tall,*
> *And stately she walks in her pride . . .*"

It was a blond woman, not very appetizing, not at all like
Lydia. But the mere representation of a female form was
provocative. He wanted a woman, and he wanted Lydia; and
nowadays he wanted them both for the same purpose. He
wanted comfort, repose, intimacy. And, failing everything else,
he wanted his letters answered.

She could scarcely be blamed, he had to admit; for recently
he hadn't given her much encouragement or much to go on.
For it wasn't done to play upon a woman's pity, to paint your
misery without a certain flippancy or cynicism of which he was
not master. It was better, fairer, to take a drink or two and write
out a few pages about the sunshine and the sand, the mules,
the horses, native customs, and what the women wore, how they
carried their babies. For it wasn't possible to be intimate and
secretive at the same time, nor to write of native customs in one
line and to devote the next to telling a woman how you loved
her. And there was no room for love in his conscious emotions;
only for self-pity, boredom and the dull pain of a dog that has
been beaten and curls itself up on its misery. So his letters grew
duller and hers less frequent. So she hadn't written for a month
and was fading back into a wistful memory; fading and growing
brighter, a jewel set in the past, irrecoverable, indescribably
beautiful.

He put the letters aside—the small pile of them that had
been inside the book, and got up off the bed, the towel clinging
to his loins, the inside of his thighs sticking together. When he
opened the door, the heat and brilliance of the afternoon
slapped at him. He winced and stepped back, and the heat
stroked him then. So long as you cringed beneath that heavy,
passive stillness, it wouldn't hurt you. You could be like the
gazelle and the monkey, huddled in the fringe of shadow; or
like the parrot, sunk into itself on the window sill of Daddy's

bedroom. In this place, you had to know when you were beaten.

They were all beaten at the fort; even the sentry across the compound, who plodded up and down his beat, topi pushed back, spine-pad unbuttoned, rifle aslant, his forearm not swinging but hanging listlessly, its fingers plucking at the shorts that were stuck to his buttocks. He showed a flicker of interest and turned his head as Tubby shouted for Ibrahim.

"*Schei* . . . tea. Hurry, blast you!"

The small boy squeaked a reply and wandered round to the cookhouse.

Later, Daddy padded into the room, native slippers hanging from his toes, also naked except for the towel about his middle. He was red and his flesh was heavy. His hair stood up from his head, showing how bald he was going. He did not smile but walked across and took a cigarette from the box on top of the yellow-varnished chest of drawers that was part of the Government furniture.

Tubby said nothing. Every day Daddy came and stole his cigarettes and took them without comment.

"Where are the matches?" Daddy asked the question crossly, a man with a right to a grievance.

Tubby threw across the box without speaking and Daddy broke the last two trying to light them. "Why do we have to have these lousy matches?" he asked. "Why can't you order us some decent ones?"

"I find them all right," Tubby said. "They're my private ones, by the way. They suit me. We can have something different for the mess if you don't like them."

"They're your private ones, are they?"

"Yes. The same as the cigarettes. I pay for them. I put them on my own mess bill."

"I don't really like these cigarettes anyway," Daddy said.

"Don't you?" Tubby said. "I'd formed a different opinion."

Neither of them was really cross yet. They were just sparring together pleasantly, unpleasantly, in a way that was dangerous.

"Blasted Scotsman," Daddy said; "grudge me an odd cigarette, do you?"

"An odd cigarette! You smoke as many of mine as I do."

Daddy ground the half-finished cigarette into Tubby's saucer and dropped it into the dregs that were in the teacup.

"Blast your soul," Tubby said. "I was just going to pour out another cup. Why can't you throw it on the veranda?"

"You can have another cup," Daddy said, going to the doorway. He shouted for Ibrahim and told him in Arabic to fetch a fresh cup for the noble officer. His knowledge of Arabic was a source of irritation to Tubby anyway. Ibrahim brought the fresh cup and Tubby did not touch it.

"Go on," Daddy said. "Pour yourself out the tea you wanted."

"It's cold now. I don't want it cold," Tubby answered.

"It's a lot colder than it was two minutes ago."

"It's just enough to make the difference."

"Like hell it is. Go on; pour yourself a cup like you said you wanted."

Tubby pushed the cup further away across the table. "I tell you I don't want it. You've put me off it, blast you. If you've got to be disagreeable to someone, why can't you stand in front of the looking glass in your own bedroom?"

Daddy walked deliberately to the doorway and gazed out across the compound. He didn't turn round.

"You make me sick," he said deliberately.

"It's pretty mutual," Tubby said.

"It is, is it?"

"As far as I'm concerned."

"It's like that, is it?"

"Just like that."

"Well, you'd bloody well better pull your socks up," Daddy said. "You're too bloody idle and I'm getting sick of it."

"*You're* getting sick of it? Christ! How do you think I feel about it?"

"I don't care how you feel. It doesn't concern me. What concerns me is the way you don't do your job and the Battery suffers."

"A lot the Battery suffers from anything I don't do," Tubby said. "I do all you tell me and a lot more that I think of besides . . ."

"That's the trouble. You think too bloody much and you aren't made for it."

"Will you get out of here?" Tubby said, speaking quietly.

"If you'd stop thinking and just do what you're told you'd be a better officer."

"Will . . . you . . . get . . . out . . . of . . . here . . ." Tubby said again, speaking very slowly.

"I'll get out just as soon as you stop thinking and do as I tell you. That's what you're here for, isn't it?"

"Get out, will you?"

"Is that what you're here for, or isn't it?"

Tubby stood up off the bed. He stood facing Daddy. "I'm a lot bigger than you," he said, "and you're fat and flabby and drink-sodden and pretty disgusting. Will you get out or do I sling you out? Make up your mind, and do it quickly."

Daddy was dead white. He stood very still and looked hard at Tubby. His eyes were small, as usual at these times, screwed down by the hate behind them. "That's a threat, is it?" he said.

"That's a threat," Tubby said in the same low voice. Then he broke. He clenched his fist and shouted. "Get the hell out of here, will you. Get out. Get out quick. Get out of here before I hurt you."

"You're not quite yourself," Daddy said gently. "You're ill, I think. . . . I'll send for that black doctor chap from the village. You'd better lie down . . . I'll leave you now. . . . I'm sorry you're not well, Tubby."

Daddy went out and let the door swing to on its spring behind him. Tubby lay on the bed, the sweat ice-cold on his forehead. Where the edge of the towel bit into the flesh of his belly, he saw that the muscles were heaving. He could not remember quite what had happened. His throat was tight and he was out of breath as if he had been running. He felt slightly sick. He pulled his hand across his forehead to wipe off the sweat and flung his arm away from him. It hit the table, knocked it over and spilled the tray onto the floor, the teapot and cup and saucer smashing into a welter of china fragments and milk and tea, with the tea soaking into the lumps of sugar, into the book and into Lydia's letters.

🌿 For a brief time it was cooler and then, as the night closed down and the room became completely dark, the heat enveloped him again. He switched on the light and, sitting up, lit another cigarette. He had lain flat on his bed for four hours and he thought that he had been sleeping. The light flickered and went out. That sapper detachment! Why couldn't they look after their batteries?

In a few minutes, Hicks came in, bringing a candle. "'Ere we are, sir," he said. "Them sappers again . . . the sergeant-major's 'avin' a word with the corporal . . ." He put the candle down and looked at the spilled table. "My word, sir," he said, "we 'ave 'ad a go at the teatray." He stooped to clear it up and then remembered: "Beg pardon, sir, I was to give you this with the Captain's compliments . . . dinner's at ten, the Captain said, unless you was wanting anything different." He handed over a screwed-up fragment of paper.

Tubby took the note and turned it over in his fingers, not bothering much about it, feeling very calm and uninterested. At last he opened it.

It was only four lines, in Daddy's small, square writing, neat except that he could not end his words correctly.

"I'm very sorry," it said. *"It's this heat or something.*
We're both a bit mad but it was entirely and unreservedly my fault.
Please come up and help me finish the whisky."

Tubby swung his legs over the bed and rubbed his face in his hands as though washing it. There was a door at the back of his room that led to a wash house, shared by himself and Daddy. It was a flat piece of sloping and grooved concrete with a hip bath on it, and there were three or four large cans of water. He sluiced them over himself. The water was never cold, but he rubbed it into his hair and down his arms and thighs and saw his flesh gleaming under the water in the light of the candle. The muscles still moved under a loose skin, the fine rippling movement of muscles; there was still some comfort in the last stronghold of his body.

He pulled on the dinner clothes that gave protection against insects and against the cool breeze that sometimes, though rarely, drifted from off the desert: high-necked jersey, grey flannel trousers, calf-high mosquito boots of soft leather, a Government issue.

He went up, then, to the parapet, taking the long, sloping ramp on which rails were laid for hauling trucks of ammunition to the gun emplacements. When he reached the top, the sky was swept with a disarray of stars that had no completion. The sand of the desert was pale below him like the mist that hangs over a river at evening. The concrete causeway and the battlements held the light from the sky, but the courtyard of the fort was in deep shadow. At the far end of the ramparts, the table of drinks and the two deck chairs and the lamp on the table were like a jewel set in the darkness, the central piece of the night.

He heard the men talking quietly from the veranda outside the barrack rooms. From the sergeants' Mess there was a shout and the crash of upset glasses. The dogs were barking in the village.

Daddy was sitting quite still, looking out across the desert, a glass in his hand, his arm on the table.

You walked quietly in the thin leather soles of mosquito boots, and Tubby went along slowly, the picture of Daddy at the table developing further details as he drew nearer. Daddy's face was still and unhappy. You could think it either clever and melancholy, or heavy and stupid. You could think it anything. It was rather too big for the short, heavy body and, superficially, had no significance whatsoever. You could hate it or love it or look through it. It was a window. Or it was nothing but a conveniently plastic medium for all the things that were Daddy; in the same way that Daddy himself seemed to be a medium for forces that were battling inside him but without his knowledge.

"Keep on noticing things, Tubby . . ." The voice came from all round him, from the stars, the desert. "Keep on noticing . . ."

"Sammy!"

"You see, Tubby, man has everything inside him—good, bad and neutral. If he's only got the strength to choose what he wants out of himself . . . and Daddy's always truthful—

remember we said that in hospital? Most people aren't. What most people say and do doesn't come straight from inside them; it's filtered on the way; they try to show off; to make you think well of them—or ill, sometimes. Truth in itself is good, even if it's a medium for evil . . . you see that, don't you?" The voice was very faint. "Truth and love, Tubby. . . ."

"One moment, sir . . . Sammy. . . ."

"Whisky or gin? The water's luke-warm," Daddy was saying.

The table was in a corner of the causeway, close to the Western gun and right up against the battlements. The light from the candle lamp, and from the hurricane lamp that stood on the parapet, killed the radiance of that star-filled night. They were enclosed within the night, sharing this principality of lamp and candle, this island that might have been anywhere in the dark ocean. Only small sounds, rare, staccato, broke into their intimacy with a warning—unheeded—that their solitude was illusion. It was a dream, in any case, complete enough to allow either hate or love, but to deny indifference. Two men alone in a world cannot ignore each other.

"I'm sorry, Tubby," he said at once. "I'm really sorry."

"No . . . don't . . ."

You didn't want apologies, not for themselves, their formality; only if they could lift the curtain of hate from between you. You wanted the intimacy to flood back; the two cogwheels of your lives to click together and to run smoothly in the lubricant of your mutual liking. You wanted it warm and easy, as it could be; so that you need not mind your words and actions; so that neither could hurt the other, each knowing that hurt was not intended. It was like that again as soon as the first words had been spoken.

"I'm really sorry, old boy. I hope you'll forget it."

"Of course," Tubby said; "it's forgotten already." And this wasn't just an easy way out of it. This was the truth. In that moment on the ramparts, all hate and anger had been swept out of him. He was clean again in a way that no scrubbing in the wash house could accomplish. But Daddy couldn't know that.

"There's no 'of course' about it," he insisted. "It isn't so easy . . . one doesn't forget that sort of thing in a moment." He spoke harshly; it was himself he was chiding this time.

"I forget things very quickly. It's all past and done with—I promise you."

"And," Daddy said, "it wasn't true, of course . . . it wasn't true what I said. You mustn't think I meant it."

"No!" Tubby said, with a sudden, unusual resolve to see this thing out, to follow it to some unimagined conclusion. "It's forgotten all right; but it was true, Daddy; you meant it."

The moon was rising, throwing the long shadow of the gun across the ramparts. The courtyard of the fort was painted a black well behind them, the tree rearing its head out of the darkness, the pale, sad light touching the topmost branches. Across the compound, they heard the sergeant of the guard changing the sentries. Then, for a pure moment, there was silence again; so that, when the dogs started barking in the distant village, the size of the night was overwhelming.

You couldn't describe it, or what it did to you—the size of an African night. Tremendous beyond words, beyond the kingdom of thought, it filled you and overfilled you with emotion. The shell of you was too fragile for such potent contents. You were bursting those bonds that kept you of the earth, that kept you human; that tied spirit and body. Spirit without called to spirit within. Apart from the spirits, beside the spirits, you were trivial.

"Tubby—you mustn't think I meant it," Daddy said, with the pleading of the world in his voice.

But lies couldn't live in that night; only the truth survives eternity.

"No," Tubby said; "you meant it all right. Part of you meant it."

"Part of me. . . ." (What anguish the spirit can suffer.)

"Perhaps only a small part. . . ."

The words died in the silence; a flame drawn out by the wind and then extinguished.

"A small part," Daddy said. "Yes. A part of me meant it. A terrible, hateful part that doesn't bear contemplation, that takes charge sometimes . . . but it isn't *Me*. . . ." (It was a cry wrung out of him.) "It's the evil of all mankind; the evil, ghastly spirit that lives in this body, that breaks loose and drives all the decent things that are *Me* shuddering into a corner." He leaned forward, gazing out over the parapet. "Some people are very good, Tubby, and some are very bad, and most are neither one nor the other. But I'm both, you see; and that's the private hell that I have to suffer. It's war all the time, I can tell you. I'm only a battlefield—nothing more than that—with every discordant element fighting within me . . . no peace, no respite— only a constant battlefield. Can you imagine it?" His voice rang in the night, but it had died before Tubby answered.

"And aren't we all . . ." he said, the words escaping him, "isn't it the same for all of us? With some people, I suppose, the fighting is pretty stiff, goes on all the time more or less. With others, with most of us—with the nice, pleasant, easy people, who don't care a lot about truth, who'll do anything for the sake of quietness—a sort of truce exists. We agree to a compromise. But if you can't compromise, if it's nothing but fight to a finish and unconditional surrender . . . if it has to be like that, there's no way out but to face it. You see what I mean, Daddy?"

The heavy face looked up quickly, the moonlight shining on it, hiding and revealing. It wasn't Daddy at all perhaps. The pale glow showed you new features—hope, fear, wonder—but flattened out the common elements, chin, mouth, nose, forehead. There was something canine in the pleading eyes that the light shone into.

"It might have been Sammy speaking . . ." he said with wonder, with longing.

One of those quick breezes that come from the desert blew in and fluttered the tablecloth. It broke up the night for an instant.

"Why?" Tubby asked, bewildered. "I didn't say anything. . . ."

"And you didn't know. . . ." Daddy murmured, speaking to himself, to someone who was standing in the night, waiting behind Tubby; speaking so quietly that most of his words were lost to your immediate consciousness. "When you learn to know, Tubby—to know yourself—there'll be a man come out of you. But it won't be a soldier. . . ." He paused and the silence

helped him. "It won't be easy, Tubby, because one day you'll
turn out to be all that you thought you weren't, all that you
didn't want to be . . . it'll be harder for you than for most, because of the way they've taught you, the way they haven't
taught you. Without your intellect trained, with all that part
of you undernourished . . . But then Sammy hadn't got much
intellect; nobody would call him clever. Or had he gone past
his intellect, built something new out of it? I never understood
that . . . but it's hard anyway, you know, to be one of the company that use adversity. Sweet uses! One of the men that climb
the mountain, stop and draw breath—perhaps—at each obstacle, but never go round it. It's a hard journey and God knows
why I was made so that I had to choose it. And God knows why
Sammy faced you to the rock and made you climb it. There
are such easy paths in the valley for happy people like you . . .
and if only I thought it was all leading somewhere—instead of
believing that it ends in darkness, in peace and oblivion, in no
more struggles, no more defeats, no more victories . . . a hateful
thought, isn't it? If only I had Sammy's faith, his knowledge
. . . his love."

There were sounds of footsteps on the rampart; hobnailed
boots and pattering feet, Hicks and Ibrahim bringing dinner.

"Food!" Tubby said. "Jove, but I'm hungry!"

   ❧ Hicks cleared the last of the dinner, replaced the whisky
and prepared to leave them.

"Beg pardon, sir," he asked, "what time in the morning?"

"The same as always," Daddy said.

"It's mail day, sir," Hicks reminded him.

"So it is. Then it will be half-past five for Mr. Windrush. Six
for me, as usual."

Then he was gone, his boots scraping the concrete ramp,
stumping across the compound, the door of his small room
shutting with a loud bang behind him.

The three-quarter moon was high above them and they were
alone again.

"You see, Tubby, it isn't fair," Daddy started. "How can
you hope for two men like ourselves—for any two men—to live

together in a fort like this without quarreling? It just isn't
possible. When you come to think of it, the relationship that's
forced on us is very nearly connubial. The details and trivialities
of the life that we have to share grow and grow until they're
just as important as they are in matrimony. A woman can't
bear the way a man wipes his mouth before he kisses her. And
he goes wild at the sight of her sitting up in bed in a hairnet.
It's the same with us. You're sick to death of the way I steal
your cigarettes—it's such a harmless, pathetic little failing—and
I'm driven to madness by your blasted imperturbability; the
way you just won't acknowledge things until a pin is driven
right into you.

"But even then we're at a disadvantage, you see. Because—
just as it is with married people—the habits of one of us become
a violent irritant to the other. But we don't have the assuagement of the equally violent reconciliation. We can't start again
with a night in bed together. We can't make it up with an outburst of passion. . . ."

He filled up his glass again; it had been a new bottle at the
start of the evening, but now it was half empty. As the drink
began to take effect, it was like a wind changing its direction.
It might take Daddy anywhere.

"It's a wicked, cruel, immeasurably false relationship for
two people like ourselves," he said; "both of us such essentially
male characters. . . ."

"And the men?"

"You miss the point," Daddy said crossly. "There's relief
in numbers, of course. And, what's more, God knows what's
going on in the barrack rooms. . . ." He emptied his glass—his
third since dinner—and looked at Tubby, a quick, furtive
glance, as if he were wondering how much further he could
carry the argument. But his words seemed to have found no
target. They had glanced off Tubby, or missed him.

"Oh! I don't know," Tubby said. "It might be worse, I
suppose."

"Could it?" Daddy said, his voice rising. "Could it? One
thing after another up against you. This damned frustration!
Everything frustrates you. Don't you find it?"

"Perhaps I do," Tubby admitted untruthfully. He hadn't thought much about frustration. Life could be peace, pain, bewilderment, yearning—but not frustration. He had never felt that the world was his enemy.

"You feel it the same, do you?" Daddy went on, hunting out an argument. "I don't see why you should . . . I don't see that you've been frustrated all along the line like I have."

"No," Tubby said. "No, I don't see that I have. I don't really see that *you* have, for that matter."

"Of course you don't. You don't know much about me. You just take me for a bad-tempered, half-witted sort of chap. . . ."

"Not half-witted. . . ."

"If you like, not half-witted; but you can't know how the bad temper gets me. It gets me so that I've no control. I just don't know what I'm doing."

"You let it get you," Tubby said suddenly, at last deciding that he might as well join in the orgy.

"That's right, I let it get me. I can't stand the way I'm always frustrated. It's frustration every way I turn."

"*I* don't frustrate you. I do what you say—and so does everyone else as far as I can see."

"That isn't the way you've got to look at it," Daddy said. (He had filled up his glass and was drinking again.) "It's just that all my life I've been thrown about and made to do utterly unreasonable things till it's become impossible . . . this lovely African holiday is only the climax. Pretty well the last straw, I think sometimes."

"I know you've had a tough time," Tubby said quietly. "Sammy told me a bit about it when I was in the hospital. But I shouldn't have thought it was as bad as all that. There must be compensations."

"I haven't noticed them," Daddy said bitterly. "Everything I've tried to do has been cut short, frustrated. I got a scholarship at Balliol, that was the first thing. Then the war came and I never went up there. When the war was over, there wasn't any money and I was supposed to be lucky to be able to stay on in the army."

"I didn't know that," Tubby said.

"Of course you didn't. You're so damned incurious that you don't worry about people. You just take them as you find them. You don't know anything. You just live from day to day, from one meal to the next, from one bloody horse to another. You don't understand life. You haven't learned to think about it."

"That's not entirely true," Tubby said. "I think and worry and grope for something . . . I don't get very far. I'm still in the dark, and the dark's pretty thick—I have to admit it. . . ."

"So was I," Daddy said, "till we came to this beauty spot. Now it's all plain. I can see it now. I can see that it's just deliberate frustration. Look at my life and try to deny it. . . ."

He was drinking steadily and, in this mood, could quickly become dangerous.

"I'd like to hear," Tubby said, soothingly.

"You'd like to hear, would you?" Daddy banged his glass down on the table. "All about my life story. Life story of a soldier; of an officer and a gentleman; of an obedient servant. That's how we have to sign ourselves, isn't it? Obedient servant!" He swung round on Tubby, bellicose, quarrelsome.

"That's right," Tubby said. "I have the honor to be . . ."

"Your obedient servant! Disgusting, isn't it? Loathsome, isn't it? That's all they want of you—obedience, nice clothes, nice manners . . . and again obedience. A nice, smart-looking footman to do them credit and not to argue. That's what I've been since the war. Kicked up the bottom, bustled about the world . . . but always obedient. . . ." He was reaching out for the decanter again.

"What happened after the war?" Tubby asked quickly, hoping to delay his drinking.

"What happened? Oh, I was a good servant to start with; a fine, keen, energetic young soldier. I was fond of horses and I didn't do badly with them, and I expected a jacket . . . in fact," he said proudly, "I was promised it." And it was clear that it gave him pleasure to recall that once he could do well those things that now he pretended to despise. "But," he went on, "just when I was expecting to go to a Horse Artillery Battery, I was sent to Aden—to Aden of all places." He said this triumphantly, scoring a point. "To the Red Sea in the middle of the summer! That was good! That was clever. They were on their form when they sent me to a lunatic major who'd gone holy and a captain who shot himself a month later. And, like a fool, I played up to them. I set out to make the best of it; learned Arabic, worked up my French and German, read economics. Improving myself, you see, Tubby? Always improve yourself—remember that! One day it might be useful. Look at me! Haven't I found it useful?" He reached again for the bottle, but Tubby got hold of it.

"No, Daddy. Give it a rest, won't you?"

You could see the anger come up in Daddy, his eyes on that bottle. "After Aden?" Tubby said. "What happened then?"

"After Aden?" He seemed to be hunting in his memory. "After Aden was . . . Mary." He leaned forward on the table, his voice low and important, his face close to Tubby's. "The only year of my life when I was really, really happy. We were married, you see, and we had a year of it together. A year on the Plain. And I had one horse, a race horse . . . we bought it in Ireland and we won a few races with it . . . Mary—she was lovely on a horse—used to ride it about, and we trained it together . . . until she was pregnant . . ." He stretched a hand across the table and drew it slowly back again. "And then," he said, "they sent me to China. Sent me to Hong Kong at a fortnight's notice because I knew languages; because I'd improved myself. They wanted French and German in the Intelligence there, and they chose me for it. And they told me to sail just about the time when the baby was coming."

He leaned back in his chair as if the memory still hurt him. As if he lived again, at that moment, through the shock of getting his orders. "The week the baby was due," he said; "the actual week, Tubby; and the doctors had warned us there'd be trouble." He was holding himself in, controlling himself, speaking with an attempt at reason. "She was a slim girl, you see. A lovely, slim girl; not built with the big pelvis that you want for having babies . . . and she was temperamental, nervous. She couldn't bear the thought of my having to go. It affected her; physically it affected her, and the doctors were worried. All the time they were worried. . . .

"I saw everyone, Tubby. The colonel, the brigadier, the general. I went up to the War Office and pleaded with them—and," (he said, his voice rising) "I'll never plead again with anyone till the day that I'm buried. I'll ask no favors and expect none. I'll fight, fight, fight. . . ." He gulped and got his voice low down the scale again. "They were kind at the War Office, polite, regretful. But they wouldn't have it. I had to sail on the day they'd told me. I had to be a good, obedient servant. . . ."

He put his hand across and took hold of Tubby's wrist; not a deliberate action this time, but a sort of blind groping. His own story, put again into words, was breaking through the liquor, breaking down the character that he'd assumed to tell it.

"I shouldn't have got married so young, you see. I'd fought for four years and been wounded three times and given up a career and a Balliol scholarship—but I hadn't the right to get married. You can't be married—officially married, that is—till you're thirty. Before that, you haven't got a wife in the eyes of the army. They treat you as a bachelor. So they wouldn't agree to Mary. So she went to hospital and I went off in the troopship."

He sat quite still for a few moments and then went on in a low, stolid voice. "We'd got to the Bay, you know, when they gave me the message. It came by wireless—a wonderful invention, wireless. . . . They just hand you a slip of paper at lunch time; and there it is, all hot and fresh from England. 'A message for you, Mr. Watson,' the Steward said, and handed it me like that" (he flicked his hand in the air) "just as I was helping myself to curry . . . you know how it is in a troopship? Curried beef, curried lamb, curried pork, curried chicken—and they all taste exactly the same; of curry.

"I can taste that curry now. I can remember it all exactly. I finished taking the curry, put a spoonful in my mouth and then opened the message. I was a bit frightened of that bit of paper, you see; and I thought that, with a mouthful of curry, it would be easier. I looked at the typewritten line on that message and at first, you know, I don't think the words meant very much to me. Just words, you know. Then the man next door had hold of my arm: 'Is there anything wrong, Willie?' he was asking. . . . Because, you see, I wasn't Daddy in those days. I was Willie . . . I was a young chap then—Willie Watson. And most people seemed to get on with him all right . . . 'Anything wrong?' the other fellow asked . . . 'Both dead,' I said. I can hear myself saying it. I can hear it at this moment. I shall always hear it. It wasn't me who was speaking, you see; and that made it interesting, curious . . . 'Mother and child both dead,' I said . . . and it sounded almost funny. . . ."

He had hold of Tubby's arm with a grip that kept them both motionless. It was so like a play that you were thankful for the darkness. But yet it was real and true and under-told. You knew there was no exaggeration; no making of a good story or painting up the details to get sympathy.

"Both dead," Daddy said again. "They both died in hospital and I had a month in a troopship. A month that made any idea of hell seem like paradise. A month of drinking and drinking. Drinking myself sick every night and starting with brandy again when I was called the next morning." He moved in his chair and put the other hand across; so that, with both hands, he clung to Tubby's forearm. "I hadn't drunk before that, Tubby, I want you to know that. I want you to believe it. Just *one* when the sun went down and a short one before dinner, I daresay . . . you believe me, don't you?"

He didn't wait for an answer. "But I went on drinking then," he said proudly. "You wouldn't think a man could hold so much and not die of it. And I went on and on when we got to China. Steady, serious drinking. . . . Because, you see, there was nothing else to do when I got there." He sat back, stretching himself, almost laughing at the joke he was coming to. "They weren't expecting me, Tubby," he said. "They'd never heard of me. They didn't want me. They didn't have me on the Staff at all. They pushed me away in a medium battery with a major who was drinking as well, and the two of us went on drinking together. Whisky and gin; but mostly whisky, and those little Chinese girls; and once a trip to Japan to try the girls there for variety. Sweet, charming little things, Tubby; but disappointing in the end; bad bodies, squat and shapeless."

He stretched out a hand beseechingly. "Give me another now, Tubby, just a small one." Tubby let him have the bottle and he filled the glass and, holding the glass in his hand but not drinking, he went on talking. "Then the major, a nice chap, got sent home to England—he'd drunk himself silly—and . . . and Sammy came out to us. He was a senior captain then. Sammy . . ." (His voice almost broke at the memory.) "The first time I'd ever seen him. I can remember meeting him off the boat, seeing him walk down the gangway; that stoop of his, that pale face. 'That's a wet one,' I thought for a moment. And then we shook hands, and I saw those eyes. . . . But you knew those eyes, Tubby. . . ."

He was silent for a long time, until at last Tubby urged him to finish the story.

"And then?"

"Then? Oh, then there was Sammy." He shrugged his shoulders as if there were no more to be said about it. "Sammy talked to me, of course. Night after night, we talked together while the drink worked out of me. Until one cool, sunny morning I seemed to wake up alive again. Somehow I was young once more—I wasn't yet thirty, you know; any more than I'm only thirty-five now. But now I'm like fifty, and before Sammy came I was like sixty. And, with him, I went back to thirty again. . . . I was happy. . . ." For a moment, he had forgotten everything else and was back in those brief days with Sammy. Then the bitterness returned. "But the generals couldn't have that. That would never have done, would it? I was going fine where I was, so they had me out of it; sent me back to England."

He became very reasonable. "It's quite understandable, you see. . . . They said, 'That man's happy. . . . Happy, is he? That won't do in the army. We don't pay our servants to be happy.' . . ."

He had drawn himself up in his chair, his chest puffed out, an arm extended to the night. The drink was beginning to take physical effect at last. Sometimes his words tripped. His face was very red, with the perspiration trickling down it. He was a wounded, mutilated man, made pitiable by his deformity, but denying your right to pity him, insisting his right to pity himself. Savage, challenging, and—with the world his enemy—he was almost romantic. It was the night that did it. Any aberrance became romantic in this greatness of sky and desert. The moon flattens out the normal till it has no existence, is absorbed in the pallid flatness. But it deepens the shadows that it picks upon.

"So they sent me away from Sammy," he said. "Sent me to the Depot. The Depot—for a man who liked horses, liked the wind and the sun and somewhere to have a gallop. The Depot! Woolwich! and all selected officers, Tubby! Remember—all selected. Chosen to tittup round Woolwich Common, to march the ruddy recruits around the square, to give them lectures on patriotism and cleanliness and sportsmanship; on 'Play the Game,' and 'God Save the King' and 'Why we salute our Officers' . . . God knows! Why do we?

"And do you know what I did, Tubby?" He was quite drunk now, talking sense because sense was in him ready to come out, but not knowing how or what he was saying. "I didn't do what you're thinking. I didn't start drinking again. I couldn't, you see. Sammy was too strong for the whisky. Sammy, away in Hong Kong, wouldn't let me." He had both arms outstretched over the table, like a priest blessing the liquor. He was suddenly very drunk. "Sammy had made me a man," he cried; "and, by God, I've been some sort of a man ever since. I've never gone down to them since then. I've never had a master. By God, I haven't!"

He brought his fists down on the table, shaking the glasses. His eyes screwed up, he looked angrily at Tubby. "No! No! Never!" he said.

"So what *did* you do at the Depot?" Tubby had to ask him. He *had* to know all that happened after Sammy.

"I worked for the Staff College," Daddy said and burst into laughter; stupid laughter that stopped abruptly and let the night close down on it. "I sweated blood at that damned examination. And three times I qualified, but I never passed in; I didn't get a vacancy. I—a Balliol scholar—couldn't get into the Staff College. Can you beat it?" He laughed again, boisterously, without mirth, rocking in his chair, play-acting.

"I don't know," Tubby said, "I thought you had to be pretty clever. . . ."

"Pretty clever!" Daddy said scornfully. "Any fool who works can qualify—like I did. Any fool, do you hear? And some of the fools get nominations. So many nominations that they crowd out the chaps who've earned a place in it. But *I* couldn't get a nomination. *I* wasn't the sort they wanted. I hadn't got a good sort of county name. I wasn't at a good school, I hadn't got any money, I couldn't give a general a week's fishing, or ask him to Scotland, or even whisper him a tip for the Stock Exchange. . . . So, of course, I didn't get a nomination. And, of course, I had none of the qualifications; only quite a decent war record, a knowledge of four languages, a Balliol scholar. . . . All the things that fit you least to be a general."

He tilted the bottle, held it against the moon, saw that it was empty and put it down again. Now, he was sobering up quickly. The changes that passed over him were amazing. You could never tell what he would be the next moment.

"And then," he said, "they made a big mistake; only the second time they'd put a foot wrong. They made their good, obedient servant happy once more; sent him back to the Plain to . . . to Sammy's battery. Sammy, who didn't think of you as a soldier, a gentleman, a servant. Sammy, who thought of you as a man, a human. . . ."

He'd put his elbows on the table, his head in his hands, and was speaking now through his fingers. "You know the rest, Tubby. The company that Sammy made of us; you and Bert and I—we were happy, weren't we?" He was perfectly sober again, speaking in a flat, toneless voice. "Then we came out here," he said; "for no reason at all. They didn't want us, couldn't ever have wanted us. If there's a European war, we put a couple of divisions against another country's forty. But they send two brigades to a tin-pot little rising that could have been put down by a hundred resolute policemen. They send a brigade to march about the mountains with a half-wit colonel leading the way and a half-wit brigadier driving us along without scouts or flank guards. They were so used to the Plain, you see, that they forgot to tell us there really was an enemy this time. . . . They were too busy thinking out a new flash for our topis, a new way of presenting arms, should gunners have an issue of bayonets . . . so they just killed Sammy. Put him on a mountain to be shot at by the only native marksman in British Africa. It was the generals killed him. . . ."

"I didn't know it was that," Tubby said.

Daddy unclasped his hands and sat up quickly. In that one movement, he changed his part again; changed the scene rather; stepping from that strange, timeless land that lies between sleep and consciousness, that may only be entered in moments of waking or in the hours when intimacy breaks down the restraint that humans owe each other.

"I didn't know . . ." Tubby had said innocently.

"For God's sake stop saying you don't know," Daddy almost shouted. "Of course you don't know. You don't think or ask questions or reason things out. How can you know? I ask you, how can you? Why do you think we got sent to this lovely fort? Why do you think they discovered this verminous ruin and made us clean it out and live in it?"

"Search me," Tubby said.

"Exactly! They couldn't think of anything better to do with us."

They stayed, then, without talking for a long time. Tubby leaned forward on the parapet, resting his arms on it and looking out at the deep shadows that were painted on the sand below, and at the scoops of shadow where the moon had discovered features that belonged only to the night. Elsewhere, the fence, the tracks, the remains of a mud wall, all these things that he knew were there, had disappeared completely. For Tubby, this was still exciting.

"Look at it!" Daddy said lifting his glass and waving it towards the emptiness before them. "Look at it!" he cried. "That's what I mean by frustration."

❋ Up to the moment of climbing into bed, he had been upon the brink of sleep. Then, lying naked except for a towel about his loins, he was awake with the keen antagonism to sleep and the quickened perception that come only after midnight. It is a strange time. You see further, but the foreground is out of focus. It is altogether a photographic simile; the night is a filter, with the cloudscapes sharpened, the distant highlights clear, but the immediate and obvious features dark and obscure, underexposed to nothing but a heavy, undetailed framework.

Sleep wouldn't come. There, in those far mountains, under those tranquil clouds, wars were raging. Was every peaceful vista the same battlefield? Sammy, Daddy, Bert, Lydia, and even the sergeant-major, even the generals? Daddy! You could see the microbes struggling in *his* soul all right; but the soul itself was shapeless; too close for a vision focussed to such long-range subjects. But then you could never know Daddy, only feel the things that he was made of. Except just at first, perhaps, when the quick, obvious picture showed you a man, pretentious, disagreeable, sometimes generous in a protective sort of way. And, after that, each day spent with him, each information added to his dossier, lessened your knowledge.

The night hung without movement. . . . And yourself? What were your own warring elements? It was only this evening, those years ago before the moon had risen, that you learned they existed; that the strangely told wisdom, ignoring reason, poured from your spirit into the stillness. Those words had by-passed thought, had been born without labor. They came from within . . . they came from without. Both were true, for there was no frontier.

Sleep would not give herself. So near she danced and each time escaped him. Lydia! She was like sleep, pitiless, provocative, elusive, offering so much only to deny it. A bitch; a fickle little dog, making friends with anyone, stealing a bone, carrying it about, only to lose it in the garden. Daddy had said at the beginning, when he picked up her photograph at Bulford . . . so much that he said was right and so much was bitter. Truth was bitter, and sweetness false. Those generals, the fort, the army, stupidity, beauty . . . these were the things that Daddy was bitter about; everything and everyone, in fact, except his brother. . . .

That brother! It was hot in here under the mosquito net.
He plucked at the net, seeing the pale enclosure tremble. He
wondered about the time, but was too far in sleep to twist himself so that he could look at his wrist watch. That brother! One
was strangely jealous of the way Daddy spoke of him; the shy,
incongruous pride, the hushed admiration. There was everything false in that sweetness . . . "My brother," he'd said.
"He's a wonderful chap, Tubby. A good deal younger than
me—my only relative. . . ."

"I've got a couple of uncles and a father I don't think a lot
of," Tubby said.

"My father!" Daddy answered. "Of course I may still have
one. He was last heard of before the war, heading fast in a south-
erly direction. We never knew if it was embezzlement or what.
There was a warrant out, I believe . . . but my brother . . ."

It was quite disgusting the way he slobbered over that boy.
For, even at your age, you thought of him as a boy because of
that irritating, maternal fondness that Daddy showed for him.
"You mustn't joke about my brother, Tubby. He's a wonderful
man. . . ." "Oh, come off it, Daddy. . . ." "No, I'm serious,
Tubby. I live for that boy. It's true. If it wasn't for him, life
wouldn't be worth the effort. One could slip away so quietly. . . .
But he's clever, Tubby; really clever. And an athlete, you know.
Did well everywhere; scholarships everywhere. And afterwards
—now—a wonderful job, a thousand-a-year man. Straight as a
saint, you see . . . he's all that I haven't got, you understand;
family, wealth, smartness. . . ."

Fortunately, Daddy had only been in that mood once or
twice, but you felt quite sick at the memory. Yet it was still
Daddy, another facet of him; and you couldn't slur it over because it didn't fit the picture that your mind projected. It was
an incongruous splash of one of the sloppy colors, magenta perhaps, against the harsh, bold reds and yellows that were Daddy.
It wasn't pleasing, but you had to expect such discordancies.
You couldn't hope to understand people . . . the cadence was
familiar: "Try to understand one person, Tubby. . . ." And then
all the other cadences. "Truth, Tubby, love. . . ." Why did
Sammy face you to the rock and make you climb it? "You're

dissatisfied, Tubby. You doubt, Tubby. It's the first stage of a long, long journey. And the moment of truth, Tubby . . . the pattern. . . ."

Would sleep never come through the heat and the darkness? For a few moments, he felt the rising panic of insomnia, the grey fear that sleep was gone forever. Without sleep, you died; just as you died without food and water. It was dreadful, this inability to sleep . . . but, if you reasoned it out, it didn't matter whether you slept or not this night. In fact, if you could achieve fatigue by noon the next day, the afternoon would pass more quickly. He did not reach this conclusion until the first light was due in the sky. At once he slept deeply.

🌸 "My word, sir, we 'ave made a night of it," Hicks was saying, shaking him to wake him. "What with me oversleepin' meself and you with the mail to fetch, we'll 'ave to 'urry."

Awake, Tubby was first conscious of the struggle behind him; of his climb from those depths where soul and body had been parted, in danger of losing each other. It was a moment of brief apprehension, of searching the cause of his fear, of attributing it wrongly—ah! it was mail day.

From then onwards, gulping tea, sluicing himself down in the wash house, pulling on shirt and jodhpurs, shaving, going out into the cool brilliance of just after sunrise—strapping on his pistol as he went—inspecting the escort, the half-dozen men with pick-handles, the sergeant with a revolver, all that time he assured himself that there would be no letter. He made it the foremost of his convictions, outshining all other knowledge. She would not have written. And he continued this assertion with increasing force and lessening conviction.

Daddy had come out on to the veranda and stood there in pajamas, screwing up his eyes at the morning. Tubby doubled across and saluted. "May I go on, sir?" he asked.

"Go on please, Mr. Windrush." This careful solemnity, this choking back of the smile at Daddy—still childlike in waking, still owl-like—this simple etiquette pleased Tubby. You knew where you were, and it was an easy relationship.

Trotting out under the archway, between the saluting sentries, swinging out with a clatter of the loose stones that lay in the sand, their ponies' hoofs throwing up spurts of sand that might have come from bullets, that hung, in the low-slanting sunlight, a golden haze behind them, he was still in search of armour, preparing for defeat, foretasting the bitterness of defeat, turning defeat into at least a verified conviction. If he could say to himself—"I told you so. I knew she wouldn't have written. . . ."

The vultures flapped off and wheeled overhead as the stench of a carcass was blown on the dawn breeze. The thin, yellow dogs came yapping. The refuse dump and then the cemetery were passed and they had reached the thorn fence that surrounded the village. The mud-brick hospital was on the right; ahead, the iron-roofed station. Lydia would not have written.

You could see the smoke of the train a long way off in the desert. The sky, that was deep blue directly overhead, dropped down to the low horizon gathering colors, somber tints of reds and browns, a heavy iridescence. It reached the earth somewhere behind a shaken veil of ocher, a mixture of sand and air, with a darker suggestion, the smoke of the train, shot into it in one corner.

At last, almost before it had materialized as a thing of dust-laden paint, crude iron, trembling steam, the train was edging into the station, pushing before it a crowd of women and children, dogs, goats, chickens. As it came to a noisy halt, the very smart, very black sergeant of Sudan Police stepped out with the mailbags, proudly showing that the seals were intact, carefully examining the receipt that Tubby gave him. He could not read English; but it was a *warrag*, a paper.

Trotting back with a mailbag across his saddle was again a bad time for Tubby. Since waking that morning, there had been a reshuffle, into a new order of importance, of the factors that ruled his spirits. It seemed now that so much depended on the contents of these mailbags; that he swung on a fulcrum with bliss on one side, despair the other; that nothing mattered but a letter, or the lack of a letter, to disturb this awkward balance, to banish forebodings or to confirm them; in any event, to finish the uncertainty. Why couldn't he convince himself that she hadn't written?

It was easy to romanticize these mailbags with their fateful possibilities. He must be carrying so much that would assuage the fears or shatter the hopes of so many of the garrison. Numbers of those men, who had called from the troopship to their sniveling women on the quayside, must—like himself—be waiting for news that would swing them one way or the other. Realization of this companionship brought shameful comfort. But it made him savage; whining men and sniveling women, each dependent on the whim of the other, all frail, despicable little people, pocked with the foul ravage of self-pity, begging mercy, lacking the one virtue—courage. What did their ridiculous worries matter to anyone? It was scorn, not compassion, they commanded. The whining of your innards was disgusting. Far better to armour yourself against others and spit at the world, like Daddy . . . "I've never gone down to them since then," he'd said; "never had a master. . . ."

"Seals all right?" he asked as Tubby took the mailbags into the Battery office.

"Seem so."

"Call the Sergeant-Major, will you?"

That was a man for you; the burly, truculent figure that swaggered across the compound; that asked and gave no favors; that didn't know mercy, pity; that wasn't a man at all—a frail, miserable human—but a fine, unfettered beast, whose strength was nourished on others' weakness, who found its prey by its poor bleatings.

"Boy! Sound orderly-sergeant . . . Sergeant Sphinx: subsection commanders at the office—and double! Form up there—look alive, Sergeant Patricks!" These were the times he liked; when the non-commissioned officers, away from their men, could be treated rudely without a contravention of discipline. "Wake up, Patricks!"

The whole tiresome business of mail distribution had to be gone through; the sergeants lined up outside; the sergeant-major waiting with a quick, and often obscene, rebuke for any who missed the name of a man in his subsection; Daddy sitting

behind a table, pulled forward to make a counter; the clerks
passing out the letters as the subsection-commanders claimed
them: "Finch . . . Oliver . . . Josephs . . . Harrison . . ."

"*A* subsection, sir . . . *B* . . . *Headquarters* . . . which Harrison,
sir?"

"Harrison, G. in *C* subsection."

"Wake yourself up, Sergeant Patricks," said the sergeant-
major unreasonably.

"Tucker . . . Wilson . . . Levy . . . Brown. . . ."

It went on and on, the letters passed from hand to hand
going steadily out into the compound. Across the compound,
the men waited in several pressed ranks, laughing and joking
beneath the barrack-room verandas. They waited helplessly
and bravely for what joy and anguish might be held in a letter.
And, to one side of Daddy's table, a small pile of official correspondence and mail for him and Tubby mounted steadily.

"Hailey . . . Trevor . . . Harris . . . Sims. . . ."

Hicks and Ibrahim were bringing across the breakfast. The
sun had climbed sharply, and the day was already heavy, solid,
formidable. Shadows were little more than dark pools that your
feet paddled in. From across the compound, the men's ribald
voices, loud at the time they were ejected into the sunlight,
came muffled, compressed. Poor, miserable humans. . . .

"Brown . . . Oliver . . . Hobbs. . . ."

"We'll do ours over breakfast," Daddy said at last, edging
out from the table and coming on to the veranda.

They went along and sat down at the table that was laid
outside their bedrooms. "That's your lot," Daddy said, throwing them across. "I hope they suit you."

Tubby was at last very calm and resigned in the certainty of
disappointment. He sat down and slowly unfolded his napkin,
poured out his coffee and pulled the scones that the native
cooks served up for bread across the table. Very deliberately he
looked through the envelopes. There were half a dozen, mostly
typewritten. In the middle of them, there was the expensive
crinkle of Lydia's stationery. Her bold writing sprawled inso-
lently across the blue paper. It was a thin letter; a single sheet,
it seemed; not the usual bulky packet. To punish himself, he

put it aside and looked through the others, bills, a circular from the Royal Artillery Institute, a long, typewritten account from his solicitors—his father wanting some more capital.

"A good lot?" asked Daddy.

"About what I'd expected," Tubby said as casually as he could. "And you?"

"Not bad. One from my brother. But I don't expect much these days."

"Nor me either."

Daddy seemed to be deliberately keeping his head turned away. When he spoke, it was with his mouth full and his eyes on the plate before him. "I'd give a lot for one decent English egg," he said. "It takes six of these beastly little things to go any distance."

"And they taste all wrong somehow . . ."

"Filthy. . . ."

Tubby picked up the letter and started to open it. "Good news from your brother?" he asked.

"It is, rather. He's coming across to Cairo for Christmas. Got rather a nice job of work to do there. . . ." He looked across at the blue envelope: "From Lydia?" he asked.

"Yes. A very short one."

"Always expect a slap in the face when you get a short letter from a woman. Go on—get it over."

Tubby opened the letter quickly:

Tubby Dear,

I'm writing to tell you that I'm thinking of getting married. You don't know him and it isn't quite settled, so I won't tell you his name; but he's in the Blues or the Greys or the Buffs or something. I never can remember. Are they good regiments?

I don't think this news will hurt you, Tubby dear, because I gathered from your letters that your ardors were cooling. I hope you've found something nice in Africa. We must meet and have a party when you come back again. Bring her along for a drink or something—if she isn't too black, that is. But I don't know. A dear little coffee-colored one might be rather sweet.

I'm just off to America for three months to make up my mind about

Freddie. He's good-looking but not very intelligent. Plays the piano rather nicely, but mostly dance music. Must stop now as I have to pack. Leaving tomorrow. . . .

He sat looking at the half-sheet, quite certain that his face was expressionless. He felt no particular misery, certainly no anger. There was even no pain; only the rising knowledge that a long, persistent pain would come later.

"Forgive me," Daddy was saying. "No business of mine, but women aren't worth it. No woman's worth a man's worry; a minute of his unhappiness. . . . Get that, Tubby! It isn't easy to laugh things off in this place, but don't—now or ever—let women use you. Use them when you want them. . . . That way, women can't hurt you."

"Give me some more of that foul butter," Tubby said.

"That's the way to take it . . . marmalade?"

Anguish, following the pause of shock, came like a burst of music. The intermission was ended. The air trembled, sweeping you into a new cadence.

It was the waste, the utter waste of so much beauty and tenderness; so much peace in which a formless vision was rooted; a tropic bloom of exquisite yearning; delicate petals, half seen through heavy foliage, shapeless, fragile, but there always; always a glimpse of its sweetness to be had through the foliage, day after day, week after week, all through the long months of heat and desert; a constant decoration, the pattern of a wallpaper. Everything, that lay behind and around and below living, had now been stripped and shredded; all the building up of half-seen pinnacles and shining towers was blown into cruel memories. There was no tune to the music; only a wild suggestion of linked movements, full of pain. It was true pain; formless, bearing the fragments of beauty.

"Angry?" Daddy asked.

"No. Not angry."

He wasn't angry; there couldn't be resentment. He had his own code, and he'd given it to her, and she had played to his ruling. There was no cause for the umpire's whistle.

"It's the waste—the uselessness . . ."

"I told you so, Tubby. I told you so at the beginning . . ." (It wasn't reproach. It certainly wasn't triumph.)

"I know, I know . . . but it was so different. *She* was so different. We were happy, you see, together. It *had* to last, Daddy. . . ."

"What fools! What fools we are, Tubby, letting our happiness depend on others. Believing that because a thing glitters it has substance, is desirable. Moths at a window; babies at the flame of a candle. It's dreams, it's hell that glitters."

"I know. Believe what you want to believe. And what you don't like *can't* be true—it's too ugly."

"Seeing's believing and only see what suits you . . . I told you at the start, didn't I?"

"Right at the start, when you saw her photograph. But I thought you were wrong. I knew it . . ."

"You're never wrong, Tubby, if you believe the worst of everything."

❀ "Give me some more of that filthy bread," Daddy said later.

Tubby passed the plate of dun-colored scones that were made by the native cooks. They were hard outside with a crisp skin that suggested a soft, fresh interior. But, when you bit into them, they were hard all through, dry and bitter. Those black cooks fashioned their bread on the model of life; all promise of sweetness, all bitter disillusionment. Expect nothing good, and the worst couldn't hurt you. That was Daddy's philosophy. That was the lesson you had to learn sometime.

"What the devil!"

Daddy was sitting with his mouth open and with a piece of the brick-like bread, covered with marmalade, raised halfway towards it. A typewritten letter was propped against the coffee pot.

"Good God," Daddy said. "Would you believe it?"

"What?" Tubby asked, jolted sharply from his own introspection.

"You read it," Daddy said and flipped the letter towards him. "Read it out to me. I think my eyes must be going funny."

Tubby took the letter and read it slowly and deliberately.

"Do my eyes deceive me?" Daddy asked. "Or has someone come to their senses?"

"No," Tubby said. "Your eyes are all right, Daddy. I take it we leave by special train on Wednesday."

"For Khartoum, Tubby?"

"It says Khartoum here, anyway."

"Why, man, Khartoum is civilization. They've got ice there and women and baths and everything. I believe there's even a cinema and some sort of a newspaper."

"Well, there it is," Tubby said. "We've three days to pack up in."

Daddy was on his feet, shouting across the fort for the sergeant-major. Tubby could hardly believe that he, himself, felt no wild elation. On the whole he was glad of this deliverance, but he felt suddenly that he would miss his legitimate suffering, the simplicity of knowing that his unhappiness was reasonable, obvious and undiluted.

The sergeant-major came running across the courtyard.

"Pack up, Sergeant-Major, pack up," Daddy shouted, as jubilant as a schoolboy.

"Pack up, sir?"

"Yes, pack up. We're leaving on Wednesday."

"Next Wednesday, sir? Beg pardon, sir, but the train isn't due till Sunday, till today week, sir."

"They're sending a special train. We're leaving Wednesday, I tell you. Don't you understand, Sergeant-Major, we're leaving —leaving?"

The sergeant-major was at last smiling. "We shall miss this place, sir. It's come to be a 'ome from 'ome for some of us."

It was the first time that the sergeant-major had made a joke in the three years that they had known him.

Chapter 11 IT WAS SOUR WAKING UP IN THE HEAT OF the afternoon after an hour's sleep in the large, shuttered bedroom of the fort at Khartoum. Tubby got up slowly and went through the door at the back that led to the bathroom. There was a shower there; and, as he stood and let the tepid water cascade on to his back and trickle down loins and belly, he became rejuvenated by a few hours, retrojected through the day to the vigor of early morning.

He sat on his bed pulling on his polo boots, while Ibrahim, knees wide apart and the whole of his small head and body sunk between his thighs, squatted on the floor and tried to help him. The little black hands were timid and anxious but not sufficiently daring to be of practical assistance. They fluttered sympathetically, or hung limp above the polished toe-caps, like a pianist's seeking inspiration of the keyboard.

Tubby fitted the jockeys to the top of a boot and tried to ease them over the end of white cotton breeches. "Ibrahim," he said affectionately, "you're just like a bloody little dog; quite useless, a blinking nuisance, but I like to have you around me."

Ibrahim understood no English, but dog-like he looked up faithfully. "Noble captain?"

"Don't trouble yourself; it's not all that important."

Daddy came in, opening the door from the veranda, the room being pierced with hard, quick light, that struck brutally as from a furnace. As if to show his reformation, he was already smoking; and, since he still wore uniform, it was clear that he had not been sleeping.

"Will you be late back?" he asked with unusual gravity.

Tubby did not take the question very seriously. "I shouldn't think so," he said. "I hadn't thought about it."

"Well, would you mind doing so now?"

Tubby at last got the boot over the leg of his breeches and stood up, stamping on the concrete floor to work his foot right into it. "Not a bit, old boy," he said. "What is it?"

"Something I have to talk over with you."

"Oh, lord," Tubby said. "What have I been doing this time?"

"It's nothing you've been doing, for a change; but we have to talk about it."

"Serious?" Tubby asked, while the schoolboy premonition came up from his belly and replaced the happy prospects of polo. It was rare for Daddy to look worried; usually his concern passed too quickly into anger for his face to show any middle emotion.

"It *is* pretty serious," Daddy said. "It concerns us both rather."

They heard a car outside, and Daddy went to the doorway. "It's Richards," he said. "You'd better get along now; but be back as soon as you can manage when the polo's over."

❀ Tubby went out quickly, saw the car drawn up in the hard sunlight of the parade ground, and plunged into the blanket of heat that hung beyond the pallid shadow of the veranda. The fort at Khartoum, though better, was constructed on the same plan as the one they had just left many hundreds of miles to the southeast. There were the ramps, leading up to the 4.7 guns that overlooked the town, the searchlight tower and the single large tree growing at one end of the compound.

Richards, waiting in the car, sounded his horn discreetly. He was always discreet; a small, fussy, nearly hairless, slightly deaf, very shortsighted little bachelor with a dark and (because of his thick glasses) rather owlish face. He was a major, second-in-command of the battalion whose barracks were at the same end of the town as the fort and not more than half a mile distant. He had come to fetch Tubby, whom he had asked to play on the team captained by himself and made up of two other members of his regiment.

The trouble with Richards was his excessive benevolence, his quite undue solicitude for everyone. His wealth gave him an almost feudal overlordship of his regiment, leaving the pauper colonel little more than a constitutional sovereign. Most requests in the army are refused on the grounds of expense; and when the colonel said "No," Richards was able to say "Yes" and take out his check book. There was not a subaltern, except for Franklin (whose father owned department stores and who had sneaked into the Army from Oxford), whose debts he had not paid at some time or other; there was not a man who had not benefitted by his gifts to Messing Funds, Entertainment Funds, Clothing Funds, Band Funds, Benevolent Funds, and all the other Funds that drain the ordinary officer bankrupt. But, his money having been decently inherited and unearned (though diminished) for three or four generations, he was not ostentatious and his charity was furtive, and began at his doorstep. The polo ponies, for instance, were nominally the property of the Regimental polo club—which Richards founded and to which he elected himself captain and treasurer. The officers paid £1 a head, a year; and Richards found the remaining four hundred or so that were necessary to balance the deficit. And the majority of the officers, who did not play polo and took no interest in the game (for it was not one of the *better* regiments), could not object to this compulsory subscription; the treasurer of the club, who enforced it, having already paid their tailors. . . .

Richards greeted Tubby with an outflow of benevolence. "No hurry, old boy, we're ahead of schedule."

"Afraid I'm late, sir."

Richards looked carefully at his watch. "Not at all; I'm early. Nearly two minutes early . . . excuse me, Tubby . . ." He leaned across to call to Hicks through the window: "You shouldn't stand about without a hat, my man."

"No, sir," Hicks said, handing in polo sticks, a whip, jersey, towel, a spare saddle. . . .

"It's dangerous, you know?"

"Yes, sir. It doesn't seem to get me some'ow. I'm dark, you see, sir, like yourself. It's the fair chaps as it gets quickest."

"I daresay. But it isn't worth the candle."

"No, sir. Quite, sir. But I never does wear a 'at, not for knockin' about like . . ."

"Go and get your hat," Tubby said shortly.

"Yessir," Hicks said and remained standing aimlessly beside them.

Richards drove off across the parade ground, through the archway and, skidding in the sand, out through the gate in the barbed-wire fence beyond. The sentry, when he had opened the gate, came from under the shade of the guardhouse and presented arms to them.

"Smart guards you turn out," Richards said. "Forgive my saying so, but it's rather unusual for a Gunner unit."

"We hadn't much else to do where we came from," Tubby explained. "We had 'em at arms drill to keep 'em busy."

"Very smart, all the same. You've got a good lot of men, I should think, haven't you?"

"On the whole, very good—and a good sergeant-major."

"Ah! That makes the difference. You want a fellow who'll be something of a father to the men."

"I'm afraid ours is hardly that," Tubby said; "but they do what he tells them. . . . A bit of a slavedriver perhaps. But we've got a tough lot—specially selected, you know—and they want an iron hand now and again."

Richards kept silent to show his disapproval and then changed the subject.

"I thought you might ride Shaheem and the Prune," he said. "The Prune's a bit of a handful, but with your weight he ought to behave himself. None of our boys can do much with him."

"Grand," Tubby said. "I like the Prune, he can get a move on. I've sent on our Professor."

They were driving past the barracks that lay on their way through Khartoum to the Omdurman polo ground. They bumped across the open, scrub-strewn sand to where the asphalt road started abruptly from nothing on the very edge of the desert. The main street was wide and there were tram lines and white and red-brown houses standing well back behind small gardens. The trees, lining the street, dropped small globules of shadow that quivered like mercury and had substance.

Turning at the Gordon Statue, they came to the Nile and took the wide road, with Government offices on their left hand, very clean and magnificent, sterile and righteous, social workers gone slumming amongst the arrogant, bacillic filth of Africa. Beyond the club and the pretentious Palace, with its guard of British soldiers, and the well-named Grand Hotel and the Zoo and the private houses of the highest placed Government officials, they turned right again to cross the river by the great bridge that leads to the native town.

They went on through narrow, deserted streets, flat and colorless, full of color that you sensed was there behind the flattening iron of the sunlight, behind the crude black-and-white contrasts. Then the squat, huddled town, with its fragile, eternal hovels, was behind them, and they were past the suburbs, past the children playing in the dust and the barracked camels, past tethered donkeys and men in single, sack-colored garments and ageless women, shrouded in their black, macabre robes—each group occupying a rare territory of shade as possessively as if it were an ancestral roothold—past the cemeteries and the refuse dumps and out suddenly into the full, unrelieved glare of the polo ground.

They left the car some way back from the boards and walked slowly towards the ponies. Swinging his whip, enjoying the nervous excitement that rose at the prospect of the game, deliberately composing himself like a stretched canvas for the complete absorption that would be laid on him, Tubby sought to enjoy this brief, leisured pause before the game started. Then he remembered uncomfortably the ominous warning that Daddy had given. It had brought a clear premonition of trouble. It worried him till he reached the ponies, saw the shine of their flanks, the worn leather of his favorite saddles, Murphy and Abdul and the small, black nephew of Abdul, importantly fussing around the ponies, the boots, buckets, leather-necked bottles, spare reins, bandages—everything that belonged to polo. Then all else was forgotten.

These few minutes before the game began were the most precious, for they held the greatest tension. Once the ball was in play, he knew with the sureness of experience that he would find repose; but, in this moment of foretaste, even the nervousness and the physical nausea were part of the promise of utter satisfaction. He did not consider in what the satisfaction lay. He didn't know that the game was a fairy tale; that he and all the players were children, who sought release—from the helpless wriggling of their lives—in this make-believe of power, of shining armour. He saw no more than the sunny land ahead; the country of pretense where men could be gods, could think —and feel with passions—only those things they chose to be concerned with; things, of course (or didn't he know it?), that were of sham importance; but things to which they were the masters. These men hadn't ever earned the unkind disillusionment of growing-up. They shouldn't have been told about Father Christmas. They should have looked to the fruit garden and the storks for babies. It was escape, you see. . . . Escape from what? Lydia had said; "From being human. . . ."

Oh, for God's sake, forget her!

He went up to Abdul, who was squatting on the ground, putting a last stitch into Shaheem's bandages.

"I'll give Professor a breather . . . I'll ride him first. The Prune second. . . ."

Professor was a big, ugly, solemn-looking pony. Tubby took him round the ground at an easy canter, right round to behind the far goal posts. At that pace you could ride him with the reins hanging loose, twist him about with scarcely a movement of the loins, control him with the power you can send down into a horse that masters him but makes him your ally. It was only when you got hold of his head and pushed him into a gallop that Professor started to lean on your hand, became awkward and was hard to stop or turn quickly.

There were a few people standing about at the end of the

ground and there were cars arriving with spectators, mostly women, coming to watch this match in the second round of the Palace Cup Tournament. There were polo balls lying about behind the goal posts, and Richards was already tapping them around in his staid, careful manner. He looked up with a serious, important face.

"Feeling in form, Tubby?"

"Not too bad, Major."

Richards tapped a ball well out in front of Tubby, and Tubby, letting Professor go at it, letting him slip into his low, easy, unpressed gallop, smacked the ball ahead and then pushed him hard after it. He felt the reins as he squeezed the pony into top speed and hit a backhander hard and clean to Richards. It took all the muscles of his body to bring Professor up short and turn him quickly; and he had him then, coiled like a spring between his legs, strong to be off again.

Two or three women were standing close by. Mrs. Clements fluttered a delicate hand and called "Hello, Tubby," and he saw her suddenly, keenly and clearly, a slim, dark, large-eyed, attractive woman dressed in pale lemon. He remembered then the hard pressure of her thighs, their knees touching, when they had last danced together at the club. At the time, he had not understood that he wanted her; his timid, still-virgin body met her offer with indifference. But now he looked back over his shoulder and, seeing that her eyes followed him with appetite, turned Professor sharply, showing his power to her, tempting her, cantering past her without a glance and leaving her, unacknowledged, to gaze after him.

He took Professor round the ground again and trotted up to the other ponies. "Let's have the Prune," he said to Abdul.

It took two of them to hold the Prune while Tubby mounted him.

"All right," he said and, as they let go, felt the discharge of the pony. The Prune jumped forward and put his head down to buck, jerking it down and hoping in that sudden movement to gain supremacy. Tubby's hand, resting on the front of the saddle, restrained him, and the pony squealed and went up on his hind legs, dancing on them, not vicious, full of his own energy and excitement. Tubby let the reins go loose and pressed his knees into him, taking him round the outside of the ground at a fast canter.

Richards, too, had changed his pony and was once more practicing his strokes with grave solemnity. He was a fussy old gentleman, he was a school mistress, he was a prim old maid who had learned to perform every action with a sober regard for its importance. All through the match, he would be equally prim and just as cool and competent, never brilliant but always reliable.

The elation was rising in Tubby. "How's the old eye, Major? Seeing it nicely?"

"Quite nicely, thank you, Tubby."

"Good old George," Tubby said. "How're you feeling?"

George had cantered up and stopped beside them. "Grand, just grand," he said, "all set for a rough house."

George was redhaired and very young and he enjoyed his polo. He rarely hit the ball, but that didn't matter. He played Number One, and his job was to mark the back, which he did thoroughly, hanging on to his man and badgering him with the wilfulness of a terrier.

"Here comes Jack, lookin' a trifle important," George said. "He takes these affairs pretty seriously, does our Mr. Franklin."

"He's a good chap," Tubby said. "It's always good to have a fellow like him on a side, someone with a natural eye for hitting a ball, someone who won't ever miss it if he gets there. It's a pity the poor feller can't ride a bit, isn't it?"

"He's a shockin' horseman," George agreed, with the worst insult he could offer to the shopkeeper's son. "It's the one thing I've got against him. He's so damn hard on his ponies; they never go well for him."

"Hello, Jack," Richards called out, "how's our Number Two feeling?"

"All right, sir," Franklin said, speaking breezily like someone who feels that it is his duty to keep up the spirits of the team, to prevent their getting nervous. He was the professional games player, the ex-Oxford blue—at cricket or hockey or something—and they were amateurs.

The four men hit the ball about between them; George and Tubby laughing and joking in their self-conscious excitement; Franklin tight and silent, using his reserves to calm and hide his nervousness; and Richards, placid and matronly, taking the game as an important piece of domestic business.

Tubby hit the ball to Franklin, leaning forward and cutting it close in under his pony's neck, and then taking the Prune on fast, twisting him in and out between the goal posts, cantering back past Mrs. Clements. When the Prune was behaving, you could put up a show on him. Mrs. Clements was watching and he caught her eye so that at last acknowledgment passed between them.

Feeling control relaxed, the Prune bucked quickly, putting in three good ones, one after another, and ending with a jump half sideways with all four feet off the ground together. Nearly unseated, Tubby shot up the pony's neck and then pulled the Prune's head up sharp with the full weight of his recovered body. It was a savage correction, and he could feel the pony jerked on to his hocks, bunched up painfully. He leaned back easily and the Prune was mastered, dominated by the strength of his body and by his skill and knowledge.

Mrs. Clements was laughing at him and at the way the pony had so nearly unseated him. She laughed, swinging her body back from the hips, her eyebrows lifted, her mouth and eyes wide as a trollop's. He grinned at her, and looked into her, knowing suddenly that it was the first time he had understood a woman's promise.

❧ The six men, the first three numbers of each team, were lined up in file, two by two, jostling each other, facing the boards and waiting for the umpire to throw the ball in. Tubby, as back, was apart from the others, waiting nearer to the center of the ground and towards his own goal posts. He faced up the ground towards the opposing back and saw Dennis sitting there with his legs pushed forward, his stick resting on his shoulder, at ease and confident.

Waiting apart from the others, as though singled out for a special responsibility, Tubby felt again his own individual importance. This feeling was overture to the game; and, where-ever he was playing, he experienced it as keenly. If he were Number One, his duties of neutralizing the back by better horsemanship were paramount. At Number Two, he was the scoring member of the team, the one who was fed by the men behind and for whom the ground was cleared by the man in front. Number Three was the key position, given to the most experienced player, the one who could be relied upon to keep his head, the surest hitter and the best horseman. But, at back, you were all important with the duties of defence; the bulwark that allowed the others to be always on the offensive.

For Tubby, this pretended self-importance was part of the make-believe that turned the game into an affair of passions. That was what mattered. It must be so vital, so true a drama as to engross your every sensibility. So that you could not be injured by the raging, unregistered worries, the clogging uncer-tainties, that made of life so rough and twisting a journey. So that the way was sure and led, at the first clatter of sticks, into a world where everything was clean, where victory and defeat were the two, and the only two, simple conclusions.

The umpire had taken a ball from his pocket. From the mo-ment that he threw it into play, Tubby would—for a short space of time—live to a single, violent pattern.

❧ A startled flurry of dust, a half-choked shout; that man Franklin wrenching at his pony, too late, missing; and their Number Two leaning far out to the sweet click of a well-hit ball; and six men and six fresh, riotous ponies thundering up the field towards him . . . Their Number One, new to the game, keen and wild, coming up lickety-split, fastening himself to Tubby, pushing and boring; all legs and arms, trying to jostle him off the line that the ball was taking.

"Hello, James. Having at me, are you?"

James didn't answer. He had his orders and all his powers were charged to neutralize Tubby. Leaning far over, he pushed into Tubby with arm and shoulder.

"Hey, hey, elbows. . . ."

James drew in his bridle arm, throwing the weight of his

body into his shoulder, kicking at his pony with his free right leg, forcing it into Professor. And Professor, the hard old whaler, the battery troop-horse, snicked back his ears and laid himself against the enemy.

With a glint of lawful malice, Tubby hooked his knee behind James's, just touching Professor with his heel and letting him slip forward.

"Hey, Tubby!"

"Quite fair, James—better pull out or you'll come a cropper. . . ."

Looking behind him, he saw Richards miss it by a foot, Franklin bounced off the line, and their Number Three coming up unmarked, steadying his pony.

Before he heard the crack of the stroke, Tubby let Professor slide into full gallop. He leaned his body slightly to the right and the pony swerved over and bumped the red-faced James out of it. Once more, as the ball came up to him, he knew the glorious suspension of time in which he exulted. He stood up in his stirrups and, leaning outwards, hit a hard, clean, easy, near-side backhander. Before he made the stroke, he knew with utter certainty that he would not miss it. With his right arm high above his head, and his stick held almost horizontal, he called "turn up" to the others; and, as he swung the stick down and—ending his stroke with a last vicious chop of his wrist— heard the exquisite crack that sent the ball up the field again, George and Franklin had turned their ponies and were galloping back ahead of it.

Professor knew what had happened. As Tubby leaned back and moved his bridle hand a fraction sideways, the old pony stopped with his hocks under him and turned sharply. Reins loose and stick swinging, Tubby followed up the ground at an easy canter.

Ahead, the backs of the ponies were half hidden in the spurts of dust that came from their thundering hoofs. There was a shimmer over the ground that made the white and red splashes of the players' shirts unreal and not quite believable. Professor was grand. He knew and loved this game. This was his world; but, for the period of play, Tubby might share it with him.

❦ The Prune was wicked, over-excited, vicious, lazy and a swine. Richards was out of place, and their Number Three had the ball, had hit it and was following it up as hard as his well-trained pony would take him. The Prune was a devil. He wouldn't get going, he wouldn't take Tubby to meet it. He was on his hind legs, he was jumping sideways shaking his head to get away from the bridle. Tubby couldn't get there, and he heard the burst of clapping as their Number Three hit the ball low between the goal posts. He kicked the Prune round and took the reins in his stick hand, and set about the pony. With his left hand, he laid in with his whip, lacing the Prune's flanks and restraining him, so that the punishment was obvious. Then he let him go, letting him release himself into a stretched gallop, still hitting him hard and quickly to drive home the lesson.

The ball went up and down the field and the dust was a haze in the sunshine. Your mouth was unbearably dry, your bridle hand numb and each movement slowed down so that you performed it carefully and with precision. The Prune, his ears cocked, watched the game anxiously. Richards hit the ball hard up the ground, checking his pony to do so, making his stroke neatly and with prim concentration. "Ride!" he shouted to Franklin, and sat down in his saddle, comically working his buttocks to force his pony into a gallop.

Tubby saw it all. For one instant the picture was enlarged and laid clearly before him, so that it was not a scene in which he was an actor, but a problem diagrammatically presented. George had their back well marked, Franklin was riding their Number Two and Richards was following on the line of the ball with the goal posts ahead of him. Their Number Three came out of the bright dust, riding all he knew for Richards, coming up at a long slant behind him.

Tubby squeezed with his loins, draining his power into the pony, knowing the outflow of power as the Prune flattened, stretched, was poised on the earth's topmost wrinkle, balanced in the speed that drew him forward. Richards' stick was hooked with a clatter, and Tubby saw the ball clear, rolling gently. He tapped it up the ground, the Prune, a twinkle of hoofs, ears back, following.

"Ride, Major, ride. . . ."

In front there was a clutter of white and red vests and dark, sweat-streaked flanks with the dust fogging everything and the goal posts beyond them. The Prune would not check and the ball lay in the dust, large and white in front of him. Up in his stirrups, Tubby hit the ball hard through the welter of ponies, seeing it soar up and pass between the goal posts, seeing—in the long moment that it hung in the air—the man behind the goal posts lift his flag and wave it, hearing the burst of clapping, knowing an instant of complete fulfillment.

If you wanted to have a hope of holding Shaheem, you had to fix him so he couldn't get his tongue over the bit; and before Tubby would swill the sweat and dust off his face with water from the bucket, he tied the tape tightly round Shaheem's tongue and then to the bridle.

Then he put his head right into the bucket and rubbed the water into his hair, the water trickling down his neck to where the polo vest was stuck to his body. In the last half minute before the chukker was due to start, he gave the pony a lump of sugar.

"It'll keep his mouth wet as long as possible," he said to Abdul. "While the sugar lasts he's all right. It's when he gets dry that he's done for."

Abdul grinned and asked God's help in Arabic.

"We need it," said Tubby, understanding that much.

He swung himself slowly into the saddle and cantered on to the ground. They were a goal down and it was the last period and Shaheem was playing his second chukker. He leaned forward and patted the pony's neck and, leaning still further, twitched at the chestnut ear that was cocked forward.

"Shaheem, this is a match; this is the last chukker. We're one goal down, Shaheem, and we have to score twice to win it. Shaheem, you must gallop like a devil from hell, with the wings of an angel from heaven."

George is so dust-caked that he can hardly grin. Franklin is still the ex-Oxford blue, professional, composed, saving himself to be played out at the last minute. Richards is precise and unexhausted. George has badgered Dennis, their back, to a state of crisis; they can never be friends again; they are enemies in the absolute way that comes from physical battle. Franklin does not smile; his thin face is hard and serious.

"Oh, boys, what a game," Tubby says, pulling Shaheem out of his canter beside them.

The ball is in play and it is all luminous dust and sweat and gallop and gallop. Gallop, Shaheem, gallop, gallop and stop, blast you.

They have scored again, and the match is all but over. We can't win now, and Franklin knows it and Richards knows. But George won't let go of the back and Tubby is lost in the game to the last minute of utter exhaustion. The game has suddenly swept up towards their goal, the players disappearing, two by two, in a cloud of dust of their own making. The ball is lying in the middle of the ground, God knows how far from the goal posts. James has been shaken off, and Tubby can see the enormous ball lying quite still with an eternity of time before him. Gallop, Shaheem. Shaheem, you haven't stopped in the last five minutes. You haven't pulled up when I've tugged and sawed at your mouth. I've had to pull you round on your forehand in wide, uncontrolled circles. You wouldn't, not once, get your hocks underneath you. Gallop, Shaheem!

Who the devil is that riding in at an angle? It's James, spurred by his conscience to a last act of duty. He can't go riding across the line of the ball like that. Shaheem won't think of stopping. *Hup*, Shaheem—for God's sake, stop, will you? "Hi . . . Hi . . . Hi . . . James, what the hell are you doing?"

"Hey, James."

"James."

"Hi . . . Hi . . . Hi . . ."

"Good God, what a smash."

"James, you damn fool!"

"I'm awfully sorry, old boy."

"You oughtn't to be allowed on a polo ground."

"James, you must be mad."

"James . . ."

"I'm awfully sorry, I lost my bearings."

Richards has hit a goal off the penalty shot, but the match is over. Richards and Franklin are disappointed. "We oughtn't to have been beaten," they say to each other. George has his face set in a foolish grin and Dennis, their back, is trotting back beside him, talking sweetly. Tubby is happy. He has emptied his soul and the energy has drained out of him to the last drop so that he is completely fulfilled and there is a warm void within him.

❀ Mrs. Clements was standing by the ponies.

"What a good game, Tubby. I did so enjoy it."

"Yes, wasn't it?"

"I was thrilled every minute of it."

"I'm so glad."

"You'll come along to the club with us?"

Tubby looked at her. He saw her without affection or regard. But, in a moment that had been of pure physical content, he was suddenly aware of an overpowering call in him for soft flesh, for further victory. The satisfaction of one appetite had sharpened another. The fear, born of ignorance, was gone. He need not be timid with this woman or afraid of his acquittance. She was the substance of all the shadow phallic symbols that, unknown, had been found in the quite trivial things of his normal living. The curtain was torn down; through the window he could see a room, well-lit in every particular.

Mrs. Clements' head was held a little on one side. Her lips were smiling at him but her eyes bore an expression that was beyond his knowledge. She was not a woman that was older than he, nor one who was married and whose husband was away on trek, nor a girl for whom he felt his usual exuberant liking. She fell into no category; she was just a woman. . . .

"I'll tell you what, Tubby. Come to the club for a drink. You can slip back and change and dine with me afterwards."

"Thanks very much. . . ."

"I'm afraid my husband's away; there'll only be the two of us. You won't be bored?"

"I don't expect so."

Richards was in his car and had started up the engine. He leaned out of the window. "Are you coming, Tubby?"

"We can drive you to the club and you can take my car up to the fort to change," Mrs. Clements said quickly. "You can have it for tonight and get it back to me tomorrow."

It didn't seem a very discreet arrangement, but he wasn't worrying. You didn't bother much about wire with the scent breast high and hounds running.

"All right, that's fine," he said, "very good of you."

He waved to Richards. "You go on, sir. I'll be along later."

❧ It was dark when Tubby drove Mrs. Clements' car past the sentry and on to the parade ground of the fort. Through the short dusk, they had sat in the club garden; and Mrs. Clements, with dainty little waves of a languid hand, and with sweet, encouraging, cultivated smiles, had attracted quite a party of men and women. Then it was night, and the lamps were lit, throwing bold patterns of shadow between the tables and from the shrubs that surrounded the lawn on which they were sitting. One more whisky and soda; and then a short one, a gin and something; and just one more fizz; and one for the road; and finally a last one in the hot dark before the party broke up and the men and women got into their cars, already late for their late dinners.

In front of all the people, Mrs. Clements leaned across and put her hand on Tubby's forearm.

"You'd better run along now, Tubby; see you in an hour, shall I?"

It seemed that she was a brazen woman, liking publicity, wanting—even at this early stage—to display a new conquest. She was not the submissive type, but the mistress in every sense. But Tubby had to reverse the roles; he was accepting no favors, serving no one's purpose. He had to be the hunter. And, if the quarry didn't mind publicity, hounds needn't worry. He swallowed the last drink quickly, putting thoughts away from him, depending on his senses. And this was something that had to be done deliberately these days.

As he drove into the fort, his headlamps lit up Daddy sitting on the veranda. It was only then that he remembered his orders and his promise to return early. His blood sank back from the surface of his skin, from the trembling tissues that had seemed inflated with expectancy. The reaction was a weakening process, depriving him of that awareness of power that had been generating all the afternoon and increasing with his physical expenditure. He slid down the wave, an unromantic tumble. He had to narrow his eyes from the wide landscape of power to all the small details within the circle of lamplight; to the whisky bottle, half empty—and how full had it been at the start of the evening? He had to look at Daddy, sitting quite still there, his hair disordered, his eye-pupils hard, his eyes fixed, wide, almost vacant, but squeezed deep into the expressionless mass of flesh, the wicked face from which all wrinkles were smoothed into tight lips, into anger.

Tubby was standing on the edge of the veranda, the thick darkness close behind him. Daddy, slumped in his chair, spoke tonelessly. "Where the hell have *you* been?"

"I'm awfully sorry . . ."

"Where have you been was what I asked you."

"At the club. I'm awfully sorry."

"Didn't I tell you to be back early?"

"I really am terribly sorry."

"Didn't I tell you?"

"Yes."

"What have you been doing?"

"At the club. Drinking and so on."

"While I've been drinking here; while I've been waiting for you?"

"Yes."

"You can drink at the club and I have to drink here. And that's after I'd told you to be back early?"

"I'm terribly sorry," Tubby said. "I promise you I clean forgot about it. It went right out of my mind till the moment I drove past the sentry."

Daddy was sitting completely still, his expression unchanging, his voice flat and dry. "Your mind!" he said scornfully.

Tubby could find nothing to answer without letting himself get angry. He was holding himself in carefully. He was in the wrong and acknowledged it.

"Whose is that car?" Daddy asked him.

"It's one I borrowed."

"Whose is it?"

"It belongs to a Mrs. Clements, if you must know."

"Mrs. Clements?"

"Yes."

"How were you going to get it back to her?"

"I was going to their house for dinner. I was going to bring the car back here tonight and return it to her somehow tomorrow."

"You can put all that out of your mind anyhow."

"Yes. I'll phone her."

Tubby started to walk along the veranda to the battery office where there was a telephone.

"Not now you won't," Daddy said. "Sit down, will you?"

Tubby sat down and Daddy, pushing the whisky bottle towards him, went on speaking in the same unrevealing voice. If you had not known him, you would have thought it was assumed and that he was pretending anger. Knowing him, you could not even guess at his feelings. He was as enigmatical as a caged animal with which you are not familiar.

"We're in a nasty mess," he said. "This can't help concerning you. . . . We'd best talk it over. . . ."

"What's the trouble?" Tubby asked, somehow unable to prepare himself for anything serious.

"Just that we've got to put the sergeant-major under arrest," Daddy said.

"Under arrest . . . the sergeant-major!"

"To start with. He'll probably get seven years to end up, and half the Battery ought to go with him."

"What on earth are you talking about?" Tubby asked, completely mystified.

Daddy picked up a file of papers from the ground by his feet, opened it, found what he wanted and handed the sheet across the table. Tubby took it, still not quite sure what he was doing.

"Good God," he said, when he had read it. And then again, "Good God, Daddy."

"Don't go on saying good God," Daddy answered irritably and in his usual voice. "That doesn't help anyone."

"Well, it's a bit of a staggerer. I wouldn't have thought it possible."

"And for the love of the Lord don't start telling me what you'd have thought possible."

"Well, I mean . . ." He didn't know what he meant, except that something very horrible had been thrust unjustly upon him. He'd behaved himself, done his job all right; and now this had smashed into him. "One doesn't expect that sort of thing," he ended weakly.

"Doesn't one?" Daddy said. "Any man with a brain or any common sense or any feelings or any ordinary appetites could hardly have expected anything different. What do you imagine the battery is—a *salon* of eunuchs? Are they men, fine, strong men, chosen for their bodies? Does a young, healthy male have appetites? Was the place littered with nice healthy girls, nurse-maids and housemaids and shop girls—or even raddled old harlots—on whom the troops could satisfy themselves? Just think of that, will you?"

"No," Tubby said. "No . . . I know it happens, of course. But not at the fort; not *our* Battery . . ."

Daddy shook his clenched fists towards the night. "Not *me*, O Lord, not *me*. Not in *my* time. Not *my* Battery. . . . We are all miserable sinners, O Lord, but not *me*, not *my* friends—only the other fellow . . ."

"But the sergeant-major!" Tubby said, his voice out of control. "All the men we know and work with . . ."

"Heaven help me!" Daddy cried. "You're as bad as the generals in India; in an out-station, tucked away somewhere and forgotten. And the bishop pays an annual visit and talks to the general's wife; and she badgers the old man silly, till he gives in and closes the brothels . . . and the regimental officers must shut their eyes till there's some flagrant case like this . . . and some wretched N.C.O. gets locked up for seven years as an example and for a so-called crime that the bishop and the general's wife and the old fool himself pretend they've never heard of . . ."

"And that's how it was at the fort," Tubby said slowly, trying to understand it.

"Just that," Daddy answered viciously. "I wonder we aren't all turned into pillars of salt, looking back at the place. Half the Battery were guilty—if you call it guilty. But what could *I* do about it? *I* didn't close the brothels—there weren't any to close. There wasn't any enterprise in that village. If I'd seen half a chance I'd have started one. . . ."

"I can't think how they do it," Tubby said. "It makes me sick to think about it."

"I'm not in the least surprised. If you won't see or hear or consider the unpleasant and common things that are right in front of you, when acknowledgment comes at last it's apt to be sickening. . . . So we call it unnatural vice because we don't like to own how natural it is; because we've deprived men of what even *we*—we, the holy, sainted emblems of authority— admit is natural satisfaction, so that they're forced to the only means that are left to them. It doesn't sicken me, because I've thought about it rationally, sensibly. It isn't my cup of tea and it isn't yours. Our appetites don't run that way. Besides, we weren't crowded through hot nights in a barrack-room; we had other interests—books, letters; we had authority . . ."

"The sergeant-major had authority."

"Yes! That's the case against him. He used it, too. He had the pick of them . . . and if they weren't willing, there were always fatigues and extra guard duties and stable pickets . . . and the sergeant-major had to detail *someone*."

"God, what a mess!" Tubby said miserably, at last beginning to grasp it.

"Yes, isn't it? And I wonder how much you've realized." He was speaking with a sort of grim humor. It was funny, really, the trick that had been played on them. One up for the world and the generals. But the malice was against himself only: "We don't come so well out of it either . . . *I'm* for it, any-way . . . but it's more than that." He spoke urgently. "You must understand . . . if it all comes out, if the sergeant-major tries to save himself by having a go at the others, if he gets nasty about that wet fish, Sergeant Patricks, who came whining to me about his driver—we, ourselves, are liable to get a smear of tar off the same brush as the others. . . ."

"I don't see what we can do," Tubby said, not realizing the content of this last suggestion. "Things must take their course. I suppose we must hope for the best and see what happens. . . ."

"Hoping won't help a lot. We've all got to tread damn carefully."

They heard the telephone ringing in the battery office. "That's probably your woman," Daddy said, "you'd better answer it. She wants her car back, I shouldn't wonder."

"All right," Tubby said, getting out of his chair and going along the veranda.

"One moment . . ."

Tubby turned back and stood, waiting for Daddy to speak, while the telephone went on ringing.

"This Mrs. Clements . . . her husband's on trek, isn't he?"

"I believe so."

"And she's alone? No sister staying or anything?"

"I don't think so."

"She's an indiscreet sort of harlot," Daddy murmured reflectively; "in view of the situation, it wouldn't do any harm if you went after all, Tubby."

Tubby blushed very red. "What do you mean? I . . . I . . ."

"Go on and answer it," Daddy said. "Tell her you'll be along as soon as you've changed, blast you."

He reached for the whisky and refilled his glass while Tubby fled to the telephone.

To be told by your superior officer to go and perform an act, half the attractions of which lie in its illicit character, cannot help making the escapade less engaging. Tubby did not reason this out; but he drew up the car in the deep shadow of a tree that overhung the road beside the river, and smoked through a cigarette, thinking it over and trying to recapture his ardor of early evening. He did not find it difficult. The trouble at the fort, about which Daddy was so worried, scarcely lived

in his thoughts. His body was still keen from its cleansing, dis-
embogueing uses of the afternoon. It was easy to refocus his
vague disquietudes into the burning point of desire for this
quick adventure.

The breeze from across the Nile stirred his hair; and the
lights on the far bank twinkled, as they had done through the
rain when the troopship steamed out of Southampton water.

Sardonically, he transformed the surge of nostalgia into a
surge of desire. Through the agency of this woman, he could
avenge himself on himself for the silly, sentimental, boyish ideals
that had once made him consecrate this occasion to Lydia. The
thought hurt him, for the two women were so incomparable.

The thought hurt him and made him savage; and still he
could not feel bitterly for Lydia . . . but he saw her now and
summoned his lust to pierce the vision; so that, in his imminent
satisfaction, he could wound himself for his own foolishness.

Mrs. Clements was wearing pajamas.

He never knew her first name, and he never spoke to her
after that night; and whether he drew aside the curls of glossy
black hair that covered her delicate ear and murmured "Mrs.
Clements," or whether it was sufficient for her to be entirely
nameless, he could not afterwards remember.

He returned to the fort at two in the morning and saw the
light in the window of Daddy's bedroom and saw that he was
in bed reading. He threw off his clothes and plunged under the
mosquito net and slept till Hicks woke him.

Chapter 12 THE COURT-MARTIAL WAS HELD IN A large, white room, heavily shuttered, dim, vaguely monastic. The proceedings were slow and important; they were immensely tedious. The evidence and all the submissions of prosecuting and defending officers had to be written down in full by the president, who was a general, and to whom a pen (except for the purpose of signing his name) was an unfamiliar and unfavored instrument. There were long periods of quiet, while the pen squeaked across the buff forms and the documents on the long table rustled under the big, slow-moving fan that was fixed to the ceiling. It was grim: matter-of-fact when you expected drama; clean and antiseptic when you were ready for something rather nasty. The whole performance was ponderous and inevitable, as ruthless as machinery; and, in your membership of it, you were no more than an obscure bolt, a spindle hidden away some-where, quite unimportant—except that the machine couldn't run without you.

The witness who was giving evidence shifted from one foot to the other, resolving to keep his testimony as short as possible, so that he could regain his chair the sooner; for him, the glamor of public appearance was already tarnished.

The staff-captain, who was prosecutor, twisted himself round, rearranging himself and leaning again on the table so as to take the weight of his head on the other elbow.

Daddy, who was defending, very delicately redistributed his papers and files, opened and shut his manual of military law, and drummed his fingers on the dome of his topi.

Tubby, the junior member of the court, looked straight to his front, looking at nothing, seeing nothing, trying in alternate waves of desperation and indifference to imbue his immediate experience with a sense of importance. But—really it was all very boring.

They were trying a man on a serious charge; so serious and so nearly proved that in a few hours (there was little doubt) he would be found guilty. In a few days, when the sentence had been promulgated, he would hear what they had decided to do to him. He might be locked up for ten years; perhaps it would be no more than five; it couldn't be less. In civil cases they gave them six months, or twelve; rarely more. But, here, a soldier's masculinity was challenged; and this most unforgivable crime must be met coldly with savage punishment. Yet there was nothing savage in their hearts—rather the reverse. They hated inflicting punishment on a fine soldier; but this was no matter of hearts, compassion, kindliness. It was the application of certain accepted standards.

And the sentence didn't matter to the sergeant-major—not yet, anyway. The pain was far too subtle to be judged by time measurements. It lay in the loss of volition, the one burning moment when the man could no longer say: "I think I'll go out; I'll come in. . . ." the quick transportation from military discipline—a discipline based on its time limitation, its cycle of contrasts from strict subjectivity to leisure hours of more than freedom, of encouraged license—to this new and utter enslavement, this dehumanization, this reduction to animal status.

Five years ago Tubby was at Woolwich, learning to be an officer, still a schoolboy; and in five years' time he might well be sour and withered in spirit, like Daddy. What would happen to the sergeant-major in that period? It was an unpleasant subject for thought; terrible, and—when you remembered the sergeant-major as you had known him—very tragic. But it was hard to feel distressed about it. The white walls, the heavy shutters, the ponderous ritual, denied emotion, forbade sentiment.

Everything was happening in a steam-roller way, and you were part of the steam roller and a steam roller cannot feel but can only act as the steam directs it.

Very slowly and relentlessly the proceedings developed in their fore-ordained degrees. Tubby wiped the dampness off his forehead; Daddy leaned back and closed his eyes; the other members of the court, sitting at the head of the room behind the long table, were twisted into the most comfortable attitudes that propriety and the hard chairs permitted. The staff-captain twirled his pencil, and tried to twirl his stiff moustaches. He tapped the pencil gently on the table and stroked his ginger moustaches, running his finger down his nose until it attained its objective and continuing the stroking movement while he turned his head very slowly to the right, to survey the line of officers who comprised the court, back again to his front, to look straight past the prisoner and escort, across the room to Daddy, and finally, refocussing his eyes without the necessity for further movement, to gaze coldly at the prisoner. It was a market-day inspection, without pity and without malice. Then the eyes dropped, the ginger moustache was left to its own mutinous attitudes while, picking up again his pencil, the staff-captain drew a flat-headed, large-headed, top-heavy figure on his pink blotting paper.

The prisoner, the sergeant-major, the man who had galloped down the hill and hustled the Battery into action, the fine, sturdy male with the big stomach and faded medal ribbons, the man who had come out of the darkness to stand, dark and burly, in the fringe of lamplight, sat now, quite still, with his large hands open on his knees and his eyes fixed straight before him. His head was square and stubborn, his face expressionless. He was the rock on which the waters split; he was untouched by the waters. The proceedings swept around him, tranquil, irresistible, a slow-moving river.

A score of responsible men were occupied with this business which hardly concerned the sergeant-major. He was impersonalized. It was all quiet, gentle and relentless; and only to the sergeant-major was it of any moment.

The president of the court, the General himself, wearily

blotted the buff form on which he had been writing. He looked up slowly, his red, square face entirely without expression, inscrutable like an elephant or an Oriental, except that—in the case of an elephant or an Oriental—there is a subtle assurance that their brains are occupied. Not only his face, but all of the General was square and solid. He was kind, sure of himself and stupid. But he knew whose advice to take and whose to reject; he was a good general. He looked across to Daddy.

"Well, Captain Watson. . . ."

Daddy stood up, his sword scraping against the legs of his chair. He fiddled with his sword and cleared his throat. He was not nervous; he was confident and yet reluctant to speak, as if he felt the atmosphere of the court was not receptive.

"Well, sir. . . ."

"One moment, Captain Watson; am I to take this down?"

"I won't trouble you, sir, just at present."

The General's voice was quiet; his words were clipped, used sparingly and not without some mental process, some reflex deliberation. It was as if their source were limited. As if, with each sentence uttered, he warned himself that one the less was left to him.

"It's not a question of trouble," he said. "You are submitting a defence?"

"Yes, sir. I was going to outline it."

"It will have to be taken down then; you must know that, Captain Watson."

"I don't think so, sir. I will put in a written statement."

The General leaned towards the member of the court on his right, an old, wizened, monkey-faced, horse-dealing major. They whispered together. "Yes, yes, quite. Oh yes, quite," the Major said too loudly.

"Don't you agree?"

"Oh, undoubtedly, sir, quite; undoubtedly."

Daddy stood, fingering his sword knot; and Tubby saw him then quite suddenly, as forlorn and unhappy. It was perhaps an unguarded moment; but, without a knowledge of the multiplicity of Daddy's facets, that idle figure, neatly dressed in khaki drill uniform (white and shabby at the edges from the laundry)

and beautifully polished, well-worn belt and field boots and
scabbard, could have no particular significance. The pink,
matter-of-fact face, over-lined on the forehead for its age, and
the thin, drab-colored hair, were uninteresting. From Tubby,
the man demanded affection. It was Daddy, his captain, bad-
tempered, hateful, brave, clever, obstinate, kind, generous,
sad, unhappy. The component clements were innumerable.
Daddy himself could not have counted them; could not have
known which of his many persons was in possession of his
scarred soul at any particular moment.

"Oh, yes, I quite agree with you," the monkey-faced major
whispered. He was clean-shaven and he pursed his thin, blood-
less lips together into an expression of wisdom. He nodded his
head slowly: "Oh, undoubtedly, General, undoubtedly."

"All right, Captain Watson, go on please."

Daddy looked at the president and spoke slowly and quietly.
His voice gained in confidence, as if he were beginning to feel
the unaccustomed part that he was playing. He identified himself with the prisoner, his sergeant-major, and yet saw him objectively, as he sometimes saw himself in moments of revealing
consciousness.

"I think, sir, that the evidence against the prisoner is not
only inconclusive, but strongly contestable. I should call it
unreliable. The few questions I have put to the witnesses have
been answered reluctantly. That would perhaps have been
natural—in view of the embarrassing nature of the charge—
if their answers had not materially altered the substance of their
evidence . . . but I think that they did. I mean that, after I had
questioned, cross-examined that is, each witness, his story was
very different from the one contained in the summary of evidence. Not only that, but the stories of the different witnesses
now disagree very materially. So much so that it would be very
dangerous to lend credence to any of them."

"To lend *what*, Captain Watson?"

"To believe them, sir."

"Oh, I see. To believe them."

The General leaned across and started whispering again. He
did not turn his head but merely bent it sideways like a pendu-

lum, looking all the time to his front, across the court, with
steady, expressionless eyes.

"Oh, quite," the Major said. "I see that. He says we can't
believe them . . . I don't know, I'm sure . . . I must say. . . ."

"Captain Watson, I have a note of all the questions and answers you put to the witnesses."

"Yes, sir; but I thought if I just recapitulated some of
them. . . ."

"Hardly necessary, is it?"

The General was not being difficult. He was anxious to help
and put at ease the defending officer. The court was, of course,
on the side of the defence; but nobody wanted a lot of unnecessary speech-making. Evidence and cross-examination were
down in black and white, or—more holy still—in black and
buff, and had acquired the sacred character that the written
word has for the semi-literate.

Daddy shifted his feet awkwardly and rustled through the
notes of his cross-examinations.

"What I mean, sir. . . ."

"Captain Watson, are you trying to submit that there is no
case to answer?"

Daddy looked up quickly. "Would you accept that submission, sir?"

"If you ask me to, the court will adjourn to consider it."

It seemed clear that a cigarette was what the General really
needed; a smoke and an adjournment, when one could stretch
oneself and get relief from the infernal hardness of the "chairs
windsor." He spoke with the monkey-faced major, and with
the short, dark, kind-looking little Richards, the other major on
the court, who sat on his left. For some time they whispered
together, while Daddy watched them anxiously, and the prisoner's face did not move but remained stony and indifferent.

"No, I'm afraid not," the General said regretfully. "We seem
to be agreed that there is quite clearly a case for the defence to
answer."

If you knew Daddy, you could see that he was winding himself up for an effort, just as he worked himself up for a bout of
evil temper.

"Yes, sir," he admitted. "I see that. What I want to say is that the evidence so far is unreliable. It must, at least, leave a strong feeling of doubt. It is almost impossible for me to produce conflicting evidence. It would have to be negative evidence, you understand? I cannot prove that these alleged offences were not committed when only the witnesses and the prisoner were supposed to be present. But I *can* produce evidence of character to show that the allegations are highly improbable."

"Evidence of character—at this stage of the proceedings?"

"Well, yes, sir. I thought I'd explained it. . . ."

There was a short silence, broken sharply by the General. "Will the prisoner give evidence?"

Daddy hesitated and looked at the sergeant-major. The sergeant-major still sat with his hands on his knees. Still he stared straight in front of him and showed no interest in the proceedings. His eyes were fixed, almost in hypnosis, high up the wall at the back of the president. If the sergeant-major gave evidence, anything might come out; anything might happen. He could scarcely save himself, and the whole fort might be incriminated. It was an important moment when a decision that had been reached in advance had to be quickly reconsidered.

"No, sir. He won't give evidence."

That sounded bad for the prisoner. In the silence—the long, heavily-charged silence that followed—it was clear that the case was as good as over.

"Evidence of character," the General repeated; "at this stage of the proceedings?"

Daddy spoke urgently.

"I wish to show, sir, that the prisoner has been married five years and has four children. I suggest it indicates that his tendencies are entirely heterosexual."

"Entirely what?"

"Heterosexual, sir."

"I see. And what may that mean? We must have plain language here, Captain Watson."

"Yes, sir, of course. From the Greek. . . ."

"We don't want Greek, Captain Watson."

"No, sir, of course not. . . ."

Daddy's voice was gentle in the slow drawl that betrayed his most guarded, deliberate moments. Only Tubby could detect the malice in his soft replies. Only Tubby knew the violent passion that Daddy felt at the unjustness of these scrupulously just proceedings.

"It seems necessary for me to give the court some idea of the conditions we were living in at the fort. . . ."

"One moment, Captain Watson, you appear to be giving evidence."

"I am trying to explain, sir. . . ."

"You are in effect giving evidence."

"There is no one else I can call, sir, who has the same full knowledge of the conditions. . . ."

"I don't see that the defending officer can give evidence. You should have been a witness." He had a word with Richards, a word with the monkey-faced major. Richards' lips just stirred in a brief affirmative; but the monkey-faced man nodded vigorously, full of wisdom.

"Quite right," the General said. "Only a witness can give evidence."

"I'm sorry, sir. The prisoner wanted me to defend him. He has the right to choose."

"Of course. . . ."

The General turned his head to speak. He was talking again with the monkey-faced major and he looked up to say "of course" and then went back to his whispering. He was clearly anxious, not only that the prisoner should be given every benefit, but that the proceedings should contain no irregularity which might be criticized by the Judge-Advocate's department afterwards. The staff-captain's chair scraped the floor as he stood up suddenly.

"Sir?"

"Yes, Captain Higgins?"

"I don't think there can be any objection to Captain Watson giving evidence providing he appears as a witness. He should do so on oath and should, of course, be subject to my cross-examination."

The General moved his head slowly, as if controlled by a mechanism of gear wheels, back across the court to Daddy. "Do you agree, Captain Watson?"

Daddy looked down at his boots and then at his papers. The silence was just long enough to reveal his embarrassment.

"Well, Captain Watson?"

Daddy's voice was low: "I agree, sir."

He stepped round the table, his sword knocking against the legs, and stood in the well of the court next to the sergeant-major. The Regimental Sergeant-Major on duty came from the back of the room with a Bible.

"I swear that in the evidence I shall give before this court, I shall speak the truth . . ."

The truth!

Tubby, watching Daddy and seeing his tired, grave, unrevealing face, knew how useless was the oath and how futile it was to believe that it would not be broken. In a matter of this sort, there was no truth. There were no facts which, viewed from all angles—or from more than one angle—gave the same picture. Daddy, more than anyone, discredited the hope that there was a basic, universal truth in anything.

Sitting in the shaded quiet of the court, while Daddy, in his gentle, even voice gave evidence, Tubby's mind wandered. Of all the unforeseen contradictions that had shattered his complacency, the continual revelation of Daddy had been perhaps the most startling. Discovering the multiplicity of spirits represented by that short, square and rather nondescript person had brought the final disintegration of his once happy belief in the simplicity of all that surrounded him. He knew now that things and people were not either good or bad. Life was rather more than living. He, Tubby, had progressed further than the General.

"The truth is," Daddy was saying, "that conditions at the fort were such that . . ."

No doubt it was the truth; for almost everything was the truth for someone. If Daddy, sitting in the cool of the battery office, saw a bombardier walking across the parade ground of the fort, saw him stepping with automatic precision through the evil brilliance of the midday sunlight, he saw a man who was making a useless journey. He saw someone compelled by the stupid routine of living to exert himself unpleasantly. The bombardier must walk across and make a quite unnecessary report, at a quite arbitrarily specified time, to the orderly-sergeant. Then he must walk back again. It was entirely trivial and harmless, and the routine of army life demanded it. But Daddy felt bitterly about it just because he felt bitter about everything; because he saw and knew everything with a gnawing bitterness that made life sour in his mouth and acrid in his nostrils.

If Sammy, who was dead and disintegrating somewhere beneath the sands of the African desert, had been sitting in the same chair and had seen the same man perform the same entirely unremarkable journey, he would have been watching all humanity enjoying the gift of purposeful movement.

If Bert had been there, he would have stiffened instinctively. He would have seen a non-commissioned officer on duty marching across the square and not swinging his arms in the way he had been taught at the depot.

To Lydia, the man would have been a rather attractive figure in that rather attractive light, khaki drill uniform, wearing a rather romantic topi. Very Empire-building, she would have thought, as she saw his brown arms and knees and quilted spine pad.

To Mrs. Clements, for instance, it would have been a male creature approaching her; someone to be stripped and regarded critically from the point of view of his animal potentialities; someone to be watched through the lens of her instinctive mind, which took each man, and all mankind, and viewed it as mechanically constructed for the satisfaction of woman.

But Tubby would have seen Bombardier Price of "C" sub-section, a chap who had a first class certificate of education and was due for promotion, reporting two men sick and one absent to the orderly-sergeant. Was there any reason to suppose that his vision was less fallacious and more truthful than any of the others?

The whole truth!

There was someone at the door, and the sergeant on duty

opened it, setting a rectangle of hard radiance at the end of the long courtroom. For a moment, before the door was shut again, Daddy appeared in stiff silhouette. He had turned and was facing the staff-captain, answering his questions.

"No, I can't agree to that."

The staff-captain leaned forward and rested his hands on the table. His ginger moustache was aggressive; he was being clever.

"But, Captain Watson, the whole of your evidence seems to me to have been directed to one end: that is, to showing that conditions at the fort were such that this offence was inevitable."

"Not inevitable."

"Then what?"

"Explicable, perhaps."

The staff-captain raised his eyebrows very obviously. He wanted everyone to see this unspoken comment. He shrugged his shoulders and felt that he ought to have been a barrister. That was what they said to him sometimes: "You're wasted in the army, Geoffrey, you ought to have gone to the Bar or something." He raised his voice slightly and tried to affect a puzzled expression.

"Explicable, Captain Watson?"

Daddy seemed to know that he was cornered. "I'll put it this way," he said. "I consider that my cross-examination of your witnesses so shook their evidence that it cannot be relied upon. I therefore suggested that there was no case to answer. Apparently the Court still believes your witnesses, in spite of the fact that they contradicted themselves and each other repeatedly."

"This seems to be rather a sidetrack," the staff-captain said softly. "We have been into this before. I think we had got to the point where, without admitting this offence, you said you considered it—er—explicable. Perhaps you would amplify that remark for us?"

"I have shown that the prisoner's tendencies are normal," Daddy said desperately. "He has a wife and four children. I am certainly not admitting that he committed this offence, much less that it has been proved against him. I am trying to say that, if the Court *does* consider he committed it, conditions at the fort were such that it might almost have been expected."

Daddy turned and faced the president. He seemed to grow in stature. "In fact, sir, I am submitting that, in the circumstances, this charge—proved or not proved—is scarcely an offence at all."

"Captain Watson," the staff-captain said quickly, "you are admitting, in fact, that you believe in the guilt of the prisoner."

"Not at all."

"I must remind you that you are not at this moment defending officer. You have elected to give evidence on behalf of the prisoner."

Daddy made no answer.

"You are remembering that you are on oath?"

Daddy faced the staff-captain again and, knowing him, Tubby could read his dislike for those ginger moustaches, the ginger eyebrows, and the thin, ginger hair that was brushed back off the slightly freckled forehead. "I am remembering that," he said.

"Then I suggest to you that you believe the prisoner to be guilty?"

"My beliefs have nothing to do with it."

"Then I suggest that you have knowledge, knowledge of facts, that leads you to believe this offence was committed. Perhaps I should remind you again of your oath. You have sworn to speak the whole truth."

Daddy hesitated.

"You must answer that, Captain Watson," the General said.

Daddy looked at the staff-captain. "Will you please repeat the question?"

"Certainly . . . certainly. I suggest that you had knowledge, specific knowledge of certain facts; and that those facts lead you to suppose this offence was committed. Just yes or no, Captain Watson."

You could see Daddy bracing himself to answer.

"Yes," he said quietly.

The staff-captain had not been prepared for such success. "There are facts which lead you to believe this offence was committed?"

"Yes. But not in particular by the prisoner."

"By whom then?"

"Not by the prisoner. It is the prisoner only who is on trial."

The staff-captain looked towards the General for assistance, but the General made no sign. His hands were on the table before him, his pen laid down in front of them. His wide blue eyes were gazing placidly past everyone to the far end of the room. Finding no ally, the staff-captain returned to the final assault. "You mean that you knew this offence was going on, was in fact being committed?"

"Not by the prisoner. I don't know that."

"But by others of your command?"

Daddy did not move. Except for his hand, which was resting on his sword hilt, he was standing at attention.

"Yes," he said.

"At the time did you know it was going on? Are you saying that all along you *knew* it was being committed?"

The silence in the room was terrible. Tubby looked desperately towards Daddy, praying for some means of creating a disturbance; for something that would break that dreadful quiet, that would put a stop to this long chain of inevitable questions which demanded these cruel answers. Once you were out there giving evidence, you were lost; your barriers were shattered; your innermost defences were open to exploration. There was no sure stronghold of secrecy for you to fall back upon.

The General shifted ponderously in his chair. "*Did* you know it was going on, Captain Watson?"

"Yes, sir."

"And you did nothing to stop it?"

There was a long, swelling pause.

"No!"

The word was hurled into the silence. There was either a clock somewhere in the room or Tubby's wrist watch was ticking sonorously, momentously, resisting the passage of each fatal second. The staff-captain was no longer leaning forward. His thumbs were tucked complacently into his belt and he was standing upright.

"*Could* you have stopped it, Captain Watson?"

"I daresay. Yes, I believe so."

Tubby was as surprised as anyone. In spite of what Daddy said to him, he had not believed this: that matters were so clear-cut and simple; that Daddy had known all the time that this vice, this crime—the thought of which raised nausea in a decent person—had actually been prevalent; that, knowing it, he had taken no steps to stop it and that, speaking the truth with a hard integrity that few men were capable of conceiving, he must admit that it had been in his power to put an end to the practice. No less than anyone in the court, Tubby asked himself why Daddy said no more to amplify this self-accusation, to alleviate the charge, to defend himself against it.

Nothing but the truth!

Tubby waited in anguish. Why did Daddy not go on? Why did he not explain, for instance, that he could have stopped it only because his men loved him and he could control them; but that, had he suppressed this particular outbreak of vice, the evil engendered by conditions at the fort would have suppurated in some other manner. Looking back on it all, that was surely the explanation.

"Captain Watson," the General said sharply, "you admit that it was going on, that you could have stopped it. Then why in heaven's name didn't you?"

Daddy's face did not move. "I did not stop it, sir, because under the circumstances I did not believe it to be wrong."

"Did not believe it to be wrong! Did you think it right, then?"

The General spoke harshly. The staff-captain had sat down, so that now it was between Daddy and the court, between him and outraged decency.

"I did not believe it to be wrong any more than I believed it to be right. I believed it to be something quite natural."

"Will you kindly explain yourself?"

"I had to face facts, sir. I was in command of a hundred and fifty men, all of them between the ages of twenty and thirty, all of them healthy and normal. A man is an animal, for all that he is a human being. He has sexual appetites which, at that age, can only be assuaged physically. I did what I could, in the way of concerts and lectures and organized games, to keep their minds occupied and their bodies tired; but that was nothing. It is a schoolmaster's theory that physical exercise dulls physical appetites. We are not schoolmasters. We face facts and we know that the reverse is the case. Nothing dulls sexual appetites except satisfaction."

Nobody moved. They just sat, solid, resistant, while the words beat up against them, rebounded, died unacknowledged. . . .

"We all know," Daddy went on steadily, "what happened to certain units in the hill stations of India when the order was given to close the brothels. I knew that the same thing would happen in my command. If I had wanted to, I could not have opened a brothel. To be honest, I thought about it; but there were insufficient women in the village. . . . Failing a brothel, I knew just what would happen; and anyone else who'd thought about it would have known the same.

"I am, of course, well aware that in England so-called unnatural vice is considered a crime. I cannot see that it is a crime in the sort of place where we were stationed, because I cannot see that it was unnatural. To my mind, it was the most natural thing in the world. In the absolute sense, the satisfaction of sexual appetites, except for purposes of procreation—breeding, sir—is to my mind always unnatural; that is if we take the behavior of the animal world as our standard. Homosexuality has no appeal for me, and I could never indulge in it; but I am sufficiently well aware of its universal practice throughout the world for it not to sicken me. Shut up a hundred and fifty young men in a fort and give them no other sexual outlet, and they'll soon find in unnatural vice a natural enough solution to their discomforts.

"That is all I have to say, sir. I was aware that homosexuality was being practiced in my command. Any experienced officer, any intelligent man in my position, would have known it. But I must insist that, beyond the evidence that has been given today, I have not the slightest reason to suppose that the prisoner himself indulged in it."

There was, of course, a long silence. Daddy waited, standing quite still and at attention. His face was white and strained, and he was square and upright, the dramatic, melodramatic figure of a hopeless crusader. All that he had said was true and so much more than true. Tubby knew it and knew that Daddy had sought a degree of truthfulness that belonged only to visions. You could not lecture generals and ginger-whiskered staff officers and certainly not the monkey-faced major. But Daddy had done worse than that; he had preached, not at them, but at the sky above their heads. He had exposed himself in front of men for whom his words had scarcely a superficial meaning.

The members of the court were decent, honest people; but when they met honesty, developed beyond the fetus, they found it sheer indecency. They knew from experience that young men, imprisoned together without feminine company, indulged too often in this vice. But it was a knowledge that was rigidly abstract, that must not be particularized, that might only be admitted in retrospect. Applied to the present tense, it must be primly disregarded; eyes must be closed, consciousness shuttered.

For them, it was more than sufficient that the practice was forbidden by law, was known to be foul, unnatural. Lawbreaking demanded punishment. It was not for them to get on terms with humanity or to fashion their own code of understanding. It was easier than that. They had, they thanked God, a simple, honest, decent way of thinking.

The General's chair grated impatiently on the floor. "Captain Higgins, have you any more questions?"

"No, sir, I'll leave it at that."

"Very well, Captain Watson."

Daddy walked back to his table, his eyes traversing the court without meeting those of any of its members. His glance passed coldly over Tubby. Pale from the reaction that followed his self-revelation, he lowered himself slowly into his chair again.

The General's voice was harsh, as though it armoured him against the dangerous atmosphere that Daddy had created. "Is there anything else, Captain Watson?"

"No, sir. That concludes the defence. If you don't mind I will put in a written statement."

"Is it ready?"

Daddy passed across a typed sheet of paper, handing it to
Tubby who sat nearest to him, refusing to meet Tubby's eyes
and to accept his sympathy. The paper was passed along to the
General who glanced at it quickly.

"Do you want it read out, Captain Watson?"

"No, thank you, sir. The substance was contained in my
evidence."

"Very well, then. The court is adjourned to consider the
verdict."

The prisoner and escort were marched out and the court
was cleared of all but its members. They pushed back their
chairs and stretched themselves, and the General came slowly
along the table to Tubby. He moved heavily and with the rolling gait of a sailor.

"No, no," he said. "Don't get up. Have a cigarette, will you?"

"Thank you, sir."

The General unbuttoned the pocket of his jacket and pulled
out a cigarette case. Every movement that he made was deliberate, heavy and important. You could almost hear him
creak as he lowered himself carefully onto the edge of the table
and sat there with one leg swinging clumsily.

"Well, young feller, made up your mind about it?"

"Not entirely, sir."

"Haven't you? Well, we've half an hour or so . . . we'll run
over the case in a minute, shall we?"

"Yes, sir."

"You have to give your verdict first, you know? Junior member always speaks first; you know that, don't you?"

"Yes, sir."

The General got up off the table and started to walk away.
Then he turned and came back and stood, almost awkwardly,
almost embarrassed, behind Tubby. He looked across the room,
keeping his eyes high up and distant, and speaking in his short,
clipped, jerky phrases.

"You mustn't take it amiss, young feller, what I'm going to
say to you. You mustn't mind it, eh?"

"No, of course not."

"Nothing to do with me really, nothing whatever. I hear you've been seeing rather a lot of that Mrs. Clements."

"How did you hear that, sir?"

The General looked down, smiled and turned away again. There was a lot of kindness in his smile and, after it, his precise speech seemed more benevolent. "We hear these things. We hear them. Is it true, can you tell me? Nothing to do with me, mind you."

"No, sir, it's not true. I've seen her on and off at the club; at polo and so on. I've only once been to her house. I went there to dinner."

"You did, did you?" the General said, speaking very staccato but quietly, his gaze across the room, very distant. "The devil you did! And I'll bet her husband wasn't there; away on trek or something."

Tubby looked up and caught the General's eye and smiled. His conceit urged him to let the General know how things stood. His code forbade that he should put the situation into words. The smile was sufficient. The General echoed it.

"You know a lot, sir," Tubby said.

"Pretty obvious, my boy."

"Is it?"

"She's a bit that way inclined—so they tell me . . . the only trouble is the whole of Khartoum hears about it. Every man, woman and child . . . wouldn't do for me to go there, would it? Never do for me. Wouldn't do at all, eh?"

"No, sir."

The General twisted up his face ferociously, as if he were playing with his children. "Why d'you say it like that, eh? I'm not as old as all that, am I? I daresay I'm not as old as you think, young feller."

"I didn't mean it that way, sir. I meant about everyone knowing. It wouldn't do for you, sir. . . ."

"Of course."

The General moved away a pace and then rocked himself back again. "I'm glad you found her, young feller, glad you got hold of her. Or she got hold of you—might be closer to the truth. Glad of it anyway. A young feller has to have his greens once in a way. Keep your interest below the navel, as we say in the Army. You'll come to no harm that way."

Tubby looked down and knew that he was blushing. He felt ridiculously like a child. The General's hand was on his shoulder, kneading it. "I'm glad it's that way, young feller. Your commanding officer's a good man; a splendid war record, you know, quite splendid. But a bit of a crank in some things. Whatever he may say, it's more natural to take your greens the way you and I do it. Don't you think so?" He gave Tubby's shoulder a twist. "More natural, don't you think so? More healthy, you know, anyway."

"Yes, sir," Tubby said, looking hard at the blank sheet of paper that was on the table in front of him.

❧ The General sat down again, and everyone stopped talking, the odd remarks that finished off a conversation straying into the silence.

"Well, gentlemen, shall we make up our minds about this business?"

He started to turn over the buff forms that were covered with his own crabbed, unnatural writing. He turned to the major on his right, the one with a face like a monkey.

"How do you feel about it, Tony?"

"Well, sir . . ."

"I don't want a verdict yet."

"No, sir, of course. But it seems fairly clear to me. The witnesses didn't behave well under Watson's cross-examination. That's true enough; but I dunno that it makes a heap of difference. You don't expect it in this sort of case. Shouldn't care to be giving evidence meself, if you take me. . . ."

"I should hope not, Tony."

The major grunted. "Haven't come to that yet, have we, General?"

"Not yet," said the General. "Then you're settled in your mind about it?"

"I'm inclined to believe the witnesses, sir."

"Very well. And you, Richards?"

The General turned to his left hand.

"I'm afraid I think the same, sir," Richards said regretfully. "If we believe the witnesses, I take it there's no more to be said about it. As I see it, Watson's remarks were, well . . . er . . . interesting but a bit irrelevant."

"And you, Porter?"

"I don't know, sir. Those three or four witnesses; they didn't face the boards too well. Watson rattled 'em a bit, I thought."

"Would you like me to read over the evidence?" the General asked. "How do you feel about it, Allardyce?"

"If you'd just read the cross-examination, sir."

"Certainly."

While the General was reading from his transcription, Tubby knew suddenly that his mind had been made up all along. It was quite obvious that the sergeant-major was guilty and that he had been proved guilty by the evidence that had been given that morning. The other members of the court must feel the same about it. This pretense at indecision was only to ease their consciences.

How much did they care, he wondered, one way or the other. He, himself—if he were honest about it—though he knew and admired the sergeant-major and had grown to consider him almost a friend, was unable to feel deeply about it. There was something in the atmosphere of a court-martial that bred a healthy indifference, that encouraged cold, clear-headed sanity, that forbade such sentiments as pity, regret and sympathy from obtruding upon your judgment. He knew that he ought to feel more strongly about it; that humanity demanded it. Having made his mind up, he tried to hallow himself into pity through the medium of thought and imagination.

Outside the court, Higgins, bristling and self-satisfied, would be chatting with Daddy. As likely as not, Daddy would no longer be the man who, half an hour ago, had spoken with such tragic vehemence. The cruel cynicism of his outer folds would have closed in upon his core of utter feeling. He would be smoking, of course, and possibly joking with Higgins, his face (if you knew it) unsmiling, hiding himself beneath its mask of deliberate inscrutability. "Poor bugger," he'd be saying with grim humor.

In the room next door, the sergeant-major would be sitting with an escort of his peers. They would have given him a cigarette, but the company would be silent in embarrassment and sympathy. He would be looking straight before him, his feelings tucked right down within his frozen self, curled up upon himself like an animal succumbed to terror. It was sad, all right, to think of the sergeant-major like that. But it didn't hurt personally. It was an offence against taste that the mighty should be publicly humbled. It was disillusionment; another castle broken up somewhere. But that was all. Compassion, poignant regrets, were quite absent.

"Well, young feller," the General said, "have you made up your mind yet?"

Tubby stubbed out his cigarette, feeling somehow as if he were going to church and that this moment demanded from him some symbol of respect, something of ceremony.

"Guilty, sir," he said, his voice ringing unexpectedly loud through the courtroom.

Once more the night confined them to the territory of their own lamplight. They sat on the parapet of the fort and, below them, the sand was pale and indefinite. Overhead, the night itself, all stars, immeasurably deep, unbelievably infinite in its tracery of stars and linked constellations and wisps of luminosity, swept down on every side, encaging them in their own world of a lamp, a table, two chairs, two glasses and a half-empty bottle of whisky.

The magnitude of the night did not reduce them to unimportance. It forbade them to expand. It confined them and, by concentrating within them all that was vital to themselves, made them more potent. They were filled to bursting. They were impregnated with power, a power which came from the reaction to the utterly unconquerable continent in which they were minutely existent. To every action there is an equal and opposite reaction. To the unbelievable force that is Africa, the soul responds indomitably.

Daddy refilled both glasses and pushed one towards Tubby.

"Thank God, today is over," Tubby said.

"Don't, for God's sake, talk about the court-martial."

"I wasn't going to."

"You mustn't, anyway," Daddy said in real pain. "You had to swear an oath about it, didn't you? You mayn't talk about it, you know. You mayn't tell me the verdict. You mayn't tell me what they're going to do to him. You mustn't say how long they're going to lock him up for. I don't want to know anyway. I'm finished with the court-martial. Something had to come out of me today and it came out. I feel cleaner—even though I made a damn fool of myself."

"No, no!" Tubby said.

"Don't let's be polite at this sort of time. Let's stick to the truth. . . ."

Tubby looked upwards, yearningly upwards at the bowed heavens. . . . "The truth!" he said. "Like the night, it's too big. So big that you can't understand it. . . . I was thinking about it a bit today while—while you were giving evidence."

Daddy smiled. "Thinking about the truth, were you?"

"I *do* think sometimes, Daddy."

Tubby was almost pathetic. The night had done for him. The storm of emotions that filled him demanded thought and yet defied thought to lessen its turbulence.

"I know," Daddy said. "I know. Like a blasted mother, I've watched the birth of thought in you. I've suckled it and weaned it and reared it and now I'm beginning to see it toddle. But truth . . . that's rather a tall order, isn't it?"

"Truth and what you believe in; they're all mixed up and you can't stop thinking about them. What's true to you is a downright lie to me. What *you* believe in just makes nonsense when *I* puzzle it out; especially when I put it against the sort of things that Sammy used to live for."

Daddy took a long drink. "Ah, that," he said. "Sammy believed in everything. He believed desperately that everything was fundamentally good. How I wish I could. But *I* . . . I distrust the world; I'm suspicious of everything in it. There's not much *I* believe in."

"Do you believe in anything?"

Daddy put his glass down on the table and stretched out his arms to the desert and to the immense night and to the deepest purple where the two were wedded. "I believe in the divinity of complete consciousness," he said solemnly; "divinely unattainable, you know. If it weren't, it would mean—that the peace of God which passeth all understanding had been comprehended. . . ."

"Complete consciousness," Tubby murmured, as if the taste were familiar; as if an echo of unknown thoughts had come back from across the valley, a thousand times louder, clearer, than it had started. Clearer—without the trammel of unspecified yearning that often filled him . . . "Passeth all understanding" . . . words of a grief that almost brought tears in a night so big, so loving, so fearsome.

"Complete consciousness," Daddy said again, so quietly that his thoughts scarcely found expression. "Infinite knowledge, infinite power . . . and . . . and, Sammy would have said, infinite love. . . ." He looked away, ashamed it seemed of so simple, so clear, a philosophy; regretting that words so plainly served, so lacking the herbs and spice of cynicism, should have been drawn out of him by a puff of sentimentality.

"The difference between Sammy and me (he was speaking in his normal voice again and his words were harsh by contrast) is that he thinks it's all attainable. He *knows* it and *I* know he's wrong . . . I know he's wrong," he said again, his voice rising so that you could feel the tension, like skin drawn tight above something evil that was demanding exit; a boil come to a head, unable to hold its badness any longer. "There isn't any Sammy," he cried. "He died, he's dead, he's buried—and there is nothing left of him . . . Nothing! Sleep! Eternal sleep. Peace. That is the rounding off of our lives. . . ."

He put his head in his hands. He wasn't acting or posing; he had scarcely drunk anything. "If I'm wrong," he said almost below his breath, "if I *could* be wrong—then life, the fight, the struggle against all the hopeless odds of cruel humanity, just mean nothing. The armour that all my life I've been forging against the last defeat—the defeat that is a victory—

wouldn't be wanted. I'd have to start again as a baby you see. A pink, clean-washed baby with all the victories taken from me. A pitiable, helpless creature, dependent on the tenderness of others. . . .

"I've fought them, Tubby," he said, talking like an old man, like someone who has glimpsed between the trees the end of a journey. "I've gone back fighting, every step of the way; and I must fight till I die, because that can be the only fulfillment —death in battle. The only way that I can have one moment of triumph before sleep gets me . . . you see that, Tubby? You must see it?" He was pleading, abjectly pleading, to be left his trust in the purity of evil. "The world's foul, rotten, and full of power. And we have one life, one tiny fraction of eternity in which to fight it. . . ."

Tubby drew breath for denial. "No," he could have said at once, responding in the hot, passionate tenor of Daddy's words. But he didn't. He was out of sympathy, disdainful at last of someone who could be so rent by passion. He didn't answer immediately. He lay back in his chair, stretching, hearing the crack of his muscles, feeling, all at once, very clean, very muscular, very superior. He knew what words fitted here; the way in which they must be uttered; breezily, like a nurse with a difficult child; like a clergyman, to whom you have gone with a hurt spirit, who puts it all right with a few God-given truths— straight from the shoulder.

"No!" he said. "You're talking rot, Daddy, and you know it. Sammy lives for all time. So do we all. What's good in us goes on—I don't know about the evil. But Sammy was so much good, so nearly all-good, that he lives completely. Why, man, I've known it and you've known it. He's stood with us. He's put words in our mouths; he's talked over our shoulders. . . ."

"You fool!"

Daddy's laughter was horrible, warning you that the man across the table scarcely clung to sanity. "You fool," he cried. "That's not Sammy! That's the good, the spirit side, of yourself that finds the words that come out of you. And the spirit is mortal like the rest—it dies with the body. Sammy's dead. Dead, I tell you. When you think it's him, it's because it was he who

started your spirit moving, stuck a pin into it and made it
wriggle, took away your smug, righteous satisfaction, gave you
the arms to fight with—if you'll only learn to use them, made
it so that you can go into oblivion fighting, losing of course,
but fighting to the last breath of that body you're so proud
of. . . ."

"Fighting for what?" The question was whipped out of
Tubby long before his thoughts had formed it. Thought followed speech now; just as it followed action in times of physical
crisis.

"Fighting for . . . for the sake of fighting. For self-respect, for
individuality. To stop yourself from being squashed like a fly,
churned up with all the muck and simpletons of humanity into
a squashed-fly biscuit. Fighting the wickedness, the adversity
that come out of the dark to strike you down, to stop you from
being a man, a single glorious creature of volition—*that's* what
they want to do to you. . . ."

"No, no," Tubby breathed; the words scarcely sounding.
It didn't do; it still didn't do. And Daddy himself had denied
it. Memory fumbled back for the answer—already spoken. He
closed his eyes, and the words were so clear that they might
have been written on the heavens, blazing the night. "Long,
long ago," he said slowly, "you gave yourself the lie direct.
And what you said comes back—comes back often—as if it
meant something that I haven't yet grasped; as if it held so
much truth that you can never grasp all of it. 'One of the company,' you said, 'who use adversity . . . Sweet uses!' "

"Yes—as an enemy." The words were rapped out as if
Daddy thought that, by a quick riposte, he could end the encounter.

"One of the men who climb the mountain," Tubby went on
steadily, parrying, hilt against hilt, locking the rapiers.

"To jump off the top into glorious oblivion."

"No!"

But there was no more to be said really; only this flat denial.
You couldn't put reason, common sense, soap-and-water rightness against this twisted dogma. You couldn't fight it; no more
than to set up the blank defence of all your longing; the beliefs

that must be true because you needed them so badly. You couldn't argue any further. "No. . . ."

"No . . . perhaps No . . . I daresay you're right, Tubby. Part of me—most of me—says you're right. But, if I give in, I'm left helpless, quite helpless. No arms, no armour. At anyone's mercy. You see that, don't you? I've got to believe in the fight, because man must have some sort of conviction. He's got to believe in something. If it can't be positive, the negative is better than nothing. If you can't find a truth you can trust, then believe desperately that everything is false; that, since there is no good, all is evil; that, without God, the world must belong to the devil. That the best of men have only neutral values. They aren't allies, but they aren't against you. They may not kick you further into the slime, but they won't help you out of it . . . if there *is* a God he is simply a part of the universe in which there is no evil. . . . *That's* something to go on. One day I may find something better. I doubt it. And in the meanwhile, I'll believe in . . . in . . ."

"In the divinity of complete consciousness;" (again Tubby was speaking beyond his knowledge, apart from his reason) "in something you can't ever get, can't ever hope for?"

"No!" Daddy said violently, waving his glass in the air. "I'll believe in whisky; it's easier."

❧ Sometime later, in a calm, quite reasonable manner, they came back to it again.

"The difference between me and Sammy," Daddy said, "is that, though we both make arms out of sorrow, he found his armour in innocence, in his belief in goodness. His defence was easy—he wouldn't admit there was a war on. Mine isn't so easy—I won't admit defeat. Time and again I'm beaten; but I call up reserves and more reserves, and I seem to find they're unlimited. And I fight on propaganda, on blazing abroad their imbecility. I mock their foulness and make swords out of my own laughter. I see the whole picture and find it funny. But Sammy didn't. He closed his eyes and deceived himself. He was romantic. I'm a realist . . . and you—Tubby—you don't know what you are. . . ."

"Me? Oh, me. . . ." Tubby was tiring of this research. It was all right, from time to time, to probe affairs for the truth of them. But they had gone deep enough for this evening. He was feeling very much a gentleman, prepared to accept things as they were, without looking for trouble. "Me?" he said brightly. "Oh, I'm just an ordinary sixty-per-cent human being. Taking the world all round, I suppose I'm a trifle over the halfway line; below the saints and above the savages. . . . Intellect? I haven't got much, but put me against an aborigine, a farm laborer or a politician, and I don't come off so badly. I'm not such a bad chap; not much of a self-seeker; I only want distinguished obscurity, as we say in the Army. And my body's good; I'm fit and healthy. Sixty-per-cent—that's me; and it suits me nicely. . . ."

"Oh, no," Daddy said. "You may consider yourself halfway up the scale of the world's human beings. But you're scarcely ten-per-cent a man—and you know it. And, what's more, it doesn't suit you."

It was Tubby's turn now to feel the sudden twist of fear. This was the leap that he'd come to so often, only to stop short without the courage to take it. He couldn't escape now; not from Daddy. He had to follow him. . . . "All right," he said, "it doesn't suit me then; hasn't suited me for a long, long time; not since my accident; not since you and Sammy and Lydia started talking at me . . . not since—as you said—between the lot of you, you faced me to the rock and made me climb it . . . and" (he asked viciously) "where has it taken me? You told me I'd stop and draw breath from time to time—and, my God, haven't I? I've been in the same place, stuck on the same ledge, for what seems a lifetime. . . ."

"In the clouds perhaps?" Daddy suggested mildly. "You can't see up or down? The sun's above, but there's a nice, warm valley below. And you can't move in any direction?"

"That's it," Tubby said, grasping at it. "The clouds. Like in a mist; you know you're lost but you haven't an idea which way to go to find the path again."

"Sammy would have said upwards."

"I know. But it's worse than that. I don't even know which

is upwards; I'm lost completely. I've learned to feel, to suffer from sadness and beauty, to be driven half mad by the ideas that whisper inside me . . . but they won't speak out! Now and again there's a sort of break in the clouds. I think I've seen something—but the mists close in on me before I've understood it. There's some things I know now that I didn't before; that what you see of a thing is the least important part of it; that the most obvious is often the least true; that the old simplicities were perhaps false, childish illusions. . . ."

"Childish?" Daddy said. "They weren't the illusions of a child. That was the trouble. A child is conscious of its growth. You had reached a static condition. . . ."

"All right. I've got past that, then. But there I am stuck; only learning what *isn't*, never what *is*. And so never getting any further."

Daddy smiled, his face in the shadow. This speech was premeditated, was the product of some sort of abstract thought. This was truly a beginning.

"You see," he said, "how the pendulum swings over; how it goes in cycles? Only this evening—ages and ages ago—it was you who put me in order; you, who were sane and masterful, while I despaired at a chipped and battered philosophy. This is my revenge! You were so sure then—and now . . . but you understand it? We're not the same men talking. It's not you and me—Tubby and Daddy. It isn't even different versions of ourselves. It's quite different people contained within our single bodies. There's you in me and me in you. It's very perplexing. . . ."

"It's all perplexing," Tubby cried. "Each step you take, you get more and more lost, further astray, entangled deeper. I'm off on a journey—you all tell me—but I'm not getting anywhere. I'm not moving; still on that ledge we talked about; still drawing breath." He laughed, a little embarrassed. "It's so easy, you see, to turn round and go back. To be a nice, simple, happy person again. . . ."

"You wouldn't be happy," Daddy said quickly, so anxious to believe it. "You'll never again be happy that way."

"Perhaps not," Tubby said; "and perhaps you're wrong—all

of you." He spoke lightly, putting a veneer of carelessness over a real distress. The well-bred part of him was very persistent this evening, restraining him as Daddy led him on, warning him, pointing him back in the old direction. "Perhaps I wouldn't be all that happy," he said, "but it would be easy anyway. Easy to go on as a good, steady, hard-drinking, hard-riding officer until I ended up as a general, making life hell for anyone who tried to be different. . . . But you've set me against that; started me off on something else. And I'm stuck in a hopeless tangle of things that hurt; and I don't want to be hurt. I want to move on again. And . . ." he felt a rising anger against them, the old anger returned, but he choked it back, forcing a laugh, taking refuge in a pretense of finding it funny. "And . . . will . . . you . . . please . . . tell . . . me . . . what . . . I . . . have . . . to . . . do . . . about . . . it . . . ?"

"You can't do anything," Daddy said at last. "You can only wait and let what's rotten crumble before your eyes and take what's left to build upon. You can only know that some day, through some misfortune, some person, some adventure, you will find an independence—my sort or Sammy's sort—that will make you free to love the world or to hate it. . . . As you know," he cried, humility flooding him, "*I* haven't the right to preach. *I* can't help anyone. But I swear to you that to remain static, smug, content with things as you find them and as you see them, is to be no better than an animal, is a denial of what man has inside him . . . I say it is the power to fight. Sammy called it—the power to love. . . ."

❧ The gift of silence fell upon them, as fine and precious as any gift of tongues; not a negative state—not just that there was no need for speech—but a positive comfort, lulling the senses, freeing the soul.

It was the more remarkable since they had played out of tune the whole evening. They had met at the start, each with a need that might well have been satisfied. For it was often that these hours on the parapet of the Fort had brought a sudden moment of sympathy, a burst of music when two spirits came at last into harmony. But not tonight. Since sunset, they had wandered up and down the scale striking discordancies. Now, in the end, they were together.

One of the lamps had died out, and Daddy was in darkness. Tubby lay back, at last contented, sprawling easily; a powerful man, with the lightly-fleshed parts of his body linked gracefully together; a certain grace in the repose of strong muscles. You could see with great clearness the modeling that had been done on him lately; as if a sculptor had started with a crude assembly of the features and had worked them into his own idealism, sensing the characters that were still embryonic in his model, finding a trace of them in each feature, tracing the link between the features, the rhythm that was coming.

And, for sometime, this knowledge of a new self had been growing in Tubby. It was not that one self was replacing the other but that the two were living side by side; the old one, a beefy, hearty chap, Windrush-old-boy; the other, darker, finer, sensitive and often timid, more truly Tubby. And these two talked together, argued, quarreled and were less and less in sympathy. They were predominant in turn; but the one who was subjugated for the moment was always just round the corner, waiting his chance to step back again.

"To hell with all this," said Windrush-old-boy; "this silly argument, these doubts, this man Daddy, a disgruntled old gentleman. Why can't we settle down and be happy. Don't we know, don't we remember—'that state of life in which it pleased God. . . .' Hang on to that, you fool. You haven't the right to go traipsing around trying to better yourself and upsetting everyone. It isn't fair on me. It was all right before, wasn't it?"

"Yes," Tubby had to admit. "It was all right before. All right, that is, at the time. But when I look back on it, I know that I wasn't happy. And, even in those days, when I looked forward I had to shut my eyes quickly."

"You make me sick," said Windrush-old-boy. "Why look forward and backwards? Don't look at all if the sight isn't pleasing. The best people live with their eyes shut. That's how the world keeps rotating."

"Oh yes, oh yes," Tubby answered; "a crowd of people on a treadmill—that's what keeps the world turning. And the convicts aren't unhappy because they want no more than food, sleep, exercise. That's what you want to be—a convict."

The argument thickened, at each retort the two men finding themselves more directly opposed to each other.

"Convicts!" said Windrush-old-man, "you're at it again. What do you want with these queer ideas, this constant likening of one thing to another? Speak plain English."

"A simile," Tubby said, "has a certain value . . ."

"Always talking about values! Similes are dangerous, only near enough to the truth to be misleading. We don't want similes here."

"You're as bad as the General—'we don't want Greek here,' he said."

"I like that! As bad as the General! You're a soldier, aren't you? What more can you want than to become a general? If you didn't want to grow into a general, why did you join the Army? We're soldiers, do you hear? And, if we were going to make fun of soldiers, we'd no right to take the King's commission. It's all that blasted fellow, Watson. A grumbling, seditious, ineffectual, bad-tempered, fat, unhealthy little man with a grievance. . . ."

"And yet," Tubby said, "there's something fine about him."

"Only what you imagine into him," Windrush-old-man said scornfully. "Other people don't see him like that, I can tell you. Put him out of our life. It's him that's caused all this trouble. If it wasn't for him, you'd be a clean, decent, healthy-minded soldier, like the dozens of other subalterns we know."

"No! There's Sammy, you forget . . ."

"Sammy's dead. Dead, buried and forgotten. See what happened to him! He's nobody."

"If you were right," Tubby said gently, "I'd give way about the rest."

"He's dead, isn't he?" Windrush-old-man asked petulantly. "You haven't gone as crackers as all that, for God's sake! Dead's still dead. As dead as a bullet through the heart can make you."

Tubby drew himself up in his chair. "Sammy isn't dead. It's something that I can't and won't argue; something that I know with a certainty that is beyond all argument. . . . And you know it too, Windrush."

Windrush-old-boy was silent.

🎖 On their way from the parapet, going down the long concrete ramp that led to the compound and thence to their quarters, Daddy took hold of Tubby's arm and held it. It was too dark for their faces to be more than pale and expressionless masks, scarred with deep shadow. But Daddy's grip was hard and urgent.

"Tubby," he whispered. "I've got to get away from here, get away from all this. You see that, don't you?"

"Why . . . yes. . . ."

"It's necessary, you see . . . I can't explain it, Tubby, but when two people have been together, have been man and wife together for a long time, and each has given all he has to give to the other, and each has taken all that there is to take in the other . . . they must separate for a time, you see. That's you and me, Tubby. . . ."

"Of course," Tubby said. "We've stirred each other up a bit. It's time to let it settle. It may be good to start stirring again later. . . ."

"That's it, that's it . . . but it isn't only that. I must make a break; a hard, sharp break. . . . You could manage here for a bit, couldn't you?"

"Sure, old boy," Tubby said soothingly. "You slip off somewhere for a month. Heaven knows you've earned a holiday."

"That's good of you, Tubby. And they'll give me leave all right—after the court-martial. They'll think I'm going crackers. . . . That's what people are always thinking about me. They get at me that way. And I *must* go somewhere where they can't. I *must* find someone who doesn't think like that, else . . . else," he drew close to Tubby, whispering in his ear; "else I *shall* go crackers, Tubby." He let go of Tubby's arm and walked on a pace or two. "I could get up to Cairo," he said in an ordinary voice, "and join my brother. He's there on business."

"Your genius brother!"

"No . . . no. Don't laugh at him, Tubby. I'm a fool about

him, I know; a sentimental old woman, if you like. But most people have a weak joint in their armour; they have one thing you mustn't laugh about. And with me—it's my brother."

"I wasn't laughing," Tubby said untruthfully. "I was only being a bit lighthearted."

"That's all right," Daddy said out of the darkness. "But there *is* something really fine about that boy; something that makes you feel you're with a great man when you go about with him. Some quality that makes the world buoyant, so that you float on top of it. I don't suppose," he said wistfully, "that you'd understand it. . . ."

"I'm sure he's a fine fellow," said Windrush. "I'm sure he's the hell of a chap. . . . But what about a spot of shut-eye?"

✤ "Our last evening together, Tubby. I wonder how you'll get on alone here. It's your first command, isn't it? It's cleansing, having a command to yourself. But it's dangerous. It's too simple and easy, like life when you start off as a soldier. It's good for you and bad for you. Good, because what you say is law, so that it matters what you say and you have to think about it. Bad, because it seems such a big thing and it's really so ridiculously easy. People say: 'He can't be such a fool, he commanded a division.' Nonsense!

"It's clever, of course, to make people obey you and follow you if they haven't got to. But here they *have* to and want to. The Army makes you into a creature that has one craving in life above all others—obedience. You eat, drink and breathe orders. And so long as you are given orders, it doesn't seem to matter a great deal what they are. You go on being an efficient soldier. And *that's* lucky for the generals. . . .

"So don't go on thinking you're clever because men obey you and nothing goes wrong while I'm away—will you? It's for your own sake; it doesn't matter in the least to anyone else. But you *can* know this—that, if you make a mess of it, you *must* be a blithering idiot."

✤ "A last whisky to wish each other luck . . . and, when I come back, Tubby, you must go off yourself. Immediately. Allow us a day for handing over, and then slip off somewhere. . . . Got anything special in view?"

"I thought of getting someone to come up the Dinder or the Rahad with me. It might be a good trip."

"Don't get someone," Daddy said quickly. "Go alone; it's important."

"Alone? That might be rather boring . . . alone!" (Windrush-old-man had come leaping forward, horrified at the suggestion.) "I'd go crazy!"

"You can't tell until you try it. Have you ever, in all your life, been alone for more than an hour or so?"

"No bloody fear," said Windrush.

"It isn't surprising. Not at all unusual. Most, in fact nearly all, Europeans have never been alone. They die without ever being alone and without ever realizing that they've never had the pleasure of their own uninterrupted company. . . .

"Of course, most people wouldn't mind if the thought *did* occur to them. They find it natural for men to be always herded together, for each to be dependent on his neighbors, for actions to be governed, not by thought or need or impulse, but by communal expediency. Love thy neighbor, you know . . . a hateful order. . . .

"But whether other men would like to be alone or not, very few of them ever get the chance of trying. The factory hand, the clerk, the professional man—it's out of the question for them. Yet they ought to have the opportunity of discovering themselves. Because, if you find yourself good company, you're a very strong man—I can tell you."

"All right," Tubby said, ejecting the more robust Windrush, "I think I'll try it."

Chapter 13 THE TAKING OF THE TIDE AT FLOOD CAN BE as fortunate in the psychological voyage of man as in his material affairs. It was high tide now with Tubby and, though he had no means or knowledge to read the waters, accidentally he caught it. Or perhaps it was Daddy who pushed the boat afloat at the right moment.

For Tubby had traveled three early stages of life, had arrived at a fourth, and was about to approach the fifth and most vital. That is to say (though the stages are, of course, not universal even for Tubby's particular variety of healthy young officer-and-gentleman) that the period of childhood fears and yearnings had given place to the simplicity and certainty of adolescence as soon as he had entered the Army. After his accident, doubts broke in and self-satisfaction began to crumble and there followed, soon, an understanding of man's duality or multiplicity, of the many warring selves that share his soul between them. But it was not till after the death of Sammy that he had begun to apply this knowledge to himself; and it was only quite recently that he had become aware of the two persons who battled within him for supremacy. The result of this conflict was not yet a foregone conclusion.

❀ Almost as soon as they were over, Tubby knew that the days and nights that came between Daddy's return to the Fort and his own leaving were important. He never knew why.

But even while they were passing—or so he thought afterwards
—he had a fear that precious moments were being wasted.
Time was so often drawn out, and so often it kept him waiting;
but now it seemed that in twenty-four hours there was compressed a vital age which he was unable to find a use for. And
this period had quite unreasonably a certain beauty and was
yet, in itself, possibly the ugliest, and certainly the most drab,
of all the times that he had spent with Daddy. But there is
beauty in aptness, in inevitability and sometimes in climax;
and something that is otherwise entirely unmemorable can
steal significance and become fine from what led up to it and
what followed after.

And the day in question was of no obvious importance. It
was rather shabby and held all the common disappointments
of reunion—when flesh, painted by memory in sweet colors,
returns sallow. Daddy, in Egypt, a thousand miles to the North,
was a glowing figure. He stepped from the train on to the platform of Khartoum station and was altogether nondescript.

❧ Tubby had ridden across the edge of the desert and, sending
his ponies home, crossed the railway line to find that he was
ten minutes too early. Standing outside the station, he looked
down the wide road that had cabs and taxis waiting on one
side, their drivers clustering in the thin shade, already listless.
At the bottom of the street, the main highway of Khartoum
split at a circular garden; and, beyond, there were neat rows
of trees, tram lines, electric light standards, the Palace, and
gleaming government buildings, shops, banks, private houses.
A lonely fragment of Europe, it was more oriental than the
remotest desert. It was futile and ineffectual, qualities that
belong to the lack of purpose of the East. It brought the impression that the world was obstinately waiting for the passage
of something, called time by civilization, but which for the
East has no significance. It was this feeling of passive waiting,
without design, with only resignation, that struck into Tubby
as a sad but true way of living. It contained peace and—
perhaps—a key to some peace-bringing knowledge. He did not

know. He never knew. But it stirred emotions and started the mind working. Then he heard the train signaled.

Daddy stepped onto the platform, smart, happy and brisk; a nonentity. He might have been anyone, a clerk, a car sales-man, a follower of any of the smug occupations, back from his holiday.

"Quite like home," he said. "How's the army in my absence?"

"Fine," Tubby said, "and how was Cairo?"

"Nicely, thank you."

They stood watching the servants collect the baggage. "Cairo was good, was it?" Tubby asked, pleased at being with Daddy again, unhappy at finding how valor was faded.

"Good? I should say it was. Gerald and I hit it a crack, I can tell you. We danced till dawn six nights a week, and only rested on the seventh because we had to sleep sometime."

"You dancing? Good Lord! I thought you didn't hold with it."

"Oh, Gerald's reformed me . . . do you know, I really enjoyed myself. . . ."

"And how *was* the kid brother?" Tubby asked. "Still knock-ing up big business?"

They were outside the station and the mule-drawn wagon from the Fort had arrived for the luggage. The driver and the lance-bombardier saluted Daddy smartly, smiling and glad to have him back with them.

"Hullo, Baxter," Daddy said. "How's the Fort these days? Mr. Windrush been looking after you nicely?"

The man grinned without answering and Tubby called up a taxi.

"We'll go by car, shall we? I expect you're hungry and breakfast will be waiting. . . ."

In a taxi they returned to their conversation. "Big business!" Daddy said. "I can tell you young Gerald's beating 'em up a bit. Where he gets it from, I'm blessed if I know, but he *is* some-body these days. He knows everyone. We lunched with cabinet ministers and dined with cabaret stars. We spent days with Egyptian princes. Interesting, I can tell you. Do you know, the boy had thousands in hard cash to hand out when he felt like it.

I don't know what he's after because he wouldn't talk about it; but it's some sort of bribery, I gather. Of course, everything in Egypt's bribery, especially if you're in on the cotton racket."

"He might have slipped us a few paltry hundred," Tubby said, "to turn the Fort into a bit of an oriental palace. We could pinch the sergeants' mess as a harem."

"You wouldn't get a half-crown of the firm's money out of Gerald," Daddy answered seriously. "They pay him a pretty useful screw, and he asks what he likes for expenses. They leave things pretty well to his judgment, from what I can make of it."

Tubby spoke wistfully. "I wish I had someone like that in my family, just to give me a sort of solid basis; just to have something to fall back upon. We need someone to make the money my governor gets through in Monte Carlo and Le Touquet . . . you're lucky that way."

"Yes," Daddy agreed, "I'm lucky. If I hadn't got Gerald as a background—as you say—as a sort of theme, perhaps, and if I hadn't got his career as the one important thing to watch and applaud—just as one cheered a house match at school—I wouldn't consider life worth the nervous cost of living."

❧ After that, there was nothing. There was much that had been generated in Tubby during the past month that wanted to come out, to be told to Daddy. But it was impossible. Intimacy had gone and they might have been in any officers' mess anywhere. Tubby handed over his command, regretfully perhaps, but he never remembered afterwards that it was so. The accounts were checked, the safe turned out. They ran through the correspondence, the secret files and the conduct sheets of the defaulters whom Tubby had dealt with. "Yes," Daddy said. "That's O.K. . . . That's fine . . . that seems straight enough."

"And look at this!" Tubby pushed across the latest orders concerning Church parade; senseless orders, making it more unpleasant for everyone but enhancing the dignity of the bishop.

"Has Sergeant Andrews seen them?" was Daddy's only comment.

"And this . . . we've got to change the flashes on our topis. Back again to the left side—that's the third reversal."

"Oh, yes," Daddy said. "Well, the quartermaster-sergeant will deal with it."

It was the dullest and most incredible Daddy. And yet he was kind, gentle and, for the first time, tranquil. For no reason at all, against every reason, he made you happy. It was as if everything was cleared up at last, his packing finished.

And then, quite suddenly, Daddy himself, the old Daddy, was seeing Tubby off at the station. The familiar, unpredictable, flamboyant Daddy was walking beside him, talking in quite a commonplace way, but dropping now and again one of his odd professions that would so often resolve themselves later into truth, evident and simple.

The train had been due to start for at least ten minutes, but they went unconcernedly up the platform again. It was early morning, cool and pleasant outside, but Khartoum station was choked with the mottled crowd that collects to attend a South-bound departure.

"This always makes me laugh," Daddy said, waving a hand at the throng of natives that surged across the platform, rocked by a wayward communal disorder, breaking and re-forming; sometimes an angry, corporate being; more often a coalescence of animated matter, in which each creature appeared to retain something of its own squirming, howling, thrusting individuality.

Watching the crowd, it was only with an effort that you could comprehend its component elements as men and women. The women—swathed in black and dark blue, dirty-looking robes, smelling pungently, uttering high-pitched inhuman noises—progressed in a series of cocoon wriggles up and down the platform but never into the carriages towards which the Egyptian officials tried hopelessly to hustle them. The men, whose only visible clothing was a single sack-colored garment, ran about full of noise and excitement, their actions—to the uninformed watcher—quite purposeless. Greek and Syrian merchants, humbly arrogant, poor traders but opulent, servile in their sly glances but lordly in their rolls of glistening sallow flesh and in their soiled baggy clothes (that were nevertheless of the best silk), and in their white, Englishman's topis, smoked cheroots and argued vigorously but in undertones. Everything about them was contradiction. They were a blend of East and West. They were poor because they wanted more money; they were rich because they had made a lot already. They respected and despised the British overlords of the East. They aped them but retained their own habits. They clung greedily to their gains, but inconsequently lost their luggage.

Two native doctors, smart in their simple khaki uniforms, strolled together unconcernedly, affirming (through the link of one or two lower-class British officials, who were seeing the train off) the continuity of species, the far but existent affinity between the gibbering mob and the high aristocracy of Sudan life—the two British officers, for one of whom a whole coach, practically a fifth of the train, was reserved exclusively. Tubby was the only Englishman traveling and, when the platform had been cleared of the rest of the passengers, he could step into his compartment and the guard might send the train off.

A high Egyptian official, the wreaths of his mud-colored face shining with drops of perspiration, his fez pushed onto the back of his head—not on account of any rakish tendency but by the force of gravity and the extreme agitation of his movements— waddled by, shouting. His remarks were addressed to a group of porters at the far end of the platform, well out of earshot but anyway unwilling to pay attention.

"You won't be off for another ten minutes," Daddy said. "We might as well take another turn up the platform."

They walked in silence, benevolently aloof from the crowd of harassed officials and presumable travelers.

"You may like being alone," Daddy said; "that is, alone except for your servants. You'll find they don't count. You'll find them nearer to the camels than to your conception of human beings. You don't know enough Arabic to talk to them anyway."

"A bit boring sometimes, I daresay. . . ."

"You *may* get bored; but possibly you won't. You may even find it quite an important experience. Strange things happen to Englishmen when they are left to their own company. . . .

"You'll probably become rather fastidious," he went on. "You won't think in the argot that we use for our everyday conversation. You'll resort to writer's English—to the English language. You won't 'get horizontal' at bedtime or consider a 'spot of shut-eye' for your midday siesta. Your last drink won't be 'one last short one.' It will all be different. You will make quite a business of your meals, not from any self-respect notions, but because eating becomes an important part of living and the whole of living is a vastly more important part of life. . . .

"Living, you'll find, embraces many more activities than you have noticed up to the present. Man, when he is alone and is unsupported by his fellows and by the routine strait-jacket he has been used to and by the vast defences that civilization has built up around him, has a greater effort to make to maintain existence. As a result he sees existence more broadly. All of him starts to function. He may even realize—really comprehend, not just sense vaguely—his own godlike magnitude and find it in his own tiny insignificance. . . . My word, Tubby, the immensity of those nights with a lion roaring in the *wadi* and the next white man a couple of hundred miles away. . . ."

The crowd on the platform had thinned and the merchants were leaning out of their carriage windows, talking to friends, bidding farewells and, it was clear, giving last-minute instructions. The fat official, at the point of exhaustion, had removed his fez and was mopping himself off with a vivid handkerchief.

"Prepare to move," Daddy said, "you'd best get mounted."

As soon as Tubby was in the corridor, the train started to draw out slowly. He leaned out of the window, and Daddy walked along the platform beside him.

"Have a good time," he said. "I'll be interested to hear what you make of it. I've got a sort of feeling that you'll come back quite a lot different. We'll have some of our famous midnight talks about it. . . ."

The train was going faster and Daddy gave up following. Tubby raised his hand to him.

"Good-by, old boy, mind you take care of yourself," he cried in a sudden flood of affection.

Daddy's answer was scarcely audible, was inaudible. His

lips moved. His face was melted into the fond, paternal smile, rare and beautiful. Words, memories of words struggled to reach you. "And remember, Tubby . . . complete consciousness . . . Truth . . . all-power, all-knowing . . . the journey, the battle, arms, armour. . . ."

It seemed there was a last cry—"Remember, Tubby. . . ."

Against the background of the white and brown figures and white bundles and the white concrete platform, scarred viciously by the shadow from the roof of the station, Daddy stood smiling, short and square and neat at a distance, his arm raised, bent at the elbow and moving slowly in a farewell blessing.

Tubby had a sudden fear; a sudden warning, as Daddy dwindled and merged with the remaining crowd on the platform. It was as though a thread had been stretched taut and broken, as though something had gone out of his life forever.

He pushed his fears away and settled himself in the carriage.

Book Three

1930

Chapter 14 THE BLACK COTTON SOIL, PATTERNED WITH fissures, like—exactly like—a monstrous, ill-fitting, jigsaw puzzle, met the sky obscurely, somewhere behind a ribbon of shuddering heat, roughly horizontal, except for one small section straight ahead where a half mirage was superimposed upon the junction. The ground was hot to touch, so hot that you could scarcely bear flesh against it; and it was hot, unyielding, iron-hard under a heavy pair of government-issue marching boots. In rare patches, its hostility became less passive as its flat surface was broken by thin, unhappy scrub that stretched out thorns as you found a way through it.

For two and a half days of this sun-killed country, there had been no sign of animal life, or of there ever having been animal life; and the only change that came across it was due to the march of the sun; the only interest to be found in it, the long, spidery shadows that lasted for an hour and a half after sunrise and came again in the last hour and a half before night. In between whiles, shadows were squeezed almost to nothing while the sun stayed motionless directly above you. Your life was tethered to the progress of the sun; and already you judged and counted distance only by sun measurements.

At ten o'clock, after something more than a four hours' march, Tubby halted for breakfast and to spend the heat of the day under the best artificial shade that he could devise from a quantity of cord, stolen from the Army, and a large canvas truck cover, borrowed from the railway department. For the last half-hour he had ridden what he judged to be the best of the baggage camels, a cream-colored animal with an evil disposition, but an action less rough than any of the others. He called the beast Egbert Effendim, enjoying the alliteration. He found Egbert an unpleasant ride and on the whole he preferred walking; for, in the crook of his leg behind the knee, he already had galls from where the pommel of the camel saddle slowly wore away the skin at each of Egbert's remote, disinterested paces.

It was only a week since he had left Khartoum station, but already everything before his departure was as memorially dead as a skin that has been sloughed, or a life that has been rounded off, completed. There was no connecting link between what was happening to him now and anything that had ever happened to him before. There was a planetary difference. None of his present circumstances stirred his memory even remotely. The only common factor between then and now was his own living, the simplest, most primitive acts of living, the common acts of eating and breathing. Even washing was impossible since he could carry only enough water for the actual consumption of himself, his servants and his animals. Even the physical processes were rendered difficult. Values were upturned; and what mattered were shade and hot tea, and whisky at nightfall, and the muscular power to cover the desolate area between the Blue Nile and his goal—the Gallander River.

✤ In the height of the morning on which he had left Khartoum, the train had made its first stop at the cotton-growing town of Wad Medani. He had stepped blithely and hatless out of the cool, gritty gloom of his heavily-shuttered carriage on to the sun-reflecting platform. Rebounding against the solid structure of heat that walled in the railway coach, he had scrambled back quickly. It was frightening. He winced at the blow. He had thought that he knew heat intimately, but now he realized he could scarcely claim acquaintance. Now he understood that Africa was like that, always able to pull out a superlative ferocity, always surpassing itself. This was a warning thought

—that you had not got the measure of so powerful an opponent; that you must be always on the defensive; that the world was no longer either the medium of your living or the stage setting of your actions. It had become an implacable enemy.

❧ Then there was cultivation, following the river, between the river and the railway. Tobacco, egg-fruit, mealies, lubia-beans, grown in terraced strips that clung to the river; so much fitted into so little with such desperate contrivance—and yet, somehow, as though nobody really meant it. Clever little water-courses and naïve irrigation tricks with boulders and great levers and bullocks, made for the photographer rather than the horticulturist. Very poor and very precious.

The sequence lacked sense or purpose: the old, reasonably savage, pre-Caliph town of Senaar, with nice, old-fashioned, burnt-brick buildings; and the genteel, garden suburb affair of Makwar supplanting it; and the lorry you had ordered not there and nobody knowing anything about it, or showing the least interest; a couple of district commissioners, who were supposed to be running the place, and providing transport for lonely travelers, playing three-a-side polo with four native officers, refusing to interrupt their game to be helpful; the first stage of everyone's first journey in Africa—sweat, bad temper, futile invective. Then the lorry appeared suddenly, innocently, in the cool of the evening, the time God made for the start of journeys. An hour's drive through sallow woods and across an umber plain. The town of Singa, and a burst of green at night-fall; clusters of trees and glowing houses; a broad sweep of the river, the deep Blue Nile, tranquil, lovely. A bed on the roof of a house with a sweet breeze stirring the netting, confusing the stars.

At dawn, the drive between woods on one side, brown and yellow trees without substance, and, on the other, the river. Then, at full noon, shouting across the river to the native village; standing between rows of tobacco plants and yelling threats, silly threats, at unseen natives. And, at last, again at the cool of the day, a sleepy, worn, decaying old gentleman poling very gently an iron punt across the water.

The lorry stood on the edge of the tobacco growth, an insolent symbol; a threat to what should be Africa.

"Good-by, lorry. And good-by, what's-your-name. I'll meet you a month from today at Abu Hashim, the nearest you can get to the Gallander River. A couple of hundred miles from here in a straight line, and twice as far by the way I'm going. For we're going to cut eastwards across the blank on the map between the two rivers and then follow the Gallander northwards. No white man has been across this way except Bates, the forestry officer, and he died five years ago. On the map, he marked in the ancient tombs, Kor Hana, and suggested that there might be water there. But nobody knows for certain.

"So, good-by, lorry. . . ."

That broke another link with the past and helped him over the frontier into timelessness. Time was no longer a precision but, if it existed at all, a vague indication, an unlikely hope. You said, for instance, that in half an hour you would have a pot of tea; and this, indeed, set a chain of events moving. The cook's boy would soon fetch more firewood; the cook would soon set the kettle; and, when the urge came, Abdul Mohamed would rise with quick resolution, briskly unlock the box containing tinned milk and sugar, arrange it all upon a tea tray, carry it nobly across the cotton soil and lay it before you with a courtly gesture. It might be five minutes, it might be an hour from the time of your order. But all was done in its proper sequence and nothing was done till the moment was fitting. And a Moslem knew from birth what moments were given for action, what for speech and what for contemplation.

For you were king, but a strictly constitutional monarch; and Abdul Mohamed was prime minister. You were exalted but powerless. Action needed your formal sanction, but your word did not necessarily produce action. Your whims and comfort were closely attended; but that was all. You could not by-pass your ministers or the custom of your country. The East acted on its instincts, often sound and always convenient for the oriental. It did not hold with planning tonight what you would do tomorrow morning—when it might not be necessary. Such foresight had no place in a kingdom of which you were undisputed, honored, nominal and disobeyed god-emperor.

You wanted camels, and on the morning of the first day gave orders for them. Sometime that night, or the day following, or the night after that, messengers sped to your command. And nothing happened. And, in the afternoon of the third day, you rose, sour and wooden-jawed from a midday sleep, and shouted for Abdul. "Abdul . . . Abdul Mohamed, blast you. . . ." And Abdul was standing, graceful, dignified and almost facetiously servile, close beside the bed on which you were lying.

"Where the hell have *you* been? Where are the camels?"

Abdul knew a little English, understanding only what pleased him. He looked away placidly, his dark, Berberine face expressionless, the tri-scarred tribal mark that was cut on his cheek reminding you that everyone had his place in a social order that was, here, as much horizontal as vertical. And, in this order, irrational anger was a sign of honored madness. Abdul's expression was tolerant, forgiving.

"Excellency?"

"When are the camels coming?"

"Camels, noble captain?" There was gentle pain and innocence in the question.

"When are they coming?"

Abdul's voice was surprised and he spoke reasonably, as if humoring a difficult child, quieting a lunatic. "They are here, excellency."

Tubby propped himself up on his elbow and looked about him. "I don't see them. . . ."

"The men are here, excellency."

"Then why on earth didn't you tell me?"

"You were asleep, noble captain."

Tubby pushed himself to his feet and looked across the arid sunlight to the big tree under which the cook, three days ago, had disposed himself. He saw that an unusually large number of men were squatting in the shade, passing the teapot from one to the other.

"I see a lot of people drinking my tea," he said. "I don't see the camels. . . . Where are they?"

Abdul made a slight gesture of disinterest; a suggestion that his master had reached a stage of such inconsequence that it could not be allowed to pass without comment.

"The camels, man, where are they?"

"I don't know, noble captain. They are not *my* camels; the men are here."

"Well, for God's sake, fetch them over."

"Excellency?"

"Bring the men here."

Abdul strode across to the cook's encampment. This did not mean that he hurried, but that his progress was dignified and forceful, his step long, his carriage imperious. Under the far tree a clamor of voices broke out quickly and was kept up in obvious argument. Then three or four men followed Abdul back again, coming up timidly, not meeting Tubby's eye, and immediately squatting down around his chair, heels together, smocks drawn tight across their widely separated knees, their arms hanging limply between their thighs like monkeys.

"Camels," Tubby said stubbornly.

"The noble captain says greetings," Abdul translated. He joined the semicircle of squatting natives and he opened the conversation, speaking first to one and then to the next, a *compère*, an editor, preventing the argument from flitting between the others without his participation. It seemed obvious that this was the first occasion on which the subject of camels had been mentioned.

"How many, excellency?"

"Camels? We've settled that a score of times. I want a dozen."

"Noble captain?"

"I want twelve camels."

The argument began again, was tossed between them, broke into high-pitched vehemence, died to muttering, relapsed into silence, revived in disjointed, staccato remarks directed at the ground with surly indifference, and then flared up once more into a wail of horror. Abdul, when it reached the height of its reincarnation, rose to his feet and quelled it.

"It is arranged, noble captain," he said with simple dignity.

"What is arranged?"

"The camels, excellency."

"Twelve camels?"

"Who can say? Perhaps twelve, perhaps more, noble captain."

"All right. When will they be here?"

"Perhaps tomorrow."

Tubby was defeated, plaintive. "Not today?" he asked wistfully.

Abdul Mohamed smiled and spoke consolingly. "Perhaps tomorrow, noble captain."

❦ When Tubby stopped for his midday rest at a little after eleven o'clock on the morning of the third day of his trek, he gave himself as his specific pretext for calling a halt their arrival at the first stunted tree that they had seen for two hours. It was not much of a tree. Not more than ten feet high and covered with thorns, it offered no sort of shade whatsoever; but it at least provided one of the two uprights necessary for the construction of his shelter. This was enough, and Tubby shouted back for Abdul and said that they would *gael* there.

He was glad that they had come to the tree, for they had been trekking without a halt since before sunrise. The march had, of course, been painful; but he had at last acquired a sort of blithe ferocity, a state in which he could view himself brutally and dispassionately and in which he could transform his vision into precise, almost verbal description. "To say that I am thirsty and exhausted," he thought, "would be so inadequate as to be a lie rather than an understatement. For two hours past I have ceased to understand even a need for water. I no longer think of the sweat which at last refuses to come freely. I am not conscious of any particular difficulty in putting one foot in front of the other. I am conscious, in fact, of very little except the complete sameness of this country. Each step, each mile—if there is such a thing—each hour, each hand's-breadth of the sun's progress, each trek, each day and, I daresay, each week, month, year, lifetime, is exactly the same as the one before it. There are no landmarks. There is no prospect. I have forgotten hope. I expect nothing. All the ingredient troubles of my state—of my mind and body—are gone into the numbing burden of self-propulsion. Unless I focus my thoughts on any of my members, I am not aware of blistered feet, of burned shoulders, of a topi glued to my forehead, of the sores at the back of my thighs where sweat-soaked shorts have chafed them. Walking has become automatic and I have a certain momentum which discourages me from halting. I just have to keep on moving up to and through an unchanging horizon towards a goal I have ceased to believe in."

For, as Daddy had predicted, lack of company had led Tubby to put his thoughts into a language that was strange to him, that was more precise than conversational. It was almost a foreign tongue, and he didn't know where he had learned it. He realized this, wondered at it and then put it away as something to be considered later. And again, this deliberate using of his brain as a storehouse was unusual.

It was good to see the tree in the distance, to see it at first without acknowledgment and then slowly to allow recognition to develop, almost photographically. They were a long time coming up with it, and it towered above its surrounding scrub, keeping its distance until it had won the standing of a landmark and, at last, the dignity of an immediate goal, a prospective resting place. Only then did it no longer wait aloof but fled rapidly; and it was only then that progress became really and consciously arduous.

A thin cloud of dust hung around the single file of crawling animals. Sadek, a very black, one-eyed, shaven-headed, villainous-looking man, who had been taken on as a tracker and who claimed to have traveled this country in the past with Bates, led the *hamla*. He carried Tubby's rifle and glasses and walked on at his own pace without ever turning to look behind him. After an hour or so, you could grow to hate that insolent back, those listless, dangling arms, the legs that moved entirely without effort or interest. Now and again a languid hand would be raised, would pluck at a branch of scrub, would (ignoring the thorns) break it off and transfer it to a nearly toothless mouth which would chew at it with all the professional impertinence of a stableboy. You could hate that more than anything.

Tubby walked behind Sadek, and immediately behind him again a ragged camel man led Egbert Effendim. One after the other, the remaining members of the *hamla* followed, the men leading their beasts and the servants illegally sitting on top, as entirely indifferent as the scornful creatures that carried them.

Only for Tubby was there any purpose in this journey, and for him the purpose was already dim and legendary. The stolid servants and the more ragged, more cretinous, camel men refused to be involved in his adventure. If the divine spark—that must make them human—lingered somewhere, it was their own secret. In their company, Tubby was utterly alone. They served him, it was true, but they were hostile. They rebuffed him politely and in silence, refusing him contact.

❁ It was close on noon when Abdul Mohamed brought him the first meal of the day which he chose to call breakfast. His second and last meal was taken at night, and he tumbled into bed as soon as it was finished. In between times, he called often for a brew of tea which he drank to the last dregs of the teapot.

A cat's cradle affair of ropes, running primarily from the tree to a jointed bamboo pole and thence to a number of tent pegs, supported his canvas shelter. The pegs were hammered insecurely into the hard, dry, ready-to-crumble cotton soil, and all movement beneath the shelter had to be made with caution. In its shadow were placed his deck chair and table, sometimes his bed, his rifle and glasses, his *zamzamia*—the flat, canvas water bottle that kept its contents cool through evaporation—and the haversack that held shaving soap, razors, compass, toilet paper and all such personal treasures. His whole world was arrayed beneath this shelter; but, because it was only of single canvas thickness, he had to live there wearing a topi whose hard brim prevented him always from leaning his head backwards. He was, in fact, no longer the same man as before; a man with a head, a body, two arms and two legs. From sunrise to sunset his stature was swollen, his members increased by the permanent addition of this hard, frustrating helmet.

The whole arrangement was inglorious and unromantic; and yet he found, in the tenure of this small, irregular patch of artificial shade, islanded by the open sunlight, the same tiddler's ground pleasure that he got at night from the isolation of his lamplight kingdom. Perhaps this strange, possessive pleasure went back for its beginnings to the games and fancies of his childhood; perhaps it went further to the childhood of animal life and the need for a lair, a last stronghold in which to find or imagine safety.

Tubby thought this out over breakfast; and thought, too, of the curiosity presented by himself, his modest conception of himself—still physically Windrush—blond, chubby, polo playing, hard-riding, exuberant but mentally limited young officer, actually analyzing a feeling. He considered himself in that way, but he did not really believe it. For now he cherished the fancy that there was more to him than that; and solitude gave his fancies substance. Daily he grew more certain that within him was a power that he had not yet discovered.

Routing amongst his most recent memories, he found gratefully the notion that had interested him that morning: Daddy's theories of the queer changes that came over a fellow in his loneliness.

It was a curious thing that an illiterate, unintelligent sort of chap like himself, suffering from all the after effects of an expensive education, should have come to pondering things in a precise, almost scientific sort of way. It was curious, too, that Daddy should have foreseen it. In regular life it was only on rare occasions that you had a sudden, demanding flash that made you find things different; a sudden shock that raised inquiries and demanded unobvious answers. When there were other folk around, you thought in the process of conversation, if at all. Other times, you slept or considered the feeding of a pony, the tactics of a match, where hounds were meeting tomorrow, what that woman would look like undressed, just how drunk you were. Or sometimes you might imagine yourself into all sorts of glorious situations, romantic situations which ended with a crowning triumph; and then, when you realized to what childish immodesties your fancies were leading, you blushed or laughed at yourself shamefacedly. But, when you were alone, thought and conversation were wedded. You had to carry on your argument without words and unaided. It was a rum sort of business.

❧ "Abdul . . . Abdul Mohamed. . . ."

Tubby looked across the harsh glitter of sunshine to the smear of shade in which the servants were huddled. The rough contrasts created confusion to the eye, which re-created it within your whole being; just as, when one sense is suddenly impaired, the whole community of senses is for a time bewildered. Everything became doubtful. When black and white were no longer separate but had merged in a trembling mist, a shimmer of heat, not a mist but a shroud of piercing oppositions containing the corpse of reason, there could be no certainty. Was it ten minutes or an hour or a lifetime ago that he had shouted for Abdul?

"Abdul . . . Abdul Mohamed. . . ."

The pool of shadow broke as Abdul reared himself up, arranging his turban as he came across the open.

"Excellency?"

"Tea . . . tea for God's sake."

He watched the man re-cross the violence of the afternoon and merge again with the other servants, losing his individuality, becoming at once dehumanized as he was taken back into the shadow. Why *were* those servants human? Still more, why were the camel men in the further group entitled to think themselves as above the animal kingdom? Did they think and love and hate; and, if so, why was he, Tubby, any better? What was the division between the supercilious camels and their saturnine owners? Between them and himself? They did not know honesty and integrity and decency as he knew it, as it was laid down in the code called cricket. But then he did not pray at sunrise and sunset; he drank alcohol and smoked cigarettes. To the abstemious Moslem, he was perhaps as inhuman as they were to the righteous, soap-loving Christian. Now that they were all unwashed and unshaven, who was the best? He or the camel men or the camels?

On the face of it, a man was an animal with a mind added; the way that you added an auxiliary motor to a sailing boat. What the man did with his mind, and if and how he used it, was nobody's business. He might employ it, as Sammy did, in conjunction with his senses and his sensibility, to love things; he might use it, as Daddy did, to hate things; or, like Lydia, to laugh at things; or, like Bert, as something to be stored away and forgotten. That seemed simple enough; but it didn't allow for one man being better than the next; and it didn't make sense for them all to be brothers in God's eyes or anybody else's. You had good men and bad men and you had to admit it. The failure of religion was due to this idea of equality; it was so clearly nonsense. But wasn't it just as much nonsense to consider that the inequality arose from wealth or birth or race or physical prowess or even intellectual attainment?

It was easy enough to understand that the quality of mind, or the quantity of brain, varied from one man to the next. It wasn't so easy to explain why one man was good and the next bad; why Sammy was a God-loving saint and Daddy an atheistic cynic—and yet both, in their last depths, were equally kind and generous; why an artist could live to create while the soldier lived to destroy; why some found a holy joy in beauty, while others found an unholy ecstasy, equally powerful, in the satisfaction of appetites.

If you examined a man critically, you were forced to admit that he had as many points to him as a horse. You didn't trot out a hunter and say "nice horse" or "nasty horse" about him; you noticed that he was deep through the heart, or well let down, or sickle-hocked, or ewe-necked, or long in the pastern, and so on. With a man, unless he were a recruit or a pugilist, it wasn't his body you were buying; it was his whole make-up that told you if he were a good chap or a bad one. You could only suppose that, without knowing it, you divided him into sections, set one section against another and saw how they were compounded together.

He applied this to the men and women he knew, reviewing them one after the other, summing them up, imagining that he was the judge and they were trotted up before him in the show ring. It was a fascinating game, and only the lassitude of the afternoon prevented him from finding pencil and paper and making notes about them. Slowly and with certainty his friends tumbled into place until, with a sudden vision, he knew that his selection was no matter of personal opinion, and that the order of his awards was not a question of his judgment but something universal. There was, then, a celestial standard? With Sammy at one end of the scale and Mrs. Clements at the other, the intermediaries formed themselves up with inevitable sureness. It was like sizing the Battery for a ceremonial parade. (You could hear the sergeant-major, couldn't you: "Tallest on the right, shortest on the left, in single rank . . . SIZE . . . on the LEFT, Higgins . . . in single rank, Jones"?) It could not be argued. One man was taller than the next, and that was the end of it. It was a question of knowledge.

He sized his friends into a single rank and walked up and down it like the sergeant-major. His own position troubled him; he had no knowledge, no instinctive feelings, on that score. He could not rank himself highly, and yet he felt, believed, hoped desperately that there was some intangible thing within himself that was slowly developing, slowly pushing him upwards, increasing his stature. He was still growing.

You viewed Mrs. Clements and found her all animal, and hustled her away down to the left with the little people. You remembered Sammy, towering on the right, ethereal, spiritual, all spirit. He, Tubby, came somewhere between the two of them.

Perhaps he had found the answer to his problem: that all men were developing from animals into spirits and that some had got further than others. But where did the development start, and what was its use when death came to cut short its progress? Or did it go on afterwards, and had it gone on for eternity before? Of course!

For a vision impinged; a rough mountainside and a track scoring through the scrub and boulders. He could hear a voice speaking in quiet, gentle tones; could see a tired, grey face. Their ponies' feet rattled the stones on the hillside path and Sammy's teeth were clenched on an unlit pipe, and he spoke between them. "And this lifetime—however far it takes us—can be no more than an insignificant stage of the journey. . . ."

"That's it, that's how it is . . ." he remembered he'd cried in answer.

He shook himself clear of his dreams and looked at his wrist watch. He wanted to make a second *shidd* that evening, a march that would keep him going until an hour after sunset. If he were off by three o'clock, he would get in a four hours' trek, making nine in all for the day. Not bad going considering the temperature. There was time for a short sleep before he need think of starting. He was nearly asleep already.

Chapter 15 FOR A LIFETIME HE HAD MARCHED THROUGH contrasts so harsh that they defeated vision. The black of the cotton soil and the colorless brilliance of the afternoon were fused into a curtain that rendered the eye sightless. There was no message for the eye to take to the brain. There was no sound; even the beat of his own passage was dulled into silence. The nose caught only the anesthetic of a changeless, arid, despairing country.

The brain was unaware, except numbly, of existence. There was a tree, for a long time there was a tree, there would forever be a tree in front of them. Somewhere off to the right of them there *had* been a tree, in the distance, in the middle distance, in the foreground; a stunted, lifeless tree, not even grotesque enough to be of interest or to be perceptible. The brain did not comprehend either the tree or its passing.

The brain comprehended nothing. The senses had lost perception or, retaining perception, could no longer articulate. They kept the brain famished of sensation.

You are not conscious of the dwindling of pain and you were not conscious that the contrasts had been toned down and that color—pale, tired color—was washing into the landscape. You did not notice that towards nightfall the scrub grew thicker; that a tree had ceased to be a landmark, had ceased at last to be even a rarity; that the black cotton soil was smeared with the pale Naples yellow of dried grasses, grasses that had sprung head-high after the rains, had retained their stature, but now were dead and withered. At first you did not even notice that the way was no longer direct, and that Sadek was leading you in ever-widening diversions; that he was threading a path through spindly tree trunks, shying away from the tendrils of thorn-armed scrub, skirting the impenetrable grasses.

The sun was low behind them and their own shadows, long and insubstantial, intermingled with those of the tree trunks. The violence had gone from the day; the pain had given way to the sedative of evening; the senses recovered perception and consciousness came back again.

Tubby called Sadek back to him.

"Kor Hana?" he asked.

"Yes, excellency."

The man showed no signs of pleasure that they had reached their halfway goal. His scarred face may have altered certain of its contours; but it was so unlike an assembly of human features that a fresh intersection of wrinkles had no meaning and could not be interpreted into any common emotion. Each time you looked at him you found some new deformity; an eye missing, half an ear gone, a scar running across the close-shaved skull, another from chin to forehead, the movement of one arm slightly restricted. Unlike the rest of the men, he was naked except for his dirt-colored drawers, so that you could see the overdevelopment of some muscles caused by the wastage of others. Right across his ribs there were the marks where some animal, lion or leopard, had savaged him.

"There is water at Kor Hana?" Tubby asked him in Arabic, and somehow expecting him to have instinctive knowledge on this point.

Sadek raised a languid hand and very delicately flipped off his shoulder a large, winged insect. "Perhaps, excellency."

"Go and see."

The man turned and trotted off through the trees. He did not perceptibly break into a run, bending his arms and readjusting his balance. One moment he was standing beside Tubby and the next he was moving quickly and easily away from him, sliding into the scrub and grasses, hidden in the nightfall.

There was no sunset. For a few minutes there was a tinge of

ocher in the sky; a haze of gold dust trembled over the hot earth; the colors softened and blended into monochrome; a new dimension came into the landscape as its flat severity melted into cumulus depths. The day was over and the early night was full of living.

Tubby did not see or hear Sadek returning. The man was suddenly beside him, standing at his elbow.

"Excellency. . . ."

"There is water?"

"No, excellency."

The man was unperturbed, disinterested; but Tubby had the nervous discomfort in his stomach that bad news brought him.

"Where is the water?"

Sadek raised his arm negligently, pointing over the tree tops on the course they had been taking.

"The river?" Tubby asked.

"The river," Sadek admitted.

"Is it far?"

"Not far, excellency."

"Is it near then?"

"Not near."

Tubby very deliberately took and lit a cigarette. It was some time before he spoke.

"You dirty black devil," he said pleasantly in English.

Sadek lifted one foot and with his big toe scratched the calf of his other leg, scratching downwards to the ankle. He lifted one arm and gently, with infinite leisure, scratched the top of his shaven head, down the back of his neck and behind the shoulder blade.

"You dirty, verminous animal," Tubby continued, "how I hate you. How I hate your damned insolence. How I detest your strong, deformed, revolting body. How I loathe the sight of your back. But you're a bit of a man, aren't you?"

Sadek stopped scratching. "Excellency?"

Tubby returned to his few words of Arabic. "The river . . . how far is it?"

"Not far, excellency."

"One day?"

"Perhaps."

"Two days?"

"Perhaps two days, perhaps three, excellency."

Tubby considered the answers with growing apprehension. He knew that margins were narrow, for they carried only two *fantashes* of water, one of which had been empty that morning. The *fantashes*, the heavy iron tanks that hung each side of a camel, were as much the essence of life as the air they breathed or the hats that protected them from the lethal sunlight. The second tank had been almost full when they started that day's march; with the greatest economy it might last for two days longer.

But what did the man mean by two days? If Sadek chose, he could go on trotting from before dawn till long after sunset, could cover forty miles in a day and a night and still leave time for sleep in the middle. But white men and servants had not that endurance, and camels had to have a journey broken. For them, twenty-five miles was a good day's march in this temperature.

It was no good worrying about it now. He would talk to Abdul after dinner.

"Abdul . . . Abdul Mohamed. . . ."

The *suffragi* came up at once.

"We'll camp here. I want dinner quickly."

It was all he could do to walk across to a single tree that stood apart from the others and to keep himself upright, leaning against the tree, while the servants unloaded his chair and table.

🌿 Abdul Mohamed moved quietly about the table clearing dinner. While he was beyond the lamp, you were conscious only of his service; but your spirit, carried on the flood of exhaustion, was undisturbed by his presence. He moved round and his shadow cut across the tablecloth, covered the green-and-white checks, the sardine oil, the soup stains and the brown circle left by a teacup. You realized then that dinner was over; that this was Abdul Mohamed clearing it, performing his last duty of the day, meeting you for the last time before he sank back through the shadows and became reabsorbed in that other world of dark, aloof figures squatting in the borders of a more distant firelight.

Your own fire crackled and revived, the flame drawn out by a passing finger of wind. It was part of the dream. You had wakened to a dream whose mystery contained a new precision.

Lying back in his chair, Tubby had thought at first that he was now utterly empty. To be tired was always one of the glories of his life; but never before had fatigue so completely deluged him, washing out of him all common sensation and all familiar potency. He had expended energy, yet it was not gone but transformed into something with which he had no previous acquaintance. His powers had changed their nature. The eyes, the ears, nose, taste, touch, failed to register; they were unimportant, and whether or not they still retained the faculties that were dormant was a matter of indifference. They were not necessary to him, for he was abstracted from them. They had been replaced by an inner sensibility, so that he saw with a new vision that sought things from behind and within, rejecting the outer surface as pale and unremarkable. He had tapped his last reserves and found them immeasurable. He had lost power and become all powerful.

In his detachment he sought, over beyond the space of darkness, the cluster of native servants by the other campfire. The two fires, his and theirs, on each of which life was centered, were drawn together. There was a community between them which was all-embracing; and within its hold, he and Abdul Mohamed and Sadek and the others became one in humanity. He knew them, now, through the medium of his own exhaustion. Through the labors of the day, he had learned the secret of their detachment and indifference, of the limitless depths of themselves to which they fled from him. For a short space of time he was in the hold of a drug which promised all knowledge. If he could but retain that state he would become all-knowing.

Something from beyond him disturbed his self-hypnosis, claiming him back insistently. It clamored from outside until reluctantly he gave it admission. The vision faded as he saw and heard and smelled again. The wood smoke was sweet and

pungent, the murmur of voices came softly from the distant
servants, the deck chair creaked as he stretched back for his
haversack. He pulled out the map and was once more a British
officer.

❦ There was little use in studying the map for he already
knew by heart the white space dividing the Blue Nile and
Gallander rivers, unsullied except by the name of the supposed
watering place by which he was now seated. But, with a map
before him, he regained his confidence. Habit—the soldier's
habit of map and compass—moved brusquely, called back his
spirit and chained it again to the senses and to the body.

Until this happened, life was being nourished on trust; on
no more than an instinctive belief, shared with the servants,
the camel men, the camels, that all things led to a foreordained
ending. You were walking to the river. Very well then, you
would reach the river or you would not reach the river. You
would live or die. God had already decided. So it needed the
Western side of you to bother about survival; it needed map and
compass and the power, regained, to measure, to calculate, to
worry. . . .

And, especially, to find fault with the map. . . .

The map was wrong, of course—you had known that for a
long time. It had shown Kor Hana as midway between the two
rivers, sixty miles from the Blue Nile and the same distance from
the Gallander. But it had taken them three very hard days—
which in English was ninety miles—to make the journey. And
this must mean that Kor Hana, being thirty miles further from
the Blue Nile than it was shown on the map, must be the same
distance closer to the Gallander. Excellent! They had only
another thirty miles to travel, another day's journey. And yet
. . . and yet. . . .

He sat up quickly, remembering Sadek's words. . . . "How far
is the river?" Tubby had asked. "Perhaps two days, perhaps
three," Sadek answered. And no native was ever a pessimist.
And Sadek knew the country.

With growing fear he studied the map again, his memory
plunging back through the sullen negligence of his marching.

Northeast, he'd said was their course, when they left the Blue Nile. That was the shortest route (for both rivers meandered in wide loops), and the one that—so the map told them—lay through Kor Hana. But, from the very start, Sadek had set his face to the rising sun and led them due eastwards. He remembered now that once, twice, three times during that first morning he had doubted Sadek, had pulled out his compass, taken a bearing and pointed away to the left of them. But Sadek had shaken his head. And, after that, you didn't bother. . . .

He knew there was some answer. They had reached Kor Hana, and there must be some factor that would reconcile the proved error in the map and Sadek's statement of distance.

He took a cigarette, but did not light it.

With first a sense of triumph, he made the discovery. The map was wrong, of course, but the error was not only one of longitude, as he had supposed, but of latitude as well. Kor Hana was not only thirty miles to the east of its showing on the map, but also a considerable distance more to the south. . . .

He looked again, and all triumph died in an instant. The course they were taking led them to a section of the Gallander River that ran in a wide sweep to the eastward—almost directly away from them. They were crossing the divide by the longest route they could have taken.

He controlled his agitation, pushing it down inside him. Panic rose quickly and must be ruthlessly handled. He must not know the hindered breath that caught at his heart, must not hear the thumping of his heart, must not feel despair rise up in him like vomit.

Very deliberately he took a pencil from his haversack, found a scale, smoothed the map down on the table and marked in, according to his own reckoning, the position of Kor Hana—his own position at that moment. He read the figure, checked it carefully and with a steady hand wrote it down large and heavy. He was not afraid of the figure; it would not conquer him. It was no good cursing blindly against cartographers or raising clenched fists to the limitless heavens. It was no good crying to the stars. He had eighty-five miles of hard, desolate, unbroken cotton soil to cover before he could reach the river. He had three long days' trekking ahead of him and scarcely two days' supply of water.

He lay back in his chair, clasping his hands behind his head, mastering himself, riding himself, thinking steadily. With care, the water should keep them alive till they reached the river. With care! He was quite calm now. The march was no longer a journey; it had become a battle.

❀ It was hard to understand this new treasure that was water. Precious beyond gems, a single ten-gallon tank of slightly muddy liquid could buy the whole outfit, could weigh down the scales against twelve camels, seventeen men and all their belongings. Gold-dust, platinum, pictures, music, science, the garnered stores of man's cleverness and artistry, were worth nothing without the four pints a day of unclean fluid that kept his spirit within its body. That, alone, was wealth. He must go and count it.

❀ It was painful to bend stiffened muscles, to struggle out of the chair and walk away from the lamp, away from the refuge of a smoldering fire into the foreign darkness. He stood in the darkness between the two fires, his own, that his thoughts and feelings had made a sanctuary, and that of the servants, which was once again strange and unfriendly. He was alone in the night; nothing called to him but the small world, contained by the fire he had left and his lamplight. Fatigue overwhelmed him, urging him back to his world, so that he was forced to summon what he thought must be his last reserves of energy. Walking unsteadily, he went across the trampled grasses to the servants.

"Abdul Mohamed," he called out of the darkness.

The servants were sitting in a half circle round the fire, Abdul Mohamed in the center. Beside him, the cook, too fat, smooth-faced, degenerate, was refilling the teapot. His boy sprawled wearily on the ground, his head lying in the crook of one elbow. Sadek, squatting motionless with the fire carving deep shadows out of his battered face, kept silence. The head camel man had joined them and a staccato, intermittent conversation was kept up between him, Abdul Mohamed and the cook.

"Abdul. . . ."

The *suffragi* showed no signs of surprise at the voice that broke unexpectedly upon them. He uncurled himself and rose to his feet in one easy motion and then stood, with the grace and dignity of a well-bred Berberine, peering into the darkness, rewinding about his head the khaki turban.

"Excellency?"

"I want to speak to you."

Tubby walked to meet him and they stood together on the edge of the shadows.

"We have not much water. . . ."

Abdul stood straight, his head level but his eyes cast downwards. He had neither been given an order nor asked a question and so he waited.

"I want to see the water."

"It is in the *fantashes*, noble captain."

"I want to see the *fantashes*."

Abdul looked away quickly and, remembering afterwards, Tubby interpreted it as a furtive movement.

"They are over by the camels, noble captain."

"They are supposed to be kept beside you . . . I've said that often."

"They are by the camels, excellency."

Too tired to argue or to recriminate, Tubby walked across to the fire around which the camel men were sitting. He passed the barracked animals, seeing them dimly in the moonless night as grotesque shapes that were unreasonably alive, smelling the bitter odor of their cud, hearing the jangle of chains that tethered them, headstall to fetlock, the dull crunch as one of them hit the ground with the boss of his chest and the windy, digestive noises as he recovered the cud for further chewing, half-coughed, half-hiccoughed and then made wind again.

The two *fantashes* were lying just outside the circle of men; and Tubby, followed by Abdul, walked straight up to them, the men scrambling awkwardly to their feet at his approach. He half lifted one and found that it was, as he expected, quite empty. The other had been almost full that morning, and he caught hold of the handle, summoning his strength to lift one end of it. It came lightly up to him, and there was a gentle gurgle.

At first it meant nothing, inspired no answer but a flat denial. It wasn't true of course. . . .

This sprang to your lips as if a man had called you a thief or a liar. You could weigh up the accusation later . . . and this had happened before, so often, in books and stories; the family solicitor came in at the door, the opened letter lay on the breakfast table—I'm sorry, Mr. Windrush, but you're bankrupt. . . .

And after that, anger and fear, two burly men at a doorway, fought for precedence, jostled each other, so that neither found exit. Tubby shut the door in their faces. Anger was good, but if he let it out, fear would be closely following.

"The camel men," he said, as he had to say something.

Abdul shrugged his shoulders. It was a careless agreement that, through his own negligence, the camel men had stolen water. But still he showed no interest.

"Listen!" Tubby said. "My *zamzamia* is full, and the cook has a *zamzamia*, I suppose. Beyond that, we have no water. Sadek says it is three days' trek to the river. . . ."

"Yes, noble captain," Abdul said indifferently. He did not comprehend, did not wish to comprehend, that danger existed. Still less would he become involved in the specific danger that faced them.

And, as for Tubby, exhaustion made a peak demand; irresistible. You would surely give way this time, since there was so little left to keep you fighting. But man, contrarily, likes the odds heavy against him; is most unyielding when all is hopeless. A new courage drives him on, a tiresome goad to his flagging spirit.

"Oh, leave me alone, can't you?"

Ah, but he envied the indifference of his servants; thought longingly of that hazed detachment, the same that had wrapped himself that very evening. And he knew without doubt that this state could so easily be re-entered; that he had only to sink back into his chair, fill his lungs with the warm night, fix his eyes on the stars or the firelight—and die happily. He sipped temptation for the pleasure of teasing his palate. He pushed the draught away from him. He stood by the fire, the servants waiting respectfully, himself rocking with fatigue, thinking numbly that he might walk ten yards, fifty, a hundred, but that eighty-five miles was not remotely possible.

"Abdul Mohamed," he said, "we must trek tonight. How soon can we be starting?"

The *suffragi* looked at the sky carefully. It was the unnecessary, purely formal gesture of the shepherd who is asked about the weather, and who has long ago made up his mind about it.

"The moon will be up soon," he said at last.

"When will it be up?"

"Before midnight, noble captain."

"If we start with the moon, can we get to the river by sunset the day after tomorrow?" Abdul looked into the darkness, pretending to deliberate. "You won't stop, noble captain?" he asked.

"We shall have to stop now and again, for an hour or two, for the animals."

The *suffragi* raised his voice and called to Sadek, speaking to him in quick, short sentences as though conducting, single-handed, a bitter argument. Each time that he paused for reply and none came, he appeared to be amplifying his question or suggesting an answer. Tubby was watching Sadek and saw that the man made not the slightest movement. Then his lips stirred and one careless word escaped them. Tubby needed no interpreter.

"My Christ," he said, "if that devil says 'perhaps' once more, I'll wring his blasted neck for him."

Abdul very nearly smiled. He spoke again over his shoulder, more urgently this time, and at last Sadek answered with another question. A conversation started, quickened and swelled into a duet, both men speaking together, their voices overlapping, becoming higher-pitched and sharper until you could suppose they were working up to an angry climax. The melody was closed brutally by Sadek; stopped on a note pitched high up the scale, cut short and—as it were—left hanging in the

air in one of those frustrating endings that come sometimes
in modern music. In the short silence that followed, you felt
that you were waiting for the second movement, something slow
and graceful, andante or adagio.

Abdul spoke quietly, still entirely without interest. "He says,
excellency, that if you can travel as fast as the camels we shall
perhaps get to the water at sunset on the day after tomorrow."

🌿 They must rest for a few hours before starting, and already
the servants and camel men had pulled their clothing about
their heads and relapsed into easy sleep. The fires burned low
and there was no breeze now, in the height of a hot, still night,
to tempt a flame from the embers. In the casual disarray of the
baggage there was an order taught by experience; everything
was accessible to a degree dependent upon its particular useful-
ness; it was the disorderly plan of an intimate desk, of an un-
tidied study. It was home; and you were safe in this small
kingdom that you had claimed out of the wilderness. You were
safe. You were urged to stay by a power that was more than
lassitude, by the paradox of a static impetus. You did not forget
the doom that hung above the place or that, if you succumbed
to the lure of your retreat, in a few hours—in a day at most—
death would be certainly imminent. You could not worry about
that, for the danger was negative; nothing threatened you
except by its absence. The habit of looking to tomorrow died in
the African night. Do nothing, be nothing; be one with the
night. Let your spirit soar to the stars, and the rest of you melt
into its setting. Drop into step with the march of a sun-killed
world. Live in the present, for the past was dead and God
looked after the future. The future was not your business.

A new light was coming into the world, a soft, languid
radiance that spread from between the tree trunks and laid
gentle fingers upon the men and their campfires and camels.
It caressed them, smoothed them out, dimmed the lights of
their making and painted their sad little kingdom with new and
more subtle shadows. It created mystery in what was already
amply mysterious. It bade the sleeping men sleep on. It held

them with maternal fondness on the breasts of sleep. It was the light of sleep, the light of visions. The moon was rising.

Tubby got up from his chair and shouted, shouted as loud as he could, emptying his lungs of this madness. He broke the quiet of the night, shattered its allure, made even the moonlight tremble. The camp stirred at his command and he hurried across to the servants and, with his toe, completed the awakening.

❀ Each time that a camel rose or knelt beneath you, the mechanics of his movements seemed equally perplexing. You were thrown back and forward and back again, and there was always one more action than you were able to anticipate. Then, if the animal were rising, you were unexpectedly looking down upon the world, godlike, detached; benevolent, but otherwise careless of what was happening beneath you. The creature moved forward into the moonlight, through the shadow and out into the moonlight again, striping you like a tiger, rocking you backwards and forwards so that you had to go limp, to submit and to let it have its way with you.

The pain, where the saddle had already galled, was unendurable. It was sharpened at each step and so became rhythmical. Each step was delayed in the slow, swinging gait of the camel; and the anticipation of the step led you up the cycle of pain, so that each time you determined that it should be the last. But, when the step was over and the next scarcely beginning, and you were able to recall the equal, the worse, discomforts of walking indefinitely across the hard cotton soil, your tired muscles refused to countenance a change of anguish; you stayed on the camel.

The camel moved on inevitably. His reared head looked over the invisible horizon. His motion was a slow cadence in the night, his shadow a grotesque accompaniment.

Your solar plexus was rhythmically shaken and the inside of you was rolled up slowly into a core that contained all your consciousness. The sores inside your knees were forgotten. You remembered only that somehow you must keep awake, for if you fell it was certain that no one would bother to pick you up again. You did not think; you had no troubles. But some part of you, with which you had only recently become acquainted, was once more keenly perceptive. What it observed was intangible and incomprehensible. It did not give, it promised. You did not know the substance of its promise; you might never know. You were only aware that it dealt with the memory direct, without bothering about your consciousness. One day, in the inconceivable future, you might recall the irresponsibility, the cradle safety of this night marching.

The day was breaking, the moon was gone, the stars dimmed. A breeze touched your check and stirred the scrub afterwards. A night ago, an age ago, you were traveling with the sun falling behind you, your shadow in front. Before that there was nothing. Now a band of light saffron was widening and growing brighter ahead. With no further excitement, with no pretentious dawning, the sun was up and, with its warmth on your face, the breeze dropped or was forgotten.

At last they halted. Tubby never remembered that he gave the order but only that the leading animals, as if by prearrangement, slowed down while those behind drew up with them. He shook the head rope and made the snake noise at the back of his throat that brought himself earthwards. He rocked forward, sharply back and then, as he was about to swing his leg over the pommel, hard forward again. In five minutes or half an hour Abdul was serving breakfast. You were not sure about time and it was scarcely of interest, for the only factors that governed you were space and water. Time was a silly business of springs and cogwheels, neglecting inclination, ignoring necessity. You had been riding a camel in the moonlight.

There was porridge for breakfast and bacon and a tin of sardines and a tin of pineapple.

"Abdul . . . Abdul Mohamed . . . we go on at once. . . ."

"In an hour, excellency?"

"At once."

"In half an hour, excellency. You won't shave, excellency?"

"There is no water."

"There is enough for that, noble captain."

"We go on at once. *Shiad* the camels."

Tubby had not shaved for four days and his beard was already a perceptible length, silky and golden. His eyes had sunk far back in his head and the hair, matted on his forehead, showed from beneath his topi. The cream camel was led up and barracked in front of him.

"Egbert, you old bastard," he said, "you've got to go on and on, all today, all tonight and all tomorrow. We may get you half-a-pint after that—if you're a very good camel."

He shook the head rope and kicked Egbert in the ribs.

"Get up, you bastard."

And yet, though it fed the memory with red, juicy meat, he could not afterwards remember very much about it. It was at no time a prideful recollection, nor was it particularly significant of anxiety. Anxiety, in fact, was remarkably absent; but even that—curious and important as it was—supplied no vivid thread of color in the general pattern of his experience. It was a time, undoubtedly, of discovery; but, far more than that, it was a time of promise. The traveler in an unknown wilderness of tangled forest saw, far ahead of him, through a parting in the overgrowth, a range of mountains, of fiery peaks, of dazzling snows surmounting green uplands. The scene, from the savagery of his forest, was unendurably beautiful. The ferocity of his experience was not echoed in the promise. The promise was the tranquillity of power, unneeded, and of knowledge that surpassed the fruits of thought.

That which he did was humanly impossible. You can go a certain number of days without rest or sleep, a certain time without food and water. You have some idea of your own powers; that you can walk ten, twenty, thirty miles between lunch and dinner; that you can run a known distance in a known number of hours, minutes and seconds. Each exploit is a measure of physical strength or physical endurance. There are world records relating to them and these are beaten only at long intervals and with acclamation. There is no world record for walking across Africa and there never can be, for the factors governing records do not concern such an experience. For the feat is not of the body but of the spirit.

The thoroughbred hunter, in the temper of a hunt, can transcend all calculable powers and drop dead at the height of his strength—of a broken heart, of a lost spirit. While hounds drive on, he taps reserves that are given to some and not to others, reserves that are quite indifferent to muscular limitations. When he comes to the dregs, he achieves release; but he can never know the capacity of the cask or how far it is tilted. Curiously enough, it does not trouble him. At any moment he may reach the dregs; but that is a matter for the future and he is living only in the present.

If you walk across Africa, the future is equally unimportant. It is gradually drawn from your hands until it no longer concerns you. If you are taxed beyond endurance, your endurance to the end seems limitless. When the muscles and the organs of the body have finally surpassed themselves, when they should —by all reason—have long ceased to function, the spirit supplies a motive power of which you were previously ignorant. You can never be aware of your own utmost capacity. Your power is hidden from you.

"Tea, Abdul. . . ."

"It is ready, noble captain."

"Abdul . . . Abdul Mohamed, *shidd* the camels."

"In an hour, excellency?"

"*Shidd*, blast you."

"We need rest, excellency."

"We need water, Abdul."

"There is still a little water. . . ."

"*Shidd* the camels."

"Dinner, Abdul Mohamed, bring dinner quickly."

"In an hour, noble captain."

"Now, Abdul."

"It is not prepared. . . ."

"Sardines don't need preparing. Tinned fruit is ready. Bread. . . ."

"There is no bread, noble captain, how could the cook bake it?"

"Tea and sardines and tinned fruit. Bring them now, Abdul."

The night wind was fresh when Abdul brought dinner and Tubby, making himself eat, forced down the food quickly.

"*Shidd*, Abdul."

"With the moon, excellency?"

"We'll leave at once. The moon'll catch us up all right. . . . You're a lazy old dog, Abdul; you want some exercise, don't you? *Mens sana*, Abdul; you know the old tag. . . ."

"Excellency?"

"*Shidd* the camels."

꧁ They stopped at midnight and for two hours they rested, and then went on again. Once more the world was dissolved in moonlight; the plain brutality of endless scrub was melted into the moonlight and became beautiful as a surface of water is beautiful, suggestive of depth and currents and hidden movement but revealing nothing. Once more, overlooking the stretch of gentle radiance and the deep shadows that found refuge in the unknown creases of an utterly flat landscape, he was aware that the obvious had no truth in it. In the country that he traversed by night there was no likeness to the country he traversed by day. The man whose shadow—coalescent with the monstrous, weaving shape that was the shadow of the camel—floated and bobbed beside him had nothing in common with the man who ate, drank, laughed, rode and mingled with his fellows.

For the second or third time, Tubby was emptied completely of all physical sensation and all knowledge of circumstance. He was utterly indifferent to fatigue and pain, to lack of food and water, to his physical need for sleep, to the object of his journey, and to the danger that faced him. He had recovered the state in which an inner perception outflooded all other consciousness. He had rediscovered the power that was in himself to know everything. He could not use the power, but he was strongly aware of its existence. He knew nothing, except that there was nothing he could not know; that things, usually inconceivable, had been drawn within the bounds of conception.

❧ The sun was just up, and so they halted.

"Tea, Abdul."

"You want breakfast, noble captain?"

"No time for breakfast. Tea quickly, and some of those biscuits."

When the biscuits came he could not eat them, but he emptied the teapot.

"*Shidd*, Abdul."

"The camels, noble captain, they want rest. . . ."

"Rest, rest, perturbed spirit."

"Excellency?"

"Hamlet, Abdul, Hamlet. Fellow called Shakespeare. A good sort of chap though he was a poet. Before my time, if I remember rightly; but he and I were at the same private school, you know. He was fly half or wing three-quarter. I can't remember. . . ."

"Excellency?"

"*Shidd* those camels."

❧ "Lunch, Abdul. Just a light lunch. Cut off the joint and two vegs, stewed prunes and custard and a lump of mousetrap."

"Excellency?"

"Oysters and a bottle of stout and a piece of Stilton. . . ."

"Excellency?"

"Tea, Abdul. My God, you're ignorant. You've no finesse, Abdul, that's your trouble."

Abdul came back and said there was no water for tea.

"What, no tea?"

"Noble captain, the camel men can't go on. They say they must drink. . . ."

"Give them a drink then."

"There is no water. . . ."

"Well, give them a whisky and soda, give them a gin and bitters, give them a half pint of champagne apiece, don't let's be stingy . . . a wonderful remedy, champagne, Abdul. Ever tried it at eleven o'clock on the morning after?"

"Excellency?"

"No? Well, you really ought to. You really ought to try it. You must take my word for it, old boy, it's the cat's whiskers. You've just no idea what it does to you."

"Excellency?"

"*Shidd* the camels."

"But they will die. . . ."

"'Tis not the whole of life to live, nor all of death to die."

"The camels. . . ."

"No, I don't recall who wrote that, Abdul. It doesn't matter all that, anyway. I had to write it out a hundred times, you see, for killing flies in a Greek lesson."

"Excellency. . . ."

"It's no good arguing, Abdul . . . The beak said that what with Aristotle and Plato and one thing an' another, life and death didn't matter . . . got me?"

"The camels, noble captain; they must have water."

"There is water at the river, Abdul, rivers of it."

"How can they get to the river?"

"We'll all get there tonight, or never. . . . *Shidd* the camels."

The cream camel was led up and barracked, groaning and snorting. Tubby climbed on and kicked him and shook the head rope.

"Go on, Egbert. Get up, Egbert. *Egbert*, what did I have to tell you last time? Abdul . . . Sadek . . . a stick, somebody."

He hit the camel over the rump and ribs.

"Go on, Egbert, this hurts me more than it does you. Be a good chap, Egbert."

The camel groaned and waved his ridiculous head on its ridiculously stretched neck from side to side. It made no effort to rise. Tubby got off its back and tugged at the head rope, trying to pull him up while Abdul and the head camel man beat him from behind.

For the last day Tubby had worn his pistol, carrying it on his hip where it chafed him, so that the top of his shorts were stuck to his flesh with blood that had been rubbed out and had coagulated.

He pulled out the pistol and put two bullets into the head of the camel. The camel dropped his head, the head falling with a dull thud on to the cotton soil and the cotton soil drinking the blood that flowed slowly out, a gentle, crimson trickle.

"Come on, Abdul, let's get going. I'll have to walk, that's all there is to it."

"Excellency?"

"Next stop Euston; step on it, man, can't you?"

"Noble captain?"

"*Shidd* the camels, curse your shriveled soul. *Shidd*, curse you."

❁ At each halt he returned to a degree of material reality. It was not a full return; and it took him no further than to a consciousness of the conditions of his journey and to an unflagging resolve that drove him onwards. He was not worried. Whether or not they arrived at the river before they had reached the limit of endurance was a matter of small concern, for its determination was too far beyond the realms of human endeavor. Already, the simple physical facts of his journey were humanly inconceivable. They were not possible, for the physical powers of the human body are limited. He had done the impossible, had surpassed all limits. And he had learned that human conception is nothing; that his knowledge of himself was an infinitesimal part of what was written.

He was quite detached about it, and he had a cold assurance of his own sanity. He even reasoned it out, remembering the exploits of men and horses which were sanely impossible. A horse that had finished a race with a broken leg—mechanically out of the question; the man who crawled out of bed, so weak that he could scarcely pull his shorts on, to stroke his crew to victory; the man who was stone dead with a bullet in his heart, but who walked across the barrack square to kill the madman who had shot him. Doctors and veterinary surgeons, perhaps, could explain these things; but they were unconvincing. He, Tubby, could supply an explanation that was a matter, not of opinion, but of knowledge.

Tubby walked on behind Sadek. In a few minutes the memory of the camel's rhythm had died out of him, and he was adapted to the process of walking. It was entirely automatic.

The sun must have edged itself across the sky. His muscles—still impossibly potent—must have been expanding and contracting. There must have been pain behind his eyes, pain where the pistol continued to chafe his raw hip, pain where the sweat-soaked shirt rubbed against burned shoulders. The ground must have been unbearably hard, his boots intolerably heavy. If he did, in fact, accomplish that march, if he and the entire *hamlah* were not transported magically that last fifteen miles, before consciousness returned to him, these things (the pain, the movement, the progress of the day) must have been and must have happened. If so, it was only in logic that they existed.

❧ Awareness came back with an instinctive action that found its origins way back in the pre-oriental era. He kicked a football. He kicked it once or twice, dribbling it through the scrub and across the cotton soil. At first he did not admit the action, and it was sometime before a vague irritation disturbed him; a querulous objection burrowed its way through to his consciousness. There was something wrong, something very wrong, about it. The football was not regulation size; not nearly. Compared to what it should have been, it was quite tiny. His step faltered; he gazed perplexedly downwards; he kicked again viciously, and the football flew into dust and into a thousand grey-brown pieces. It was most irregular.

Then he halted and looked around him. Sadek halted; Abdul halted; the head camel man drew up beside him. Only the camels showed an inclination to press forward.

The ground was littered with clusters of grey, dry balls, larger than a polo ball, smaller than a football, sun-dried dung that flew into fragments when you kicked them violently.

"Oh, boy," Tubby said, clasping Abdul's shoulder, seizing Abdul's hand and shaking it with vigor. "Oh, boy—it's rabbits."

Abdul Mohamed was smiling. "Excellency?" he inquired automatically.

"Look, Abdul," Tubby shouted, "do you see what I see? Is it or isn't it? Make an effort, Abdul Mohamed, and try to understand me. Be a good chap and concentrate for just one minute. Use the old grey matter and do a spot of heavy thinking. Listen, Abdul Mohamed, do you see what I see, or don't you?"

"I see them, noble captain."

"Well—you say it first—what are they?"

Abdul's smile was gone. The joke was over. He answered quite without interest. "Elephants, noble captain."

"Ah, I thought so, elephants."

In a few hours at most they would reach water.

❦ Once more the trees thickened. There were occasional birds, a solitary gazelle, and then the first sight of one, two, three, a dozen giraffe, domestically graded in various sizes—father, mother and child, two grown-up brothers, three lovely sisters, a spinster aunt and a bachelor uncle—disturbed by the *hamlah* and cantering away with their quite unbelievable slow-motion movements, the last phase of the vision.

The day was gone and they were walking in half darkness. The trees broke and they were following a game track through towering grasses. The grass thinned and they were on a short-cropped plain, riddled with tracks, littered with dung and studded with ant hills. It was quite dark when, half a mile on, they reached the river. He had expected a smooth-flowing current, wide and sedate like the Blue Nile he had left behind him. They came to a steep, cliff-like bank, black and alarming in the night. It dropped vertically down to the pale sand at the bottom. The sand looked clean and sweet in the starlight and stretched out into the darkness. It might have been Margate; but there was no water.

Wearily they headed northwards again, following the game path that led along beside the river. It was the worst, the most desperate, the most utterly impossible hour of their journey before they saw the stars shining up from the sandy bed of the river and knew they had reached water.

Chapter 16 NOW THAT HE WAS ON THE RIVER, HE started to kill, started filling up his licence with the trophies that could be got on the Dinder.

Each morning he was awakened before sunrise, with the first light just in the sky and the stars growing less significant, fading every moment, the dawn breeze sweeping the sky clear of them. The fire was a heap of wood ash with a half-burned log on top of it; and, from his bed, he watched Abdul Mohamed bending down, testing the heat that was still left within the grey ruins, very delicately arranging a stick or two and putting his head to the ground to blow a small flicker and then a steady flame out of the apparently dead embers. He threw on the branch of a tree and the fire blazed up, starting fresh shadows, recalling the night and competing with the day that was hard upon them.

They were fine moments in the very early morning; and Tubby, waking clean and fresh as a child wakes and as he had not wakened within clear memory, swung his legs out of bed and walked barefoot across the cotton soil, feeling with his toes the short, stubby grasses and the cracked ground, that was now at its coldest but would soon be heated so that bare flesh could scarcely suffer its contact. Between sunset and sunrise the land rested, and just before dawn it seemed to treasure the precious minutes that were left before it would again be submitted to the sun's torture. You did not feel, then, the world awakening; you

339

felt it composing itself for the dogged sleep in which it would sweat through the hours of fierce daylight.

He dressed primly, slipping on shorts and shirt and jersey discreetly, so as not to expose himself and offend the Moslem servants who were prudish in this matter. Abdul brought tea, and he drank it by the fire, ignoring the deck chair that was solicitously placed there, squatting on the ground with his knees far apart and his body hung down over them, sucking in the warmth of the fire and energized by his closeness to the earth and by the unusual stretching of his muscles.

All around, skulls lay drying on the ground and skins were slung on ropes that were stretched between tree trunks. The trophies were at moments in silhouette from the coming day, and then the fire burst upwards more fiercely, throwing light and shadow on the half-bleached bones, picking out eye sockets, painting in the ridges of flesh that were left on the inside of the great lion skin. It touched the buffalo, all that now was left of that evil, magnificent animal, the vast hump of his shoulder muscle, the menacing head that was carried low and thrust out aggressively. It lit on the poor, clownish Tiang, the buffoon of the river, the village idiot, owlish and stupid. It left in shadow the proud reed buck who had stepped out of a clearing with his fine, delicate little head raised arrogantly; who had stamped his foot once at the intruder; who had snorted once and half turned to gallop back through the tall grasses; who had rolled over dully, a heap of crumpled limbs and slumped muscle, when the bullet smacked into him—nicely behind the shoulder.

Deep in the shadow were the water buck, the ariel, the wart hog, that had died without memorable incident in the normal course of killing. But the fire, catching at a last rotten branch or some resinous deposit in the wood, flared once more—and still more strongly—to light the remnants of the roan antelope, to display the long skull and great curving horns (the horns that stretched backwards in their grey corrugations, the horns that swept backwards in the fine, free curve that was all pride and beauty), and to recall the triumph of this, the best and most worthy of all the trophies.

It was indeed a worthy trophy; theoretically a perfect trophy because it was the fruit of effort and endurance. Because it had behind it the full weight of the journey, of hardship, exhaustion, of that unbelievable march, of three days' hunting, during which all except the quarry merged out of consciousness, and of a final stalk that continued in somber heat from sunrise till near sunset. Because, too, the antelope was a superb bull, old, driven out of the herd, living a solitary life between forest and river; so that the time had come for death at the height of his powers, his death hurting no living creature except himself and his killer, and—at the end—coming to him painlessly from an almost impossible shot at two hundred yards that lodged a bullet in the only square foot of neck that was visible between the tree trunks. And, after that, his flesh had been cut up and eaten, his liver and kidneys served up as breakfast dishes, his skin dried in the sun, his head and headskin preserved for decoration. So that, even in death, he lived and gave life and was useful—which was more than you could say for miserable humans. . . .

Oh, yes! He was a good trophy. Because of all that, and, especially, because of the moment when the black, fur-edged foresight, seen through the sweat lens that covered the eyes, came onto the grey neck and held there, and of the moment when—the trigger pulled steadily to conclusion—the shock of recoil blanked out everything in a blind knowledge of death, and again of the moment when Sadek stood at his feet and cried "Praise God, *hallas*, it is finished," and ran forward the two hundred yards and pulled his knife from the sheath on his forearm to hack and saw through the tassels of thick hair and through the thick, grey, black-marked skin to let the crimson blood gush and froth out and slake the eager cotton soil—because of the moments of hunting, of death, of finality, that were all unforgettable.

Unforgettable, as well, were the large, liquid eyes, the gentle, brown eyes, that looked up with strange wonder; the eyes that gazed reproach while Sadek hacked through the still quivering neck muscles of the dying antelope. You didn't forget the eyes.

Reasonably, there was sense in the killing; the world acclaimed it as a sign of healthy manhood, applauded fine trophies and the exploits that had won them, praised unreservedly the killing of a fine, old, solitary, bull antelope.

There were, of course, critics. There were prim old ladies, lank-haired spinsters, pimpled youths, smug parsons, self-righteous tradesmen, none of them healthy and hard living, who condemned killing noisily and knew nothing about it. They did not count at all for if you could not admire their persons you could not respect their views. They were entitled to their thoughts, as he was entitled to his passions; but the uninformed violence of their ranting incited you against them; made you kill the more, to prove their impotence.

This killing was a deep-rooted instinct. And, whether it were ruthless or careful, its fulfillment relieved an appetite that was no more bestial than any other of man's cravings for food, drink, lust or hysterical religion. Bloodletting was a personal matter. It brought either satisfaction or disgust, and—until you tried—you could not tell whether or not you had yet transcended the instincts that required it. Didn't they say that, until you had tried God, you could not know whether or not you wanted Him?

There were men who *must* find brutal assuagement, against man or against animals; there were others who couldn't.

The lion skin swung gently, very slowly, as the dawn wind stirred the trees that held it. It was stretched loosely, as it had been stretched on the frame of the wounded lion; just as it had been when the lion leaped the *wadi* and hung in mid-air, rampant, spreadeagled in an heraldic device, one paw raised, the other folded, its pale, amber eyes deep and angry, its curled lips and long teeth framed by the dead-white whiskers, its great chest pale behind the foresight.

It was a moment of last trial, man and beast facing each other, and the beast falling to the rifle. But the rifle was held steady—in that quick, urgent fraction of a second—by all the delicate nerve and muscle and tissue that were the essence of man. He, Tubby, had faced the lion, had undergone the ultimate trial, had known his own power and its fulfillment. It was a necessary experience. But now he was done with killing.

He did not know why. He did not know all that was himself, his lower currents, his profundities. He was only aware that the depths were unfathomable. He had learned that there was so much more to him than the surface water of appetites, vague desires, animal instincts and their simple appeasement. There was, for discovery, an unknown land of promise; a country where killing—and all the triumphant assuagement and keen experience and vital living, that it meant—was already explored, registered, indelibly mapped and left behind him. Blood had been let and the body was peaceful.

The teapot was empty so he picked up a lump of sugar, toyed with it, put it in his mouth, sucked it, broke it with his teeth, and crunched it. A sharp pain went through his head; his tongue followed the pain, explored it, found a cavity and a hard lump of loose matter. The pain became less general and attached itself to one of the maxillary molars. The filling had come out.

He had dabbed iodine on it, groping with cotton wool and a matchstick into the hinterland of his mouth. He had chewed aspirin, pushing the sodden powder into the sharp-edged cavity that his tongue insisted on exploring. Round and round he worked his tongue, torturing himself for the exquisite relief of turning dull, invariable pain into something fierce and remarkable. He had finished his stock of sedatives and had found whisky useless. He had pushed the pain right away into his inner recesses and had tried to ignore it. But it would not be ignored. Like a child, it persisted in its intrusions. Its trespass forbade thought or oblivion; prevented enjoyment in its simplest form, in the satisfaction of appetite, in the pleasures of a cigarette, in sleep.

Then he concentrated on the pain, regarding it with consideration, visualizing the white, grotesque affair that was a tooth, contemplating the ugly roots that must be thrust down into the water pink of his gums. Again like a tiresome child, once it had obtained recognition, the pain became tractable. It would not go away; it demanded a place in, and a part of, his life, but it was on its best behavior. For a time it would recede and make room for other feelings of enjoyment, annoyance and even other pain. So long as it was accepted as a companion, it did not demand pre-eminence.

"*Shidd,*" Tubby shouted and the loads were lashed on to the camels and the *hamlah* pushed on again through the spindly trees, across the pale shadows, over the hard, hot soil, with the river running parallel to their path, sometimes to the right and sometimes to the left of them. Often they scrambled down the steep bank to take a long cut diagonally across the sandy bed, and to climb again and plunge into the barren forest until they met the river once more on its return from a wide, meandering, purposeless loop through exactly similar country.

Endurance was not now taxed as it had been before; and Tubby traveled fast but easily, and with a double purpose, anxious to complete his journey and, by nightfall, to achieve sufficient fatigue to make sleep come quickly. There was glory in the fatigue that was so studiously contrived and that, each day, demanded increasing endeavor; glory in the pain that, now it had been acknowledged, allowed him a triumphant detachment and permitted, commanded, the subjection of the body to the will and to the spirit. He could see pain now—in company with hardship, danger, fear, unhappiness—as the main element of common experience. Pain was the purest experience; and experience was the simplest element of life, the only element that you had to spend your life acquiring.

When you thought back and tried to consider life without the experience with which you had filled it, you found that there was nothing left to consider. So you contemplated experience, concrete experience, your memory leaping from peak to peak, traveling by the crags that projected memorially above the sea of all that you had done and heard and seen and felt deeply. Dryshod, you made your way through the spate, back through the long perspective behind you, marveling at the stepping stones that you had left on the outward journey. You regarded them critically and were astonished at their curious structure and their unfamiliarity. They were not the stones that you remember placing, the wistful sunset, the gold cup that was handed you beneath the arc lamps, the dive between the posts in the last two minutes of the match, the path of moonlight that led you seawards to the horizon; not even the moments of utter clarity, when you hit a goal or slung the battery into action while time went into slow-motion and waited for you. These were nothing. They scarcely broke the surface of the water. The intensity of your feeling at any moment had nothing to do with its ultimate value as experience. It was a surprising discovery.

You followed it up and were surprised, too, to find that important experience was nearly always painful, nearly always misfortune; that it seemed to be measured, not by its glory, but by the demands it had made on your resources, on your courage and on the temper of your spirit.

You could face a wounded lion. You could bring the animal to the finality of death and, in a hot, liquid elation, see him roll over snarling and lie still. Yet, a few days afterwards, the elation and the vital excitement were as frigid and uninteresting as cold porridge. All that remained was the moment of final demand, the portrait of the lion reared heraldically as he leaped the *wadi*, the fraction of a second in which you had to collect your powers and kill him. And even that had become insignificant; so trifling that the dried skin packed on the camel had only a conventional importance. It would do to fall over in a sitting room. It could remind you that the experience attached to it lay only in the revelation of its own cheapness, was all disillusionment, was as trivial as the taking of a woman whom you have had and who remains in memory only as another conquest. The two contests were similar.

Tragically you found it was always the same. You made your way back to your beginnings and, repassing your landmarks, found that time had unpredictably swollen the most trifling misfortunes into unforgettable adventures, into experience. A quarrel with Daddy Watson; an excessively foolish remark made to someone whom you wanted to impress; the embarrassment of a forgotten name and of someone important introduced quite wrongly as a complete nonentity; the indignity of a mild beating by a boy who was very nearly your own contemporary; the horror of discovering that you had to walk nude down a long

corridor into the dormitory bathroom; that you had to sit on the
toilet with the door open. The last day of holidays, and the
smell of heliotrope while the dog-cart was waiting to take you
to the station; seeing the new nannie and wetting your pants. . . .
These were what were left of all the successes; all that remained
of a prodigious infancy, a boyhood of athletic triumphs, an
early manhood of popularity.

These were the relics and, as such, were also trophies. Trophies
of what? Of shame and sadness and frailty, but acknowledged
and conquered. And they were such trivial things and such
famous victories. You wetted your pants for the last time; you
restrained tears and found courage; you were humiliated and
learned that humiliation was only a product of your own weakness. Slowly your strength emerged from trial and acquittal.
From weakness came strength. From strength came the beginnings of peace and understanding. These were the fruit, but the
seed was unhappiness. This was what Sammy knew, what
Daddy had yet to agree to. Daddy valued unhappiness, but for
false reasons, for false objects . . . "As an enemy," he had said.
But before that, he had murmured "Sweet uses. . . ."

Tubby slept deeply and woke cleanly as the darkness was
just trembling. He woke the servants and shouted to the camel
men. Before the dawn he was trekking northwards through the
sinking night. He did not want tea or tobacco; he was content.
If peace and understanding were built on misfortunes, nothing
mattered, nothing could hurt you. What was it Daddy had
said? Wasn't it that he believed only in the divinity of complete
consciousness? It was reasonable now.

Looking back on the last month, Tubby found that he had
learned, quite simply, how much there was to a man, and how
little what happened to him mattered. Circumstances could
never injure him for he was beyond circumstance. All that it
could touch was the outer shell of him that was concerned only
with the mechanics of living. He had only to retreat inwards
to find impenetrable defences, to achieve new consciousness,
a knowledge of new powers, and to discover a strength that
need not fight misfortune but could use it. Daddy had talked
of "the divinity of consciousness," meaning—one supposed—

that it was desirable and unattainable. Well . . . you'd agree
that it was a long way distant—even for the best of mortals.
But couldn't Daddy see that it was only unattainable so long
as you persisted in regarding misadventure as an implacable
enemy? That when you had once conceived pain as the essence
—the primary element—of experience, you had turned a corner
with a new and limitless vista before you. Couldn't Daddy see
that? Or had he done so at last? Was that the reason of the
gentleness, the tranquillity, on his return from Cairo?

Eref el Dik, the site of a long deserted village, was behind
and they had left the river at last. Abu Hashim, where the
lorry was waiting, was three days ahead. He must hurry back
to the Fort and to Daddy Watson. He wanted to share his
knowledge with the man who had set him on the path towards
it. He wanted to sit on the battlements of the Fort, and empty
a bottle with Daddy Watson. He wanted Daddy now; he
needed him. He was very happy.

"Abdul," he shouted back from the head of the *hamlah*,
"we'll stop for breakfast."

🌸 In the evening, as they came upon it, Abu Hashim was not
an ugly village. During the afternoon, the cattle dung and the
hoof marks along the track had promised them the end of their
journey; but the characterless nature of the country had in no
way changed, so that they had followed on through the drab,
tired forest, through the half shade that, in its breathlessness,
increased the heat rather than lessened it, until a sudden twist
in the path had shown them at once the complete village, the
thorn fence with the pointed *tukuls* growing out of it, assembled
behind it, huddled together as though—out of all Africa—man
had only been allowed to claim for his home this tiny, valueless
territory.

Drawing closer, they could see the flat, square, grass-mat
erections, the homes of wives and children, clinging to each
central hut. Then the village opened itself out into a main street
with the dwellings grouped, not altogether without pattern,
along it. Further on there was a central space, which—except
for its polygonous shape—might almost have been called a

square and on which were built the two mud-brick houses, clearly government buildings, a school and a hospital.

The native doctor who came out to greet them was very black, but dressed, still a little self-consciously, in khaki uniform.

"How are you?" he asked politely in clipped, careful English.

"Bloody ill," Tubby said, grinning, "and how are you, Doctor?"

"I am well, thank you, sir. But you are ill? Oh, sir, that is bad. . . ."

"It's the toothache," Tubby said, "it's given me hell the last week or so."

"The toothache can be very bad."

"Don't I know it, Doctor."

"But it cannot be disaster; so it may be fortunate."

Tubby could not help laughing. The doctor's imperfect English had allowed him to approach the truth so closely.

"There, you see, sir, you can laugh—so it may not be serious."

"You're right," Tubby said, "toothache can't be serious. But then nothing can be very serious, can it?"

The doctor spread out his hands pathetically. Tubby's smile led him to suppose that he was being teased, but Tubby's eyes were sober.

"That, sir, is something I may not say. There is perhaps illness that may be serious."

"We won't argue that," Tubby said. "The point is, can you pull a tooth out?"

The doctor smiled deferentially.

"Oh, sir, very well indeed. It is a very small thing, you know. It is even less, sir, than pulling out a baby. It is not nearly so much as pulling out an appendix. I do that very often. I am very good at that. I do here many operations each week, on the stomach, on the head, everywhere."

"That's fine," Tubby said, "let's start on the tooth, shall we?"

The tooth was difficult and the doctor had given a cocaine injection in the gums. But the lorry was there in the village and, with the drug still strong in him, Tubby had insisted on paying off Sadek and the camel men and making a four hours' journey towards Singa that evening.

The lorry was piled high with his kit and with the servants and with the trophies, the skins and skulls of the animals he had shot on the river. The lorry jolted and swayed along the little-worn track and the drug began to work out of him. He was frightened of its going and of meeting again his fellow officers. He had to—wanted to—hurry back to them; but he grasped at the last precious moments of his own company.

For the last month his solitude had altered all the values of life that he had previously accepted. He thought something out and then, because he was alone and there was no one to draw him back on to the path of unreason, he believed what his brain had told him. There had been no formal code of behavior to discredit his thought or to be discredited by his thinking. He had lived in a golden age where things were based on what they were and not on what tradition called them.

First his journey from one river to the other, and after that remorse, and then the toothache, had elevated him still further above the ordinary design of living. Now, at the last, the cocaine was keeping him mercifully apart from his homeward journey. With the passing of the drug, he was timid of plunging once more into human contacts, teased with doubts of his own security, attacked by the fear that what he had come to believe, to feel, to suspect, to know—which was it now?—would not stand the wear of normal existence. Would his knowledge of himself wither and die in a life that ignored the nature of man and denied him nine-tenths of his being? How could his knowledge exist within the lunacy of civilization, where men and women suffered and were unhappy and lived, worked, wept and died—to no ultimate purpose and without reason—within the traditional pattern of their setting?

Then the memory of Sammy came to him and he clung to it eagerly, clutching at it for the credit of his newly won knowledge. Sammy had known and had reasoned; but he had still believed in the decency of man and had lived happily. If it had been like that with Sammy, so it could be with Tubby. Sammy had not mocked and despised the men who had ordered his life. He had not bothered to; he had ignored them. He ignored all that happened to him and it could not touch him. Circumstance ruled his actions but it could not touch his living. Wherever he was, whatever he was doing, he created a world in which he could live according to his own fashion. That was the essence of his greatness. . . .

The lorry crashed on, throwing a tunnel of light into the darkness ahead, painting the ruts of its predecessors with deep shadow, lighting up the trees on each side of the track to a one-sided existence. The wind that blew in through the open wind-shield was cool and sane, but the night all around, the heavy darkness that they rent open and that closed in behind them, was full of madness.

If only he could believe like Sammy; if only he could achieve his aloof happiness. It began from somewhere, it had a vital source like every line in a great picture. All beauty, all truth, all emotion must begin somewhere and lead somewhere with a purpose. Sammy's power began with some belief that was to him an unshakable truth. If Tubby could only find it.

As the lorry rocked along the path, the pain that his tooth had left behind it grew once more insistent. Once more it demanded recognition. Tubby grunted as he twisted himself about in the hard seat of the lorry. The driver crashed his gears as they charged down the bank of a *wadi* and up the other side again. Branches of trees clung with their thorns to the hood, slid downwards and ripped at his bare forearm. The biting ache that came from the soft, still bleeding cavity stabbed in rhythm to the jolting of the lorry. But it was a trivial thing. He and the doctor had both agreed that it could not be serious. They hadn't meant the same, but that did not matter.

"Pain doesn't matter; it's experience, you see."

"Excellency?" the lorry driver inquired.

"It's all right, I was only talking to myself."

"Excellency?"

"Oh, nothing," Tubby said in Arabic. "Drive faster."

❦ Towards nine o'clock the track widened and the head-lamps threw increasing shadow before them as they lit on cattle dung and on the scars of many footprints. They topped a hill with the horizon of the road cutting in a hard line the black night beyond it. Then they rocked downwards, the lamp beams grasping at tree trunks and at the upper arms of thorn scrub, groping for the road but projected above it. The ground flattened out and the wheels skidded in the thick sand. Away to the right there was a huddle of dark shapes that must be *tukuls*. Then on the left there was the same.

"Abu Harrar," the driver said; "do we sleep here, noble captain?"

"No, we'll go straight through."

"I must stop for water, excellency."

"All right, stop for water."

Dogs ran out yapping; men, women and children ran out excitedly, and the lorry pushed its way slowly through them to the open space in the center of the village. There were no native houses here, but behind a mud-brick wall and a pleasant garden there was a British bungalow. From the extra height of the lorry, Tubby could see a white-clad figure on the lit veranda. With despair he realized that he had returned to civilization.

He saw the man look up at the sound of the engine and shade his eyes as he peered into the darkness. A small brown figure uncurled itself from the floor and slipped into the black cavity of the house. The man came away from his table of bottles and glasses, down through the garden towards the lorry.

Tubby climbed stiffly out, feeling suddenly and for the first time in his life a sad loneliness. He was alone again amongst his fellows. He dreaded this meeting.

"Hello . . . who's this?" the man called out.

"Hello . . ."

"Why, bless me if it isn't old Tubby. Last saw you in London . . . isn't that Tubby Windrush?"

Tubby peered at him, seeing at first only that he was tall, thin and dark, and remembering the voice as familiar. Then something in the stoop of his shoulders allowed recognition.

"It's Benjamin," he roared. "I didn't know you hung out here. Good old Benjy; my word, but I'm glad to see you."

"I heard you were in these parts, but I didn't expect you'd take this road; the other's shorter."

"I had the toothache. I didn't bother about maps. I left it to the driver."

"Well, it's great to see you. Come on in. As you see, the alcohol is waiting."

They walked up to the veranda and sat down in the deep chairs while Benjamin poured out the whisky.

"Dinner," he said, "is punctually between seven o'clock and ten-thirty. I haven't had mine yet, so you're lucky. You'll stay the night, of course?"

"Of course," Tubby said. "That's what I came for. Can I have a bath before dinner?"

"I expect you'll find it waiting."

❦ Benjamin led Tubby off the veranda, away from the cluster of bottles, the sherry, gin, vermouth, whisky, home-made soda and lime juice, across the garden to the large guest house.

"You'll have to make the best of this somehow," he said, opening the door into the large white room. "I hope you'll be comfortable. Just ring down to the hall porter if you want anything."

"A bit tough," Tubby said, looking round him; "but I can't object to roughing it once in a blue moon, can I?"

The guest house was a large, native-style *tukul*, but built with mud walls and the usual thatched, conical roof. To one returning from a month on trek, it offered all the half-forgotten luxuries for which a traveler can be homesick while sincerely applauding their absence. Homesickness is one of the attractions of travel that gives it a spice of limitation and adventure. You must have something to get back to. If the adventurer has no roothold in his home country, if there is no intimate curve of a hillside, no cluster of park trees to beckon him homewards, or if he does not hunger for the tremor of the omnibus and the jostle of the Piccadilly crowd, and the lights high up, flashing vulgarity and merchandise, it will be the elegance of luxury that feeds his nostalgia.

With a sense of homecoming, Tubby entered the large room that had been prepared for him. Abdul Mohamed was waiting, already transformed into the perfect servant, laying out clothes.

preparing a bath, moving noiselessly and with an unction that
came from his own love for the niceties of living. Already the
silent patter of an African night, the grunt of a lion over by the
river, the Southern Cross hung above the tree trunks like the
sacred picture at your bedside, the solid atmosphere of space—
as real, though as intangible, as sound and smell and color—
were completely forgotten. Abdul was made of them, and they
must have called him homewards through no more than one or
two generations of dark ancestors. But he was glad to leave them
again. He laid out Tubby's white tussore suit with joy and
tenderness.

When the *suffragi* had gone, Tubby threw off his clothes and
stood naked, stretching himself, filling himself with the returning
familiarity of his surroundings. The rough camel-hair rug welcomed his feet; the enclosing walls were kind to eyes that had
been recently accustomed to the infinite depths of night. The
table, the tablecloth, the washstand, the chest of drawers, the
pictures, the ivory elephants, the ornamental fly whisks, the
futile little native toys, were all objects made precious by the
knowledge that they were not essential to living. As he looked
around him, he was aware with pleasure that he could put his
watch down in one place, his cigarettes in another, his pipe and
matches somewhere else without deliberating his actions. He
need no longer consider just where an object would not be lost,
would not become clogged with dust or attacked by insects.
He did not have to husband space, to treasure each square inch
of table as a haven where his personal possessions would not be
lost or injured. He was guarded by walls, protected by a roof,
enclosed with light and comfort. He had come home.

He lay in the hip bath with the warm water lapping at his
ribs, regarding with tolerance the curious gentleman who, two
hours ago and under the influence of a cocaine injection, had
been plunging northwards in a lorry. The fears and doubts and
the yearning that had assailed him were very ridiculous. It was
time that he returned to sanity. It had been dangerous, he
thought, this dabbling with queer ideas about truth and experience, misadventure and knowledge. He had been pretty
close to becoming a God-botherer, a religious sort of bloke who

made hell for everyone by insisting on a full attendance at Church parade; one of those chaps who objected to foul language in the barrack rooms; a good, cranky sort of abnormally normal muscular Christian; the sort of person who joined the padre at being heartily righteous in a quiet corner of the anteroom. It was splendid to be back to sane comfort, and to the sane welcome of good old Benjamin. He finished dressing and went across the garden back to the veranda.

Dinner was a long-drawn hour of physical delights and of recollections.

"Old Baxter now, he went crackers in Hong Kong. I don't blame him. . . ."

"And James—James Brewis?"

"James chucked it a couple of years ago. He was at Gib in that fellow Carter's brigade. Seven subalterns asked for a transfer at the same time, but of course the Brigadier sat on it. . . ."

"James had a bit of cash, didn't he?"

"He feathered his nest all right; married one of the Turtles—soap or something. . . ."

"Tommy Taylor chucked it too, didn't he?"

"He got sent to the Depot and couldn't stick Woolwich. He tried selling cars, but wasn't sissy enough for the job; so now he sells insurance."

"I suppose dear old Raikes is time expired by now?"

"They kept him on half pay for a couple of years and when he was nearly bankrupt he chucked it. . . ."

"He was a nice chap, Raikes."

"A dear chap and a damned good officer. . . ."

"Do you remember the guest night when we took that big grey mule of yours into the Colonel's quarters?"

"Do I not, Tubby! That was Paddy Wilson's stunt, not mine. He deserves the credit. . . . I'd like to see old Paddy again."

"You won't see him again," Tubby said. "He fell out of a fourth-floor window of a hotel in Calcutta. Nobody knew what he was doing there; they said it was probably suicide."

"Poor old Paddy. . . ."

"You've done as well as anyone, Benjy, getting a nice soft job in the Sudan Government."

"Yes, I was lucky. I was about the last soldier to get taken. They stopped it after that, of course."

"Larry Gerrard was out here for a bit, wasn't he?"

"Larry Gerrard?"

"You remember, that queer fish who was in my House at school. The fellow who got a painting prize for a portrait of old Mrs. Dingle. You must remember; we had the hell of a lark, cut up the picture and papered the quad with it."

"Larry Gerrard, of course. He wasn't out here long. He went cracking off to Everest or somewhere and fell off it."

"Poor fellow. Probably all for the best all the same; he was a cranky sort of chap, never happy anywhere. But Baxter and Tommy Taylor and poor old Raikes and Paddy Wilson—they were damn good fellows; normal, healthy sort of chaps, if you get me. . . ."

Yet each was ringing a cracked church bell; there was no honesty or belief in their words; they were dressed for character parts that they had rehearsed from infancy, and they gave a splendid performance.

"Champagne in your honor, Tubby."

"Do you remember . . ."

"Do I not?"

"And that time we went up from Aldershot . . ."

"When old Buster threw the sofa out of the mess window. . . ."

"When Pansy's dog got into the mess and cocked his leg against the General's overalls . . ."

"My God, that was funny . . ."

"I shall never forget . . ."

"One more glass, Tubby . . ."

"All right, then. Well, Benjy, here's to it all. My God, those were the days, weren't they?"

"Those were the days."

"We used to knock it a crack now and again."

"My God, we did."

"We had a bit of fun, didn't we?"

"We had a bit of fun," Benjamin said and drank deeply. Over the top of his glass he looked with wide, serious eyes across the table. Tubby looked back, flinched and looked downwards at the tablecloth. He crumbled at his bread and sat in silence. Then he drank again.

"Those were the days!" he cried almost hysterically. "We knocked it a crack now and again. We had a bit of fun. We had a hell of a time, Benjy—or didn't we?"

❀ "But you were always a brainy sort of chap, Benjy . . . in the sixth, head of your House, prizes; all that sort of thing. It beat me why you ever went into the Army. . . ."

"Coffee?" Benjamin said. "Brandy? Kümmel?"

"I don't mean to say, old boy, that you weren't a success as a soldier. On the contrary . . . but you were too good for it, if you take me . . ."

"By no means," Benjy said. "Nobody's too good for anything —and certainly not me. And certainly not the Army. The Army's a fine, splendid institution. Fine, generous men; a fine, clean life. It's like nothing else in the world; and nowhere else do you get the same decency, the generosity, the openness . . .

"We were good to each other, you know. We were a splendid company. We took a man at what he was, not at what his father was, or what money he had, or if he had a title . . . *we* were the Army; and *we* were all right. It was the people who ruled the Army—the politicians, the War House, the generals—who were rotten, rotten, rotten . . ."

"Ah! Now you're talking like Daddy . . ."

"Yes! And Daddy knows what he's talking about! The generals just aren't the Army at all. . . . No more than the profiteers, the crooked merchants, the round-bellied financiers are England. The generals are a self-elected clique; father to son, one pair of nice boots to the next, one county family to another. A clique rotten with success in the way that success rots everything. . . .

"And *we* could have been in that clique, Tubby. *You* still can be, if you want to . . . that is, if the thought of what you'll have to turn into doesn't make you vomit. If you don't mind carrying on the system of the survival of the least fit; tapping the good ones on the head when they've done a dozen years or so, and giving a hand to the handsome boot-lickers, or the fellers with the cash and the families. . . .

"No, Tubby! It's the system that stinks. And for some extraordinary reason it still attracts the best, the cleanest, the decentest chaps in the country. They seem to *want* to commit suicide. They join the Army for six years of a simpleton's glory and a life afterwards of misery and disillusionment . . .

"We're all right, fellows like you and me who've got names that people know and a bit of money behind us. We can struggle clear of the birdlime when we want to. But look at the ordinary decent sons of clergymen, doctors, lawyers . . . caught for life!"

"Yes," Tubby said slowly. "I know all this. And I know it's true. You get some devilish hard cases. . . ."

"But it isn't a question of hard cases. It's ninety per cent hard cases. The rest are the exception. Look at the ordinary officer! He's told that he needn't have a private income—but he hasn't a hope of living without it. He scarcely gets enough to cover his Mess bill, his uniform and his compulsory subscriptions. If he wants a pair of pants he's got to give up smoking to pay for them. . . . He's told he has the right of appeal to the King against the decision of the generals. But let him try it! He gets a note from the Secretary of State for War, saying that he can see no reason for bringing the matter to the notice of His Majesty . . . King's men! If we only were, Tubby, it'd be a heap different. . . .

"Look at the things we say and the songs we sing in Mess! The tradition of drink and women; that fornication is the mark of a gentleman; wine, women, horses . . . and in half the stations abroad neither officer nor man has any chance of sexual satisfaction. . . . So he pops into bed with his captain's wife—if she'll let him—and when it comes to the divorce court he has to resign his commission. . . .

"And look at the older fellows! One straight remark to a general—and a major's finished. After twenty-five years, he gets a pension that's cut and taxed till it's little more than a junior clerk's salary. So that the old man hobbles round Cheltenham or Tunbridge Wells, told all his life that he has to be a gentleman, and trying to end his days as one. . . ."

"You're talking to the converted," Tubby said. "Remember I've had two years with Daddy Watson."

"And I hope," Benjamin answered, "that you believed what he told you. I used to think him a crank. But then, one day, I saw he was right. . . . Remember, I got an inside view as A.D.C. to that general. And that was why I got out of it. *You* do as you please. You're all right either way. But you've got to choose between being a successful soldier and being human. . . ."

"I saw you the day before you sailed," Tubby said; "in your club. Do you remember?"

"I do. . . ."

"And after that?"

"After eighteen months in the Eastern Arab Corps, I got the chance of transferring to the Political. Of course I took it. . . . You go out on trek, you see, and that starts you thinking; lets you think. It clears the eye too. . . ."

Tubby lay back in his chair and looked at him. "And it's changed you," he said.

"And you've changed too, Tubby. In a lot of ways. But, mostly, you've got receptive. You've learned, haven't you, to absorb things. . . ."

"I saw Sammy killed, I was at a couple of forts, I got turned down by Lydia. . . ."

"Lydia . . ."

"Yes; but don't let's talk about it."

"It still hurts, does it?"

"I tell myself it doesn't."

"All right," Benjamin said, "and you've been on trek yourself, haven't you? That helps."

"Yes. It's rather a voyage of discovery. . . . If only what one found was substantial, believable. . . ."

"Ah!" Benjamin said, his glass arrested halfway to his lips, his eyes peering between the bottles. "You've gone further than I thought. Let's move to the veranda, shall we?"

🌿 They went through onto the veranda and Benjamin walked to the end and shouted into the darkness. A servant answered and they spoke together quickly in Arabic. Then they settled down again in the chairs they had occupied before dinner.

"I'm going to pay you a compliment," Benjamin said. "I'm going to introduce you to Khadiga. I usually see that she makes herself scarce when there are visitors. She's frightened of strangers anyway."

Khadiga slipped onto the veranda, passing them shyly and at a distance, slipping by quickly with her head turned away like a child who is self-conscious before a visitor. She was young and slim and lovely. She sat at Benjamin's feet, sinking down in one movement, not squatting with all of her contained within her thighs in the common but not ungraceful way that most natives compose themselves, but spread lightly on the ground, her hips twisted and the weight of her torso taken on one slender, chocolate-colored arm and outspread fingers. Her orange robe, which she had held demurely in front of her breasts and the lower part of her face, fell apart and her full, tiny breasts quivered when she moved, when she laughed or when she became animated in her chatter.

"She's really my wife," Benjamin explained. "Of course she knows that when I go it's finished. But I'll set her up for life, I suppose, so she thinks it's worth it. She's a dear little thing, but we don't own to having them—you know—as a matter of habit."

Tubby sat back in his chair with his face twisted into the smile that he felt was proper to the occasion. He hoped that he was radiating sympathy, amusement, kindly tolerance; but he only succeeded in looking embarrassed. Benjamin laughed at him.

"Feeling shy about it?"

"No, no," Tubby said quickly. "After all, you expect that sort of thing, so one may as well be open about it. I mean to say, you can't ignore sex and appetites and all that, can you?"

"Sex!" Benjamin said scornfully; "that's got very little to do with it. Of course, she sleeps with me. But I really keep her as a sort of pet, so as to have someone, something, to talk to, to laugh with. You get pretty fond of your own company when you live by yourself, but you have to have a companion sometimes."

"Yes, old boy, I suppose you do."

"Suppose as you like. It's the way most of us find it."

"It's what Daddy used to say," Tubby answered. "You can only get really intimate with someone of the opposite sex . . . and man needs woman to complete himself . . . to outpour what's superfluous, like the waste pipe at the top of a bath . . . and a lot more of that stuff. . . ."

"And you believed it?"

"I don't know. I expect I believed it at the time. . . ." The question had somehow stirred it all up again. For no particular reason, he couldn't let drop a casual, untruthful answer. "How I wish I did know," he said desperately. "I believe a thing, you see, and I build up everything on it. It seems a fine, solid sort of building—if you understand me—but there must be a barrel of gunpowder in the cellar. For, a week later, someone shoots out an odd remark that seems to put a match to it, that sends the whole lot up in pieces. Then I'm left with nothing. . . . No! I can't say I believe it. For I believe nothing, Benjy; absolutely nothing. If you knew how I wanted something to believe in. . . ."

"You must believe something, for God's sake!"

"For God's sake and my own, I wish I could. There's no single thing I can honestly and truthfully believe. Being with Sammy, with Daddy, and then being alone, and thinking and imagining and so on, has upset all the old ideas I had; and, now that I've got back to a roof and a hot bath, I mistrust all the new ones. If I could believe in one single thing—even that this chair is a chair, that this body is human—believe it so that I knew it and knew that it was absolutely and utterly true and without qualification . . . but I can't, you see. . . ."

"God, or the existence of a soul in man, or that there's something divine in life. . . ."

"But how can you know it?"

"Take it the other way round then; that's the common cure. Get something negative, something that can't be made or explained by the scientists. Can they ever create a conscience?"

"No," Tubby said, "let's take it that that's a bit beyond them."

"All right. Then man *is* rather more than just an animal with underdeveloped senses and an overdeveloped intellect.

He *has* other instincts beyond those of self-protection and propagation. Why?"

"Oh, I dunno," Tubby said uncomfortably. "I suppose he's not such a bad sort of chap after all."

"Hell take it!" Benjamin cried; "just look at the age we've got to. Three hundred years ago we'd have been tied up and burned in the market place for denying God. Nowadays we daren't mention Him. We can talk about copulation and lavatories and unnatural vice and our loathsome complexes and miserable repressions and our ambivalence and introversion in any sort of company. They're all right as subjects for conversation because we can be clever about them; but we can't be clever about God—He's been done already. There's only one subject we have to blush about and sheer away from, and that's the soul and the destiny of man. There's only one name we daren't utter in public, except as an expletive, and that's God's. We have to get hysterical before we can pluck up courage to mention Him."

"One doesn't bandy Him about the mess a lot," Tubby admitted. "He's useful when ordinary language fails to express our annoyance. . . ."

"Oh, shut up, Tubby. It gets boring to go on trying to be funny as the only object in life. Why can't we say in an ordinary, matter-of-fact way 'I believe—I know—that there is something divine in me; that the animal side, that goes on living mechanically and satisfying passions, is only a minute part of me'? If we say that, we acknowledge that we are fundamentally good, that we have more than utilitarian instincts. Of course we are often bad. . . ."

"Yes," Tubby said suddenly, "when the animal side to us gets above itself. . . ."

"Exactly! But bit by bit, if we once get started, our animal side becomes less important. We learn to replace it with something else. It crops up again and again and, if you ask me, there's more animal about human beings today than there has been for the last two thousand years. The world seems to be increasing in evil, increasing in pain and suffering, and man more often succumbs to it. . . ."

"Yes," Tubby interrupted, "we succumb to misfortune instead of using it, instead of seeing that it's only a chance to exercise all sorts of powers we seem to have inside us. Misfortune makes demands on us. It calls for something. Our usual answer nowadays is that we're sorry but we're right out of stock at the moment. We've got no guts left, but if we can rake up the guts to find what's wanted, to supply the demand, we seem to take another step forward—if you get me."

"I get you all right," Benjamin said. "You and I have just about caught up with the beliefs of our great-grandfathers. They said all this in church when they declared that troubles are sent to try us. Now we say that they're sent to try the scientists. If you and I progress much further, we'll get back a few more generations and start believing in God again."

"It's not our fault we don't," Tubby said. "Look at the chaps who preach God to us. Look at half the clergy of all denominations and all the religions that we've got in England! They're a pretty poor lot anyway. The sort of creatures that get put up at Tattersall's without a warranty as 'the property of a gentleman!' "

Benjamin laughed at him. "You're as bad as the old colonels who say that the hunter isn't what he was. In point of fact he's a lot better; it's the pace and the fences that are stiffer these days. We ask so much more of a good half-bred hunter than we used to and we ask a hell of a lot more of the clergy. In the old times, all a clergyman had to do was to pass on the truth of God. Now, every utterly brainless individual in our era of ultra-civilization has to reason everything out before he'll believe it. Do you wonder he can't do it? For centuries the best brains of the world have been working out systems of religion— the Jews, the Christians, Moslems, Buddhists . . . and they've all reached the same ideas in principle. We refuse to accept their findings because we can't follow every step of their reasoning . . . but we take the discoveries of the scientists without a murmur. We'll agree with any ha'penny general practitioner who says we've got a disease with a long enough Latin name to it. . . .

"But some of us—you and I, Tubby, let's be conceited about

it—have got back fifty years or so. We *can* suspect the scientists, and we can at least believe that there may be something to believe in. We can at least begin to build up some sort of simple, idiot-boy's philosophy that helps us along sometimes; something that allows you to be quite a nice, ordinary, healthy sort of chap with a bit of armour against troubles and misfortunes. It makes you sort of independent. Men were independent a century or so ago when they believed in God; when they said 'God wills it so what do we do next?' instead of 'there's nothing to be done, the doctor says it's hopeless.' It's only now, when nobody believes in anything, that we get so bowled over by a spot of trouble. . . ."

"Yes," Tubby said, "if life isn't to be hell, you have to be independent—like Sammy."

"Ah—Sammy."

"Sammy taught me more than I care to admit. More—I sometimes think—than I'll ever discover."

"A man above men," Benjamin murmured.

"But a man, an ordinary man. Made of the same pieces as you and me, but arranged differently."

"Unbelievably human. . . ."

"No," Tubby said. "What's unbelievable is the way the rest of us hide our humanity."

"I agree," Benjamin said, getting up from his chair. "In fact you can't live alone and think differently. Your own company makes you honest. You can talk a thing over without blushing about it. You can see all your various selves drawn up in front of you, choose the one you want, and kick out the others. It's easy while you're by yourself; but see what happens when we meet our fellows again. Remember what we were like when we came out of our solitude—out of ourselves—to greet each other? It was only three hours ago that we were boasting about cutting up a man's picture and papering the quad with it! And earlier in the evening we were both human beings."

"Yes," Tubby said. "I was afraid of it. All the way home I dreaded plunging back into friendships . . . but it was easy; easy to forget what I'd hoped I'd become and to turn into an officer again."

"Often and often," Benjamin said, "it'll be the same thing. We mustn't expect too much of ourselves. . . ." He stood on the edge of the veranda, looking into the darkness. "But, once you've started, people and things seem to turn up to help you along from time to time. . . ."

"Daddy said that—and Sammy said that."

"Yes! They would; both of them. And it's a queer thing, but once you begin to see your life as a sort of pattern, you'll begin to trace the threads in it. All the time, when you look backwards, you'll find that there's been something purposeful—even inevitable—about what's happened; inevitable, that is, within your pattern. You meet a man; you stay with him for a day, a few years, a lifetime, or only a few minutes; but he leaves his mark on you. He supplies a thread in your pattern."

"Lydia, Sammy, Daddy, a dead lion—and yourself, Benjy. . . ." Tubby stretched himself, yawning and speaking through his yawn. "So what about a spot of shut-eye?"

"Exactly my idea. Come on, Khadiga."

He spoke in English, but Khadiga rose swiftly and easily, unfolding herself, stretching and standing for an instant with her body taut and reaching upwards, full of beauty.

"Forrard, forrard, little bitch," Benjy said, "get along in, little bitch, leu in with you."

He smacked her fondly on the buttocks as she slipped through the French window into his bedroom.

Chapter 17 THE LORRY SWAYED, ROCKED AND JOLTED on, skidding sideways in the sand, shuddering across the hard, ridge-and-furrow tracts of cotton soil. Singa was passed and they were back at Makwar and the railhead.

Then it was the train, and Tubby lay once again under the fan in a darkened sleeping compartment. The window was open a crack behind the shutters, and the dust drifted in and covered everything. He slept little that night, but lay composed, rhythmically assuaged by the even jolting of the train. He was going back to Daddy. . . .

When it was daylight, Abdul Mohamed, important and leisurely in civilization, came along bringing tea, solicitously handing cigarettes and lighting matches, laying out clothes, collecting baggage in the corridor. He half raised the shutters and the flat, brilliant morning pressed against the window and slid into the carriage. The train shook itself over the points, slowed down almost to a halt, and then crept onwards.

"Bloody old Khartoum," Tubby said, with an unhappy, uneasy feeling in his stomach. It was the end of the holidays, the beginning of term again. But there would be Daddy. . . .

"Khartoum, noble captain," Abdul Mohamed said happily.

As the train drew up, Tubby stood on the compartment step and scanned the throng of busy, useless, black, chocolate, yellow and white individuals who attended their arrival. He

365

looked eagerly for the small, square person who would be hurrying up the platform, his head on one side, greeting Tubby with the smile that was always twisted.

A tall, freckled officer with a Gunner flash on his topi came up to him. "Hello, Windrush," he said; "I don't know if you remember me, we met once at the Royal. You had that big chestnut. . . ."

"Hello," Tubby said, "where's Daddy Watson?"

"I don't expect you *do* remember. After all, we only met once. My name's Chapman."

"Chapman, of course. How are you? What are *you* doing in these parts and where's Watson got to?"

"Come along," Chapman said, "and I'll tell you all about it. I've got a car and there's a G.S. wagon here, if your fellow can see to the baggage."

Outside the station, in the hard, crisp light of the clean town, the grey wagon and the two well-groomed mules in their well-polished harness stood waiting. The tall men in khaki drill uniforms stood stiffly to attention and saluted. You had to own it was a smart turnout; you had to be proud when you came back to it.

"Hello, Baxter," Tubby said, "how's the Fort these days?"

As he spoke, he had a sudden, very vivid sense of repetition; a knowledge that some scene out of the not-distant past was being re-enacted in detail. The light, the cool hour, the quick brilliance of early morning were the same. The taxi cabs were still waiting, their drivers indolently apart from their vehicles. The wagon and the men were there, under the hard sunlight; and the purposeless natives were still squatting under the flimsy trees that bordered the street to the station. Not much more than a month ago he had met the train from Wadi Halfa that brought Daddy back from Cairo.

"How *is* Daddy?" he asked again.

"I'll tell you all about it in the car."

They drove away from the station, accelerating swiftly up the wide street, taking the corner without slowing and swinging into the still wider street that led between the tall government buildings, the well-grouped trees, the neat gardens and the clean flat-roofed houses, along the tram lines and up to the point where the tarred surface would end suddenly in the beginnings of the desert.

"Well, tell me about Watson."

Chapman cleared his throat uncomfortably.

"He was rather a pal of yours, wasn't he?"

"Yes, he's a friend, a great friend."

"Then I'm afraid it'll be a bit of a shock for you, old boy."

"What do you mean?" Tubby said. "Nothing's happened to him, nothing serious, has it?"

"I'm afraid he's had an accident."

"An accident! Not hurt or anything?"

"I'm afraid he is, old man. It's hard to have to tell you. I'm afraid he's dead."

❧ They stood on the parapet of the Fort beside the long gun in the western angle.

"It was here he went over," Chapman said; "God knows how he did it."

"We used to walk along the top wall sometimes," Tubby said absently.

"Well, there's nothing dangerous in that. It's wide enough and there's no projections or anything. Of course it was night time but he never made a sound, at least no one heard him. They found him in the morning with his neck broken and the doctors said he must have died instantaneously. It was a funny business. He wasn't the sort of chap to commit suicide, I suppose?"

"No," Tubby answered slowly, "I wouldn't say he'd commit suicide."

"Of course there was a lot of talk about it and they went through his papers and everything. I got sent down by air from Cairo, but it was all over by the time I arrived; the funeral and everything."

"Did they find anything—in his letters, I mean?"

"Nothing to suggest suicide. A few bills and receipts, all quite ordinary. He was halfway through a letter to his brother. They found it in his bedroom. He was fond of his brother, wasn't he?"

"Gerald? He thought the world of him."

"The police commandant said it wasn't the sort of letter you'd expect a soldier to write. I got rather annoyed when he seemed to find it funny."

"He found it funny, did he?"

"It seemed Watson was quite extraordinarily happy. His letter was full of how happy he was; the police bloke used the word 'exalted' . . . and the General said perhaps it was all for the best if officers were going to get into an unhealthy state of mind like that. He said he didn't want any exaltation in *his* command."

Tubby walked down the ramp to his quarters. Abdul Mohamed had unpacked his things and arranged them exactly as they had been before; and Ibrahim—the little black boy who had been left behind—was still fussing round opening and shutting drawers and trying to find some way of being helpful. The room was unchanged, the same in every detail as it had been when Daddy had wandered in to steal a cigarette, to chat about the routine of the Fort, to complain about the messing, to start an argument or a quarrel, to discuss the mail, to rant against the idiocy of his superior officers, to lend Tubby a book or even to sit smoking in silence, hunched up in a chair, his head on one side, his hair untidy and all of him radiating the quiet sympathy and affection that sometimes had tied the two of them together.

There was a knock at the open door and the room darkened as Hicks stood in the entrance.

"Beg pardon, sir?"

"Come in, Hicks; what is it?"

Hicks stepped into the room and closed the door behind him with theatrical caution. "I thought you ought to see this, sir."

He fumbled in his pocket, pulled out an unopened envelope and handed it to Tubby. "It came for the Captain, sir, the same day as the accident. I found it after the funeral, sir; it was in his jacket pocket."

"Unopened?" Tubby asked.

"Yes, sir, it hadn't been opened. I'm sure of that, sir."

"That's funny," Tubby said. "The Captain always opened all his mail as soon as it came, and this must have arrived in the morning."

"Perhaps he forgot it, sir."

"Perhaps he did, Hicks."

"I thought as how I'd keep it for you, sir," Hicks said. "They'd all bin rummaging about in the Captain's papers and such, and I thought like as anything come to light after they'd finished wasn't no concern of anyone's—not anyone's outside the Fort like."

"Quite right, Hicks. . . ."

"That's as I thought, sir. I thought of giving it to Mr. Chapman, sir, but he not knowing the Captain, I thought I'd best keep it till you got back, seeing it was only a matter of a day or two. I hope I did right, sir?"

"Quite right, Hicks—and thank you."

Tubby looked at the envelope again, examining it carefully.

"You're quite certain it hadn't been opened?" he asked, for he had recognized the writing.

"Quite certain, sir, there wasn't a doubt about it. You can see for yourself, sir. . . ."

"Funny. . . ."

"Yes, sir; if you asks me it *is* funny, and that's why I acted like I did. . . ."

"Thank you very much, Hicks."

"I hope you understand, sir, that I didn't want to do anything as wasn't right; but knowing the Captain pretty well, sir, and knowing yourself, and knowing how it was, as you might say, between you, sir, I thought. . . ."

"Yes, yes," Tubby said impatiently. "You did perfectly right. Thanks very much, I'll attend to it."

Hicks went out and Tubby sat down on his bed, slowly turning over the envelope. It was a cheap, thin envelope of greyish paper, obviously blue lined inside. The writing was bold and slanting forwards, writing that Tubby now remembered he had often seen in Daddy's correspondence on thick, expensive stationery. He slit the letter open carefully.

"Dear Willie . . ." it started, and for just a moment Tubby

found it hard to recollect that Daddy had not been Daddy to everyone. . . .

The letter was short, just running over the single page, and he turned to look at the signature. As he had expected, it was signed "Gerald." As he had known all along, the letter was from Daddy's brother. He read the first few lines with amazement and then, with a sense of complete perplexity, put the letter on to his knees, put his head in his hands and tried to understand it. The envelope fluttered onto the floor and a newspaper cutting slipped out, drifted away, and lay on the camel-hair rug that was beside his bed. He picked up the cutting. It was the report of a police court proceedings.

"Gerald Watson . . . appeared before Mr. . . . on charges of fraud and embezzlement. . . . Superintendent Richards said that it was expected that further charges would be preferred, and that the sums involved would ultimately be very much larger. . . . Watson was remanded for a week, bail being allowed in two sureties of five hundred pounds. . . ."

Tubby folded the letter up and slipped it into his pocket as he heard Chapman coming along the veranda.

"May I come in, old boy?"

"Come in, Chapman."

Chapman stood awkwardly in the doorway.

"Sorry to butt in, but I forgot to tell you, Windrush, that you've been posted home—with effect from tomorrow."

"Really," Tubby said indifferently. "Where are they sending me? Do you know that?"

"I'm afraid I don't, old boy. They've given you a couple of months' leave to start with."

"Decent of them, but I don't want it."

"Oh, I don't know. One can always do with a spot of leave, can't one?"

"I suppose so . . . I don't know what I'll do with it."

"You'll find something," Chapman said.

"I expect so."

Chapman started to go and then turned back again.

"Oh, I say, old boy," he said awkwardly, "what about your ponies and things?"

"My ponies?"

"Well, I might take some of them off you; and I suppose you'll want to sell the rest, and so on."

"Take what you want, pay what you like, and put the rest up for auction," Tubby said wearily. "For the moment I've rather lost interest in ponies."

He was alone on the crowded train that took him up to Wadi Halfa, alone on the river steamer, alone again on the train that went from Assuan through Luxor to Cairo. He was not interested in the women who were returning home for the hot weather, in the poker and bridge and parties, in the crowd of acquaintances who drank at the various bars and collected for meals on the journey, in the dam at Assuan, in the ruins of Philae, in a glimpse of the tombs at Luxor. Alone he retraced Daddy's last journey. They tried to tap him about the Watson affair, skirting round the subject, approaching it tactfully. He said he knew nothing. He said it all the way from Khartoum to Cairo, from Cairo to Port Said, Marseilles, Calais, Dover. They thought him surly and stupid.

He was not interested in what they thought. He was busy searching for the truth, searching for a pattern. Daddy had been happy before he died—they had even said "exalted." He knew nothing of his brother's troubles yet the letter was in his pocket telling him about them. The letter was unopened and there had not been a suicide. What had happened?

On the face of it, a man had tumbled off the parapet in the dark, had broken his neck in falling, and had died instantly. That was the obvious explanation, supported by every outward appearance. But Tubby was no longer interested in outward appearance and face value. He was searching inwards, probing and seeking in the deepest recesses of himself, in the deepest recesses of Daddy. What had happened? What had happened?

It did not matter to anyone. It did not matter to Daddy. It certainly did not matter to generals and staff officers, for whom there was a certain relief that one who was so dangerously capable of exaltation had been painlessly removed from the Army. But it mattered to Tubby. It mattered desperately that he should know about it with certainty, that he should trace the pattern of Daddy's life, that he should positively identify the "moment of truth" about which Sammy had spoken on the morning of his death on the Red Sea hillside. . . .

He saw Sammy and Daddy as two interlocking bricks on which his own life and his own peace rested. If he could only be sure that it was a stable foundation, he could build on their lives a life of his own. He could achieve the precious detachment that he had glimpsed and coveted. He could know what mattered and what didn't. He could know himself.

It was curious what a personal thing that was. The death of Watson mattered to Tubby and to no other person. From the told and untold inhabitants of the earth, these two had been drawn inevitably together. There was already a strange thread of purpose in the pattern that was being woven.

The texture was so fine that you could not tell the weft from the warp. Peoples, things, knowledge, feelings, were woven together without meaning. And he could not distinguish a tonic color. A thread was started and seemed to end; another and another. Lydia, Sammy, Daddy, Benjamin, played their part and went from him. What was left? The glory was old and faded. All hues were somber. What was left to him?

Groping in the deepness of his misery, sick with his own emptiness, abandoned, lost, with no light ahead, nothing that beckoned him from either hand, he traveled homewards without purpose. The insistent questions beat in his head like the drums at night from the village; like the dogs yapping from the village; like the sounds of night that came off the desert. There was no answer but confusion; no end but misery; no life but dying.

Clouds came on a cloudless sky. Slowly the grey days washed into his azure memories. The sun receded. There was drizzle, rain, wind and high seas that rocked the ship. The rain splashed against the windows of his railway carriage. The wind tore at him on the quayside at Calais. Dover was hidden in the rain.

He could not keep out the memories. They seeped into him.

They poured into him, filling him with the sadness of a quiet evening. Sammy, Sammy, Sammy—when we stood on the deck of the troopship, and the dying music followed us, and England faded sadly in the darkness. Daddy—why, why didn't you wait for me? Lydia—you said, you said . . . where had you all got to in this empty night? There was no one, nothing, that remained in this dark pain.

❦ The seas kept the ship tossing in the harbor. Oh, yes! That was Dover Castle. This was England. The white cliffs, the shining roofs, the rain beating in on you. Who cared?

They tied her up at last and he waited his turn patiently, and at last walked down the gangway. On the quay, he stood bewildered. This was a foreign land, a foreign people; nowhere to go, nothing to do, no one to see. His house was fallen to pieces. All had been taken from him.

"Tubby," she said, and caught at his arm. "Tubby . . ."

"You?"

"Oh, Tubby—I've met three boats and Bert is waiting at Folkestone."

They laughed. He tried to laugh but it caught in his throat and only his lips twisted.

"How did you know?" he asked.

"Benjy. He wrote and then he cabled."

"But I spent a night with him. And we scarcely mentioned you."

"Perhaps that was why. . . ."

"Sammy . . . Daddy . . ."

"I know; he told me. When he wrote, when he cabled."

"And you? You're in America . . . no, you've come back. And you got married."

"No. I couldn't." She looked up at him, frightened; the pale face and large eyes that he'd seen in an upturned automobile. "Tubby, Tubby—what *are* you?"

"Blessed if I know," he said; "scarcely a soldier. . . ."